DAWN OF THE ELITE
Book One of the Brennen Series

Andrea Barringer

Dawn of The Elite
Copyright 2021 Andrea Barringer
ISBN# 9798730910171
Paperback ASIN# B091F5QCJ6

ALL RIGHTS RESERVED. No part of this book publication may be reproduced, stored in a retrieval system, or transmitted in any form or by any means — electronic, mechanical, photo-copy, recording, or any other — except brief quotation in reviews, without the prior permission of the author or publisher.

This is a work of fiction. Names, characters, places and incidents either are the product of the author's imagination or are used fictitiously, and any resemblance to actual persons, living or dead, events or locales is entirely coincidental.

Cover by Daniel Adorno

Prologue

Twins across many galaxies have a special bond that is quite unique from the rest of the population. Here, on the big bright blue planet of Vilmos, twins – specifically fraternal twins of opposite genders – have the coveted ability to communicate without words, a term commonly known as duo-com.

Table of contents

Chapter 1
Chapter 2
Chapter 3
Chapter 4
Chapter 5
Chapter 6
Chapter 7
Chapter 8
Chapter 9
Chapter 10
Chapter 11
Chapter 12
Chapter 13
Chapter 14
Chapter 15
Chapter 16
Chapter 17
Chapter 18
Chapter 19
Chapter 20
Chapter 21
Chapter 22
Chapter 23
Chapter 24
Chapter 25
Chapter 26
Chapter 27
Chapter 28
Chapter 29
Chapter 30
Chapter 31
Chapter 32
Chapter 33
Chapter 34

CAST OF CHARACTERS

Nerida Kortez (Nair-EE-dah) - Wife of Alastair. Lives and works at Marez Cave.

Alastair Kortez - Husband of Nerida. Lives at Marez Cave. Works at the University in the City of Clivesdail.

Evia Kortez (EH-vee-ah) - Daughter of Nerida and Alastair Kortez. Twin sister of Ensin.

Ensin Kortez (EHN-sin) - Son of Nerida and Alastair Kortez. Twin brother of Evia.

Doctor Perry Kortez - Brother of Alastair. Doctor at the palace.

Rayah Jur (RAY-uh) - Twin sister of Ondraus. A nurse in the military.

Ondraus Jur (An-DRE-us) - Twin brother of Rayah. A nurse in the military.

Kaled Behr (KAL-ed) - Twin brother of Aymes. Goes by Kal. Vehicle specialist and pilot in the military.

Aymes Behr (Aims) - Twin sister of Kaled. Vehicle specialist and pilot in the military.

Ameena Noxx (Ah-MEEN-ah) - Twin sister of Wilstead.

Cook and nutritionist in the military.

Wilstead Noxx (WILL-stead) - Twin brother of Ameena. Cook and nutritionist in the military.

Tru Ryder - Twin sister of Tye. Communications and technology specialist in the military.

Tye Ryder - Twin brother of Tru. Communications and technology specialist in the military.

Bo Xulu - Twin brother of Lina. Engineer in the military.

Lina Xulu (LEE-nah) - Twin sister of Bo. Engineer in the military.

King Tarrington Branaugh (TAH-ring-ton) - King of the country of Brennen.

Queen Ellandra Branaugh (El-ON-druh) - Queen of the country of Brennen.

General Elden Peterson (EL-den) - Highest-ranking military figure in all of Brennen. He works and lives at the palace.

Guyad Lurca (GUY-ad) - Head of security at the palace.

GLOSSARY

Brennen - The country ruled by King Tarrington Branaugh.

Brennish - The language and people of Brennen.

Diagnostica - A small handheld medical device used to quickly diagnose any immediate health issues of a patient.

Duo-com - The language that fraternal twins use, which allows them to communicate with their minds as opposed to speaking out loud.

Duo-com Master - Someone who has multiple years experience as a duo-com instructor.

Gaoled (pronounced like *jailed*) - A mental dream-like world where only fraternal twins can visit. This world is not physical and normally would appear like a dark, empty space. Typically, someone might get stuck in a Gaoled if they are having trouble communicating or trusting their sibling and are experiencing an anxiety attack. It feeds off emotion, and the only way to get out of a Gaoled is to trust the sibling.

Monktuary (MONK-shoo-ary, pronounced like *sanctuary*)- An establishment where Duo-Com Masters live with their fraternal twins and can be a place of refuge and teaching to other fraternal twins in the country of Brennen.

Mono-block - The act of one twin building a temporary mental wall so that the other cannot communicate with them through duo-com.

Nemi - A handheld sidearm weapon. It can switch between stun and kill functions and uses electric impulses to deliver a charge to the opponent. If the opponent is not wearing a protective vest, a direct hit to the chest will cause immediate cardiac failure and death. However, if it is not a direct hit or if the person is using a protective vest, the weapon will deliver electric second and third-degree burns, which if not treated properly can lead to death.

Susa (Soo-zah)- The country that borders Brennen close to the city of Benal.

Vilmos - The planet on which this story takes place. Residents are called Vilmovians.

CHAPTER 1

Nerida

Marez Cave, a hidden gem nestled deep within the Wild Deltarra Forest, buzzed with action. Ten-year-old twins Ensin and Evia ran around the cave's living room with toy laser guns and vests, shooting at each other and trying to get as many points as possible. Their mother, Nerida Kortez, made dinner in the kitchen, her hips swaying to the rhythm of the steel drum music that played through the built-in surround sound system. The music reminded her of dancing barefoot on the beach while on her honeymoon fourteen years ago. Her husband, Alastair, sat in the corner of the living room reading from an old dusty book...at least until her swaying caught his eye. He got up and tried, comically, to copy her movements, which made her and the children stop and burst out laughing.

Nerida was a petite thirty-eight-year-old woman with light blue skin – like all the people on the planet of Vilmos – as well as light purple eyes and matching hair that reached her waist. Pale blue swirling lines began at her wrists, making their way up the sides of her arms, neck, and temples and seeming to shimmer when the light hit her skin just right. She had small ridges on the bridge of her nose and on her pointed ears. A radiant smile and joy for life and family added to her natural striking beauty.

Nerida draped her spatula-holding hand around Alastair's shoulder while they danced, trying in vain to lose herself in the moment. She relished the tender way his hand rested on her waist and the intimacy he displayed with his serene cerulean eyes. It would have been a romantic moment except for the ruckus being made by their two children. Having a few seconds to themselves was a rarity these days.

"Please say it stopped snowing," she whispered into Alastair's ear.

"Let me go check." He headed toward a small digital screen set on a massive cavern wall and placed his palm on it. The clear screen beeped quietly as it lit up, and the large cavern wall disappeared, revealing a forest blanketed in snow. The wall, a hologram engineered to look and feel like solid rock, was the entrance to their abode. Alastair peered outside. "Looks pretty calm."

"Aha! I got you again! That's twenty million points for me," cheered Ensin victoriously. His sister Evia pretended to pout and then shot him with her laser gun, which sent both of them running around the kitchen and bumping into Nerida *again*. She loved her children dearly, but being stuck indoors for too long made them go stir-crazy, and they were definitely past that point. They had been sprinting around the house since before the snow began falling four hours ago. They'd already finished their chores earlier that morning, and now they needed some time outside to burn that energy off.

"How about you guys go outside to play?" suggested Nerida. "Dinner is in the oven. It'll be ready in thirty minutes, and I could use a break from my own chores. Let's get some fresh air."

Her children needed no further convincing. They

zipped out of the living room and into their bedrooms to find their winter coats. Nerida put on a warm cloak and told her husband to stay inside and finish grading his school papers. The family was supposed to have a vacation in three weeks and already had prime seats to the Winter Games, and the last thing Nerida wanted was her husband being forced to spend time thinking about work. She grabbed a pad of canvas paper and her painting kit, giving her husband a peck on the lips on her way out.

As Nerida exited the large mouth of the cave, she felt the midwinter chill seep into her bones and wished she would have thought to set a pot of coffee to brew so she could enjoy it while outside painting. The stunning landscape beckoned her to capture its beauty on canvas.

Freshly fallen snow covered the entirety of the vast forest, and supple mounds of white topped even the tallest of trees. The Wild Deltarra Forest was home to ferocious animals such as thirteen-foot-tall Wooly Bears, which sported tusks and sharp claws that could disembowel an unsuspecting prey. During the warmer months, Trance Snakes slithered about with hypnotic eyes, luring their next meal into lairs far beneath the forest floor. The Wild Deltarra Forest was not for the typical wanderer, and it was certainly no place for a home...which made it perfect for the Kortez family.

Inaudible high-pitch sensors, strategically placed in a one-mile radius around the cave entrance, kept the massive animals away while still allowing the smaller ones to pass through. Large pink birds with turquoise colored breasts flew overhead, making Nerida wish they would hold still long enough for her to paint them. At the same time, small furry mammals hopped from one tree to another, trying to find nuts and in-season Icy Pears that grew in the winter. Everything seemed fine, like a typical afternoon outdoors, until Nerida's world flipped upside down.

She was sketching out the landscape, hoping to capture the essence of the stillness, when out of the corner of her eye she saw her son Ensin try to climb a tree. "Careful, Ensin," she called out from a distance.

"Just trying to get our ball, mom," he responded.

Nerida's mother's instinct kicked into gear as she put down her paintbrush and eyed him carefully; she could feel trouble looming around the corner. Ensin climbed several branches and reached for the ball, accidentally bumping a small enclosed nest. Nerida couldn't tell what type of nest it was and hadn't even seen it before Ensin jostled it, but something within her demanded that she get up and move closer to the kids.

"Careful, Ensin!" she yelled. The ball and the nest both thudded to the ground right by Evia's feet. A cloud of angry wasps flew out of the hive and began to swarm toward the children.

"Ouch!" exclaimed Ensin, still perched on a branch. "Ow! I just got stung!"

Nerida could hear the panic in her voice. "Evia, step away! Ensin, get down the other side of the tree!"

Twenty bright yellow-gray wasps surrounded both children, seeming to sense Nerida's presence as well. "Run!" she yelled, sprinting toward the kids. Five wasps plunged their stingers into her, yet some distant part of her mind noticed that their sting was not as bad as she had been expecting. She'd never seen this particular type of wasp before, but she'd been stung plenty as a child, and those stings had been much more painful.

Her children still weren't fleeing, paralyzed by indecision or fear. Nerida reached Evia, who was on her knees and wobbling as if about to faint. Ensin fell from the tree, landing face-first in the soft snow. He didn't cry out and didn't get up. *Okay,* she thought, *this is an emergency!* Nerida flicked her forearm, and her wristband lit up, projecting a comm screen onto her skin. She smashed the spot on her arm that would make the wristband call her husband, then waited half an eternity for the connection to click open.

"Hey babe," said Alastair, utterly unaware of the dire situation taking place outside.

"I need your help!" Nerida yelled. "The kids were stung, and they're having an allergic reaction!"

Her mind raced for options. They were in the middle of nowhere. Even with their hovercar, it would take thirty minutes to get to the hospital. Alastair appeared at the main entrance of the cave without bothering to put on any winter clothes. Even from more than a hundred feet away, Nerida could see the concern twisting his face.

In the two seconds she spent looking at her husband, she heard a sound like choking. Both children were now on the ground convulsing. Foam dribbled out of Evia's mouth, her eyes blinking open and closed while her small body twitched helplessly. Nerida turned Ensin over and saw he was exactly like his sister. She dialed her brother in law, Perry Kortez, the doctor at the royal palace.

"Answer! ANSWER!" she screamed as the phone rang for a full minute. In the time it took for the phone to ring, Alastair had made it to Nerida and the children, his jaw dropping when he saw the children foaming and shaking.

"Hey, Ner. What's up?" said Dr. Kortez, his voice light and airy as usual.

"Perry, we have an emergency! The kids and I were stung by these wasps, and now they're convulsing!" Nerida swiped at the projected image on her forearm and turned on the video feed. "See?"

The alarm in his response echoed her own as he blurted a succession of questions. "What do the wasps look like? How many stings?"

Alastair picked up a dead wasp that lay dead near Ensin's twitching body and let his brother see it. Dr. Kortez turned around, barking orders to his two male nurses.

"Birchram, look up this type of wasp. I want to know everything you can find about it. Zendo, get three stretchers ready, and call the local police station. Let them know we'll be having a civilian vehicle on an emergency approach to the palace. I'll alert the guards. Ner, are you feeling ill as well?"

"No, not at all. Maybe a little woozy, now that you mention it, but not like *that*. What if we don't get to you in time? It's a thirty-minute drive!"

"Not today it won't be," insisted Alastair, already running toward the mouth of the cave as his wristband lit up.

He swiped and tapped at his forearm until two doors, which had perfectly matched the snowy landscape until that moment, hatched like an egg and began to spread apart. A sleek hovercar emerged from the interior, and Alastair ran toward it, hopping in and speeding over to his family. With a swift motion, he picked up Evia and stuffed her in the side door, then went back for Ensin almost before Nerida even saw him move.

As soon as both twins were safely buckled in, Alastair shouted, "Let's go!"

Alastair switched the autopilot off and performed a command-level override of the speed restrictions, which activated a beacon to alert the local authorities. "Hold on," he warned.

In a flash, they zoomed up above the trees. Nerida gripped the edge of her seat until her knuckles began turning white. Everything within her screamed a silent warning to drive carefully, but she didn't dare speak and break Alastair's concentration. It looked like he might not even hear her if she spoke, so intently were his eyes focused on where the car was going. Nerida had never seen Alastair this way, nor had she ever been in a vehicle going so fast. They zoomed past multiple cars once they had arrived in populated areas above the nearest city, Capenia, and then toward the capital, Clivesdail.

"There's a cop," she said in a warning tone.

"I see him," he responded, still gripping the steering wheel and his foot slammed down on the accelerator.

"Are you going to stop?"

"Don't plan to."

Nerida glanced back at her children. Their bodies were slumped over and still convulsing. Her heart raced erratically; if they didn't do something, those officers were going to slow them down, and this was not the time for *that*.

"They're really gaining on us, and I can see them pulling out their HoverCraft Stopper."

"They can try," he said determinedly. "I thought Perry said he was telling the police to clear the way for us."

Nerida rolled down the window and waved her arms to the cops that raced after them. She yelled in a shrill, panicked, frantic mother voice. "We're headed to the hospital wing of the palace. It's an emergency!"

"Pull over," demanded the cop.

"It's an emergency! Our kids are very sick and we can't stop! Call Dr. Perry Kortez, or you can arrest us for all I care when we get there, but we are not pulling over!"

To her amazement, a second cop car pulled up near them in the sky barely a second after she had yelled at the first one. "I'll escort you to the palace. We've confirmed with Dr. Kortez."

"Oh, thank the All Creator!" Nerida breathed. It was the first thing that had gone right for her since Ensin first climbed that tree.

All three cars – one cop car in front, one bringing in the rear, and Nerida and her family in the middle – raced toward the palace. After what felt like hours, they landed in a clearing where a medical team met them.

Dr. Perry Kortez ran to them and started checking the kids' pupils, then circled the sting marks on their skin with a marker. He did the same with Nerida, who still felt perfectly fine.

"Hook the kids up to get vitals," Perry barked to his aides. "Get them on a stretcher and give them a point-one-five milligram shot of epinephrine!"

The medical personnel worked quickly to follow Dr. Kortez's orders. In a flash, the team rushed indoors, talking among themselves in the choppy cadence of doctors and nurses on a mission as they pushed their catatonic patients on hovering stretchers. Nerida, Alastair, and the cops were left standing silently outside. The entire situation felt like pure mayhem, and Nerida noticed that her hands were shaking. The adrenaline that had fueled her for nearly twenty minutes was working its way out of her system, and she couldn't decide whether to try and look strong or whether to sit down and start bawling.

"We're sorry about your kids, folks," whispered one of the officers.

Neither parent could speak. Both simply nodded in unison.

The officer continued. "But if you don't mind me asking, why didn't you take them to Lexel Hospital? You passed it on the way here, and you could have saved ten minutes."

Nerida looked at her husband, wondering if he would answer first. Maybe she should speak up, or perhaps they should act dumb as if they didn't know full well that they had passed a perfectly good hospital on the way to the palace.

CHAPTER 2

Rayah

Stepping out of a hover vehicle and onto the snow that crunched under her feet, Rayah Jur and her twin brother Ondraus took in the majestic view of Maw'Qai Mountain before them. Towering at fourteen thousand feet, it was a popular skiing destination during the frosty months of the year, except for the two weeks in late winter when it hosted the most anticipated sporting event in all of Brennen: the Winter Games. A bright blue sky gleamed above the snow-capped hulking mountain. Rayah and her brother had never had the opportunity to enjoy the view in person, and she found she couldn't take her eyes off it. Crisp, cool air filled her lungs while the wind nipped briskly at her face. Her brother had a jump in his step; he was clearly as excited and intrigued as she.

Rayah and Ondraus had received an unexpected invitation to participate in the Winter Games. Their company commander had surprised Rayah by approving the leave request without hesitation, even though she and her brother had already used up their limited vacation days. To call the invitation *unexpected* was a serious understatement, she thought. In all her years living in the great country of Brennen, there had never been a Winter Games event like this one: for the first time ever, fraternal twins had been single-handedly picked out and asked to join the Games for one day.

Normally the Games were only open to professional athletes who had been training for years. For someone like Rayah – even though she and Ondraus, as soldiers, were in top shape, with strength and reflexes far beyond the average person's – this was a once-in-a-lifetime opportunity. Even as excitement surged through her, she couldn't help but wonder what had brought about this sudden change in the invitation process.

Her brother Ondraus could not pass up the chance to compete in the games and had hardly talked about anything else since their invitation arrived. Rayah, on the other hand, didn't have a competitive bone in her body, and the thought of winning a trophy didn't interest her as much as the mere thought of participating in all those events she'd only ever seen on the tele-screens.

Even so, something about the situation just felt *off* to her. "Don't you think it's odd that in a hundred and forty-three years of the Winter Games, this is the first time they've ever invited...you know, ordinary people like us?"

"I don't care about the reasons," Ondraus said with a wide grin. "I just want to win."

That was her brother, alright. He'd always been the one to run headfirst into something without overthinking it. "Besides," Ondraus continued, "we passed all the simulated races they put us through. The real thing should be easy as pie." He paused. "Great. Now I want pie."

"We've only had two weeks to prepare, though," Rayah protested. "Okay, simulations are one thing, but we don't even know how to ski, let alone how to ride a Bitroika. We could get badly hurt or even die."

Her brother shrugged his shoulders. "You worry too much, sis. If I really thought we couldn't do it, I wouldn't push it at all. I have faith in us. We're a pretty great team." He gave her his usual beaming smile.

They'd had this same discussion, in various forms, nearly every day since those invitations first arrived. What was the point in trying to convince her brother to pull out now that they were here? Rayah always fought against this part of her personality. She knew she tended to worry about safety and would often overthink all the possible outcomes – even the ones that stood almost zero chance of actually happening – before agreeing to something that seemed slightly off. The part of her that was brave and strong lived side-by-side with the part that exercised caution and over-analyzed everything.

Throughout their lives, all their free time had been invested in military training. Even when they were young, their father, who at that time served in the Royal Army, would wake them early for a run through the wooded trail behind their high rise apartment. At home, he insisted on proper military decorum; Rayah and Ondraus were always expected to stand up straight, shine their shoes, and make their beds so crisply they could bounce a coin off the covers. By age twelve, they were enrolled in the Junior Military Academy, located an hour from their home. They only got to visit their parents on weekends, extended holidays, and summer break.

Rayah knew that if she had wanted out of this type of lifestyle at any point, her parents and brother would have supported her decision. Truth be told, though, she loved being on this journey with her twin, and she felt as though it had been written in the stars ages ago. She couldn't imagine her future going any other way.

Fraternal twins across the planet of Vilmos – for reasons no scientist had yet been able to determine – were able to communicate mentally without words, a term commonly known as duo-com. Ordinarily, it took months and sometimes years of practice to become proficient, but the skill was extremely valuable, especially for soldiers.

Her brother did nothing to prevent his thoughts of infectious enthusiasm from bombarding her, and as a result, she felt and heard everything that went through his mind.

You're practically whistling, she duo-commed.

I know. I can't help it. I can't wait to get up there and show them our moves.

She shook her head; that irrepressible personality was one of the many reasons why she loved him. As they made the long trek toward the meeting place at the base of the mountain, Rayah took in all of the sights and sounds. Thousands of people milled around the grounds and spectator seats as hundreds of vendors beckoned people in for hot drinks or souvenir clothing. Swirls of smoke from food stalls wafted up into the sky, permeating the entire area with the delicious smell of grilled meats and vegetables. Folks in line at the famous Yemley's Yummylicious Shoppe waited to order the local favorite, Choco Moo Brew.

Nearly everyone had a shirt or a flag sporting their favorite athlete or team's colors, and the whole mountainside was awash in colorful clothing and decorations. From Rayah's position, she could see the course that she and her brother would be trying to conquer.

Bright gold streamers marked out the boundaries, and Rayah followed them up the hill with her eyes until they disappeared into the trees. The course, which dropped eight hundred vertical feet over its three thousand foot distance, was known for being punishingly hard and causing massive wipeouts – which was why hundreds of spectators were already making their way to the viewing areas that lined the most challenging parts.

Rayah hadn't seen anyone carrying a banner for Team Jur or for any of the other sets of twins, which was no surprise to her. The twins were, after all, almost an afterthought, hastily included less than a month before the Games began, and most people viewed them as an opening act to the *real* Games. Rayah didn't even know who she was going to compete against; she hadn't been given a full list of the twin category entrants. That was yet another element that added to her growing wariness and suspicion concerning the true reason for their invitation. This all felt so last minute, so rushed, and she wanted to know why. What plan had been hatched so suddenly that the twins couldn't have been invited six months ago – or even six weeks?

Rayah Jur was twenty-three years old, and even a bulky snowsuit couldn't conceal her curvy, athletic build and graceful movements. Her thick, curly hair was a mix of dark purple and turquoise, and she'd set it in braids so that she didn't have to worry about any loose strands getting in the way while she competed. Ondraus Jur was a muscular man with broad shoulders like their father's. He preferred to keep his dark purple hair in short sculpted curls with a tapered fade, and his face was accented with a thick short beard. Both he and

Rayah had amethyst-colored eyes that lit up when they smiled, which was often.

As they finally reached the base of the mountain, the joy and excitement she'd been feeling immediately swooshed out of her, as though she'd been gut-punched. It wasn't the size of the mountain or the daunting task of competing in a sport she's never actually done in her life. No, it was the face of someone she recognized: Kaled Behr. She froze on the spot, utterly shocked; she had so expertly removed him from her life that he might as well have been a ghost. For less than a split second, she'd felt joy and wonder at seeing his face, followed by fiery anger and painful memories. Her fists automatically balled before she even realized it.

I see him too, duo-commed her brother in a gentle tone.

Why is he here? Why him of all people? She had not expected this, and now she wondered if she would be too flustered to properly think or function with him there. If she had her way, she would demand that he be removed from competing in the games on the grounds of being a sleazy, good for nothing –

Okay, okay, interjected her brother. *I hear you loud and clear, sis. But we need to do our best here, no matter what happened between the two of you. Stay focused and take care of business.*

Rayah loathed Kaled on a deep, personal level, whereas Ondraus had remained good friends with him. Of course, her brother could be buddies with whoever he wanted...as long as her ex-boyfriend stayed well away from her. Today would be drastically different. For the first time in two years, she was face to face with the man who had been the cause of so much heartbreak.

It felt as if the universe were intent on making her overcome both physical and emotional challenges today. One or the other was fine...both together did not sound like a good time.

Even from a few paces away, she could see how Kaled's body language completely changed when he noticed her walking up. He tensed, took a step back, and even gulped. His twin sister Aymes, standing beside him, seemed exhilarated at first to see her old friends. When she noticed her brother's reaction, though – or maybe sensed it through duo-com – the excitement instantly disappeared from her face, and she walked tentatively toward Rayah and Ondraus.

"What a nice surprise," said Aymes, holding out her arms.

Rayah took in a deep breath and smiled; it was nice to see Aymes again, and she went in for the hug that her friend was offering. "It's a surprise, alright," said Rayah just below a whisper. Then, looking Aymes in the eyes, she said, "It's been too long, my friend."

Aymes nodded in agreement and hugged Rayah again. Rayah's heart soared with the warmth of her friend's embrace, which felt like a tangible energy source filled with longing, pain, and joy. Rayah had not spoken to Aymes in over a month, and more than a year had passed since they'd seen each other in person. They should have been out grabbing drinks and catching up on personal matters instead of enjoying an unexpected reunion; regardless, the moment's sanctity and beauty prevailed.

Things hadn't always been like this. There had been a time when Rayah and Aymes were inseparable. They'd been friends as long as Rayah could remember, and

Aymes was there in most of her happiest memories. Together they'd discussed crushes they'd had on guys, cried on each other's shoulders after each heartbreak, and borrowed the other's clothes to dress up and go to a party. For almost ten years, they were inseparable. All of that had taken a back seat after Kaled had broken Rayah's heart one too many times.

Cutting him out of her life had meant cutting Aymes out, too, which tore Rayah apart, but she couldn't, simply could not, take any more chances with her heart. The two friends still spoke, but it wasn't like before, and she knew that neither of them would again share deep matters of the heart with one another. Rayah missed Aymes with every fiber of her being, and seeing her friend made her wonder why they had gone a whole year without flying out to spend a day together. It was a terrible pity that Aymes was the sister of the one guy Rayah loathed.

As soon as Rayah and Aymes let go after their lengthy warm hug, Ondraus swooped in to greet Aymes. Rayah couldn't help but smile; she knew her brother liked Aymes, and the poor guy had been dropping hints at Aymes for years without her even batting an eye at him in return. Yet here he was, turning up the charm. Their voices faded into the background as Rayah's heart began to beat violently against her chest.

She stood there, watching warily as Kaled approached her, dreading the upcoming interaction. Rayah had not spoken to Kaled or even seen him in two years, and yet here he was, in the flesh, walking toward her. Unfortunately, he'd somehow gotten even more handsome than she remembered.

"Hi," he greeted with a sheepish smile on his face,

reaching out with his gloved hand as if to wave. Rayah rolled her eyes; she wanted to walk away, but he pressed on. "Please, Rayah. It's been two years. Please, just talk to me."

Her brother's voice in her head was annoyingly mature. *Sis, don't lose your temper. Business, remember?*

Rayah turned to face her nemesis and huffed impatiently, placing her hands on her hips. "What, Kal? What could you possibly want to say to me?" To her dismay, she didn't sound as mean as she had wanted to. Instead, she was certain she had tripped over her words as a sob threatened to creep out of her mouth.

"I...I just want to say I'm sorry."

"You already did that years ago. It doesn't magically make things better."

"What can I do?" he pleaded, "I had hoped by now you would have forgiven me; it's been two –"

"Yes, yes, two years, I know. Trust me, I know." She looked down, unable to look at his light green eyes, knowing that if she did, her heart might give way all over again.

"So, that's it? We'll never be friends again because of one error that I –"

"One error? Is that what you're calling it?" She could feel the heat rising, her blood bubbling. "Plus, need I remind you that *you're* the reason our friendship ended?"

To Rayah's surprise, Kaled made no attempt to defend himself. He just stood there, his head down, looking pathetic like a boy being told he couldn't go outside to play.

"You're right," said Kaled. "All the blame is on me. I would settle for just being an acquaintance, but I can see you're not interested in that either."

Rayah wanted to dismiss Kaled; she was sickened even by the thought of him being a mere acquaintance. She wanted him out of her life forever, but part of her wondered if she were capable of holding on to so much hurt and rage for so long. She couldn't predict what the future held and knew it wasn't healthy for her to keep holding a grudge. It was like punching herself in the face and expecting Kal to cry out in pain.

"Maybe one day, but today is not that day," she whispered.

His head perked up, eyes glistening. "Then I'll wait patiently."

To her surprise, he had the audacity to touch her. His hand was on her shoulder, and she could feel herself on the edge of falling apart under his tender touch. "I miss you, Rayah."

She nodded, holding back a flood of tears that threatened to force their way down her cheeks. But she stood her ground; she would not let him see that she still felt something, and that part of her battered heart would always belong to him, for better or for worse. As he walked away from earshot, she couldn't help but think how much she had missed him too. Unfortunately, that chapter had closed for them a while back, and there was no way she would open herself up for him to hurt her ever again.

Rayah watched from afar as Ondraus and Kaled finally greeted one another with a hug; most guys would resort to a handshake or fist-bump, but not these two. There was too much history between them; they, just like Rayah and Aymes, had grown up together and at one point had been as close as brothers. Unlike Rayah and Aymes, they hadn't drifted apart even after *the inci-*

dent. If this were a reunion like it had been years prior, all four of them would be huddled up together, hugging and laughing. Now, the greeting was an awkward dance, as Aymes and Ondraus did their best to keep Kaled away from Rayah.

CHAPTER 3

Rayah

A man in a military uniform, with a high and tight haircut, approached the Winter Games competition grounds and called all the sets of twins to him.

"My name is General Elden Peterson. I see some of you have already been talking to one another. That is good. I am also happy to see that you all arrived thirty minutes prior to the appointed meeting time."

General Elden Peterson? The highest-ranking official in the entire royal army? Rayah didn't understand why the Winter Games, a mere sporting event, would interest a general. Surely he had more important things to be doing with his time. Now that Rayah didn't have to deal with Kal the Impossible, she found herself glancing at the other competitors as General Peterson spoke, trying to see who all was there.

Do you recognize everyone as well? asked her brother, his thoughts in her head as seamlessly as if they had been talking out loud.

I feel like I've met them all before in the army, but I'm not sure.

Rayah's mind spun. She was quite sure indeed that all the teams around General Peterson were soldiers like her. The more she surveyed the faces, the greater her certainty grew. The small hairs on the back of her neck stood up momentarily as her thoughts automatically jumped to the worst-case scenario. What would they want with all military twins? Who set it up this way, and why? What had she and her brother gotten themselves into? She looked at Ondraus, wondering if he were going to respond with some throwaway line about how she over-analyzed everything. Instead, he stood there, equally puzzled.

"I am not your twin," said General Elden Peterson, "but I might as well be able to read all of your minds right now, so allow me to address your concerns."

Rayah had never met General Peterson in person; she'd only seen him on secure video conferences when he delivered important information to military personnel. She'd always had the impression that he was an all-business type of man who spoke assertively and whose presence commanded attention. Today, however, he seemed to be concealing tension. Perhaps he would have fooled any average person, but fraternal twins were experts at reading faces and body language.

"Yes, you are all military," continued General Peterson. "You've probably all crossed paths at one time or another. We've brought you all here because we believe you are the best, and we simply wanted to showcase the resourcefulness of our athletic soldiers who work so well together that they might as well be one mind. You all will be competing in two events. The first is the mountain Bitroika race. You'll get points both for finishing quickly and for collecting flags, which have varying point values depending on color. You'll have to showcase your tactical thinking by deciding quickly, in the heat of the moment, how to strike the perfect balance between speed and points.

"Second is the ice maze, which is a lengthy and devious labyrinth relay race with plenty of dead ends and surprises I can't reveal. Each of these tasks will test your mettle and your ability to communicate and work with your sibling effectively under pressure. Please put on your gear and get ready for the first task."

Rayah and the rest of the competitors reached into their equipment bags as General Peterson moved away to take a phone call. She removed her helmet from the bag and began to strap it on, thinking again about the announcement General Peterson had just made. She wasn't buying it one bit. The soldiers – all twins – hadn't been invited to the Games just because the Royal Army wanted to let them have some fun together. There was more going on, but Rayah couldn't figure out what.

She eyed Kaled and felt another wave of emotion coming down hard on her, forcing her to take a deep breath and look away. These thoughts were not the type she wanted her brother to know about, so she focused her energy on building a wall in her mind so that he couldn't sense her feelings. That was called monoblock, and it was one of the duo-com skills that all fraternal twins learned. This time it was for Ondraus' protection; the loathing Rayah felt toward Kaled was all-consuming, and the last thing she wanted was to bore or exasperate her brother with her constant inner monologue right before a life-or-death race down a mountain.

Her brother must have felt the mental block; he nudged her and whispered, "We got this. Just push him out of your mind. Whatever energy you might be spending on thoughts of him, use it to win against him instead. Come on. Let's show these people what we're made of."

Bless his heart, Rayah thought; her brother really tried to encourage her, as if a few sweet words would make a difference. Still, she owed it to Ondraus, and certainly to herself, to try her best. Now that General Peterson was no longer there, the sets of twins felt more at ease to converse with one another before they had to make their way to the starting point.

Bo Xulu, a massive man with bulging muscles and a shaved head, might have appeared at first glance like an unapproachable thug, but there was no hiding the kindness in his face or the way his eyes and mouth were lined with wrinkles from frequent laughter. His sister Lina Xulu was also quite tall, but nowhere near the stature of her barge-like brother. She had powder blue hair and hazel eyes. They were both captains in their early thirties and worked in the engineering field in the army. Rayah had met them a few months before when the Xulu twins traveled to the city of Benal to help build the new medical center where Rayah and her brother were currently stationed.

Ameena Noxx and her brother Wilstead were lieutenants in their early twenties and had dark purple eyes with straight hair of the same color. They were slender despite their jobs as cooks in the army; they must have had incredible self-restraint not to gorge themselves on all the free food they made. Ameena, Rayah recalled, had a bubbly, positive personality. Her brother Wilstead tended to walk a fine line between being a joker and accidentally hurting someone's feelings.

Tru Ryder and her brother Tye were good-looking soldiers in their late twenties, serving in the army's Info-Tech department. They both had straight silver hair with icy blue eyes, high cheekbones, and lean, toned bodies. She'd met them once at a party several years ago and remembered with a chuckle that Tye had tried to hit on her. Rayah had been extremely uninterested but too polite to say so, and Aymes had swooped in and pretended to need her for something urgent. The memory brought a smile to Rayah's face. Those were the good old days before Kaled had ruined everything.

Metvier and his sister Uma were short and wiry; neither Rayah nor Ondraus had met before, though it was evident that some of the other teams knew them. The same was true for Sherell and her brother Zerod.

Last came Aymes Behr and her insufferable brother Kaled. Aymes had a sporty, petite build; her left arm had been decorated by a sleeve tattoo of flowers with intricate spiraling vines and stems. She'd gotten it the day after her father died, with Rayah by her side. Her scalp had a fade on one side while the other grew long, showcasing her ombre of bright blue, purple, and fuchsia hair. On days like today, when she wasn't in uniform, she wore multiple platinum earrings on the same side of her shaved head. The look was striking and accented her femininity in a way that simple long hair never could have.

Aymes Behr was a confident and beautiful twenty-four-year-old woman who never said no to a good time. She and her brother Kaled both had light green eyes, but that was the extent of their similarities. Kaled had abundant light purple hair, tousled on top and shorter on the sides. Rayah knew from intimate personal experience that he had washboard abs, muscular thighs, and defined arms. Rayah felt her cheeks warm as she discreetly watched Kaled and imagined running her fingers through the short and well-trimmed beard that clung to his squared-off jaw. Both Behr twins worked as pilots in Fleet and were experts on every military or civilian vehicle, whether it moved in the air, through the water, or on land.

Rayah and her brother left their bags in the competitor staging grounds at the base of the mountain and followed the other teams toward a ski lift. Rayah could hear the crowd now as she and her brother stood in line waiting for their chance on the lift. Something was odd about such a massive group of people cheering for her and the rest of the sets of twins; she was certain no one at this point had even mentioned their names yet. Rayah saw a drone flying past her and up the steep mountain as it provided a live feed for the curious crowd to watch.

Finally, Rayah and Ondraus climbed aboard the chair lift; the majestic view took her breath away, and the beauty finally pierced her tumultuous thoughts. It felt surreal to be so high up and not in the safety of a hovercar, or even a parachute on her way down during a training exercise. Tall trees led partway up the mountain then thinned out, so the only thing left at the top was bare snow.

Rayah's heart raced uncontrollably with a mixture of fear and excitement as she got off the ski-lift and walked carefully toward the group of people that were near the Bitroika snowmobiles...or, as Rayah liked to think of them, the *death buckets*.

Death buckets? Really, sis?

Convince me otherwise.

Ondraus laughed and then greeted the event workers, who were there to ensure things went smoothly. Her brother was extremely charismatic, Rayah knew. He had a face and a demeanor that most people automatically liked and trusted. Though Rayah was a friendly person, she much preferred to let her brother use his magic instead, so she followed him and allowed her lingering anxiety to sift away so she could enjoy this moment. The other teams arrived and settled beside each other at a small clearing near the starting line.

Aymes sat beside Rayah, and together they stretched their legs and lower back. "Is it me," asked Aymes while she touched the tip of her snow boots, "or has your brother gotten insanely hot since the last time I saw him?"

Rayah threw her head back and wheezed with laughter. "Gross! That is my bro–"

Mortified, Aymes quickly stuffed her hand over Rayah's mouth. "Girl, be subtle," she hissed, and then she lowered her hand.

"Sorry, Aymes," replied Rayah as she wiped a tear from the corner of her eye. "You just really took me by surprise. I swear if you tell him that, he'll follow you like a lost puppy all day. He's had a crush on you since forever."

"I know, but he's always looked like a *kid* before now…"

"It's the beard," Rayah said. "He started growing it to cover up his dimples and boyish face."

"Mmm," grunted Aymes quietly. Rayah threw a lump of snow at her, which only made the two women laugh uncontrollably.

Overhead they could hear the speakers come alive. "Alright, folks, thank you for your patience. Welcome to the one hundred and forty-fourth installment of the Winter Games, the most anticipated sporting event of the year! This year, as we teased earlier this week, we've added an additional day to this spectacle. We have seven teams of twins competing for the prestigious Winter Games Cup!" The announcer's exaggerated tones got the crowd screaming and clapping but had no effect on Rayah, who continued to stretch and then checked her watch. She had five more minutes before she and Ondraus had to settle themselves into the death buckets.

"Are you scared?" Rayah asked Aymes.

"I don't scare easily," Aymes replied with a confident smirk.

"I know," continued Rayah, "but it's not like any of us have actually done this, other than in that ridiculous low-budget simulation they gave us a few days ago."

"Yeah," chuckled Aymes, "Niklas could probably put together something more realistic."

"Niklas? Who's he? Do tell."

"Umm," Aymes smirked, "it's a bit complicated. I'll have to tell you later when we have more time. What about you? Are you dating anyone?"

"I was, but we just broke up two weeks ago," replied Rayah. She glanced over her shoulder and noticed Kaled had been looking at her.

"Oh, I'm sorry to hear that," said Aymes.

"Hmm?" Rayah snapped her attention back to her friend. "It's all good. He got a new job at a hospital in Devino."

"So he broke up with you because of that? Devino is only like an hour from Benal, right?" asked Aymes.

"I have a strict rule against long-distance relationships. Nevdier and I enjoyed our last night together and then went our separate ways. The long-distance thing sucks; I won't put myself through that ever again."

Aymes grew quiet, then wrapped her arm around Rayah's waist. "If I recall," said Aymes gently, "things didn't all suck when you tried it with Kaled."

"You're right," said Rayah leaning her head on her friend's shoulder. "But the ending did."

The announcer continued his speech. "Unlike our usual competitors, these teams have never physically been inside a Bitroika, nor have they had all year to hone their skills. Of course, there's the advantage that these individuals can communicate in a way normal folks can't, but will that be enough? I'm sure this will be an event that we will all remember."

As the announcer blathered, Rayah and the rest of the competitors walked up to the starting line, where they met with the event workers. In just a few minutes, the seven teams would be barreling down the snowy mountain, trying to capture as many flags as possible. Unfortunately, all this mayhem would be happening simultaneously, and there was no specific path for each team, meaning every flag all over the course was free for any team to grab.

With help from one of the event workers, Rayah settled into the back of the Bitroika, a sleek two-person snowmobile that had bucket seats, a steering wheel, and a lever that controlled the speed of the vehicle.

She and her brother had decided several weeks ago who would be in the back capturing flags and who would steer from the front. It was an easy decision for both: Rayah would be on flag duty. If she were in the front steering the death bucket, she wouldn't go fast enough, nor would she make the necessary split-second decisions to take sharp turns and daring courses. In the back, however, she would have to trust her brother's judgment.

They balanced each other out in this event, just like in every other area of their friendship. Rayah kept Ondraus reined in from making brash decisions, while he kept her grounded and calm when she was getting carried away with wanting to control everything. Without each other, they would be completely insufferable, or at least that was what they always said to each other in a half-joking manner.

"Careful, miss," said the event worker in a warning tone as he bent down to check her safety belt. He must have been wearing at least twenty scarves, and they kept slapping Rayah in the face as the wind whipped them back and forth. "Last year one of the riders suffered a fractured spine doing this course." The man patted her on the shoulder and then tended to Ondraus's seatbelt.

Wow, that was very reassuring, she joked. The pat on the shoulder felt like a strange omen from the lanky, overdressed man.

Yeah, we need a new seatbelt guy, Ondraus chuckled. *This one is terrible.* She could see her brother in the side mirrors now as he adjusted them. *Seriously though, we should pray. You know, just in case.*

She agreed instantly. In truth, she had been feeling the same thing. She put her hands on Ondraus' shoulders while they both bowed their heads to say a quick prayer.

The roar of the crowd climbed up the mountain and filled the air with enthusiasm. Rayah looked to her left and saw Aymes and Kaled laughing and giving one another an encouraging slap on the helmet. Now that Rayah was seated precariously on the incline of a steep mountain face, she saw the course stretching out before her. In the few moments before the event began, she tried to memorize as much as she could, because she knew full well that it would be utter craziness once the starting signal went off.

She could see multiple flags for capturing and ramps for getting a daredevil jump into the air to reach higher flags worth significantly more points. Boulders and trees dotted the course to act as obstacles. Whatever fear or anxiety she had been carrying finally left her completely, and instead, she was filled with excitement. This course looked fun, and she was glad her brother had dragged her out here, even if she'd had to tolerate an unfortunate encounter with Kaled beforehand.

Right on schedule, the announcer bellowed, "Let the countdown begin! Five, four, three, two, one!"

As soon as the bullhorn made its sound and the gate released, all seven teams launched out from their starting points and down the mountain. Rayah's heart thumped madly against her chest as she gripped the sides of the sled, the scenery already racing past her so quickly she could barely see it. Through duo-com, she could sense that her brother was in laser focus mode, his head crouched down and nearly level with his visibly tense shoulders.

Forty feet ahead, a bright red flag hung under a lean pole, and there was Ondraus' thought in her mind: *I'm going for the red. Get ready.*

The sled yanked hard to the right, and Rayah flexed

her fingers to prepare for what might be a painful contact. She extended her arm above her head and barely managed to catch the flag, snapping it loose from the quick-release line that tied it to the pole. Rayah stuffed the small flag in her jacket's front pocket and readied herself for the next one.

Ouch! Did you see that? asked Ondraus as he looked in the side mirrors.

No, what?

Someone almost wiped out near that large boulder. They got knocked way out to the left. I didn't see who it was.

A great way to scramble your head early on, responded Rayah.

Ondraus must have slowed down, even if just by a little bit, because two teams rushed past them as they were duo-comming. The Bitroika's speed, combined with the steep incline down the mountain, made Rayah feel like she were jumping out of an airship with a parachute on like she had for her eighteenth birthday, at Ondraus's insistent request, of course. Her stomach had leaped into her throat and seemed quite content to stay there. She shook her head and focused her eyes on the course in front of her.

Far right, forty-five feet, yellow, she said as a smile crept to the corners of her mouth. With that instruction, her brother quickly slammed the sled into a hard turn so that Rayah could reach for the flag.

They continued at lightning speed down the face of the mountain, grabbing flag after flag. Ondraus accelerated when they were going straight down and didn't ease up for the sharp turns, letting the Bitroika's skis grip the snow and slow them down by friction alone.

We need to get that flag on the ramp, said Ondraus. *You*

ready?

Let's get it!

Ondraus maneuvered the Bitroika toward the ramp. Rayah felt a hard thud as the sled hit the ramp, and in the next moment, they were soaring five feet in the air, which let Rayah grab the bright fuchsia flag that was taunting them from a high pole. Rayah and her brother were like a machine. Left, right, straight, another hard left. She could anticipate every sharp turn and every decision Ondraus was making. A few flags slipped through her fingers, and she wished she could have used some sort of adhesive or double-sided tape on her gloves to make them more grippy.

Is that a white flag? asked her brother in a confused tone. *I haven't seen any of those yet.*

Let's go for it.

Is it me, or is that flag shining? asked her brother while they inched closer to it.

I see it too. Only one way to find out. She took a deep breath and extended her arm as high as possible, and reached for the flag, which didn't move. It was too late; there was no way to attempt a second grab.

I couldn't get it. It was lathered in grease. Rayah tried to wipe off the excess onto her pants and readied herself for the next flag instead.

Kal and Aymes got the white flag, said her brother with annoyance.

Of course they did, she responded. Rayah wasn't as bothered as her brother. She wasn't competitive and could care less whether they won...but then again, she reminded herself, this competition didn't feel so innocent. Maybe winning was critical.

Her face was numb from the ice-cold wind that

rushed at her constantly as they continued their steep decline. Out of the corner of her eye, she saw another Bitroika twirl around uncontrollably.

I think we're almost at the finish line, said Ondraus. *Pretty sure I'm hearing the crowd right now. I don't see any more flags.*

I do! White, far left, near the tree, thirty feet. She made the unwise decision to undo her seatbelt. She knew, even from this distance, that the flag was too high up, and with the added grease, it would be nearly impossible to grab.

As they hurtled toward it, she hopped out of her seat and stood precariously on the rear body of the sled, sticking both arms out to balance and steady herself. She could hear her brother's alarmed thought: *WHAT ARE YOU DOING?*

Just keep it steady; I got this. No pressure.

No pressure, she says!

Rayah could feel the anxiety in her brother, but she blocked it out and readied herself.

Together they counted: *Five, four, three, two, one!*

On one, she jumped. It was quick but far from graceful. Her feet landed in the seat, and she nearly fell, dropping to her knees and smiling to herself.

I swear, Rayah, you better have that flag after that crazy stunt you just pulled.

She laughed victoriously. *You bet I do!*

That jump had cost them some time, and as a result, Kaled and Aymes made it across the finish line first. After accounting for the clock and the added points for all the flags, Rayah and her brother came in first. Kaled and Aymes finished a close second, with Ameena and Wilstead in third and Bo and Lina in fourth. The roar of the enthusiastic crowd made Rayah smile even wider as she and the rest of the contestants stood at the finish line, happily receiving their accolades.

"It's not every day that people cheer us on. I kinda like it," said Ondraus with a smile as he waved at the crowd and the flying drone cameras.

"Why am I not surprised?" responded Rayah with a grin.

"Way to go, twinkle toes," said Aymes as she and Kaled approached them. "This is why I rarely believe you when you get nervous about something. You always conquer your fears and do it in style. I don't know how you didn't fall, though. You seriously had me worried there for a second."

"Thank you, thank you," said Rayah as she bowed dramatically and waved.

Kaled had stayed a few feet away from them, remaining silent but smiling in encouragement. She appreciated that he kept his distance from her, as she was having a hard enough time keeping her composure, knowing the man she'd once loved had appeared in her life again. All the twins congratulated one another as they began their trek toward the Ice Maze.

CHAPTER 4

Ondraus

His sister had amazed him with that stunt she'd pulled. Annoyance roiled inside him because she had done something that could have gotten her hurt – and he knew *without a doubt* that she would have screamed at him for days if he'd done the same thing himself – but he also swelled with pride at her resourcefulness. She'd always been quick on her feet thanks to all the dancing and combative fighting she practiced in her free time; he had only been successful in knocking her down with a foot-sweep twice.

The Ice Maze now loomed in front of them. It was notorious for being filled with different types of obstacles and courses each year. In theory, the main objective was easy: get from the starting point to the ending point in the fastest amount of time. The difficulty came from the ever-changing walls, icy floors, and whatever other surprises the Games Master had in store for the competitors that year.

Although Ondraus was enjoying himself, he agreed with his sister that something felt strange about their invitation to compete. Ondraus had seen plenty of Winter Games in the past, and the Ice Maze was one of his favorite competitions due to its complexity. He still didn't understand what these events had to do with being a twin, though. The instructions from the

Games Master were unclear, and none of the competitors knew any more than Ondraus did.

After winning the first event down the mountain, Aymes surprised Ondraus by giving him a lengthy warm hug. Aymes had always been a good friend to him and a kind woman, but this hug felt different somehow, and he liked it. He wondered if he could score an equally amazing hug regardless of who won the Ice Maze event. Aymes, Rayah, and the other females had been blindfolded and sent somewhere in the maze. Ondraus assumed they would do some sort of "pass the baton," since he'd been given a small rubber stick to carry. No one had yet explained what the stick was for, but he stored it in his cargo pocket so he'd be ready for anything.

Ondraus flexed his fingers and stretched his legs while he stood on the starting line at the entrance to the maze. Each time he exhaled, a puff of warm white air escaped his mouth and trailed away. All the other men stood at the starting line as well, and as fate would have it, Kaled was the one closest to him. Ondraus knew what had happened between Kaled and his sister and truly understood why she wanted nothing to do with him ever again. However, Ondraus wasn't comfortable ignoring him, no matter the strength of Rayah's hatred. Kaled had been Ondraus' best friend growing up, and they still spoke regularly, but there was no denying that something huge had changed. It felt like they could never return to that true camaraderie they had had in the past.

"Good luck, friend," said Ondraus.

"Thanks. Same to you."

The announcer's voice filled the open space once

more, this time giving a quick run-through of what the Ice Maze held for the competitors. He reminded the viewers that Team Jur was in first place, with Team Behr in second and Team Noxx in third.

"Here's a little tip for my eager competitors," declared the announcer in a sing-songy teasing voice. "It would be beneficial if you are on your guard and remember every move you make."

That sounded like more than a tip to me, said Rayah from somewhere within the maze.

I agree. Hey sis, do you know where inside the maze you are? Any hints you can give me?

I actually have no idea, but they have us sitting down. I guess that's their not-so-subtle way of saying this is going to take a while.

A while was right. Ondraus had heard that the maze was thirty acres in size, which meant it could take a full hour or longer just to get to the middle. Where the previous task required nerves of steel, this one might call for perseverance and strength of mind. Thankfully, Ondraus was quite good at puzzles.

The Ice Maze's walls were actually crafted from metal covered with ice, and Ondraus knew – from watching this race on the tele-screen every year as far as he could remember – that some of the walls could be moved hydraulically, changing the layout of the maze even while the competitors were inside. It was great to watch, and he was betting it was even more fun to experience. As soon as the bullhorn sounded, Ondraus and the rest of the men ran toward the entrance of the great labyrinth.

He kept to one wall and then made the choice to go right instead of straight at the first crossroad, slowing to a jog as he did. Ondraus knew if he went too fast, he wouldn't be able to stop in time if the walls changed direction, and then he would just slam his face into an obstacle. The last thing he needed was for every single woman in all of Brennen to see him accidentally smash his face, with instant replays in slow-motion from every imaginable angle. Somewhere to his left, he heard someone crash into a solid wall and curse in pain.

Behind him was Kaled, who had somehow reached him despite initially taking a different route. Ondraus didn't know if that was a good thing or a bad thing. Together they came to another fork in the maze, and each of them took a different path. As Ondraus ran, he couldn't help looking at the height of the walls on either side of him.

I bet if I climbed those walls I could see the whole course from here.

O, you know if you do that, we'll be disqualified, scolded his sister from an unknown distance.

Ondraus chuckled and picked up the pace, only to stop a few seconds later. *Do you feel that?* Instinctively he looked up.

I do. But, I watched the forecast this morning, there were no predicted Sonic Storms.

Same, he responded.

Now he felt an even greater desire to get out of the maze, or at the very least to reach his sister so he could shield her from the incoming storm. Not because she needed it and couldn't take care of herself, of course; she was as capable as anyone he knew, but still, she was his sister, and he liked watching out for her when he could. He sped up just as a strange humming sound pierced the air, giving him and everyone else a mere split second to react. Ondraus was caught in mid-stride and couldn't react quickly enough when the sonic energy slammed into him. He fell to the ground with the weight of the invisible wave pinning him down.

A moment later, he got up and caught hold of his bearings, trying to run, although he felt disoriented. He didn't know how this affected the crowds outside the maze, since it wasn't like they all had a safe place to wait inside. All he knew was that he needed to get to his sister.

Ondraus pushed through his daze, no longer caring if he went face-first into a wall. He saw another fork up ahead and ran as fast as possible, taking a left this time. As he did, he felt the hum of another wave about to hit, and this time dived into a corner with his hands over his neck. The wave smashed him to the ground even from that defensive position. It must have been way stronger than the previous one.

"Argh!"

Ondraus heard the sound of someone in front of him. It was Bo, that tall tree of a man, lying on the floor and holding his leg. "I fell and landed on my ankle," he cursed while he rubbed the joint repeatedly. "This Sonic Storm came out of nowhere."

"You think it's strange, too?" asked Ondraus, standing near Bo and catching his breath.

"Oh, yeah. I'm thirty-two years old, and in all my years, I've never experienced an unannounced Sonic Storm. Not once."

"You think you can put weight on your leg?"

Bo got up, but winced in pain and cursed again while he shook his head. "I'm gonna finish this race. I'll just...hop."

"Let me take a look," said Ondraus.

Bo lifted his pant leg, and Ondraus saw that his ankle was already starting to swell. "You should wrap that. If not, you'll be in a whole world of pain later." Ondraus removed his neck gaiter and tore the fabric, quickly kneeling and wrapping it tightly around Bo's ankle. "That should do for now, but you'll want to rest it later. Now let's get out of this blasted maze."

"Thanks, doc. I appreciate it."

Ondraus gave him a friendly nod and said, "I'm a nurse, not a doctor, but you're welcome. Catch you on the other side!"

He then sped off, trying to make up for lost time. Helping out Bo was a good thing, and Ondraus didn't regret stopping, but he did hope it wouldn't be the difference between winning and losing this race.

In front of him, he saw Kaled come out from the right and suddenly wobble as the floor underneath him began to totter.

"Whoa!" Kaled fell to the ground, tumbling left and right.

Ondraus ran toward him and jumped onto the shifting floor, keeping his balance by swaying his body weight each time the stone moved beneath him. He reached down to the man his sister hated most on the entire planet of Vilmos, helping Kaled stand up again.

"Thanks, man," replied Kaled as he gained his balance. "I hope we don't get hit by another wave. It always knocks the air out of me."

"I feel you," replied Ondraus as he put his hand on the wall to help stabilize himself. The floor wobbled more violently than ever, seemingly intent on knocking them both down.

"We must be really lost," said Kaled. "We've been at this course for over an hour, and I know we've both been running almost the entire time, but I don't see our sisters. Aren't they supposed to be in the middle?"

"Yeah, I was thinking the same. I was sprinting for a bit, too," replied Ondraus.

Ondraus chanced a look at his watch and winced at the time; they had been in the maze for an hour and thirty minutes, and the end was still nowhere to be seen. He wondered if anyone else had made it to the other side, but when he duo-commed his sister, she assured him no one had arrived yet. After several minutes of inching along, Ondraus finally escaped the wobbling floor, and he picked up the pace once more.

He saw a digital sign that pointed to the left and wasn't sure if that was a trick or an actual tip. Not wanting to waste time, he quickly decided it was a tip, and took the left turn at lightning speed. Suddenly, someone dropped onto the snow-laden ground in front of him. Ondraus looked up and deduced the person must have been perched on top of the ice wall before dropping down precariously close to Ondraus' head. The opponent wore an all-white snowsuit and kept his face hidden with a neck gaiter that he had pulled up to his nose. Only his mischievous eyes were visible.

The man took out a rubber rod, one similar to the one Ondraus carried in his cargo pocket, and pressed a button to extend the rod automatically. The man in white beckoned Ondraus with his hand, and within a fraction of a second, he began to twirl his weapon menacingly. Then he ran toward Ondraus, ready to attack.

"You really don't want to do that," warned Ondraus with a smile. "I'm pretty good at combatives."

The man didn't slow down nor respond; instead, he used the rod to land a solid strike on Ondraus' thigh.

"Fine; have it your way," replied Ondraus with a smile.

Ondraus enjoyed a game of good old-fashioned stick fighting. He twirled his own rod and then spun his body around so that his weapon hit his attacker on the back. The other man fell to the floor but bounced right up, rocking his arm back for power and bringing it down hard with the intent of smashing the rod against Ondraus' face. The attack was too slow. Ondraus blocked the hit and stepped back, waiting for the other man to overextend himself.

His opponent thrust the rod forward, and Ondraus moved back again, then sprang onto his right leg and counterattacked, his rod pounding the other man's midsection. Puffy padding absorbed the worst of the blow, but it was still enough to make the white-dressed man bend over, giving Ondraus just enough time to swing his leg up and over to kick the man in the back of the head. As soon as the man was down, Ondraus fled, not wanting to spend his precious minutes fighting if he could help it. After ten minutes of running, Ondraus encountered yet another fighting man, even more tenacious than the last. Ondraus gave him a good beating, but received several strikes to his face and arms and had a bloody lip to show for it.

O, is that you? I think I hear a few people.

"Rayah, do you hear me?" he asked out loud.

"Yes!"

He was delighted to hear her voice; that maze had been absolutely ridiculous. He looked behind him and heard Kaled fighting that second opponent.

"Come on, Kal! I think our sisters are up this way. Let's get out of here!"

"Bo!" yelled Kaled. "You're almost at the end. Just a few more feet!"

Ondraus and Kaled raced as fast as they could toward the halfway point of the maze, with Bo hopping loudly behind them and cursing every few steps.

"Okay, now it's time to switch things up a bit!" That was the announcer's voice again, echoing from somewhere outside the maze. "Since you've been through this once already, you will guide your sisters back the way you just came in. I sure do hope you were paying attention!"

I don't like this guy, thought Rayah.

Neither do I. No time to dwell on it, though. Ondraus gave his sister's wristband a tap with his, synchronizing their timing data, then passed the rubber stick to Rayah and quickly showed her how to extend it.

With that, she was off, duo-comming her brother everything she saw. *I see a small drop of blood here,* she said.

Okay, be on the lookout. This is your first obstacle. There's a person waiting to fight. Get out the stick and just beat the snot out of that one as fast as you can. They were laying the pain on pretty thick with us.

Thirty minutes later, she reached out to her brother again. She said she'd passed a sign that told her to go right, which made Ondraus pause for just a moment – *it told me to go left* – before realizing it was opposite because he'd been coming from the other end of the maze. Past that was the part with the shaking floor, which he warned her about, and suggested that she use the wall to balance herself.

Ondraus was pretty certain he had been paying attention to all the lefts and rights he'd taken during his leg of the race, and even with all the distractions, he was still pretty confident he could talk his sister through it. By now, all the men had arrived at the midway point, unable to influence the competition any further except by guiding their sisters as best they could. Ondraus hated just sitting around doing nothing, and he was sure he wasn't the only one.

"That Sonic Storm was fake," stated Wilstead while rubbing his bloody temple.

"What makes you think that?" asked Ondraus.

"I looked up as the first wave hit and saw a reflection above me. It's like an invisible dome is over this entire maze."

"I'm not following. What do you mean?"

"I think," said Winstead, a little lower, "I think the Sonic Storm was fabricated for this event. And for the record, they've never had something like this during the real Games, so I don't know why they would do it for us."

"It's like they're trying to prove something," added Zerod. He too had some blood on his face.

Metvier and Tye nodded in agreement. The minutes crept by at a snail's pace. Ondraus provided as much accurate detail as possible to Rayah, but things kept getting all muddled in his mind. Several times she asked him for guidance at a crossroads, and he spent several long seconds imagining what it would have looked like from the other direction when he'd seen it himself. He didn't think she'd gotten lost – yet – but maybe it was only a matter of time...

This is different, she said after an hour had passed by.

I think this is where you had the Sonic Storm, but here we have to creep over and under laser beams. There's even a sign posted saying that if we touch the lasers, we'll be disqualified.

Ondraus looked at his watch and confirmed it was the exact place in the maze where he would have encountered the Sonic Storm. He wasn't concerned about her touching the lasers; he'd seen her scurrying under enough barbed wire and low obstacles in her army training. The prize was in the bag. After a few minutes of silence on her part, she spoke up again.

O, I think I see the exit, but Aymes is well ahead of me.

Ondraus took a quick look at Kaled, who was pumping his fist in the air. *Yeah, I think I see Kal celebrating. Aymes must have crossed the exit.*

Yup! Oh well, good for her, said Rayah.

That last sentence made Ondraus smile. Even though it was clear that Ondraus and Rayah had wanted to win, they would still celebrate a win for their friends. Aymes and Kaled ended in first place, with Rayah and Ondraus in second, Bo and Lina in third, and Tru and Tye in fourth. All seven teams got a few minutes of screen time with the announcer and the cameraman, who were casting live. Ondraus enjoyed the attention flashing his notorious pearly smile. As his interview ended, he glanced to his far left and saw Aymes looking at him. Her gaze felt nice, and he wished they could be granted the opportunity to hang out longer instead of going home right after this strange, albeit fun, competition. He was going to smile back at her but noticed she was talking with Rayah, her attention no longer on him. The two women were laughing and enjoying each other's company, just like old times.

After the teams were awarded their medals, the announcer told them that General Peterson wanted to meet them at the same place he'd addressed them earlier that morning. The clock read thirteen hundred hours when they met up at the clearing. There, General Peterson praised all of the teams for their hard work and gave a small cash prize to Metvier, Uma, Sherell, and Zerod. After those two teams left, he ordered the remaining five teams to meet with him later that night at eighteen hundred hours sharp. A vehicle would pick them up from their hotel at that time to take them to the palace, and they were to be dressed in their military uniforms.

Before he dismissed them, he said, "If you're late, don't bother calling for a ride. You're still a soldier. Your punctuality matters."

"So, what do you think, sis?" asked Ondraus. "Wanna hang out here a bit or go relax at the hotel?" They had left the meeting area by now and were back out in the spectators' paddock, where the festivities were still in full swing.

"Maybe a little bit of both? I'm exhausted, but I also want to enjoy this. Just look," she said as she raised her hands, as if to embrace everything around her. "Look at all of this. We're always training or working, and now we finally have a few hours to do whatever we want."

Ondraus agreed wholeheartedly, and so they set off, still in their Winter Games uniforms, with their bags of gear slung over their shoulders. Behind them followed the other four sets of twins, who were also deciding what to do with their free time. To Ondraus' pleasant surprise, Aymes was very close behind him. It had been two years since he had last been near her, and seeing her here stirred back to life some feelings he thought he'd buried long ago.

Her voice alone sent sonic chills up his spine. But how to play it off so that his sister didn't notice... that was another thing. He didn't necessarily want to fraternize with the enemy. He knew that Rayah never considered Aymes anything other than as a sister, but where there was Aymes, there was Kaled, and he knew Rayah would give a rapid veto to any plan that involved the chance of her running into him again.

"Mind if I tag along?" asked Aymes, picking up the pace to walk next to Ondraus and Rayah. Kaled trailed a few steps behind, fully obscured because there was some lady with her hands all over him and her lips on his.

"There's always room for you, Aymes," said Rayah with a smile. Ondraus noticed the flicker of annoyance in her eyes when she caught a glimpse of Kaled.

"Thanks," replied Aymes.

Rayah extended her hand, and the two women hooked arms as the group continued together. They only made it a short distance before stopping at a vendor to get some food in the outdoor seating area. They opted for grilled lamb with mint sauce, freshly baked bread with melted butter, and a large pint of the local ale. As they ate, Ondraus noticed his sister staring out into the crowd, and he didn't have to read her mind to know what she was doing. He figured he'd save her the embarrassment and ask the question he knew was burning within her.

"Hey, Aymes, who's that girl that your brother was kissing earlier?"

"Oh, her. You saw?"

"Kinda hard to miss it."

Aymes looked at Rayah for a moment before responding. "Her name is Vellah, and if there is one thing she likes doing, it's making out with my brother. Like all of the time. You'd think that one of them would get tired of it after a while. They've been dating for four months. Sorry you had to see that." Again, Ondraus noticed the apology was directed at Rayah and not necessarily the two of them.

"But why is she here?" Ondraus pressed. "I don't remember being told we could bring a visitor. The flights only allowed for two tickets."

"She insisted on coming," replied Aymes as she washed down her food with a swig of the frothy ale. "So my brother paid for the flight and made the arrangements."

"Hmm." Ondraus didn't know how to respond to that, so he left the matter alone. He noticed that Rayah was blocking her thoughts and trying her best to ignore the fact that Kaled was out with another woman. If she was using mono-block, there was no point in continuing this conversation about the mystery woman.

Aymes finished her food and fixed her gaze on Rayah. "So, can I ask you guys a question? Kal and I have been wondering something all day, and I don't know if it's just us."

"That something here seems a bit suspicious?" added Rayah with an arched eyebrow.

"Yes! Why in all of Vilmos is there a general talking to us at this event? General Elden Peterson is pretty much King Tarrington's right hand."

Aymes took a deep breath and shook her head. "Why these games? Why all fraternal twins?"

"I don't buy this *friendly competition* bit for one moment," said Rayah.

"Exactly." Aymes put down her drink and cleaned her lips with a napkin. "Did you notice how the teams that didn't win got their cash prize?"

"They sure did," agreed Ondraus." But I felt strange asking about our payment, so I kept my mouth closed."

"Kal said the same thing. And now we're all going to the palace, in our uniforms," said Aymes as she looked at her two friends.

"Maybe," said Rayah, "they're gonna offer us a job at the palace. Can you imagine that? It would be our dream come true. Do you remember how we always talked about that back in the academy?"

"How can I forget?" asked Ondraus with a huge grin. The idea brought back all those memories of the four of them, so young, and the only sets of twins at the academy at the time. They'd always talked about one day being good enough to work at the palace. Was that goal finally at his fingertips?

CHAPTER 5

Ondraus

After eating their delicious lunch, the three of them decided to walk around a bit. After a while, though, everything caught up with them: the excitement of the competition and the physical and mental toll it had taken.

"Please tell me I'm not the only one who just wants to go and take a nap while there's still time," said Ondraus.

"Damn, that sounds like a mighty good idea to me," said Aymes as she bent forward and stretched her calves and back.

"Same, please," agreed Rayah.

"I don't know what I want to do first, take a warm bath or pass out on my bed," replied Aymes, still stretching.

"Well, I guess that settles it. Let's go back to the hotel. Wanna catch a ride with us?" asked Ondraus as he took out his keys.

"Yeah, give me a second." Aymes went quiet for a few moments and looked out into the distance. Ondraus knew she was duo-comming with her brother. "Yeah, I'd love a lift. Kal says he and Vellah are going to hang out a bit longer. Although, honestly, he sounds exhausted."

"Something tells me it wasn't his decision," observed Rayah.

Aymes didn't answer out loud, but she did seem to nod in agreement. They all hopped into the hovercar, and Ondraus didn't miss the fact that his sister automatically went into the back seat, allowing Aymes to ride shotgun.

She's our guest, was Rayah's excuse. He shrugged, thankful for the gesture.

Ondraus was also glad they had all been provided private suites at the hotel. He had not been to many hotels in his life – barracks, yes, but hotels, not so much. Though he didn't have much of a standard for comparison, he knew this one was luxurious. Whoever had orchestrated all of this must have spared no expense.

The Hotel Maraviya must have been at least twenty stories tall, Ondraus thought as he and his passengers disembarked and entered the hotel. The entrance had clearly been designed to impress; Ondraus counted eight different fountains, lit with color-shifting lights. An elegant marble staircase circled up to the second level, and palm trees lined the lobby. Ondraus found himself examining the windows, trying to figure out how there was enough natural light to allow anything to grow indoors.

But the thing that interested him most was the needle-like revolving restaurant that pierced the sky. He'd seen it from the air as he approached, and even then he'd thought it would be a great place to bring Aymes on a date...if only he had an excuse to date her.

The interior of Ondraus' room had thick, intricate rugs that prompted him to remove his shoes and let his toes relax into the luxurious fabric. He treated himself to a scalding hot shower, which did a great job of loosening his sore muscles. By midafternoon he plopped himself onto the massive bed, set a timer, and promptly fell asleep.

After that much effort, and in a bed that comfortable, he could probably have slept for days had his alarm not beeped incessantly to wake him up. He grunted as he swiped to turn the alarm off, as if his wristband could hear his verbal protest. Fatigue aside, this was already one of the greatest days of his life. First, he'd gotten to compete in the Winter Games – which of his friends could say *that*?! Even better, he and his sister had been invited to the palace, in uniform, *and* his crush, Aymes Behr, had once again entered his life. This only meant one thing: he needed to make himself look presentable. He trimmed his rich purple beard so it wouldn't look unruly and applied oil to moisturize the hair.

A look at his watch told him it was late afternoon, and he knew it might be a while before his sister emerged from her room. Experience had taught him, however, that he didn't have to worry about her being late. With nothing left to do, he decided to go out into the lobby and wait for Rayah there. If he was lucky, he thought, he might see Aymes and strike up a conversation with her. Instead, out of the corner of his eye, he saw Kaled hand in hand with his girlfriend Vellah. Kaled looked exhausted while his girlfriend seemed to be fluttering with excitement.

"Oh!" she said while stopping in mid-step. "I forgot to put on my makeup!"

"You're already wearing makeup," said Kaled, looking confused.

"Not my evening makeup, silly! We're going to the

palace! I might just need to do a full wardrobe change. I'll be right back."

"Hey, you only have about fifteen minutes."

"I'll be back in a shake!"

Ondraus kept watching Kaled, who yawned and looked around for a seat in the lobby. "There's a free spot here if you want," offered Ondraus with a wave.

"Thanks, man," replied Kaled as he made his way to the empty seat and kicked up his feet on a footrest. "Boy, I wish we'd left when you guys did. I could have used a good nap. But Vellah, she wanted to see and do everything, so we stayed a few extra hours."

"What time did you get up this morning?"

"Three."

"Same. I'm surprised you're functional," said Ondraus.

"I'm not. It's a total front. I'm dead inside," chuckled Kaled.

Ondraus had so many questions for his old friend. The two of them did talk from time to time, and Ondraus recalled hearing that Kaled had started dating someone new a few months ago, but he couldn't figure out why he would have brought her here. Then there was the crushing weight of questions he had swimming in his mind regarding the strange reasons they were called to this Winter Games in the first place and why they were all getting ready to go to the palace. His thoughts about the mystery were cut off by Kaled, who had piped up with a question.

"So...does your sister have a boyfriend right now?"

"I thought you and I agreed years ago that we wouldn't discuss my sister," warned Ondraus.

"I know, bud. It's just, you know, I still think about

her. I can't help it."

"No, she's not dating anyone at the moment," replied Ondraus. A surge of guilt coursed through him as he responded. If Rayah knew he had just dished out this personal detail, she would be livid.

Kaled nodded his head and followed up with a second question. "Does she ever talk about me or ask about me?"

"Don't do this to yourself, man."

"Please. I just need to know."

"No, she doesn't. Not once in the two years since the incident has she ever asked me about you. And when she talks about you, it's not something you want to hear. She's still pretty peeved."

Kaled sighed and slumped further into the oversized armchair. "I figured," he said in a resigned tone.

"Dude, why are you asking about her when you literally have a gorgeous woman worshiping you? Why did you even bring her, anyway?" Ondraus was feeling a bit fed up with his friend. He tried not to let the annoyance show, but the whole situation really rubbed him the wrong way. He didn't like it when guys checked out his sister, especially not if those guys were already dating someone. It was a major lack of respect.

"I miss Rayah so much. I miss being her friend, all of us hanging out. I miss all the fun we used to have. I messed up, big time, and I lost one of my best friends in the process."

Ondraus noticed that Kaled had dodged the question completely. He just gave his friend a nod because there wasn't much he could say that would be helpful at the moment. Kaled wasn't the only one who missed all the fun they used to have. Growing up in the academy together was part of what had given all of them the kind of connection that only the closest of friends could share. Ondraus just listened as Kaled continued.

"And Vellah, she's...you know, she's great. She wanted to come to this because I never have time to really take her out. She's so supportive of my career, and I wanted to show her a bit of fun. But, damn, had I known that Rayah was going to be here..." He trailed off and shook his head.

"You wouldn't have brought Vellah?" asked Ondraus, disgusted.

"I know what that makes me look like," said Kaled, pinching the bridge of his nose.

"Kinda like a sleaze-ball."

"I deserved that. And speaking of which..." said Kaled looking to his far right.

Out came his girlfriend in a tight dress, heels, and different makeup. *Something* must have set it apart as evening makeup, but Ondraus couldn't figure out what, and he wasn't about to spend time staring at another man's girlfriend.

"Hey, babe," said Vellah as she flipped her bright silver hair flirtatiously with her hand. Seeing no other available chairs, she sat on Kaled's knee and kissed him on the lips. "This place is so fancy. Did you see those thick steam towels they had available in the rooms, O?"

Ondraus almost flinched when she called him by his nickname. Only his closest friends and family called him that. Now that Vellah was right in his face, he could see why Kaled was attracted to her, at least on a physical level. She was outrageously beautiful, like the type that would have been popular in school. Oddly enough, it looked like she was the one who called the shots in the relationship.

"I did notice it. Very nice indeed," replied Ondraus with a cordial smile.

"So," she said, as if she had been chummy with Ondraus for many years, "why do you think they've called all of us to the palace? Maybe you all did such a great job that they wanted to thank you in a special way. Maybe you'll all get promoted!"

Ondraus arched an eyebrow. *All of us?* he thought to himself. This Vellah was quick to include herself, as if she had been there competing alongside him and the rest of the soldiers.

"Hmm, I'm not sure if it works that way," said Kaled, patting Vellah on her thigh. Vellah responded with a playful slap on Kaled's shoulder and rewarded him with a lengthy kiss on the lips.

Just then, Rayah walked into the lobby and spotted them. Ondraus could feel the literal heat bubbling up within his sister. She was blocking her thoughts again, and he didn't blame her. As she walked by, he swore he saw a flicker of flames in her eyes. Kaled, not thinking, got up and stared stupidly as Rayah covered the length of the lobby to the entrance. She wasn't in a dress like Vellah's; instead, she too wore her uniform, yet that seemed to get Kaled's attention more than the woman who had been on his knee. Rayah had, however, lost the braids she had worn earlier that morning, opting to wear her hair down in its natural curly form.

"I almost fell, Kal," chided Vellah, sounding annoyed as she straightened her dress.

"Oh. I'm sorry."

Ondraus had seen the whole debacle happening in slow motion: Rayah on the other end of the room,

Kaled fumbling his way through his feelings, and Aymes following Rayah outside but stopping momentarily to give Kal a dirty look that spoke volumes. Yet all the while, Vellah remained utterly clueless that her boyfriend was thirsting for another woman right in front of her.

After a moment, Ondraus deliberately looked at his watch and then stood up. "If you'll excuse me," he began, then walked toward the entrance.

Outside he saw both Rayah and Aymes talking to a good-looking man in a military uniform. The man was smiling at both ladies, and they seemed content with his company. Ondraus had hoped to get a few moments alone with Aymes, but felt the other man had beat him to it. He spun on his heels to re-enter the hotel lobby when he felt a hand on his arm.

"Hey you," said Aymes with a dazzling smile. "Leaving so soon?"

Her touch had stopped him in his tracks, while her smile made his body warm up despite the cold weather. Aymes walked closer to him; her eyes twinkled in a way he had never noticed before. Ondraus couldn't help but notice that all of her attention was on him and not on the palace soldier she had been talking to moments before.

"Hey," he responded, taking a step closer to her, wondering if she felt the same vibes. "No, I'm not going anywhere. The company here is too good to leave."

Wow, that was perfection. Rayah tore her infatuated gaze from the handsome man and looked at her brother for a second. She must have audibly heard him talking to Aymes.

"I think your sister is flirting," said Aymes, unaware

that Rayah was well within earshot.

Ondraus motioned for Aymes to follow him closer toward the hotel doors so they could speak more candidly. "Yeah...she does that."

"I hope she's not doing it just because my brother and his clingy girlfriend are playing kissies in public."

Ondraus wondered the same thing. Rayah knew how to amp up the charm and bat her eyes just the right way to get most men to fall over themselves. It didn't take duo-com to tell from her body language how upset she'd been earlier with Kaled. Perhaps Rayah was only swooning over this new guy because she'd seen Vellah sitting on Kaled's knee and locking lips with him. One thing was to smile and flirt like Rayah and the soldier, but to kiss and be affectionate the way Kaled had done with Vellah moments earlier was a huge no-go while in uniform.

Rayah's conversation partner had light blue hair and dark purple eyes. His bulging muscles were visible even through the fabric of his thick winter uniform. If Ondraus didn't know any better, he'd have thought the man was intentionally standing in a way that flexed his biceps. If this were any other girl, it would be funny, but his sister? Gross.

"I might seriously get nauseous if your sister and my brother are throwing themselves at other people all night long," said Aymes with a smirk.

"I'll be sure to hold the vomit bucket."

Aymes laughed and slapped Ondraus' shoulder playfully. "So gross, but thank you for the offer and also the vivid picture."

"My pleasure."

Ondraus heard the glass doors swoosh open and saw

the rest of the soldiers exit the hotel lobby. Everyone was present except for Kaled.

"Hey guys," said Ameena. Her brother Wilstead stood beside her, waving and then immediately shoving his hands into his pockets.

"I'm not used to this weather," said Tru.

"Yeah, the capital has colder weather than the places we've been stationed for the last few years," said her brother Tye, who was visibly trembling.

The temperature had not been such a bother earlier that morning due to the protective cold-weather gear they wore to compete in the Winter Games; the military uniform, on the other hand, did not offer the same level of warmth.

The van driver looked at his watch. "We still have another five minutes. Is this everyone?"

As those words were spoken, Kaled and his girlfriend walked out, still wrapped halfway around each other.

"Yes, that's everyone," said Aymes, rolling her eyes.

"Great," said the driver. "Let's get into the vehicle and out of the cold. I need to see the digital invitation that General Peterson sent each of you so I can scan the encrypted barcode."

One by one, all the soldiers displayed the screen from their digital watches.

"Who are you?" asked the driver as Vellah approached.

"I'm his girlfriend," she said importantly.

"I'm sorry, ma'am, but no visitors. Only military personnel."

"Oh," said Vellah, looking like it had been the first time in a long time that she had been told *no*.

"I'll just meet you afterward, okay?" offered Kaled,

with visible embarrassment on his face.

"Um, sure. Bye."

Ondraus took a seat next to his sister. She was no longer looking annoyed. Instead, she was staring at the muscular man she had been talking to earlier. The man settled into the driver's seat, entered the coordinates to the palace, and raised the hover van into the air. A moment later, he hit the autopilot button and left the chair to face the group.

"Hello, all. My name is Sergeant Guyad Lurca, and I'm Head of Security for the palace, so we'll –"

Stop undressing him with your eyes, thought Ondraus as he nudged his sister playfully.

Be quiet and listen up, replied Rayah.

"...and once we reach the palace, we'll go through security. From there, you'll meet General Peterson. You'll receive further instructions at that point." Guyad flashed his smile again at Rayah, who unfortunately was in the same direction as Ondraus, and he didn't much appreciate the look. He saw his sister swoon...but her eyes flickered toward where Kaled was sitting, and Ondraus saw a satisfied smile creep onto her face when she noticed her ex-boyfriend's reaction.

CHAPTER 6

Rayah

The Hotel Maraviya had been the definition of classy-chic, thought Rayah, but it paled in comparison to this breathtaking view of the palace and its grounds. She'd seen video images of Istina Palace before, but being there in person was a different thing altogether. The complex sat on high ground, making it appear to be suspended above the ancient town below the walls. That town, known as the Heart of Clivesdail, had snow-capped mountains behind it, adding to the image of power and beauty. To the far left, beyond a wall around the Heart of Clivesdail, ran a cliff that dropped off to the crystal blue waters of the ocean beneath. Though the outer city of Clivesdail was the image of new technology, the historic Heart of Clivesdail still had an old-style touch with shorter buildings, cobblestone roads, and quaint shops on every corner.

The view from above, in the safety of their hover van, was enchanting. Rayah enjoyed hearing Guyad's commentary on the history of the architecture of the Heart of Clivesdail and how it had stood, basically untouched, for centuries. Hundreds of lights twinkled from the homes and shops below, perfectly matching the multitude of stars in the sky. As the vehicle descended, she chanced another look at Kaled and noticed he was still pouting. Rayah's covert glance had gone undetected; she only hoped the pleasure she took in seeing him sulk wasn't too obvious.

Even if Kaled hadn't been there, Rayah might still have taken a liking to Sergeant Guyad Lurca. The man was ruggedly handsome, with an irresistible smile that could melt any woman's resolve. But the fact that Kaled was there did complicate things. She didn't understand why Kaled kept looking at her and Guyad when they were chatting, or why he was pouting now. Was Kaled jealous? A part of her secretly wanted him to be jealous, while the other part of her, the part that was so over him, wanted him to finally be over her too.

The hover van landed gently, and Guyad helped Rayah and the other soldiers to climb down since the flooring was icy by the grand entrance. Once Rayah was indoors, the rich warmth of the palace thawed her within seconds. Guyad removed his heavy winter coat and gave it to a maid who had been standing there to greet him. Now that he no longer had on the bulky snowsuit and Rayah could see him better in his regular uniform, she took the time to appreciate the size and shape of his physique...which *definitely* deserved the appreciation.

"I was supposed to take you all directly to the meeting room," said Sergeant Lurca to the group, "but I just received a notification that we have a few minutes to kill. Who here would like a quick tour of the palace?"

As everyone except Kaled eagerly nodded their heads, Guyad led the group toward a marble column with a digital screen. The sergeant then tapped the screen several times to summon a holographic projection of the palace. From her position, Rayah noted the descriptions on each of the towers. The directory displayed a service tower, a royal suite tower, and a large Fleet department that occupied several floors. Memories of visiting Kaled in Fleet, back when they had been dating, flashed before her eyes. Rayah sighed and tried to refocus her attention on the tour.

After pointing out several important locations on the holographic map, Sergeant Lurca guided the party to a large high-ceilinged room adorned with gold trimming. The walls were decorated with life-sized oil paintings of previous monarchs, and glass cases held various priceless artifacts. Rayah heard both Tru and her brother Tye gasp in unison as their eyes landed on a particular item that caught their interest.

"Is that what I think it is?" asked Tye, his eyes widening as he took a step further.

"Yes, it is," answered Sergeant Lurca with an air of self-importance. He flashed his smile at Rayah and beckoned her to come closer to him. Though he addressed the group, his eyes and attention were on her and her alone. Standing so close to him, she couldn't help but smell the wonderful scent of his cologne.

"This is Rancor's Relic. Twenty-six years ago, Rancor and General Peterson fought and –"

"We know the story, Sergeant," said Kaled.

Rayah looked back over her shoulder just in time to see Kaled roll his eyes and then get awarded with a swift stomp on his foot by Aymes. Rayah could not believe he would dare be so rude to anyone, let alone someone in uniform.

"Of course you do," replied the sergeant, completely unfazed. "Well, this is the rod that Rancor lost during the legendary fight. As you can see by the placard's description, the rod is made of smooth rock and not wood. We've had some of Brennen's most prestigious scholars and scientists conduct studies on this item, but all results have been the same. It's just an ordinary bit of rock that has been shaped into a walking stick. There isn't anything special or magical about it."

"Oh," said Tru, a little disappointed. "I've always wondered if the tales were true."

"No," replied the sergeant. "Not true at all. I know; I grew up with the same wild stories as well. I suppose we all did. But there is nothing magical about this rod at all. That being said, it is still a product made with excellent craftsmanship. We don't know why Rancor had it with him during the battle, nor why it was so important to him, but we keep it safely guarded here as a memorial to that fateful night."

Rayah examined the smooth relic, wondering how long it would have taken to make such an intricate item by hand. She noticed the sergeant's handsome reflection on the glass case as he took a few steps closer to her.

"Are you doing anything later tonight?" whispered Sergeant Lurca.

"I don't know," replied Rayah with a grin, "what do you have in mind?"

Guyad took another step, his arm brushing up against hers, sending hundreds of delightful impulses throughout her skin. Rayah turned to face Sergeant Lurca but caught sight of the pitiful look on Kaled's face. Kaled stood alone, far from the group, who were all gawking at Rancor's Relic. Instead, Kaled fixed his attention on an oil painting of a man enveloped by bramble and vines as his wild, desperate eyes looked up at an elegant woman holding a pair of shears. Kaled's shoulders drooped, and his face was visibly distraught.

"We could go out for drinks," said Sergeant Lurca, interrupting Rayah's thoughts.

"That sounds wonderful," she said. "I don't know how long our meeting with General Peterson is, but –"

"I guess we'll just have to wait and see where the night takes us," he said smoothly.

If Rayah weren't wearing her uniform right now, she would be highly tempted to kiss Sergeant Lurca. He had a way of carrying himself that she found irresistible.

After a short while in the museum, the ten twins and Guyad continued up a corridor. Rayah saw an old man pushing a cart with treats, which filled the hallway with the decadent scent of rich chocolates and pastries. He looked exhausted but was humming quietly to himself, and he waved at her when he passed. Rayah followed the rest of her group to an intimately sized room just big enough for everyone to take a seat and be comfortable, but with not much space for anything else.

"You still haven't learned the ancient practice of subtlety when checking a guy out," teased Aymes. She had just taken a seat next to Rayah, who apparently was still *very obviously* checking out Guyad's muscular body.

Rayah didn't look at her friend but playfully hit her lap and whispered while still looking forward, "Please. You can't keep your eyes off my brother."

"I'm off my A-game. I'm usually the master at this fine technique," said Aymes in an exaggeratedly defensive tone.

"It's okay, Aymes; Ondraus is checking you out too. How long do you think we'll be here? Sergeant Lurca and I are going out for drinks later."

"Hmm," said Aymes. "He doesn't strike me as the type of guy that ends the night with just drinks, if you catch my drift."

"Good point," added Rayah. "I should definitely shave my legs before I meet up with him."

"Wow, Rayah," said Aymes in surprise. "It's not like you to go after a guy so quickly."

Rayah looked at her friend and noticed there was no judgment in her eyes. "I've changed a lot in the last two years," she said quietly. "Anyway, I just need a bit of a distraction, and who could say no to that eye candy?"

A respectful low murmur filled the room while groups of soldiers sat discussing things too quietly for Rayah to discern. The exciting revelation that Aymes had finally taken a liking to Ondraus, and the looks Rayah herself was getting from both Sergeant Guyad Lurca and Kaled, kept her thoughts divided into many avenues. Sergeant Lurca stood by the doorway, sending seductive signals toward Rayah while he waited for General Peterson. Kaled, on the other hand, sat on the other end of the room, brooding.

As her mind continued to swirl with emotion, the sergeant's phone began to ring. "I'll be right there," he said importantly. Before he left, however, he approached Rayah and smiled hungrily. His eyes didn't bother hiding what he wanted. "I have to go, but here's my number."

"Thanks," responded Rayah, curling her hair around her finger flirtatiously.

Sergeant Lurca's satisfied smile grew wider, and then he addressed the room, the lust in his eyes suddenly gone and his voice professional. "General Peterson will be here shortly. I need to attend to some time-sensitive matters. I'll see you all later after the meeting."

Aymes put her hand on Rayah's thigh, then leaned in and whispered, "Are you really going to bed with a guy you just met because you need a distraction from my brother? Or is it because you just want Guyad and that's it?"

"I don't know, to be honest." Rayah looked over at Kaled and saw him shaking his head. Kaled's eyes were on her; he had watched the whole thing, and somehow his reaction made her feel exposed in a way she couldn't fully explain. She turned her gaze back to Aymes, who was still watching her with concern. "A one-night stand isn't really my thing, but that guy is insanely hot, and I'm newly single. I'm all for committed relationships, but let's face it; they're all doomed to end anyway. I'm gonna seize the night. "

"You were once such a hopeful romantic," said Aymes. "I guess it's just jarring to hear you think that way."

Rayah chuckled half-heartedly. "It's okay. I no longer feel the need for something as trivial as love. That part of me died long ago. It's better like this. Strong emotions have a way of ruining everything. I find that honesty and open communication are far more important."

"Wait a minute," interjected Aymes, "how long did you say you and Nevdier dated?"

"Five months," said Rayah evenly.

"Five months? And you broke up because he had to move, and you're okay with this? You don't seem sad at all."

"I'm fine, honestly. What? Do you want me to cry or something?"

"No," added Aymes quickly. "I guess I didn't realize my brother had impacted other parts of your life. Man, he did a number on you. I'm so sorry."

"What are you talking about?" asked Rayah, thoroughly confused.

"Rayah, when was the last time you cried over a guy?"

"I don't know," said Rayah. She thought hard for a moment, trying to recall the last time she had felt the heart-ripping emotion of falling in pure love and then breaking up. "Maybe two years ago?"

"Yeah, that's what I thought. It was when my brother crashed and burned everything to the ground."

Rayah did not know how to respond to that revelation. Instead, she stared at Aymes for a few seconds in complete shock. Had she truly built a wall around her heart to prevent any more pain? Was this the reason why none of her previous relationships amounted to anything permanent? Now that she thought about it, Nevdier was the complete package: handsome, intelligent, great career, got along well with Ondraus, and Rayah's parents approved of him. Rayah had thoroughly enjoyed her time with Nevdier; they were a great couple, but she didn't even shed a single tear when they broke up. She'd made the decision the same way someone might change the channel on their tele-screen. It was simply what needed to be done, so *click*, new channel.

Rayah wanted to get Aymes' attention off her for the moment, so she deliberately changed the topic. "Looks like we still have some time before General Peterson comes in. Who is Niklas?"

Earlier that morning, before the mountain race on

the Bitroikas, Aymes had mentioned a guy named Niklas but didn't have the time to explain who he was. Even now, when she said his name, Rayah noticed a sparkle appear in Aymes' eyes.

"He's the love of my life," answered Aymes.

"Then why are you digging on my brother?" If there was one thing, Rayah could not stand, it was infidelity. She knew she had lost touch with her friend, but this was not the Aymes she remembered.

"Calm down, love," she answered gently, "Niklas is my son."

How was this possible? How was it that Aymes, her friend of over ten years, had gotten pregnant and had a son without Rayah knowing?

Aymes seemed to sense Rayah's confusion. "Look, I'm sorry I didn't say anything. I learned I was pregnant right after you and Kaled had your falling-out. You just weren't in a loving, cry-on-my-shoulder mental state. You shut me out, Rayah, and I had enough on my plate without trying to figure out how to fix things with you. I had a son to raise."

Stunned, Rayah sat motionless for a second, her mouth hanging open. How could she have been so insensitive to her friend? Only now did Rayah understand how beastly she'd been to Aymes and how deep the wounds went. "Aymes, I'm so sorry. I –"

Aymes placed her arm around Rayah and gave her a reassuring squeeze. "It's okay. We were both in a terrible state, and we did the best we could. It's water under the bridge. Let's just never let boys separate our friendship ever again."

"Deal." Rayah leaned her head onto Aymes' shoulder and closed her eyes for a second, relishing the closeness of her friend. She had missed Aymes so much, and this was almost – *almost* – like making up for lost time. Maybe Sergeant Lurca wasn't the person she should be spending her night with. Rayah's heart and mind needed a distraction from Kaled, but she also had a friendship that needed a lot of love and attention.

General Peterson came in, and all of the set of twins stood up and saluted him. "At ease, soldiers. Please take a seat."

CHAPTER 7

Rayah

General Peterson looked like he had the weight of the world on his shoulders, sitting heavily down and rubbing his forehead for a moment, as if at a loss for words. He didn't seem as jovial or even as intense as he had earlier that day. It was as if he'd been stripped of whatever pretense his rank forced him to put on, ready to speak freely in a way he didn't often get to. Rayah couldn't help feeling that things were about to get real.

"I know you are all intelligent and have been asking yourselves a multitude of questions. I will finally be forthcoming with you, and I only ask your forgiveness for the necessary deception from earlier." He paused and took a breath while looking them all in the eyes.

"Three weeks ago, a very strange thing happened. Two children, the nephew and niece of our palace doctor, became gravely ill. The two had been outside playing and were stung by more than a dozen Lucid Wasps. I don't know why the children became as sick as they did, but it was an emergency and they were brought here for urgent medical intervention. When they arrived, the children were convulsing and non-responsive. While here, however, they proceeded to make predictions about the future while still in their catatonic state." He paused again, allowing the group of soldiers in the room to take it all in.

"I know we have two medical soldiers in the room, but for the rest of you, I'll give a brief run-down on these types of wasps. They are only active in the winter and are usually only found in dense wooded areas. Their formal name is *Ampiainen qobiliyati*, but they are commonly known as Lucid Wasps. Anyone who is stung experiences very realistic dreams while asleep, due to a particular enzyme in their venom that interacts with the neurochemicals that transmit brain impulses across synapses. Many years ago, Brennen's agricultural ministry tried to eradicate this type of wasp because stupid teenagers kept daring each other to get stung so they could trip out on the dreams.

"Apart from the dreams, however, the only effects of these stings are some localized swelling and occasional severe reactions. These children, however, have experienced things that none of the medical staff have ever seen or heard of before, and no one quite knows why. Even while in the hospital bed and with their eyes closed, the two children began to speak, and they said something over and over again."

General Peterson, his hand trembling, reached into his pocket and pulled out a small strip of paper. "I had to write this down; our computer system is not responding for some reason." He cleared his throat and read from it. "'He comes at night by flight to strike; heir of throne turned to stone. We, the jewels are hunted down, but royal's twins will save the crown.'"

He pocketed the piece of paper and looked once again at the group before him. Rayah knew her mouth was agape, and she couldn't help it.

"I have been in the military all my adult life," said General Peterson, "I've been in many battles, and served my country with my own sweat and blood. Yet for some reason this has me spooked. Maybe it's because I'm a father, and I've come to care for King Tarrington as if he were one of my own children. King Tarrington and my son, Captain Yosef Peterson, grew up together and are as close as brothers. So this lucid dream, if we may call it that, feels like not only an attack on our crown, but a personal warning to me.

"As I mentioned, these young children keep chanting this strange saying over and over again. The doctor has never seen a recorded case like this one. The phrase almost sounds like an omen or even a prophecy. I'm not the type that buys into something that is not tangible or backed by science, but I can't ignore my gut, which is telling me this is terrible news that requires immediate action."

The room fell silent. The general had the attention of every single person there, and Rayah noticed her brother sitting on the edge of his seat. King Tarrington Branaugh was universally hailed as a great and honorable ruler, and his wife, Queen Ellandra, was said to be just as wonderful. It felt jarring to hear that anyone might want to do them any harm.

The general continued. "Whatever your first thoughts about this are, they are probably the same as those of the medical staff, namely that all of this is extremely strange, but that the words *vision* and *prophecy* are where you draw the line. Lucid Wasp dreams, after all, often have nothing to do with reality. However, Dr. Kortez, the royal physician, took the matter very seriously and immediately sent the queen for a sonogram."

Rayah heard someone move behind her and saw that

Tru had raised her hand.

"Yes, Lieutenant Ryder."

Tru stood up, as was required when asking a question of a higher-ranking individual. "Sir, I had read that our queen was barren. Why then would the doctor do a sonogram?"

"A very valid question, soldier," replied General Peterson, nodding his head. "You are correct. It was believed, after her near fatal fight with the Utroba Virus, that she would never be able to bear children. However, the sonogram was indisputable. Not only was the queen four and a half months pregnant, but she was carrying twins...just as the children had spoken in their trance. Now, we may, if we desire, believe that all of this is merely a coincidence and that the children randomly babbled something that just so happened to be true. Quite frankly, I don't have enough faith to believe in a coincidence that large. If the part of the statement that we can verify turned out to be true, I feel we have to take the rest of it seriously as well."

"Amazing," whispered Rayah, her mouth still wide open.

"You are all free to talk and ask questions without having to get up. Frankly, I'm too tired to deal with decorum at the moment."

"It's a miracle, sir," said Ondraus in awe. "Modern medicine still has no way to remedy the type of infertility caused by Utroba. It was a miracle that she even survived it, let alone to get pregnant after so nearly dying."

"You would know, wouldn't you, Captain Jur? You and your sister, Rayah, are nurses, after all."

"Excuse me, sir," said Aymes, "but how exactly did

she not know she was four months pregnant? It's not the type of thing a woman wouldn't notice."

"I have no doubt that she noticed *something*, but there would have been absolutely no reason for her to assume pregnancy was the cause of her nausea and food cravings. For years, she had been told by every single one of the best and brightest doctors in the land that she was infertile and there was no medical remedy. Why would she have even considered the thought that she might be with child? Now, I don't know much about the pregnancy itself, since I've never been in the medical field. I'm primarily concerned with protecting the crown at all costs if it turns out these children are speaking some kind of truth. Yes, Captain Jur?"

"Sir," said Rayah, "what became of those two children that gave the prophecy? Have they been questioned further?"

"Unfortunately not. They are still in the hospital bay, still unconscious. Every day or two they mumble the same phrase they first chanted weeks ago. Dr. Kortez, their uncle, has tried everything."

Rayah sat down, feeling terribly helpless. As a medical soldier, her passion and duty were always to help heal others. Here were two innocent children, with something inexplicable happening to them, and there didn't seem to be much that she or her brother could do.

General Peterson spoke up again. "And that is why we have brought you all here. We have great soldiers and officers in our Royal Army, but King Tarrington and I are desperate to create an elite group that will safeguard his children. If the hospitalized kids were right about the queen being pregnant, then there stands a chance that her twins will be hunted down as well. These royal babies are fraternal twins. We don't fully understand the significance of that, but if it's more than just a coincidence – and I believe I've made my position on that quite clear – then we want people like you around them. Even if all of this *is* merely a coincidence, at least your ability to duo-com with your siblings will give you a tactical advantage in the unlikely event that someone attempts to harm the royal twins."

This was a lot for Rayah to process. She took a moment to examine her comrades and saw they were equally as stunned. What did this all mean? Were they being asked to work for the palace after all? For how long? The royal infants aren't born yet, so would she and the other soldiers come back later in the year or wait here the entire time?

Then a terrible thought came to her: *Oh no! Does that mean I have to be in the same city as Kaled for the foreseeable future?* She truly hoped not. Maybe she was completely misinterpreting what General Peterson had said and was, like always, letting her thoughts get carried away. It had been easy to cast Kaled out of her mind and live as if he didn't exist for the past two years because they'd lived in different parts of the country. Living and working in close proximity to each other would bring its own multitude of problems. She glanced up at Kaled and saw that he looked mortified; maybe he was coming to the same conclusion she was and didn't want to spend a second more near her either.

General Peterson seemed to be finally concluding his remarks. "You will be on a separate pay grade from the rest of the Royal Guard. You'll be assigned duties based on your military occupation, but you'll also be in the palace performing guard duty. But being part of this group, which we are calling The Elite, is top secret. No information about it leaves this room, including the fact that it exists at all. The only people who know about it are me, the king, his wife, and all of you. We'll most likely have to tell Dr. Kortez sooner or later. No one else, not even my son Yosef or our Head of Security, Sergeant Lurca, knows of this group. Is that understood?"

All of the soldiers stood up and responded, "Yes, sir!"

"Good. Are there any final questions before we continue?"

Rayah still had one thing on her mind. "General Peterson, sir, can we see the kids in the medical ward? I..." She trailed off for a second, not knowing how silly she was going to sound. "I feel a great desire to see them."

"I do, too," said Ondraus.

General Peterson agreed, and The Elite walked toward the medical ward, located on the first floor in the rear of the palace. Large automatic doors opened as soon as the group approached; the ward was fully integrated with the most up-to-date technology and had ten beds, with large digital screens hanging on the walls above them. The walls, floor, and ceiling were all white, giving the room a pristine and antiseptic look. The ward was quiet, save for the soft rhythmic beating of the two ventilators and monitors in use on the far end of the room.

From afar, Rayah could see the small bodies, covered in crisp white blankets, with tubes down their throats and wires all coming in and out of every visible patch of skin on their arms and chests. The names listed on the two monitors were Evia Kortez and Ensin Kortez. For reasons that Rayah could not put into words, she felt compelled to be near these children and hold them as if they were her own. She had been in the medical field only five years, but had seen terrible things in that time. This, for some reason, was pulling at her heartstrings.

"Dr. Kortez," announced General Peterson, "I have a group of soldiers here who are new to our palace and were curious about the status of the two children in your care."

The doctor had on a wrinkled white uniform. His rank of Major was pinned on the uniform's collar, but the metal insignia bars were dull, as if he hadn't polished them in quite some time. He had bags under his puffy red eyes and facial hair hadn't been trimmed lately. The condition of his niece and nephew had obviously taken a physical and emotional toll on him.

He stood up and tried to snap his body to attention when General Peterson came in, but the general waved him off. "At ease, Doctor, at ease. They just want to take a look and we'll be out of your way. And go get Birchram to take over so that you can get to bed, because you look terrible. You're not technically in my chain of command, so I can't give you an order...but that's an order."

"May I?" Rayah asked the doctor as she got even closer to the little girl. "I'm a nurse."

"Go ahead," replied Dr. Kortez.

Without a second thought, Rayah reached for the little girl's hand and closed her eyes. Perhaps she had planned to pray for the child, or just to center her own thoughts, as if she could somehow pass along some peace to the girl. Instead, a flurry of blurry, frightening images flashed through Rayah's mind at lightning speed. She saw a snake chasing the children's heels and could hear the eerie chant that the general had read earlier. *He comes at night...*

"Ah!" exclaimed Rayah, letting go of the child's hand and staggering backward.

"Everything okay, sis?" asked Ondraus, looking concerned as he watched her rub the palm of her hand. He took it in his and examined it.

"I..." she stammered and looked first to the group, then to the general, then back to her brother. "I think I saw their vision. And when I tried to pull away, I got a shock on my hand."

With a face of concern, the doctor approached the bed where Evia lay and looked at the monitor. "Yes, look here. There's a spike of activity. Whatever you did seemed to...wake up her brain for a moment."

The general spoke in a hurried tone, "Can you try that again? We should try again, right, doctor?"

"We'd need a lot more of that brain activity to pull her out of the coma," Dr. Kortez replied, speaking to the general but looking at Rayah with eyes that were pleading for help.

"What if," suggested Ondraus, "I held my sister's hand while she held the girl's hand? Like form a chain? Maybe that would prevent actual burns on our hands if we share the burden."

"Well," said Bo, "what if we all do it? You hold the girl's hand and we make a chain. Someone else – me, since I'm the biggest, maybe – I stand in the middle holding the girl and the boy's hands."

"That...sounds like an idea, I suppose," said the doctor. "Wait a minute, did you mention you are siblings? You look to be the same age."

"Yes, doctor. We're twins. In fact, everyone here is a twin," replied Rayah.

Then, after looking at the medical insignia on Ondraus' shoulder, Dr. Kortez asked, "How long have the two of you served as nurses?"

"Five years of experience, the last two at Benal," responded Ondraus.

"If this works, these kids are going to wake up to find tubes down their throat," said Dr. Kortez. "As you can see, I don't have any of my other nurses here at the moment, so I'd appreciate some help."

"Of course, doctor." Ondraus grabbed a small aerosol can of hand sanitizer and two pairs of gloves, setting them on the bed near the little girl. "You ready, sis?"

Rayah sat down and rubbed her temples. "Let me think for a second."

She grew quiet, focusing on the memories of her duo-com training at the age of fourteen. Every fraternal twin in the kingdom of Brennen who wanted to learn duo-com had to register for a class with the Monktuary. Brennen's Monktuary was a place where twin monks lived; it was a center for all different sorts of physical and spiritual enlightenment. Its most important purpose was to teach the disciplined practice of duo-com to twins throughout the land, and its secondary purpose was to provide a sanctuary for twins free of charge. Rayah was busy recalling her Gaoled experience, and wondered if perhaps something like that was affecting the twins who were hospitalized in the palace medical ward.

"Did any of you experience a Gaoled when you were

first learning how to duo-com?" Rayah asked, then waited for a fraction of a minute while she surveyed the crowd. The doctor cocked his head to the side and furrowed his eyebrow. "I figured as much. It affects only a small portion of the fraternal twin population.

"A Gaoled – it literally means prison – is when you are stuck in the mind world of duo-com. You normally can't see this world at all; you just talk with your sibling without being aware of the realities around you. But sometimes, when you're first learning this difficult merging of minds, you can actually get your mind stuck in that world. It's a mental world, not an actual physical place, but it can keep your mind prisoner. It's easy to get out once you know how, but you have to be taught the technique, or else you'll just panic and get more and more stuck.

"When I was fourteen and first learning duo-com, I was having a minor anxiety attack from the pressure of all of the practical exams we had to pass in order to get our entry-level duo-com badge. During the exam I freaked and got stuck in the mind prison, the Gaoled. The duo-com master, Andrei Iyoshi, was able to pull me out by simply talking me through it."

Dr. Kortez looked at Rayah and then back at the two monitors that reported the children's medical status. "Do you think somehow they are experiencing a Gaoled?"

"I'm not sure. If Master Iyoshi were here, he would probably be able to give you a better answer." Rayah paused, collecting her thoughts. "Doctor, I'm just making an educated guess, but these kids seem younger than fourteen, meaning they haven't had duo-com courses at all. There's a reason why you can't start the classes until you're older. The ability is actually quite difficult to learn. I think that the combination of the Lucid Wasp venom, their young age, and the fact that they are twins all worked itself into the perfect storm and possibly got them into a severe Gaoled. It's just a theory, but it feels plausible."

"Plausible indeed," said Dr. Kortez. "How can this knowledge help us? I'm willing to try anything."

"That's what I'm still trying to figure out." Rayah began to pace the medical ward, feeling everyone's expectant eyes on her. She hadn't been in a Gaoled in so long, and she didn't even know if she could intentionally get herself into her own Gaoled, let alone into someone else's. An idea was beginning to form in her mind, though. She knew she was close to the answer; maybe talking through her logic out loud would get her to the correct conclusion.

"When I held the girl's hand, I got shocked," said Rayah, "I think we need something that will be a good conductor. It's a tactic I learned from our Master Iyoshi when I was younger, and it helps a person communicate better."

"Um, please don't say what I think you're about to suggest," said Tye from afar.

"What?" asked both the general and the doctor in unison.

"She's going to suggest we use earwax," inferred Ondraus, as he watched his sister and shook his head.

You agree?

Yes, responded Ondraus. *I think you're right. This is a twin problem and it needs a twin response. This might just work.*

"I think my brother and Bo had the right idea," said

Rayah, "as far as connecting with the kids and creating a link. But if we don't want to get fried, we need to use our earwax the way we were taught when we were first learning how to duo-com all those years ago."

"It was just as gross back then," said Tye, already putting his index finger in his ear.

"Okay. Let's get in position," ordered Ondraus.

"We will need to try and link minds as well," said Rayah. "I think all we need to do is concentrate on Evia and Ensin. I'll try to pull us all into their Gaoled."

No further instructions were necessary. Everyone in The Elite dabbed a wad of earwax onto the bridge of their nose and linked with the others. One by one, they closed their eyes and grew quiet. This time, when Rayah regained her senses, she didn't just see a bunch of mental images as she had previously. With the linked duo-com capability of the entire team of twins, she was able to transport her mind into the strange dream-like world. She felt like she was physically there, and could see everyone else's body as well. She never remembered things being this vivid when she was stuck in her Gaoled, but maybe the link made things stronger, as if she were seeing the combined images from ten pairs of eyes.

After a few moments, Rayah's mind was settled enough that she could begin looking around. She nearly jumped when she turned behind her and saw two children standing close by.

"How are you here? Are you stuck too?" asked the alarmed girl.

"We're here to get you out," replied Rayah.

"We can't," said the boy in a whimpering voice. "We've tried so many times."

"Come on, kids," said Wilstead. "All you gotta do is believe."

Rayah shot Wilstead a look; his words were obviously not helping. He was mostly right, though. Master Iyoshi had told her ten years ago that getting stuck just meant that she was feeling scared and anxious. The only way to escape the Gaoled was to trust her brother and to sense the safety in their mutual connection. Now Rayah had to encourage Evia and Ensin in the same way.

"Hi, Evia. Hi, Ensin. My name is Rayah." She bent a little so that the two children were at eye level. "As I said, we're here to get you out. I've been stuck in one of these mind prisons before, and I got out, so I know it's possible.

"How?" Evia asked desperately.

"The way to get out is to release fear. I saw a glimpse of the nightmare or vision you two have been experiencing over and over again, and I think that's why you can't get out of here. Those visions are scary. But we're here now. You see all of these people? This one is my brother, and the rest of these folks are my friends, and we're all twins in the military. We won't let anything hurt you."

The two children clung to her. Rayah dried the tears off both of their faces. "Are you ready to bust out of this place?"

The girl nodded, tears swelling in her tired eyes.

"Do you trust your brother?" asked Rayah, still holding both of them. The girl nodded her head.

"And you, Ensin, do you trust your sister?"

"Yes, ma'am," he managed to respond while his lower lip quivered.

"Excellent. Here; hold hands." The kids did, and then all of the adult sets of twins put their hands on each of the kids' shoulders. "All I need you to do is close your eyes. Think of the love and trust you have for each other and say out loud, 'I trust you.' Okay?"

CHAPTER 8

Kaled

Kaled opened his eyes and immediately stared at the children on their hospital beds. Rayah and Ondraus were already in motion, with Rayah checking on Evia and Ondraus examining Ensin. Both kids had snapped awake and were squirming in anxious alarm, but Rayah and Ondraus were doing the best to soothe them while also applying alcohol-based foam to their own hands and donning sterile gloves.

"Hey sweetie, it's okay. I'll take that out for you, alright? Okay, on the count of three. One, two..." In the next moment, Rayah removed the long tube that had been inside Evia's throat for the past three weeks.

Dr. Kortez looked ecstatic. "Welcome back, kiddos!" he shouted, kissing each of them on the forehead before going to work on them.

Amid all the happy chaos, Kaled wondered if anyone had called the kids' parents or the king and queen. At last, he summoned the courage to put the question to General Peterson, who looked like the thought had never crossed his mind. In a matter of minutes, the twins' parents were rushing into the medical wing, their pajamas rumpled and their hair uncombed, followed shortly by the king and queen and several members of the royal guard.

"My babies!" exclaimed the mother as she went to

the beds and kissed her children through tears of joy.

Even their father seemed to be overcome with emotion and was holding his hands over his mouth. King Tarrington and Queen Ellandra were more businesslike, quietly asking the doctor what had transpired, though they couldn't hide their collective sigh of relief. Dr. Kortez praised Rayah's quick thinking and explained how the group of new palace soldiers had worked together to find a solution to their problem.

"This is such excellent news!" cried the queen.

With all the free-flowing tears, hugs, and kisses around him, Kaled couldn't help but be filled with satisfaction at the minor part he'd played. He didn't even bother drying the tears that rolled down his face as he watched the happy reunion.

A male nurse walked in, with the last name Birchram pinned to his crisp white uniform. He nearly dropped the cups of coffee he was holding when he saw all the unexpected commotion. "They're awake?" he asked in disbelief.

The Elite were later ushered out of the room to let the kids and their parents rest. The doctor unclasped the buttons on his collar. The expression on his face was one Kaled had seen in his own reflection in a mirror before after he'd finished a mission that took a toll on him and was finally given a moment of reprieve.

As they left the ward, the doctor said to both Ondraus and Rayah, "I don't know where you guys came from, but if you want a job here, there's a spot open for the both of you."

"We can arrange that," said General Peterson as he put his arm around the doctor and gave a good, friendly squeeze. "We can certainly arrange that, my friend."

"I think I might sleep for twenty hours straight," said the doctor as he yawned.

"Likewise. Listen up, crew," said General Peterson as he addressed The Elite. "Go to your hotel rooms and rest. I'll have someone from personnel arrange for all of your belongings to get packed and shipped here while we obtain the appropriate paperwork to get your current duty station assigned to the palace. Don't expect a call until nineteen hundred hours tomorrow evening. At that time, come dressed in your uniform, with your overnight bags packed. Call room service and get the most expensive meal you can find. Today, we celebrate this win. After that, we get back to work, for there is much to do and discuss."

Kaled was more than happy to follow those orders and spent most of the following day in his hotel room lounging around, eating exquisite food, and enjoying the complimentary spa session with a hot stone massage that had been arranged by the palace. Vellah had wanted to attend the second day of the Winter Games, when the real athletes would finally be competing. Instead, Kaled managed to persuade her to stay in the room with him, watching the games on the tele-screen and enjoying the other fine amenities the grand hotel had to offer.

In truth, Kaled was exhausted from a sleepless night. He had not expected to see Rayah ever again in his life. When they'd parted ways two years before, she had made it painfully clear that he was to stay clear away from her. He'd been blindsided – they'd *both* been blindsided – by hearing General Peterson announce that they were being asked to stay on as a team of soldiers to help protect the royal twins. He wasn't sure if he could work in the same place as Rayah without spiraling into an unhealthy mindset.

He dressed and decided to visit his sister. Perhaps, he thought, Aymes had come to the same conclusion he had, and she would suggest that they decline the tempting offer of working at the palace, even though it had been their dream since childhood. He wouldn't ask her outright, of course. He'd just talk to his sister and see where the conversation went. So Kaled went to his sister's hotel room and knocked. Rayah answered the door, her smile vanishing immediately upon seeing him.

"Never mind; I'll just talk to her later," said Kaled, trying to ignore the daggers her eyes hurled at him.

At nineteen hundred hours sharp, The Elite were once again at the palace. Kaled placed his phone on do-not-disturb mode as his girlfriend, already en route to her hometown, continued to bombard him with video messages. She had not understood how he and the rest of The Elite could just be told to move and start a job elsewhere at a moment's notice. Even though he'd tried to explain numerous times that he had a contract with the army and they could send him where they wanted, she'd always failed to see it his way. At last, they'd just agreed to see each other the next time he had a day off.

He did think he handled the matter with finesse as she tried to ask *why* they were being told to work at the palace; he'd simply replied with, *That was the reward for doing so well in the Winter Games. We got to work in our dream job—nothing else.*

Much to Kaled's disdain, they were met once again by the insufferable boy toy, Guyad. Just like the night before, he was paying special attention to Rayah, and she couldn't seem to peel her eyes off him.

Cool it, said Aymes to her brother.

I'm sorry. I just don't like that he's all over her. Besides, what does she even see in him?

Really? asked his sister in a sarcastic tone.

But he's enlisted, replied Kaled childishly. *Enlisted aren't supposed to date officers. You know that.*

I don't see a problem, as long as it doesn't interfere with her work.

Guyad led them to the medical ward where General Peterson was already waiting. The general's expression looked brighter, and so did the doctor's. Evia and Ensin were still in bed, accompanied by their parents, who held a cup of a blue fruit smoothie with a straw so the children could drink from it. As soon as the group walked in, the parents stood up. The father approached The Elite and addressed them all.

"I cannot thank you enough for what you did to save my children. My name is Alastair, and this is my wife, Nerida. These past three weeks have been a living nightmare, quite literally, and thanks to you, we have our children and a reason to hope."

"Thanks, Al," said General Peterson before turning toward The Elite. "I've already spoken to the parents and the children. I told them we'd need to interview the kids to have a better understanding of what they saw in their Gaoled, but we did not want to do it until you were all present with us. We're just waiting on the king and queen; they too have requested to be here for this."

They only had to wait another five minutes before the royal pair showed up. King Tarrington looked better rested than he had the night before, with his hair freshly trimmed and his face full of hope and anticipation. Queen Ellandra, as always, seemed the picture of elegance.

Kaled looked at Rayah and saw that she had been staring straight at him. As soon as their eyes locked, she turned and faced the children. For a brief moment, his heart leaped, but just as quickly, it fell.

Nerida was the one who asked the opening question. "Okay, my darlings, please tell us what you saw and heard."

Evia began, her voice strained. "We awoke in a clearing in that Gaoled, and we saw the queen holding the two babies, a boy, and a girl. Then we saw a creepy guy come and take the babies. Each time we heard the babies cry, we felt their fear, their thoughts."

"And when we tried to escape from that place, we got chased by a big snake with huge fangs," said Ensin.

"When you were in the Gaoled," said Nerida, "you chanted something over and over. 'He comes at night by flight to strike, heir of throne turned to stone; We, the jewels, are hunted down, but royal's twins will save the crown.' Do you know what that means?"

"No," repeated both children.

"But," asked Tru, "not to sound harsh, but the part that says 'royal's twins,' that part sounds like improper grammar, does that matter?"

"Grammar? Really, sis? At a time like this?" said Tye, exasperated.

"No, not like *that*," Tru responded. "I mean, could that strange phrasing be a clue, or was it accidentally said that way?"

"We don't remember saying the chant at all. Our uncle even showed us the video recording, but no, we don't remember saying it. We only remember what we saw when we were inside," protested Evia.

General Peterson wrote something down and said, "Regardless, it's worth keeping in mind."

"Do you remember what the man looked like? Can you describe him?" asked Nerida.

"He was tall and very thin," said Ensin, balling up the pillow in his hands. "He had a strange, eerie voice."

Evia took in a deep breath and closed her eyes, bending her head before she spoke as if reliving the events. "His hair was dark purple, straight, and shoulder length. His eyes were light gray, and he had a big scar or burn mark on the palm of his hands. He would have had a handsome face except...except," she trailed off, hiding her face.

"Except his smile looked evil. It gave me the chills. It felt real," added Ensin, shuddering.

General Peterson had stood up while Evia was talking and had remained still as a statue. Was he confused, or had he seen a ghost? Kaled could not tell, but the general seemed transfixed on Evia's portrayal of the creepy man. Quickly, though, General Peterson regained his composure and addressed the children.

"Did you see or hear anything else while in the Gaoled?" asked Nerida.

Ensin furrowed his brow as he concentrated. "No," he said, "just the babies crying. The creepy guy didn't speak at all."

"Okay. Thank you, children. We won't bother you again for the time being. Please continue resting," said General Peterson as he ushered out The Elite with a quick hand movement.

Right as the group started to leave, Ensin asked, "Say

that again?"

The group stopped. "Say what, dear?" asked Nerida.

"I thought a kid had said something," said Ensin.

"Me too," said Evia. "I thought I heard kids talking."

Perplexed and looking around the room, the general said, "You are the only kids here."

Kaled watched Rayah and Ondraus, who seemed to be looking at the kids and the queen. He'd known his friends long enough to sense that their brains were trying to connect certain dots.

"Um," said Rayah, "Queen Ellandra, this is going to sound strange, but can you come closer?"

"Dear, at this point, nothing sounds too strange," replied Ellandra with an encouraging smile as she walked toward Rayah and the kids.

"With your permission, I'd like for the kids to place their hands on your belly. I think...well, I don't know for sure, but I *think* they have a connection with your babies."

"Do you think what they mentioned about my children, in their Gaoled, was literal? Do you think they can actually hear the babies' thoughts?" asked King Tarrington.

"That's my theory. I guess we'll find out in just a second," replied Rayah with a shrug.

The queen nodded her head and stood in between the beds. Kaled watched as the kids' parents helped them up into a sitting position, holding them as they reached over so they could place their hands on the queen's abdomen. Instantly, they closed their eyes and began to smile.

"I can hear their voices!" exclaimed Evia with glee.

"Me too, me too!" croaked Ensin.

The queen looked at them and then back at her husband, King Tarrington. He seemed perplexed. "I feel them moving," exclaimed Ellandra.

"That should be impossible; they're too young for you to feel them," said Dr. Kortez, now grabbing a device that looked like a sheet of stickers and placing it on the queen's belly underneath her shirt. Heartbeats instantly popped up on a nearby monitor, and small images the size of a bean seemed to be swimming around her womb.

"Do you see that, O?" said Rayah looking at the screen. "The babies look excited." Her brother nodded, eyes glued on the monitor.

"What are they saying?" asked the queen.

"They're saying, hmm, wait, something about elite... works," replied Evia. "Well, that doesn't make sense. I'm sorry, I don't know what that means."

Suddenly she and her brother let go wiped at their eyes as if trying to clear their vision.

Kaled noticed King Tarrington, Queen Ellandra, and General Peterson all glancing at each other. There was no way Evia and Ensin would have known about the term The Elite since it had not been mentioned in front of them at all, not even to the doctor. King Tarrington ran up to his wife and placed his hand on her abdomen as she wept happily in her husband's shoulder. After a few seconds, both Evia and Ensin let go of the Queen.

"What's wrong, sweetie?" asked Nerida.

"I'm tired all of a sudden," Evia murmured.

"Me too," said Ensin as he drew back into his covers. "I think that wore us all out."

"Yes, Queen Ellandra," said Dr. Kortez as he started to remove the stickers from her belly. "Looks like your babies are taking a nap as well. I'm sorry that what the children said makes no sense. I'm sure they can try again tomorrow, but for now, we must let all four kids rest."

The Elite reconvened inside a meeting room. Several tables of food and drinks lined one wall, and the middle was occupied by an oval-shaped table surrounded with chairs. Queen Ellandra took her leave, while King Tarrington remained standing next to General Peterson, ignoring the chairs. That meant The Elite stood, too, and Kaled found himself elbow to elbow with his sister while they waited for everyone else to enter the room. Once the doors were closed, the king addressed the group.

"I cannot express to you how hopeful I am right now. Outside of these walls, the only one who has heard any mention of The Elite is my wife. I don't know how my children are communicating with the doctor's niece and nephew, but I am a man of faith, and I will take this as a sign. General Peterson will provide you the full details of our plan thus far, although things are likely to evolve with time." The king then moved closer toward the exit doors and whispered to General Peterson, "If you need me, I'll be in my prayer room."

The general nodded. "After this meeting, I'm going to call the prison in Susa to make sure Rancor is still locked up. That description earlier sounded just like him."

"I was afraid of that, too," said the king.

After the king left, General Peterson turned to face the group. "We might be here for several hours, so please make yourselves comfortable. Get some food and take a seat." He led by example, unhooking a series of buttons on his uniform and grabbing a seat.

"The main goal for The Elite is to protect the royal children, whatever the cost. You are free to share ideas, not only in this room but out of it as well. Just make sure that any business regarding The Elite or the royal infants is not shared with anyone other than the king or me. In the corner over there, you'll find totes with new gear for each of you, including a secure mobile phone and smartwatch, which you will carry on you at all times. You'll also find a new set of uniforms to use while here. The barracks are located outside of the palace, and I trust you will find the accommodations more than reasonable.

"Those of you with spouses or children will be given a housing stipend to find an apartment nearby; Captain Aymes and Captain Bo, please see me after this meeting for more details. For the rest of you, the barracks are two-person apartments; siblings will be kept apart since we know you tire of seeing each other and hearing each other's thoughts all day."

A collective "Oh, thank you," floated up from the sets of twins.

Kaled noticed the look of confusion on Ondraus's face when General Peterson had called out Aymes for the separate housing, though he also noticed that Rayah had not seemed surprised. There was a time when the four of them had been close friends; now, though, they were so out of touch that Ondraus didn't even know Aymes had become a mother a year and a half before. He had a feeling that Aymes had told Rayah only yesterday.

Kaled listened intently as the general spoke nonstop for nearly an hour, with only sporadic pauses for food.

The Elite had been assigned jobs throughout the palace, doing whatever they usually did in their regular posts throughout the country. This meant that Kaled and his sister would be working in Fleet and getting to know every single vehicle. He knew, of course, that Rayah and her brother would work in the medical ward. The Ryder twins, Tru and Tye, would work on anything electronic, especially the communications equipment. Ameena and Wilstead Noxx would work primarily in the dining facility, preparing meals for the soldiers and palace staff. Finally, the Xulu twins, Bo and Lina, would work on all special projects regarding building and infrastructure.

The Elite would also pull guard duty weekly so that others did not become curious about their presence. Another portion of their time would be spent at Primeda Fortress, located five miles away. Whenever they weren't working in either of those two places, they would spend quality time getting to know Evia and Ensin, since it seemed that destiny had chosen to bond them with the royal babies. This was the first time that Kaled's military job had entailed being around children. He knew it would be far different than taking care of his nephew Niklas, but figured it wouldn't be too hard. Based on the little he'd gathered by observing Evia and Ensin, he supposed they were good kids and expected to get along with them just fine.

After a breakdown of the duties, preliminary schedules were drafted, and then General Peterson called for Guyad to show the soldiers to their lodging.

"It's just a mile from here, and it's a clear night. Would you guys mind if we walked it?" Guyad asked the group.

Kaled could see right through his intentions. The sleazeball just wanted a nighttime stroll with Rayah so he could sweet-talk her, especially because she'd chosen to hang out with Aymes the previous night instead of taking him up on his offer for drinks.

I can't believe this is really happening, said Aymes, breaking into his thoughts. He had not even noticed that his mind was so deeply immersed in what Rayah and Guyad were saying that he nearly jumped when his sister's thoughts popped up in his head.

Can you repeat that? he asked.

Oh, Kal, are you thinking about her? Knock it off, bro. You know how you got last time. Aymes stopped walking and put her hand on her brother's shoulder, gazing into his light green eyes with concern. *You can't go down that road again. It nearly ruined you.*

Kaled didn't respond with words, simply nodding his head in silent agreement.

Do you need us to walk back and tell General Peterson we can't accept the job? she asked in her typical motherly tone. Ever since she'd become a mom, she couldn't turn off that part of her new personality. Kaled found the quality endearing. He desperately yearned to accept her offer, to drop all of this and move far away from Rayah, but he couldn't do that to his sister.

No, it's fine, but thank you. I'll let you know if it becomes too much.

Okay, but I'll talk to Rayah as well. I won't tell her about your...past...but I'll just ask her to be mindful since it looks like we will be spending time around one another for the foreseeable future. But you need to promise to not talk to her other than for work. And keep your distance. You made that girl miserable, too. Agreed?

Agreed.

Besides, said Aymes with a wink, *you have Vellah to keep you occupied. She looks like a handful.*

Kaled didn't smile or wink back. In truth, he was only with Vellah – or any previous woman – to fill the gaping hole Rayah had left in his heart. He had not even thought of Vellah at all since placing his phone on do-not-disturb mode several hours ago.

After fifteen minutes, the group arrived at their new apartments, and Kaled watched as Rayah waved Guyad goodbye with a flirtatious smile. Rayah stood still and rounded on Kaled as he approached the building.

"We need to talk," she said in a business-like tone.

Kaled didn't respond verbally; instead, he stopped a few feet away from her. He could tell by the crossed arms and stern look on her face that she was upset.

"Just because you have my number now," she said, pointing at her new phone, "doesn't mean you are allowed to call or text me for any reason other than for work. Do you understand?"

Kaled nodded. The desire to contact her, something he had not been able to do in ages, was forever out of his grasp. He knew this.

"This is ridiculous," she continued, "I can't believe, of all the people in the Army, you are here. If you so much as try to pull the same shit from the past, I will –"

"Rayah," he said quietly, "you don't have to worry about that. You can pretend I don't exist, and I'll stay clear away from you the way I have for the last two years. I know this doesn't change anything."

"Good. We are not friends, and as far as I'm concerned, we're barely co-workers. Let's just be professional about this, okay?"

Kaled took another step backward. He saw Aymes and Ondraus talking underneath a street lamp on the sidewalk. Kaled knew he had no choice but to be strong and not ruin his sister's career and her chance at being with someone she has started developing feelings for.

"Understood," he said evenly.

"Fantastic. Have a good night, Captain Behr."

Rayah turned on her heels and entered the building, leaving Kaled standing alone by the entrance. Aymes rushed past him and met up with Rayah. Kaled turned around and saw Ondraus still standing underneath the street lamp, with a wide-eyed smile on his face. He knew that face; Kaled use to walk around feeling that way back when Rayah was his. Within a few seconds, Ondraus caught up, the grin still present.

"Wanna room together?" asked Ondraus. "You know, like old times."

"That would be great," responded Kaled.

CHAPTER 9

Nerida

Nerida, her husband, and her two children were staying in the lavish high-rise apartment of her brother-in-law, Dr. Perry Kortez, in the bustling city of Clivesdail. It was the second week of late winter, and from her perch on the balcony, Nerida could see snow still crowning the mountains that rose behind the palace. She wore a pair of house slippers and a warm cotton sweater that belonged to her husband, along with a pair of worn-out jeans and a blouse.

Perry's apartment stood near the boundary of the city of Clivesdail and the ancient Heart of Clivesdail. Tall buildings surrounded the apartment, their metal and glass facades giving the structures a mirror-like appearance when the sunlight hit them. Most of the buildings had incorporated nature into their infrastructure, with greenhouses or gardens on their roofs. Though most of the population drove hover cars, there was an electric-powered train hub that serviced the entire city, which helped minimize the number of vehicles during peak hours of the day. It had been *ages* since Nerida visited Clivesdail; she did not realize until now how badly she had missed the beautiful city.

Nerida's husband, Alastair, opened the large glass-paned double doors and walked onto the balcony holding two mugs of coffee. "Hey, gorgeous," he said, placing the mugs onto a small glass table and then wrapping his hands around her waist. She kissed his lips, resting her head on his chest and breathing in deeply. He rubbed the small of her back and kissed the top of her head. "How was it last night?"

Nerida shook her head, and a tear rolled down her cheek. "Evia had nightmare after nightmare. And Ensin...I know he's not as affected as her, but he's pretty spooked, and it took forever to get him to fall asleep."

"I still don't understand why all of this happened. Why did those wasps create such a strange situation? None of this makes any logical sense," said Alastair.

Nerida shrugged her shoulders, not wanting to make too large a movement and risk disrupting the warmth of his embrace. Alastair sighed. "Since it's my turn with them tonight, I think I'm just going to wear them out first and wait until they're at the point of exhaustion before I send them to bed. Maybe they'll be too tuckered out to have bad dreams of that creepy guy."

"It's just been a rough month," agreed Nerida, finally stepping away from her husband and reaching for the hot mug of coffee. "And I feel like it's not over yet. Also, I'm a little wary of taking them back to Marez Cave just yet. What if they get into another...what was the term the doctor used?"

"Gaoled," replied Alastair. "I agree. I've already talked with my brother, and he said we can stay here as long as we want. He told me he's rarely home because of the long hours at the palace, and he'd prefer the kids to be nearby for the time being anyway."

"Mom," said Ensin opening the balcony doors, "Sergeant Lurca is at the door for you."

Both Nerida and Alastair entered the house immediately and saw Sergeant Guyad Lurca standing by the entrance. Nerida had seen this young man around the palace on several occasions and wasn't sure how she felt about him. His dashing good looks had no effect on her; something about him rubbed her the wrong way.

"Good afternoon, Sergeant," said Alastair. "My brother, Dr. Kortez, is not home at the moment. How may I be of service?"

"Queen Ellandra is here and would like to know if she can meet with you all for a few minutes," he said.

"Of course; it would be an honor," said Alastair. "Would you like to come in as well? It's pretty cold out there."

"I'll go get the queen. Thank you for the offer, but this is a private matter."

At once, Nerida tore off the sweater she had been wearing, straightening up her blouse and running her fingers through her hair. She ran to the kitchen, took out a kettle of her recently made Choco Moo Brew, and put it on the stove. Ensin took out a few small iced cinnamon cakes.

Evia had been sitting in the parlor, making a bracelet out of moon crystals that she'd shaped into beads with a specialized quartz tool kit.

"Evia, for goodness sakes, put that stuff away! We have company!" hissed Nerida.

By the time the queen arrived, plates were set at the table, with mugs full of piping hot chocolate and the cinnamon cakes. Nerida could tell the queen was pleasantly surprised to receive such hospitality on barely a moment's notice.

"Thank you for having me in your home," the queen greeted them, then looked behind her to make sure

Guyad was gone. She wore an A-line lavender coat dress that hugged her petite frame nicely. "I've come to discuss some matters that have been on my mind. They involve your children."

"Would you like to take a seat, Your Majesty?" asked Alastair.

"Yes, that would be wonderful. Thank you. And please, for now, Ellandra is fine. We must observe proper decorum outside of these walls, but here in private, I much prefer my actual name."

"I prefer my name too unless my mom is calling out my first, middle, and last name because that usually means I'm in deep trouble," blurted Ensin while stuffing a slice of cinnamon cake into his mouth.

This made both the queen and Evia laugh while Nerida and her husband stood there like embarrassed statues.

Evia popped a small piece of the cake into her mouth and closed her eyes as she savored the sweet treat. "Wow, mom. These are so yummy. Can I have another slice?"

"No, darling. You've already had enough sugar today," Alastair cut in.

Queen Ellandra made small talk with them for a while, sampling the cake and the chocolate drink, before getting to the root of the matter: the safety of her children.

"I imagine you two might be suffering some measure of bad dreams or possibly anxiety regarding your recent experience in that strange Gaoled," she said as she eyed Evia and Ensin. Her face echoed the concern she seemed to have for them.

"I do not want to make light of what you two have

gone through. At this time, we do not know if what experienced in your Gaoled has any validity to it, even though I'm sure it felt very real, and even if it looked very real from our end." She paused for a moment and then continued. "The prudent thing to do is not to dive off the deep end and allow this possible revelation to prevent us from living and enjoying all the beauty this life has to offer. On the other hand, we can't take this lightly either."

"Yes, Your Majesty," said Nerida, putting down her mug to listen more intently.

"I am glad you see this as I do. The king has some ideas about how to plan and prepare just in case...well, just in case that phrase the both of you chanted over and over again does come to pass. In the meantime, though, I want to explore something else: a relationship between you two children with my own."

"Your Majesty, we will do whatever it takes to keep the prince and princess safe," said Ensin standing up to his full height. Nerida was a little surprised to see her son react so positively even though just a few hours ago he had been terrified of falling asleep and seeing images of the creepy man.

This gesture made the queen smile warmly. "You have no idea how much I appreciate that," she said while reaching over and placing her hand on his for a moment. "It seems like our two sets of kids have some sort of ability to communicate with one another. I don't know if that was a one-time thing or not, but in any case, I feel there is a connection, and we should continue to nurture it. I would like for you all to move to the palace. We have a suite big enough for the four of you. We also have a teacher in the palace, and there are a few kids around your age who you can get to know." The queen looked at everyone, with hope and pleading in her eyes. "This might be a long shot, but I feel very strongly that we should attempt it."

Evia raised her hand, but she looked embarrassed at doing so.

"Yes, dear?" said Ellandra.

"I don't know about Ensin, but I don't think it was a one-time thing. Your babies mostly speak in images or...how do I say it?" She looked at her brother for help.

"Sometimes they speak by repeating something they heard."

"Can you," asked the queen, "talk to them now or whenever you like?"

"I think it's the other way around. It's whenever they want," said Ensin. He then started giggling, and so did Evia.

"What's so funny?" asked Alastair, his face flushing further, as if he had not recovered from the last silly thing that his son had said.

"They want more of the yummies. I think they mean the cakes."

"Oh?" said the queen, amused. Ellandra took another bite of the cake and washed it down with the hot chocolate, and saw that both Evia and Ensin were smiling.

"They like that," said the kids in unison.

****

Rayah

Rayah stood outside the rear entrance of the palace near the landing pad. She was wearing her new uniform, which consisted of a white high-collared top with red trimming and buttons on the side, along with black pants and black boots. On her left leg, she wore a strapped bag, where she stored her sidearm, known as a Nemi, and a small remote-sized medical device called a Diagnostica used to quickly assess someone's health. Only medical personnel used white tops for their uniforms; everyone else used a charcoal gray with gold trimming.

She flicked her smartwatch and the band lit up, projecting an image onto the skin of Rayah's forearm. She scrolled through the projected screen and saw that Aymes had texted her a photo of herself and Niklas with a caption that read, "Mommy says hello." The notification brought a smile to Rayah's lips. She looked up at the sky and noticed a hovercar approaching the landing pad. After it settled down smoothly, Kaled stepped out of the driver's seat and walked around to open the passenger doors.

"That is hilarious, Captain Behr. I can't believe it really happened to you," exclaimed Alastair as he wiped a tear from the corner of his eye.

"It was not funny at the time," chuckled Kaled. "You should have seen my face when that massive dog came charging at me, and my foot was stuck in that hole. I really thought I was done for! Then to my surprise, it just started licking my face, and my hair got extremely goopy from dog slobber. I still get postcards from the dog every year. I think it has a crush on me."

The last statement made Evia and Ensin laugh hysterically. Rayah brought her hand to her mouth to hide the fact that the memory had made her smile momentarily. She'd been there, of course, when it had happened years ago. Kaled's demeanor completely changed when he noticed Rayah standing there waiting for the group. He stopped laughing, and it was abrupt enough for Nerida to notice, prompting her to look at Rayah and then back at Kaled.

"Thank you, Captain Behr, for the ride and for also helping us pack our things to move here to the palace," said Alastair.

"It was my pleasure. But please, only military people have to call me Captain Behr. I prefer Kal."

Rayah watched as Kaled greeted a few members of the palace staff, who were there to take up the luggage, and then opened the hovercar's trunk so they could unload the vehicle. The Kortez family said goodbye to him and approached Rayah, who stood nearby. Nerida was fussing about something on the side of Evia's neck, probably a stain or something, before finally sweeping the girl's hair toward the front of her shoulders and whispering, "That should cover it."

"Hi, Ms. Rayah," said Evia with a bright smile.

"Hi! Are you excited for your first day at this school?"

"Excited, but also a bit nervous," replied Evia.

"I'm excited," added Ensin. "We've always been home-schooled, and other than my uncle, we don't have any friends."

"Oh," said Rayah, a little taken back. Not many people home-schooled their children, and those who did made sure their children had a vast line-up of friends who were also home-schooled. She couldn't imagine being that age without any friends beside her sibling. "Well, hopefully, you'll consider me a friend. I'm here to escort you to your class, and I'm sure you'll fit right in with the kids there."

As she was about to leave with the kids, Rayah glanced toward Kaled and noticed he had been looking at her.

"Have a good morning, Captain Jur," he said while preparing to leave. He had already turned before she had the opportunity to respond, which saved her the hassle of deciding whether she needed to.

After saying goodbye to Nerida and Alastair, the children and Rayah continued through a hallway that led into the service tower. Certain parts of the palace were the definition of elegance, and those were the places where royalty, noblemen, or guests could be found. Other locations, such as the third floor habitation suites and classrooms, lacked the same sophistication while still maintaining a charming appearance. The walls had a cheery yellow color and the floors were made of a mosaic tile. Large windows lined the hallways at regular intervals, allowing for natural light to bathe the area in a warm glow. Rayah spotted Sergeant Guyad Lurca at a wall panel, holding an electric screwdriver with a built-in flashlight.

"Hi, Sergeant Lurca," Rayah said while approaching him.

"Just a second, soldier," he said distractedly. He continued drilling for a few seconds and then tapped on the digital screen of the panel. "There we go. All fixed." He turned to face her, and instantly his demeanor changed; he cleared his throat and straightened his back. "Oh. Captain Jur. How are you this morning?"

"I was wondering if you knew what time Mr. Pilmen's class started. My schedule says zero eight thirty."

"Well, if you need a private tutor, Captain, I'd be more than happy to give you some lessons. My apartment is on the first floor of the barracks." He smiled deviously.

Rayah was appalled that he had just spoken that way in front of two children. Perhaps he had not seen them, so she stepped to the side to allow him an unobstructed view of the entire corridor. "It's not for me, Sergeant. It's for those kids down there by the classroom door."

"I see. The class starts at zero nine hundred. How come you're walking them around? Where do I sign up for you to be my escort?"

Rayah could feel her ears go warm with this double meaning of a comment. It didn't take much to realize he had a one-track mind. Part of her was amazed that he had enough brain cells to have a job since all of them were concentrated on one thing. "I volunteered."

"I don't know what's going on around here. As the Head of Security, I should know why those children and their common family are living in the palace, and on the second upper floor, no less. Instead, General Peterson has been tight-lipped about the whole thing."

Rayah was on the verge of telling him off. She knew the kids wouldn't have been able to hear their conversation since they were a few feet away and the ears of Vilmovian children did not mature properly until the age of fourteen. Still, it bothered her how he had been so dismissive of them. "I heard Mr. Kortez was offered a job here as Royal Scholar in Residence," she said neutrally.

"Oh. I see. Well, good for him. Makes sense, because Mr. Pilmen is old as dirt. Maybe that's what the Queen went to discuss at Dr. Kortez's apartment. It just bothers me when I don't know what's going on, since it's literally my job to know everything. You know, for safety reasons. Can't ever be too careful."

Rayah agreed with him and smiled pleasantly. "Yes, understandable."

"Hey, so when are you and I going out for those drinks? On the first two nights here, you seemed quite keen on a date, and yet you haven't called."

"Nor have you," she replied. If the children weren't there with her, she might have been tempted to act a little more flirtatious.

"I don't have your number," he said, taking a step closer to her. His dark purple eyes roamed up and down her form. "That new uniform fits you nicely."

"As Head of Security, I would have imagined you had a way of acquiring a number if you wanted it badly enough. Besides, *Sergeant,* now that I'm working at the palace and not merely visiting, it would best if we let *this* cool down a bit. I wouldn't want you to think I'm anything but a lady."

Sergeant Lurca was about to respond when his phone rang. "Duty calls, my *lady.*" He bowed exaggeratedly and then left.

Rayah returned to the children, who were sitting on the floor and eating azule berries. She sat down beside them while trying to wipe the silly grin off her face. Sergeant Lurca's smooth, albeit scandalous, words had left her feeling stupidly giddy. Rayah didn't like the idea of a one-night stand with a man who worked at her place of employment. The last thing she needed was to get a reputation for being easy. If he wanted her, it would need to be through a relationship, and something told her he wasn't the type who liked being with just one woman.

Rayah gave the kids her personal cell phone and let

them play games until their teacher arrived. Mr. Pilmen was a short, tubby man with wild gray wispy hair surrounding a mostly shiny bald head. He had small beads of sweat resting on his scalp and eyebrows, which he dabbed with a cloth he pulled out of his pocket.

"Ah! You must be Evia and Ensin Kortez. Welcome to my classroom. I'm sure we'll have a great time. Please, do come in."

When Rayah looked up, she noticed the light in the room had turned on, even though Mr. Pilmen had not yet opened the door. She peered through the glass pane to see four children sitting at their desks, talking excitedly.

"How did they get in?"

"They come in through the secret tunnels. I used to always tell them it's supposed to be a secret and that no one should be using them, but I stopped trying to convince them long ago. You see that young man right there? The one with the short cropped hair? Yes, that is General Peterson's grandson, Jerah. His father, Yosef Peterson, and King Tarrington were in my class together many, many years ago. Those two discovered most of the secret passages in this palace. They loved having adventures. Oh, my. Here I am going down memory lane, when I have a class to teach."

CHAPTER 10

Kaled

Kaled watched as the two Kortez children came out of the building and onto the palace grounds. It was early – zero five-thirty in the morning, to be precise – and he assumed those two were not accustomed to being awakened before the first sun rose. Kaled didn't mind running nor waking up early; he enjoyed having something constant in his life, and running allowed his mind to wander. It also did a great job of working off the pent-up energy he sometimes carried within him. The looks on the children's faces, however, gave away some very different feelings. The late winter chill didn't stop Kaled from wearing just his running shirt and shorts instead of a tracksuit; he knew that within minutes he'd be sweating, and his body would be warm all over.

"Good morning, kids," said Rayah. "I know it's early and last minute, but we talked with General Peterson late last night, and we all agreed it would be smart if we included you in some athletic training."

"And," continued Bo, a massive man the size of a tree, "since you two have school and we have our other duties, we decided that this training would have to take place very early. Are you familiar with the term *zero dark thirty*?" He chuckled at the question.

"No, but I assume it means the butt-crack of dawn," said Ensin with a yawn.

"Ensin!" reprimanded Evia with a slap to his shoulder.

But his statement made everyone in The Elite laugh. Soldiers were accustomed to being up very early in the morning. In fact, Kaled had been up around zero four forty-five to pray, run the mile to the palace, and then meet up with the group.

"Don't worry, young man; you'll get used to it," said Bo with an encouraging clap on Ensin's back.

"Have you ever done any running, like in a race or something?" asked Ondraus.

"No, not anything like that. We just try to catch each other around the house when we play. We've never done a race, and we've never run with anyone else other than with each other," responded Evia.

"Okay. We'll take it easy on you for now. Let's start by warming up our muscles, and then we'll go on a short run around the palace and back. After that, we'll have you stretch out to cool down, and then you can go back to bed until class," said Rayah.

Not thinking much of it, Kaled stood beside Rayah to try and warm up his muscles before the exercise, although he had already run a mile earlier. Rayah, however, moved away from him with an apparent look of disgust on her face. This made Aymes and Ondraus laugh quietly.

Sure, sure. Go ahead and laugh. Man, it was an honest mistake; it's not like I would try and be near her on purpose, said Kaled to his sister.

She really doesn't like you, bro, said Aymes delighting in his misery.

After warming up, Rayah tapped the screen on her smartwatch and yelled, "Let's go!"

She had mentioned earlier that this wasn't a race. It was only a test of their fitness level for the kids, whereas, for The Elite, the run acted as a warm-up for whatever they had in store for themselves for the remainder of the workout period. The children were at the front of the line so they could set the pace of the run. To Kaled's amazement, Evia and Ensin started running much faster than he had anticipated. He even noticed Evia looking behind her, confused about why the rest of The Elite were so far back.

Kaled sped up and overtook the children. "How are you running so fast?" he asked, his lungs heaving.

"Um, I don't know. We always run like this," replied Ensin.

"Are you up for racing?" asked Kaled with a grin on his face.

"Sure!" said both kids enthusiastically.

"Okay, on three. One, two.....three."

All three of them started rushing toward the rear of the palace grounds beneath the mountains. Behind him, Kaled could hear Rayah saying, "I'm gonna get you, kids!" while roaring with playful teasing. He chanced a glance behind him; Rayah was nearly within arm's reach of Evia, with the rest of The Elite running much faster and catching up as well.

"Let's make a bet, shall we?" said Wilstead above the noisy laughter and commotion. "I will reward anyone who can outrun Kaled to that tree with an extra serving of roast hog tonight."

"Y'all can certainly try!" said Kaled, intentionally slowing down and making a show of it.

Kaled waited until Rayah and several others passed him. Ondraus and Aymes appeared to be in no hurry while they jogged side-by-side, immersed in a private conversation. Rayah looked back at Kaled, arching her eyebrow. He took off, fast as lightning, past all of the runners, fully intent on winning his extra portion of meat for dinner. He had expected Wilstead or Tye to give him a run for his money; instead, Rayah sped up.

The Rayah he knew wasn't competitive, but extra meat wasn't something a hard-working soldier would ever turn down. Kaled saw that Ensin had slowed down considerably behind him, while Evia had stopped running altogether and was bent over trying to catch her breath.

"My lungs!" whimpered Evia.

As soon as Ensin saw his sister pull out of the race, he did the same, except that he took matters a little further by lying on the cool grass with his arms and legs splayed out.

Kaled made it to the tree a fraction of a second faster than Rayah, but she nearly collided with him when she finally reached it. There was an uncertain moment when he turned around and saw her directly behind him. Their faces met, but she quickly side-stepped and was out of his way in a flash.

"Wanna run back to the palace?" asked Rayah as she crouched down beside Ensin, who still lay on the cold grass with a thin layer of snow on it.

"I'm dead," responded Ensin while barely lifting his head to meet her eyes. His head plopped back down to the ground.

"What about you, little Miss Evia?" asked Bo.

"Help! I can't move!" said Evia.

"Want a back ride?" offered Bo.

"Yes! I haven't had one of these in years!" exclaimed

Evia, instantly revived with a reserve of energy at the thought of being given a back ride. She shot up as Bo bent his large body down so that he could swoop her up in a single movement.

"I have daughters back home; they love back rides as well. We haven't been properly introduced. My name is Bo."

"Hi, Mister Bo! Thank you for saving me."

"Anytime."

The pair met up with the rest of the soldiers surrounding Rayah and Ensin, who had finally sat up with much difficulty.

"I thought," said Kal, "that you said you had never raced before. You two were fast. Here I thought we would have a light jog as our warm-up to go easy on you kids, but surprise, surprise. You guys brought your A-game."

Rayah looked at Kal. He wasn't sure if she was about to say something, but instead, she opted to move away from him…again.

"Surely, you ran track at school," said Ondraus.

"What's track?" asked Ensin.

"Oh, we're going to have fun training you guys," said Wilstead.

"Wilstead is right," added Ondraus. "We are going to have loads of fun helping you get faster and stronger. I've never seen a kid run that fast before unless they were actually sprinting, which you weren't doing. I can tell you'll go even faster with some practice. I don't know how, but you two are ridiculously fast."

****

Ondraus

Ondraus sat beside Wilstead and Kaled at the faculty dining hall designated for military and regular palace staff. The three of them were still in their workout uniforms, enjoying breakfast and discussing that morning's workout with Ensin and Evia.

"Those two were incredibly quick," said Wilstead, shoveling a spoonful of eggs into his mouth.

"I'm fast, but I was never that fast at their age. I think, when they train up a bit, they'll easily outrun any of us," commented Kaled.

"Hey, did any of you get to see the last day of the Winter Games? I was working the entire day at the medical ward and didn't get to watch any of it," said Ondraus.

"Oh, boy, you missed it! Team Hollen-Beck were able to pull into first with their freestyle ski jumps. It's worth watching the highlights; that's how good a show they pulled off," said Wilstead.

Ondraus was going to comment on how he planned to watch the highlights of the Games online when he got home, but was distracted by the way Kaled scanned the dining hall as if on the lookout.

"Dude, stop it," said Ondraus. "She's not coming until after she showers anyway."

"I don't know what you're talking about," said Kaled, pretending to be innocent.

"What's going on?" asked Wilstead.

"Kaled is about to strain his neck, looking for my sister. It's not like it matters, bro; she's not going to sit here if you're here," said Ondraus while shaking his head.

He wished his friend wouldn't do this to himself. Ondraus could see him starting to regress, and it scared him a little bit. He'd promised Aymes that he would keep an eye out for Kaled, and she, of course, would do the same.

"Wait, don't you have a hot girlfriend? I swear you told me you planned to see her this coming weekend," asked Wilstead in confusion.

Ondraus butted in and answered for Kaled. "He does, and now he's not paying attention to you because my sister just walked in."

Rayah had indeed entered, flanked by Ameena and Aymes. The women were already showered and dressed in their duty uniforms. Guyad approached Rayah, gave her a small white carton box, then smiled and walked away after caressing her hand. The three ladies took a seat at the same table as the guys, though Rayah sat on the other side of Aymes so that she was as far from Kaled as possible. Ondraus could tell all of her small modifications such as this one were intentional.

"Where's the rest of the group?" asked Ameena as she sat down near Kaled.

"They had to get to work early; they all got a text from their unit," said Ondraus. "What do you have in that box?"

"I don't know. Let's find out." Rayah put aside her cup of coffee and power-bar before opening the small box. Inside there were a few donuts with shimmering icing that changed color depending on how the light hit them.

"That's got Mister Yemley's Yummylicious Shoppe written all over it," said Wilstead as he eyed the treats like a child on his birthday.

"You all want some? I can't eat all of this myself," offered Rayah.

Everyone at the table agreed, and soon the donuts had been cut into fourths so everyone could have a share. The bite that Ondraus took had bacon in it; he'd never had bacon in a donut before, but was instantly made into a believer. It was ridiculously delicious – perhaps even *yummylicious*. Kaled acted as if he would pass up a slice of the donut until Aymes kicked him under the table. When Kaled finally reached into the box, Rayah's hand accidentally brushed against his. Ondraus did not miss the fact that she grew suddenly quiet and sipped on her coffee.

"Have you noticed that Mister Yemley's sweets are literally the best in the entire country? Like seriously, you could fight me on this, and I would win the argument," said Wilstead as he stuffed another piece into his mouth.

"Well," said Ameena, "I suppose it would make sense if the rumors I heard earlier this week are true."

"What rumors?" asked Aymes, leaning into the conversation. Instantly, everyone else did the same thing; there was nothing like a juicy rumor in the morning to get a person pumped up for the long workday.

"I heard that yesterday was the twenty-sixth anniversary of his son's disappearance. He had two sons. Brett is the one you see at his shop, but the other was named Barnabus, and he went missing when he was about nine."

"That's terrible," said Aymes, shuddering. "Does anyone know how it happened?"

"There's plenty of speculation, one being that Barnabus got tired of his brother Brett and ran away, but most residents of Clivesdail don't believe that for a minute. Sure, Brett is autistic, but ol' Mrs. Welsh, the main cook for the palace, says the brothers got along very well. According to her, they were inseparable."

"Well, what's the other theory?" asked Ondraus.

"The other one," answered Ameena, "is that someone kidnapped Barnabus, and that he might still be alive because a body was never found."

Silence fell among the group at the table. A collective breath was taken in as they mulled the words in their minds, and then Aymes asked, "That's horrible, but what does that have to do with his baked goods?"

"Folks say that he's just concentrated a lot of his efforts into his food. His wife and Brett were deeply affected by Barnabus' disappearance, and they all work at the bakery shop. Sometimes working hard on something helps you take your mind off the thing that hurts," replied Ameena.

"I can attest to the latter part of that," added Kaled. "Sometimes staying busy helps keep your mind from thinking about something you rather not think about."

Ondraus, wanting to change the subject for Kaled's sake, asked the group, "What do you all plan to do this weekend?"

"My boyfriend is coming to visit," said Ameena excitedly. "Nearly a whole week without him has been hard. It's too bad he doesn't have a job here. That would make things so much better."

"I hear you, sister," agreed Aymes. Ondraus perked up his head, but she caught his eye and quickly added, "Been there and done that. I'm not dating anyone now, but I remember how terrible it felt."

"How about you, Kaled?" asked Wilstead.

Ondraus looked over at Kaled, who had not answered yet, and was staring off into the distance. Rayah looked equally lost in thought. Ondraus supposed he'd prefer them quiet instead of lashing out at each other.

"Oh, I'm sure he's going to visit that girlfriend of his," said Ameena with a wink. "Did y'all catch how beautiful she was? How about it, Kal?"

"Huh?" he said, finally aware that his name was being called.

"Are you visiting your girlfriend this weekend?" repeated Ameena.

"Yeah, I am. I'm taking her to see a musical. Should be fun." Kaled's words said one thing, but his tone of voice said another.

Across the table, Ondraus saw Rayah check her smartwatch and then touch the wireless device in her left ear so she could have a private conversation.

"Hey, Odin," greeted Rayah in a happy tone. She squeezed Aymes' shoulder in delight. Ondraus couldn't help but notice that Kaled dropped his head to the table in defeat. "Yeah, I'm free tonight. Hmm, okay. Sounds good. I'll see you at my place at six. Catch you then."

Rayah turned to Aymes and Ameena with a triumphant smile on her face.

"Wow, I gotta tell you, I'm happy he asked you out; hopefully, that will be enough to get Guyad off your tail. That guy just doesn't seem to understand that you're not interested," said Aymes.

"Oh, I'm interested," said Rayah playfully, "but Guyad has bad news written all over him. Each time I try to strike a conversation with Guyad, he automatically starts hinting that I go to bed with him. As *yummy-*

licious as he looks, I need to avoid that man at all costs."

"Not a bad plan," commented Ameena. "That being said, Odin sure is easy on the eyes. Where does he work?"

"Mmm, he sure is," agreed Rayah. "I actually don't know where he works. We met last night at the barracks when I was doing my laundry."

"Actually," said Aymes, "he works in Fleet with Kaled and me."

The mention of Kaled's name made Rayah look down the table, but Kaled had already left.

CHAPTER 11

Rayah

Only a few weeks had passed since she'd learned the true purpose of the twin version of the Winter Games. The queen was nearly five and a half months along in her pregnancy, and it was getting harder to conceal the fact that she was expecting. Rayah stood in the palace's medical ward, scrolling through a tablet to ensure the inventory on hand matched the data on file. The occasional bird sang near a window, breaking the silence and stillness of the quiet morning.

This military post differed from her time at Benal, the duty station she had worked at for two years near the kingdom's border with Susa. There, a medical emergency occurred almost every day, whereas here, the most interesting thing that happened was that they woke a few kids up by holding hands and using earwax. Though it had been exciting, it paled in comparison to the daily adrenaline rush she had experienced for so long at Benal.

Part of her was glad to have a change of pace. She reminded herself that she and her brother had always dreamed of working at the palace, and maybe her feelings would have been completely different if Kaled wasn't there to ruin everything with his mere presence. Rayah tried in vain to keep her mind focused on the task at hand, but her thoughts kept landing on her dating life. She'd dated Odin for three weeks; he was handsome and a sweet guy, but he was also insufferably dull. She couldn't even make out with him without almost falling asleep. He droned on and on for hours about the different makes and models of ships and hover cars and anything else he worked on. Aside from his rambling monologues, Rayah found Odin a pleasant person to be with, but that was it – not charming, not romantic, just *pleasant*.

She might have considered dating Odin longer except that he worked in Fleet, which meant that anytime she went to visit him, she usually saw Kaled as well. She didn't want to see Kaled, but she also couldn't stand the pained look on his face each time she dropped in on Odin. Kaled tried to hide it, but she knew him too well and noticed how his countenance changed each time she walked in. Kaled would suddenly go quiet and avert his eyes; his shoulders would visibly tense, and he would find an excuse to leave.

For some reason, it bothered her. She'd thought seeing her ex-boyfriend squirm would have the opposite effect on her; there should have been joy in seeing him suffer, but oddly enough, that was not the case. At any rate, up until now, Kaled had done a pretty good job of respecting her space. They'd barely said more than a cordial hello or goodbye to one another in the month they had been working at the palace.

Her phone vibrated, and when she looked, it was Guyad; he had sent her a picture message of his bare chest after an intense workout. He must have heard that she and Odin had broken up. Rayah shook her head in disgust. When she had first arrived in Clivesdail, she had found Guyad interesting and deliciously handsome; plus, she'd needed a distraction from Kaled and his ditzy girlfriend. Now that she'd been around Guyad for more than a month and gotten to know him a little better, she had a much greater understanding of what a pig he truly was. She had no intention whatsoever of dating him.

Though Guyad never shied away from being overtly on the prowl for his next conquest in bed, Rayah sensed a slight change in him. She had noticed him become even more insufferable than before. Even Evia and Ensin had mentioned how he acted when Rayah was not around. Tye and Tru, who worked with communications and technology, encountered Guyad and his team a lot during their line of work, and had told Rayah that even the soldiers in his department were saying he seemed like more of a douchebag than usual.

Rayah felt it was best to keep things between the two of them on a professional basis. It didn't stop him, however, from trying to "charm" his way into her life. Rayah sat down while a familiar, albeit painful, insecurity crept into her heart. She breathed in deeply and steadied her thoughts, but no amount of encouragement or lies could cover up the suffocating doubts within her. There were times, like right now, when she wondered if something was wrong with her.

Her relationship with Odin had ended before it amounted to anything. Rayah replayed the conversation she'd had with Aymes a month ago when they first arrived at the palace. Okay, so a lot of Rayah's relationships – all of them since Sy, in fact – had ended before reaching the point of real long-term commitment. But even that admission wasn't entirely honest, though, was it? Saying that they "had ended" made it sound like

Rayah awoke one morning to find the relationship over. What she meant to say, what she needed to admit to herself, was that she had ended them before any deep attachment developed.

She'd convinced herself that she had been thriving, living her best life as she dated these incredible guys, and now she had to face the reality that her *best life* was all a lie. Instead, she had been merely surviving the trauma left in the wake of Kaled's carelessness with her heart. Commitment issues had dogged her ever since that night in Sy's apartment, and if she didn't confront them head-on, she might as well stop dating altogether.

Rayah wanted to cast all the blame on Kaled; he had single-handedly ruined her innocence, her belief in love, and her capacity to trust a man's intentions. Kaled had never been an evil or mean-spirited guy. All of the pain he'd caused was collateral damage due to his own shortcomings. Had he been stronger, all of the drama could have been avoided. The thing that hurt the most was knowing they had truly loved each other. But love just wasn't enough; experience had taught her this the hard way.

"I need help," Rayah murmured. "If there's something wrong with me, I need to know it."

Resolutely, she picked up her work tablet, signed onto the medical platform, and scrolled through the vast list of counselors available through her network. She made an appointment for one located at Primeda Fortress, hoping the distance would help with her desire for discretion.

"Please," she prayed out loud, "help me heal. I want to love again. Teach me how."

Nevertheless, she felt that she should try and date

someone else soon. One silly notion she hung onto was that if she remained busy with a guy, Kaled would see it and leave her alone. If he left her alone, she could continue her job and do it well. But if he so much as looked at her or talked to her, it could set her off into a rage or something worse, something she had vowed would never happen again: she might develop feelings for him.

Rayah had busied herself with taking inventory and putting in a request for additional supplies. A big emergency stash had been useful at her last post but seemed to be lacking in this one. Her mind was entirely focused on numbers and potential scenarios that might require immediate medical attention when, suddenly, the medical ward's automatic double doors opened. Guyad stood at the entrance.

He was dressed in his uniform and looked hungry for attention. "Hey, gorgeous," he said in greeting, walking in and letting the doors shut automatically behind him. Guyad closed the distance between the two of them. "I heard you're single again. When are you going to let me take you out? I could take you dancing."

As he said that, he grabbed her hand, twirling her around effortlessly and ending with a perfectly executed dip. Rayah loved dancing; Guyad's actions had certainly gotten her attention. *Too bad,* she thought, *that he seems the type to take what he wants and move on.* While they were still in that position, the doors opened again. This time, Kaled stood on the other side. His hands were down at his sides, and there was no hiding the look of total shock on his face. Guyad snapped Rayah back up to a standing position, looking behind him at the doorway...which was now empty.

"That's funny. I thought I heard the doors open,"

Guyad said, confused.

"It was a soldier. Never mind that. How can I help you, Sergeant Lurca? Are you really here to ask me out, or did you need medical attention?" she asked. Rayah didn't know why, but she felt irritated that Kaled had walked in on them.

"Well," he started tentatively, "there's a rumor going around the castle that the queen is pregnant. I was hoping you could confirm or deny that."

"Sorry to disappoint you, but I can't talk to you about the queen's medical status. Patient confidentiality. It's an oath and responsibility I don't take lightly."

She saw a flicker of disappointment and rage in his eyes that went away just as quickly as it had come. "Surely," he tried again, "if she was, the kingdom would know by now, or at least the palace staff."

"I don't know," said Rayah playing dumb. "Every woman is different, and situations vary too much. Some women don't even tell their best friends."

He watched her, or so it seemed to Rayah. She felt as if Guyad were inspecting her to see if she could be hiding something. As he did, the small hairs on the back of her neck stood up. She felt uncomfortable but did not allow her concern to reach her face. This was something, however, that she had plenty of experience with. Being a twin, she'd poured incredible amounts of mental focus into mastering duo-com and mono-blocking. She knew how to control her mind and face to keep her thoughts private. In the end, Rayah merely smiled at Guyad, which seemed to put him at ease.

"I just got curious," Guyad said, trying to excuse himself. "It would be so exciting if she were. Catch you later?"

"Of course." She walked him toward the door, eager to see him leave. She didn't know why, but his questions had not felt innocent; the sooner he left, the better. She noticed the zipper to his pants was undone. "Your fly is down," she said.

"Thanks." As he turned around to fix his zipper, the automatic doors opened, and there was Kaled once more. "Careful," said Guyad to Kaled, who stood there, transfixed, "she's feisty."

Rayah shook her head. It didn't matter to her what Kaled thought, but she didn't like men insinuating that something had happened, when the opposite was true. She waited for Guyad to be out of earshot before looking at Kaled, who seemed statuesque, apparently unable to move, looking furious.

"How can I help you, Captain Behr?" she asked, aware that her attempt at professionalism still came out in an annoyed tone.

"We were summoned here. I'll just wait outside until the rest of the group comes." Whether he'd meant it or not, his words came through laced with disgust.

"No, by all means, come in. Take a load off. Besides, it looks like you have a lot on your mind," she said sarcastically.

They were standing a few feet from each other. Kaled looked her up and down and then shook his head in frustration. "Forget it. It's none of my damn business."

"You're right; it's not," she replied with an icy tone.

He spun around as if to leave and then turned back to face her. "Look, we're both adults. What you do behind closed doors is your prerogative. But on duty and in uniform, Rayah? Seriously? What has gotten into you?"

She approached him, shaking with anger. "What

exactly do you think you saw? Hmm?"

"I don't think I need to paint you a picture." He shook his head again as if to rid himself of the thoughts creeping into his brain. "Just next time, make sure the door is locked," he spat.

Enough was enough. Rayah was livid. How could Kaled think she would do something like *that* while at work? He, of all people, would know how she behaved behind closed doors, and the fact that he thought her capable of it made her furious. She could feel her fiery eyes boring a hole into him.

"Nothing happened," she retorted. "How dare you come in here and jump to conclusions? Never, *ever* question my work ethic again, or you'll see a side of me you don't want to meet."

Rayah seethed with anger and indignation. Was that what he thought of her, that she was some hussy who couldn't wait to disrobe herself? She felt so disrespected by his assumptions. She knew she should be angry at Guyad, but instead, all her anger was focused on the one who knew her better.

Geez sis, what's going on? I can feel loads of anger coming through, said her brother through duo-com.

Ugh. Kal is insufferable. Please get here as soon as you can before I kick him in the teeth. Also, please stay behind after the meeting; I need to talk to you and General Peterson.

What about? he asked.

I can't concentrate now with Kal here. I'll tell you after the meeting.

Hmm. He does have that effect on you.

Rayah decided to ignore her brother's playful jab at her. Kaled moved away and stood by the double doors, watching her from afar.

"I'm sorry," he said after a minute of silence. "You're right. I jumped to conclusions. It just looked –"

"I know what it *looked* like, Captain," she said a little less defensively. "I may be many things, but a bad soldier isn't one of them."

She thought of telling him off and finally giving him a piece of her mind about *the incident* that had caused that rift between them. Years ago, when everything had fallen apart, she'd been far too shocked and emotional to rip him apart with the words that desperately needed to be said. But then there were the other thoughts, the vivid memories of their passionate relationship and the wonderful friendship they had once enjoyed, all mocking her because she knew it could never be that way again.

Kaled's demeanor relaxed slightly, "You speak as if I believe you have any negative attributes," he said tenderly. "You are one of the kindest, most compassionate, and honorable women I know. I apologize if my actions have ever made you think otherwise. This isn't easy, by the way. We were never supposed to cross paths again."

Rayah couldn't agree more. Having him in her life truly complicated matters. To her dismay, she felt a pang of loneliness and longing for him. She hated that she still harbored feelings for Kaled, even after so much time had passed. He was, after all, her first kiss and her first lover. He had at one time been one of her closest friends. No matter what she did, a part of him would permanently stay with her, just like a tattoo.

"Thank you," she said. Kaled's kind words felt like an ointment to her raw emotions. "It isn't easy for me either," she admitted.

Kaled smiled, but Rayah could see the sadness in his

eyes. She wondered if he could see the conflict in hers. "I'll just sit over here quietly. I promise not to bother you," he assured her, taking a seat in a solitary chair in a corner on the far end of the medical bay. He retrieved an item that looked like a flat stone from his pocket and twirled it absentmindedly in his fingers.

Rayah looked at her watch; the rest of the group weren't due to arrive for another fifteen minutes. There were many places she'd rather be instead of in the same room as Kaled, with no one else around to diffuse the tension. Squeezing a lemon onto an open wound, for example, would be preferable. She pretended to continue with her inventory, though truthfully, her mind was preoccupied with conflicting thoughts of Kaled.

The minutes passed with agonizing slowness, and she could feel Kaled looking at her every so often as if to continue their conversation. She was done, though, and didn't want to hear his voice for another moment. Looking upon his face and those green eyes had a hypnotic effect on her; the last thing she needed was to lose her composure while at work. Mercifully, Dr. Perry Kortez and the two young twins, Evia and Ensin, appeared shortly after.

"Hello, Captain Jur," Dr. Kortez greeted her. He and the children walked in, and then he did a quick head turn. "Oh, hi, Captain Behr. Didn't notice you there. It was so quiet that I thought she was alone."

Rayah took a deep breath, exhaled, and then smiled. "Yes, the captain and I were just enjoying some peace and quiet before the rest of the group arrived."

"How are you guys?" asked Kaled as he approached the kids.

"Doing good," said Evia, "but my legs are hurting a

lot after those runs."

"Have you been doing the warm-up and stretches I've taught you?" asked Rayah, concerned.

"It doesn't help," said Ensin.

"Show me where it hurts," said Dr. Kortez.

Both kids pointed to their hamstrings. Kaled looked at the doctor and Rayah, confusion on his face. "I've never hurt there after a run. Have any of you?"

"No," they both answered.

Rayah asked the children if they thought the pain was due to running or something else, but they assured her the pain only began a few weeks ago and had increased after each run.

"Okay, well, maybe we figure out a way to stretch that muscle. Can't be too difficult for us to figure out. Do as I do, and let me know if any of it feels good."

Rayah moved side to side, then sat down and lifted her leg, but that seemed to have no effect. Then she placed the leg behind her, which highlighted her flexibility, but again it didn't seem to do anything for the kids. Next she stood up and bent over to reach her toes. Both kids hollered in a mix of pain and pleasure.

"Was that it?" asked Rayah.

"Yes! That's the spot!"

Moments later, the rest of The Elite trickled in. First was Ondraus, who ran up to Kaled and placed an arm around his friend.

"Hey, buddy. You still going out with Vellah tonight?"

Kaled eyed Ondraus and then looked at Rayah, who was close enough to hear the conversation. "Yes," said Kaled dispassionately. "I was thinking of taking a stroll with her through town, and getting some food at a cafe."

"Do you mind if Aymes and I tag along? Like a double date? If she says yes, I mean. I feel like we've gotten along pretty well lately, and I'm going to give it a shot."

"Of course," said Kaled with a big smile. "Just don't make out with my sister in front of me."

"How's that fair? You and Rayah were always at each other's faces. A crowbar couldn't take you two apart."

"Wait," interrupted Ensin, who was sitting much further away and should not have been able to hear the conversation. "Are you saying that you and you used to date?" He pointed at both Kaled and Rayah.

"It was a long time ago," said Rayah, trying to sound nonchalant.

"But you two hate each other," said Evia with bewilderment.

Rayah couldn't dispute that logic. "It would not be an appropriate conversation for two youngsters to hear," she replied. "Now, how did you guys hear them talking? They're clear across the other side of the room."

The two kids exchanged a look with the doctor, then shrugged their shoulders. Rayah wondered why she had never experienced such anomalies with any of her previous patients. First came the reaction to the lucid wasps, then the pain in their hamstrings, and now this.

Before Rayah could ask any follow-up questions, though, General Peterson walked into the room, ending the conversation. "This shouldn't take long; it's just a quick meeting. As you may all remember, Dr. Kortez is the uncle of these young twins. He was here when the children chanted the so-called prophecy, and was present when you all woke the children up. As you can imagine, one thing led to another, and we have filled in Dr. Kortez with full detail regarding The Elite and what your function is here. Doctor, you have the floor."

Perry Kortez looked at the soldiers and then cleared his throat. "Thank you, General Peterson. Once I understood the purpose of this group and what you were attempting to teach these kids, I felt it was my duty to inform you of the following. My niece and nephew have a broken link, meaning they cannot duo-com."

Silence fell in the room. Sure, there were plenty of twins in all of Brennen and throughout the world of Vilmos who were not proficient in duo-com. It was a very time-intensive language and required both twins to exercise self-control and maximum focus to learn how to communicate. But it was one thing not to practice duo-com, and another thing entirely to have a broken link. In all of the years that Rayah worked as a nurse, she had only heard of one set of twins with a broken link, and it was due to the siblings hating each other. After years of not talking and trying to kill each other to gain possession of their late father's land, their ability to duo-com came to an end. A broken link wasn't unheard of, but it was extremely rare.

Dr. Kortez continued, "I didn't say anything sooner due to my duty to keep patient-doctor confidentiality. I also needed to speak with their parents to get their consent before sharing this information with all of you."

"We can't communicate the way you all do," said Ensin looking at the group, "but I can sense my sister in a way that most non-twins cannot. It's not words like you hear with your sibling in your head. With us, it's more like a feeling. I can look at her and sometimes read her eyes to know how she's feeling or what she's thinking about something."

"If you don't mind me asking," interjected Rayah, "if that's the case, why were you able to get into a Gaoled in the first place? Only fraternal twins with an intact link would be able to get stuck in one."

"That remains a mystery," replied Dr. Kortez. "I assume it's because of the strange connection the royal infants have with Ensin and Evia. We don't know why or how this is all happening."

"Hmm," said Tru as she looked at the children. "Can you communicate in some other way? For example, my brother and I know seven different languages, and not just spoken language. For example we know the Tapp language, which is really just a bunch of beeping and tapping sounds. Here, watch." She tapped the table near her using various short taps and some of them seemed to have a longer space between the other tapping sound. "Tye, could you please translate?"

"She said 'I'm hungry,'" replied Tye without even looking at his sister. Rayah could see the wheels of his mind were turning. "My sister's got a good point here. Do y'all have your own language that you use?"

"No, not really."

"If you're willing, I'd be more than happy to teach you sign language," said Tye.

"I didn't know you knew sign language," remarked General Peterson. "It's not in your personnel file."

"That would be because I don't know it yet. But I'm a quick learner when it comes to languages and anything that involves communication. I can learn and teach the kids. I'm sure my sister would love to help, right?"

His sister nodded. "Most certainly."

General Peterson made a note on his phone. "Excellent. It's settled. Children, please work your schedules to include time with Lieutenants Tye and Tru Ryder. They'll teach you as they learn. Lieutenants, please provide me a weekly update report on their studies. I think this will be beneficial. We don't know what the future holds, but if there ever comes a time when these kids have to communicate with each other and can't speak out loud, knowing sign language may be the key."

Both Ryder twins nodded their heads in agreement, and so did Evia and Ensin. Rayah was happy that they'd all found such an easy solution for something that could have been truly problematic. It was strange how these two young children were far more different than any set of kids she'd ever had the pleasure to meet before.

General Peterson gave the Kortez kids a set of new smartwatches, which could make secure phone calls and sent encrypted messages. They were similar to the ones he had given The Elite a few weeks back. "That is it for now. I won't take any more of your time. Have a nice weekend, everyone."

"General, Dr. Kortez, can I see you all once the others leave?" asked Rayah quietly. The two men nodded and waited patiently while everyone else made for the door.

"Hey Tru, if you're hungry, I made some really good shepherd's pie tonight at the cafeteria, and there's a slice available with your name on it," said Wilstead with a smile.

"Wil," she replied, "I'm famished. How about we meet in fifteen? I want to get out of my uniform first."

"That sounds great. I'll walk with you to the barracks," he replied.

"Coming, O?" called out Kaled.

"Yeah, I'll catch up, bro."

"Okay."

Once everyone except for Ondraus, Dr. Kortez, and General Peterson had left, Rayah took in a deep breath and shared with them her thoughts regarding Guyad and the conversation they'd had earlier. "I don't know," she concluded, "something is off. I don't know if he's always been like that, but the way he was watching me really set off all the red flags. I don't trust him."

"This is very strange," said General Peterson. "Sergeant Guyad Lurca has always had a faultless personnel file. Sure, he's abrasive, but he's an excellent soldier. I've only known him for two years, but his dedication to our king and nation is evident in all of the notes from his previous commanders."

Rayah was afraid of this. Her thoughts would go unnoticed and set to the side. Maybe she was overthinking what she had experienced earlier, as she did so often, but her gut told her otherwise. How could she press the matter further while still maintaining her military bearing?

"Sir, I can't deny the odd feeling in the pit of my stomach."

Her brother Ondraus stepped in. "Would it hurt to keep an eye on him, just in case my sister is right?"

"No," said General Peterson thoughtfully, "it wouldn't hurt. I don't want you to think I'm not taking your comments seriously, Captain. I'm just trying to think of how to handle this. Sergeant Lurca is the head of security here; he has access to everyone's personnel files and quite a bit of other sensitive information. He and my son Yosef are friends. Maybe Yosef can let me know if something seems odd with Sergeant Lurca. I don't think this will be as easy as we think. Sergeant Lurca is not a newbie soldier; if he has something to hide, he is trained to do so."

"I can think of a way," said Rayah before she had the opportunity to ponder it all the way through.

"What's that?" asked Ondraus.

"I plan to date him."

"What? Absolutely not," said Ondraus, shaking his head. "You've lost your mind, sister."

"I have not lost my mind. General Peterson, Sergeant Lurca has been pursuing a relationship with me since I got here. Why not take the bait?"

"No. I don't like it," said Ondraus. "I don't want my sister dating some guy specifically if she thinks he might be hiding something. No way."

"Brother, I can take care of myself. Besides, you are just a mind-thought away. If I sense something wrong, I'll duo-com you."

"I don't like this either, soldier," said General Peterson, "but I think it's an option we need to consider. Let's keep this in our back pocket for now. No need to date him just yet."

"I plan to string him along as much as possible," said Rayah.

"Okay. Just let me know if you find anything out. Was that all?"

"No, sir. When can we share the news about the queen's pregnancy? If Sergeant Lurca came here with rumors, that means other people are talking."

"I agree; she only has another week or two before her belly really shows," said the doctor. "King Tarrington does not want to reveal anything until we can be certain that we've taken care of this prophecy, but the belly will show long before that, and we don't even know if the words Evia and Ensin chanted are going to come true."

"I will talk to the King and Queen. You are right; we must announce the pregnancy before people come to that conclusion themselves," said General Peterson.

CHAPTER 12

Ondraus

Ondraus still could not believe the conversation he'd just had with his sister. Even as they left the medical ward, he urged her to reconsider her rash decision, but she remained headstrong. He already didn't like Guyad, and now with this added suspicion that the sergeant might be up to something suspicious, Ondraus' loathing deepened. He'd known men like Guyad: the extremely good-looking, young, arrogant type with a high-paying job. A guy like that usually expected certain things behind closed doors from a woman he dated and wouldn't accept anything less, or at least not for too long before becoming frustrated and leaving her.

How was Rayah going to handle a man like that? What would she have to do to get him to talk? He shook his head and tried to get the disturbing thoughts out of his mind.

"Hey, what was that all about?" asked Kaled at their shared apartment.

"Believe me, brother," said Ondraus, "you don't want to know."

"Did she complain about me? I said something insensitive and –"

"No, that's not what the meeting was about," Ondraus assured him.

After changing out of their uniforms, the two men

sat in the living room to wait for their dates to get ready.

"Have you been attending your meetings?" asked Ondraus.

"You mean the Sobriety Society meetings?" Kaled clarified.

"Yes. Your sister and I have been worried about you. It can't be easy with Rayah being around."

"I've been going," said Kaled evenly. "If anything, I've been going far more frequently now than I had in quite some time. Plus, my sponsor knows about Rayah being in my life again, so he's been checking up on me a lot as well."

"You're good, then?" asked Ondraus, afraid to hear the answer.

"Yes. I just need to be sure I make healthy decisions, and staying clear away from Rayah is definitely one of them."

"When are you going to make amends with her, bro? You know that's the only step in your sobriety program that you haven't done."

"I'm not ready to face her," croaked Kaled.

"Face who?" asked Vellah, her hair still wrapped in a towel but otherwise dressed to go out.

"Nothing, babe, nothing at all," Kaled replied. He then looked back at Ondraus and said, "My sister said she's almost ready," while pointing a finger at his temple.

Though Rayah's idea bothered him tremendously, Ondraus also had something else on his mind: Aymes. He had liked her for as long as he could remember, but she'd always been dating other, older guys. Never in all their years had she given him the chance to ask her out until today. He was surprised she'd said yes and wondered, in the back of his mind, if she'd only agreed because she thought he was asking as a friend rather than as a guy who liked her.

A few minutes later, a knock sounded on the door.

"Sorry I'm late," said Aymes, hugging Ondraus and Kaled. "I was busy bathing my son. I had on a totally different outfit, but it got wet and this was the only thing I had clean," she added, flustered.

"I think you look beautiful," Ondraus assured her. She had on a pair of form-fitting jeans and a long-sleeved shirt. He offered her the flowers he had purchased on his way to the apartment.

"Oh, you're too sweet. How did you know I liked bluebonnets?" she asked, inhaling the sweet perfume of the flowers.

"There was a time, back in school, when you used to wear them in your hair all the time after hours. I just kinda figured you might still like them."

"Wow, that was so long ago. I must have been fifteen at the time."

Kaled bit into a bright red apple. "Might as well take a seat, you guys. Vellah still has to dry her hair."

After fifteen minutes of waiting on the couch and conversing about their day, Vellah finally emerged from the room, and they all set out. Ondraus could not have asked for a more romantic stroll or better weather. The first sun had already descended, and the second one was well on its way toward the horizon. The cool spring weather made it so a long-sleeved shirt was comfortable and a bulky jacket was no longer needed. Several gusts of wind caught them in the face, and Ondraus took the opportunity to wrap his arm around Aymes.

To his delight, she leaned into him.

"Thanks. I was getting cold," said Aymes.

"My pleasure."

They walked the Heart of Clivesdail and heard street musicians playing wind and string instruments, which was a welcome change from the usual synthesized electronica sounds of most modern Brennish music. A few artists were painting the romantic evening scene on canvases they'd set up on the sidewalks.

"I love this song," said Aymes as she walked and snuggled against Ondraus.

"Well then," he said, "may I have this dance?"

"Are you serious?" asked Aymes.

"Of course. Why not?"

Vellah started giggling and applauding as Aymes and Ondraus began their dance near an antique book shop. "Dance with me, too," pleaded Vellah.

Kaled obliged, taking her hand in his and twirling her around. The two couples were the only ones dancing, but many others on the street stood and watched happily as they enjoyed the impromptu concert and dance. The musicians were elated to see a crowd forming, and copper and gold coins began accumulating in their donation hat.

"No one's ever just danced with me like that. At a dance hall, sure, but like this...never," commented Aymes once they had begun strolling again.

"Well, I'm not most guys."

"I can see that." Aymes grew quiet and pensive but placed her hand around Ondraus's waist and leaned into him once more. "Maybe you can take me dancing for real one of these nights," she said quietly enough so that her brother and his girlfriend could not overhear.

"Just you and I."

"I'd love that."

The two couples walked toward a street vendor who sold small fried meat pies in half moon shapes. With meat pies and a soda in hand, they made their way to a bench under a street lamp.

"Oh, these are good," said Aymes licking her lips. "I should have gotten a few extra for Rayah. She would have loved them."

"Who's Rayah?" asked Vellah, adding more lime sauce to her meat pie.

"She's my sister," said Ondraus before anyone had the funny idea to say that she was also Kaled's ex-girlfriend.

"Oh, yes. I knew the name sounded familiar. Why is it that I never see her? Is she that busy?"

The other three exchanged glances and grew quiet while they devoured the rest of their food.

"Ah, look who it is," exclaimed Ondraus, thankful for a diversion.

Both Kaled and his sister followed his eyes, smiling when they saw the Kortez family walking up the street toward them.

"Hello, Mr. and Mrs. Kortez. Hi, kids," said Ondraus while waving his hand.

"Hello!" said Alastair Kortez.

"We're on our way to my mom's old job, back when she was a teenager in the summer," said Evia happily.

"Oh, are you from Clivesdail, Mrs. Kortez?" asked Aymes.

"Please, call me Nerida. Yes, I'm from Clivesdail, and I used to work right there," she said, pointing further up the road. "At Mister Yemley's Yummylicious Shoppe."

"Do you all want to join us?" asked Alastair.

Ondraus and the rest of his group agreed and followed the Kortez family toward a two-story cobblestone store. As they walked in, a delicious aroma engulfed them: hot chocolate, fresh-baked pastries, and treats like the blood-orange cupcakes with raspberry white chocolate icing. Three employees worked diligently behind a polished wooden counter, serving the many customers seated at the four-person tables throughout the shop. Drawings by children from all over Brennen covered the walls, creating a cheerful ambiance.

"What's upstairs, Mama?" asked Evia as she stood watching the happy commotion all around her.

"Oh, that's where you go to just have a drink and read. No talking is allowed up there. It was perfect for when I was in college."

"Wouldn't the sound carry up the stairs?" asked Kaled.

"No. Mister Yemley installed a sound barrier that automatically seals itself after you walk through. You can't even see it."

"Oh, that's got to be useful, huh, babe?" asked Vellah with a grin.

Ondraus noticed how Kaled's face and ears turned red at the suggestive comment.

"Oh hey, there's Rayah! Can I say hi to her, mom?" asked Evia, already jumping up and down.

"Sure, darling," said Nerida.

Rayah was sitting at a two-person barstool with Guyad and had her hand on one of his flexed biceps. Ondraus couldn't hear what Evia said to Rayah, but he saw his sister look up and lock eyes with him and the others. Rayah waved, then looked back at Evia and chatted with her. Evia threw her arms around Rayah in a parting hug before trotting back to her mother. Just as quickly, Rayah turned her attention back on Guyad and continued to flirt with him.

"Oh, that's your sister, isn't it?" asked Vellah, waving back a little too late.

"Yes, it is."

"I knew she was going to get with that guy. You should have seen how he was all over her that day at the hotel when he told me I couldn't go with you to the palace. He barely took his eyes off her. They make a cute couple. Don't you think, babe?"

Ondraus turned to see Kaled twitch uncomfortably. "Yup," Kaled answered.

Oh my goodness, O. I saw you and Aymes dancing earlier. That was so romantic! exclaimed Rayah through duocom. Ondraus did not miss the fact that she had not mentioned seeing Kaled and Vellah dancing as well.

How come you didn't stop and say hello? teased Ondraus.

Me? Get anywhere near Kal voluntarily? No, I'd rather squeeze lemon juice in my eye, thank you very much. Besides, you all looked like you were having such a wonderful time; I didn't want to intrude.

Speaking of good times, how are things going with you and Guyad?

Rayah responded with a laugh in her mind. *Bro, this guy has literally talked about himself the entire time. I've been here twenty minutes, and I've barely said a thing.*

I didn't think you were going to go out with him so soon, commented Ondraus.

I know. Neither did I. But this is technically not a date. I paid for my drink and met him here as opposed to having him pick me up.

Ondraus felt nostalgia emanating from his sister as her thoughts grew quiet in his mind. *Everything okay?* he asked.

It's beautiful the way Aymes is looking at you right now, sighed Rayah.

Ondraus turned to look at Aymes, whose eyes seemed to twinkle. Without thinking twice, Ondraus took her hand, lifted it to his lips, and kissed it. For a fleeting moment, he forgot about Rayah, Guyad, Kaled, and everyone else except for Aymes. The room dissolved around him; only Aymes remained.

Geez, you see what I mean? asked Rayah. The magical moment vanished like morning dew; Aymes took her hand back with a slight smile, leaving Ondraus standing alone, longing for more. His sister's voice continued. *Look at how long our conversation has been; I'm not even paying attention to Guyad because he's droning on and on about his workout routine. Like, I get it, dude. I work out too.*

Ondraus laughed out loud so hard that Aymes and the others asked him what was so funny. "Sorry. Rayah just told me that he's talking to her about his workout routine. That just sounded funny to me."

Finally, their group was next to order treats and drinks. Ondraus noticed a gangly man, about forty years of age with headphones in his ears, come out from the back room with a vat of hot and frothing chocolate milk.

"Brett!" exclaimed Nerida as she jumped up and ran toward the man. At first, he looked confused, and then a wide smile spread upon his face.

"Nerry!" He placed the large vat of hot chocolate on

the counter and clapped joyfully.

Nerida came up to the bar. "Can I hug an old friend?"

Though it appeared Brett was happy to see Nerida, he stood silently and smiled, seeming to think about the question while his eyes roamed around the room instead of looking directly at her. After a pause that lasted nearly a full minute, he nodded his approval.

She hugged him tenderly and asked, "What are you doing working so late? I thought your dad only had you work the quieter morning shift."

Brett nodded, his eyes looking past her as they conversed, and then pointed to his headphones. "Dad's on a trip. I have to work." Brett spoke in a slightly nasal tone and with an unusual, singsong cadence.

"Oh, well, that's too bad. I know how much you like playing your video games at night. Can I have a Choco Moo Brew?"

He giggled and clapped his hands again. "Say it right, Nerry!"

"Oh, I see. Not even an old childhood friend like myself can get away with it, huh?"

"Nope! Nuh-uh!" He giggled again as he hopped with excitement.

Nerida took in a deep breath and then said, "Can I have a Choco MOOOOOOOOOO Brew, please? Oh, and a few azule berry tarts, please."

The howl caused even further laughter from Brett, who was now doubled over and snorting. The employee next to him smiled and handed over a large cup of the hot drink, along with a peppermint straw and multi-colored marshmallows. Brett walked away without saying goodbye, but Nerida didn't seem fazed by his lack of social etiquette.

"Mom," asked Evia quietly, "what's wrong with that man? Why does he act like that?"

"Brett is not like you and me, darling. He's different, and he learns differently. He doesn't like large social gatherings or loud noises, which is why he's wearing his headphones. As you can see, though, he's a sweetheart."

"Yup, your mom and I took him to our prom our senior year. Technically, he was her date, and I just tagged along," said Alastair with a smile.

Nerida kissed her husband on the lips. "Oh, my goodness. Remember all the trouble the three of us got into that night? It was so fun. Come on; let's go get a seat before they're all taken."

Now I'm learning about the different protein powders he likes to use. Someone shoot me.

Ondraus laughed out loud once more. His sister's terrible date, or rather not-a-date, was disastrously hilarious.

"Hi! I like your headphones," Evia said to Brett, passing him as he wiped up one of the counters.

"Thank you. They keep down the noise. I like your bracelet, too. It's pretty."

"Oh, thank you! It's a moon crystal bracelet. It shimmers in the dark and in direct sunlight!"

"Cool!" Just then, Brett's mother came out of the back room, and as soon as he saw her, he stopped her and said, "Mama, I want one of those bracelets. It shimmers in the dark. Can I get one?"

"Oh, I can make him one, Mrs. Yemley," Evia offered.

"That's sweet of you, dear. I would hate to impose, though – oh, my stars; it can't be! Nerida, is that you?" asked Mrs. Yemley as Nerida approached.

"Yes! Hello!"

Ondraus ordered a cup of gingersnap hot cocoa and a salted caramel cookie with broken pretzel pieces on top. He found his group a table that had just been cleared off when Kaled tapped him on the shoulder and asked, "Can we talk outside real quick?"

The two of them stepped out the door while their dates remained in the warm, cozy shop.

"What's up, man?" asked Ondraus, already sure he knew exactly what Kaled was going to say.

"Hey, look, when we get back to the barracks, can you just take my sister home? She lives in an apartment about fifteen minutes from here. I need to break up with Vellah." Kaled looked sick to his stomach.

"Why? I thought you liked her. She's a nice girl."

"I know she's a nice girl." He looked up at the dark inky sky and then shook his head. "I can't stop thinking of her. Rayah has gotten so far into my brain again that I can't function, and it's not fair to Vellah; she deserves better than a guy who is pining over someone else."

"Not this again, man. Come on. You've come so far."

"I know, dammit, and I'm back. I hate it so much. No offense, but I wish I wouldn't have seen her again. I lose myself every time she's involved."

"Breaking up with Vellah isn't going to fix anything," said Ondraus. "It's not like Rayah is going to come running back to you."

"I know that. She hates me. She's made that clear, and I don't blame her. For as long as I'm here at this base, on this mission, I just don't think I can date anyone, because the entire time, I'm going to be thinking of Rayah instead. Besides, I need to make healthy decisions. I have to do whatever it takes to stay sober. I can't bring Vellah down with me; I have to let her go. It's what's best."

"Dude, we could be here for years. What's your plan? Be celibate the entire time or something? Let's face it, all the problems you're talking about started because you couldn't keep it in your pants."

"I know." Kaled looked down at his shoes and pushed a pebble across the sidewalk with his foot. "What other choice do I have? Subject Vellah to a relationship where each time I kiss her or make love to her, I'm thinking of another woman? That would be vile. Or how about a revolving door of women? Endless one-night stands? There's no other way, man. I'll be okay. I'll make this work."

Ondraus eyed his friend. Concern filled his mind as he recalled the arduous journey Kaled had already undergone in his battle with sobriety. It scared Ondraus; what if Kaled failed? "Kal," he said cautiously, "what can I do to help?"

"Just be my friend, even when I'm insufferable," said Kaled with a weak smile; his lip trembled slightly.

"I love you like a brother," said Ondraus with conviction. "I will not abandon you, no matter what." His tone changed as he added, "But how are you going to go without sex?"

Kaled shrugged. "Honestly, I don't know. I suppose I'll just have to stay busy all the time, you know, keep my schedule full, so there's no time to think about her or alcohol or anything else I'm not allowed to have. I'll be fine."

There was a short pause before Kaled asked, "Do me a favor?"

"Sure," said Ondraus.

"Don't tell Rayah about this. The last thing I need is

her pity or any snide remarks. She doesn't need to know I'm incapable of keeping a girlfriend due to my own emotional malfunction, while she, on the other hand, is dating one of the hottest guys in the entire kingdom."

Ondraus wanted to spare his friend these feelings and tell him the real reason why Rayah was out with Guyad, but he had promised to keep it secret. Instead, he nodded his head and swore he wouldn't tell his sister about Kaled's relationship status.

CHAPTER 13

Nerida

"Mmm," purred Nerida, "you were amazing." She sat up and retrieved her bra and blouse from the bedpost.

"I love you," said her husband Alastair as he kissed her neck from behind. His hands traveled up and down her bare body; his touch re-kindled her desire for another round.

"I love you too, darling. Let's do it again after the kids go to sleep," she said while dressing herself.

"I'm counting down the hours," he responded with a smile.

Dreary gray skies had a way of making Nerida want to lay in bed with him all day; unfortunately, motherhood and its attendant responsibilities did not allow for such luxuries. Thankfully her children were fully immersed in their quiet activities, allowing Nerida and her husband to escape to their bedroom for a few stolen moments together. After making sure she looked presentable, Nerida padded down the hallway to check on her kids.

"How's the reading going?" she asked upon seeing her son sprawled on his bed with a bored look on his face.

"I've been at this for hours, mom," he whined. "There's so much to read about the Vengard Revolution. Like, just get to the point so I can start on my research paper."

Nerida laughed and kissed her son on the forehead. Ensin preferred to use his hands and explore the world, unlike his sister, who enjoyed reading. Evia sat on her bed on the other side of the large room, working on more moon bracelets while bobbing her head to the music coming out of her wireless headphones.

Nerida would have liked to join her daughter and make bracelets, but she still had work to do. She continued into the living room, where three transparent screens surrounded Alastair. Each screen displayed portions of a lesson plan for his university students. Nerida brought him a cup of coffee and wrapped her arms around her husband's neck. She rested her chin on the top of his head and sighed dreamily.

"Thanks, babe," he said while caressing her hand.

"My pleasure. I'm going to start going through my files now. Do you need anything while I'm up?"

"No. As soon as I'm done with all this," said Alastair, pointing at his coursework, "I'm going to give you a back massage."

"I'll hold you to it," responded Nerida.

The Kortez family had taken up residence at the palace a month or so before, and in that time, Nerida had been able to speak to the queen on several occasions. More than once, the two ladies had sat on a bench in the garden under the twinkling stars, enjoying a cup of hot chocolate. It was evident that royalty always had to be *on*, for there was no way Nerida could be convinced that someone sat so perfectly straight and ladylike at all times. Still, in the short time since Nerida had come to know the queen, she felt a closeness to her. Oddly enough, she also felt the queen was hiding something.

Nerida couldn't quite put her finger on it, but there were times when she'd look at Queen Ellandra and notice a twitch of worry or even guilt over something. Every time it happened, Nerida was tempted to press for details, to see if she could do anything to help the queen. But she'd always cut off the words before asking. After all, Nerida and her family were guests at the palace, and though she had come to care for the queen, she knew they weren't exactly friends. It wasn't Nerida's place to nose in on the queen's business like that.

She stood up and looked out the window, toward the back of the palace grounds; the snow had finally melted away, leaving bits of frost here and there. Cold rain pelted the city, and for some reason, the rhythmic raindrops falling onto the windowsill reminded Nerida of sitting near a warm fire with her parents when she was younger. She missed her mother and father and sighed heavily at the thought of their departure; next week would mark five years since they had died of the virus. Nerida wondered what her parents would have said if they found that their daughter was living in the palace. Surely it would have made them very proud, and the thought of that brought a smile to her face.

Nerida knew she couldn't put off reviewing her data any longer, so she walked over to the kitchen table, which also served as her workspace for most of the day. The transparent computer screens came to life as files of raw data began opening. To the untrained eye, the pages and pages of information appeared as numbers and decimals of no importance. For Nerida, those reports represented a year's worth of work showcasing the growth and potency of her power crystals.

She was thankful that harvesting season had occurred in early winter, or she would've had no other option than to stay behind to finish the job, family emergency or not. She clicked on another file and reviewed the slight increase in revenue, making a mental note to contact the kingdom's treasurer to report her findings. She would have to schedule a time to visit Marez Cave soon, but would rather not go by herself if it could be helped, since the massive cave had a way of making her feel lonely and isolated.

Her thoughts were interrupted when Ensin came out of his room and sat on the couch. "I'm bored," he said as a greeting. "This homework is never-ending."

"Well," said Nerida, "I could use some help with these numbers if you want to pull up a chair. I've been trying a new formula for growing the energy crystals, and I just ran a report this morning. There are pages of data here," she said, pointing at the screen.

Ensin huffed a loud whine. "Why can't you hire people to do this, mom? It's not like we don't have the money."

His father looked up from his lesson plan. Alaistair taught history at the university, but one of his favorite things to do was research old dusty books and ancient languages.

"Son," he said, "I thought you told me you were learning about the Vengard Revolution."

"I am. I just don't want to read anymore. I don't know how Evia did all her homework so quickly." He slumped further, as if the couch were devouring him.

"You just asked your mother why we don't hire someone to handle the energy crystals. That's literally the main reason the Vengard Revolution took place."

Ensin cocked his head and looked at his father for

a minute. "Are you sure, dad? Because I thought it was about King Yerod wanting more power and land."

Nerida laughed. "Oh son, I appreciate how much you joke around. You actually asked your father, a historian, if he knew about the very episode in history that requires our family business to be a secret."

Alastair straightened his back and cleared his throat. "Yes, King Yerod of Tanpenica, modern-day Susa, wanted more power and land. But so did our king, and all the various countries near us, such as Montavlio. For more than eight years, all these nations were at constant war, but one of the biggest reasons was the supply of energy crystals. Before these crystals were discovered, we relied on things like wood for fire and coal for fuel, and the byproducts were destroying our planet. A few years before the great wars, an alchemist by the name of Anozie Durazzo discovered the power of energy crystals. That is when all of the kings decided to send their soldiers to fight for the land where the crystals grew naturally, so they could have a monopoly on this new resource.

"Your ancestor, Bevan Marez, found that a certain cave produced large, superior crystals. People started calling it Marez Cave for simplicity. At that time, its location was not a secret. Bevan and his entire family, except for his youngest son, Na'eem, were slaughtered by Yerod's men in order to take control of the cave and its precious cargo," said Nerida solemnly.

Ensin looked at his father and mother with astonishment. "So, what happened to Na'eem? How did Brennen get the cave back from King Yerod?"

"Na'eem was about nine at the time. He escaped through the waterfall exit by diving into the pool below and then ran to the nearest town to ask for help. Our king sent an entire division of soldiers to the cave and was able to take back control, but only half of the soldiers came out alive. Many died protecting that cave and its resources. After that, the king swore that he would keep the cave secret from everyone, including our own countrymen. Only a select few know of its location and how to get in."

"But then how did Na'eem keep working the crystals? He was just a kid when his family died," Ensin pointed out.

"He kept a diary, you know, back when people wrote on paper. Honestly, son, Na'eem was a bright young man. He took the pain and ashes all around him and worked tirelessly to make a successful business out of them," said Nerida with pride. She didn't like the dark parts of her family history, but she certainly prided herself to know that Na'eem's blood ran through her veins.

"By himself?"

"Yes, by himself," she replied.

Alistair, seeming to notice that his son had grown quiet and pensive, added, "A few years later, when he was about twelve, Na'eem became quite ill and went into the village for some medical attention. While he was staying at the small hospital, a widowed woman came to visit every night to read to him. Sometimes she would bring her two children, a daughter and a son. When he regained his full health, he went back to living in his cave and working it day and night, but he also visited the village frequently to spend time with the woman and her children. The woman provided him a measure of joy, and he felt like he was part of a family once more. It was nearly three years later that her house was burned down due to a lightning strike. Seeing that they would be destitute, he offered them a place to stay at his cave."

"Then what?' asked Ensin, completely enthralled by the story of his ancestors.

"The rest is history, my son. Na'eem and the widow's daughter fell in love and married when they were both nineteen, and it's been a family business since then. An entire hundred and sixty years. There used to be a lot of hands that helped, mind you; it's just that your grandparents only had your mother, and that Utroba Virus killed them all as well as your great uncle. Uncle Perry helps out when he can, but he's busy, as you've seen. So a lot of it falls on your mother...and, of course, we all help too. That's also the reason why she's taught you and your sister so much about crystal harvesting. At this point, there are very few people who know how to manage them. All other countries keep their crystal growing locations a mystery as well."

Nerida remained standing, watching her son as he pondered all of that history. Perhaps if he had known all of that at the beginning of his assignment, he would have devoured the story a lot quicker and been done with his schoolwork already. Nerida was about to comment on that when a knock sounded at the door.

"Hello, may I speak to you and Alastair?" It was the queen. She wore no makeup, and her eyes were red and puffy from crying. On the other side, Nerida saw Guyad standing behind her. As soon as he noticed eyes on him, he straightened the collar of his uniform and then turned the other way.

"Of course, Your Majesty," Nerida responded after a

quick pause. She moved out of the way to allow Queen Ellandra to enter their suite. Ellandra carried a small leather book in her hand and walked directly toward Alastair. Guyad remained on the other side of the door and did not enter the suite.

Sensing the gravity of the forthcoming conversation, Nerida asked her son to go back to his room so the adults could have some privacy.

"Alastair," Queen Ellandra said quietly, "as you know, my uncle died two weeks ago."

"Yes; I was sad to hear of his passing. My condolences," responded Alastair.

"Thank you." Ellandra looked at Alastair and Nerida. "He left this book to me in his will. It looks like it's my great grandmother's. I...I read through some of it, and it sounds almost like a fairy tale, but she is making it out as if it were a real account. Could you take a look at it and tell me what you think?"

Alastair received it and furrowed his brow with curiosity. "Who else knows about this book?" he asked quietly as he thumbed through it.

"All my other family members are dead, so I think just myself and my husband. And now the two of you."

"Does Guyad know?" asked Alastair.

"Who?"

"Sergeant Lurca, Your Majesty," said Nerida.

"Oh. Um, well, he saw me carrying the book, and he accompanied me here since he was working out the details for me to go to the orphanage. I didn't tell him anything specific about the book. Why?"

"This looks authentic, although I'd have to study it closely to know for sure. I'd like to compare it to some other literature I have at our home at Marez." He turned to one of the pages she had bookmarked and read it quickly.

"But it's not like any of it is sensitive information, right?" asked the queen.

Nerida heard a door creak behind her and turned to see both of her kids with their heads peeking out of their bedroom, trying to listen in on the conversation.

"Children," said Nerida in a no-nonsense tone, "please go back into your room." This time, however, Nerida crouched down beside a small button near the door frame and turned on the sound barrier so her children could not listen in.

After another ten minutes of hushed conversation, the queen commented that she should tell Sergeant Lurca she would be a few more minutes. Nerida volunteered to speak to him so that Ellandra could continue discussing the important matters of the book with Alastair. Guyad was on his phone in the hallway, and looked stiffer and creepier than usual. His eyes gleamed angrily at Nerida and she felt uneasy under the scrutiny of his glare.

"Hello, Sergeant Lurca," she said tentatively. Nerida noticed that he seemed to snap out of his terrible mood, looking around for a moment as if confused, and only then seeming to notice the phone in his hand.

"Hey, I didn't see you there," he responded in his typical arrogant tone. He started to walk away before Nerida could speak up.

"Um, aren't you going to wait for the queen? She said she would be a few more minutes."

"The queen?" responded Guyad in confusion. "I arranged for her trip to the orphanage. She should be there."

"No..." added Nerida, equally confused. "She's right in there with my husband. You brought her here." After noticing the look of disbelief on his face, she added, "You can check if you want," and opened the door.

Guyad peered through and stood by the open door in shock. "How the fu..." He trailed off and then stepped away to the spot where he had been waiting before.

Nerida watched him for a few moments before letting herself back in and locking the door behind her. She decided not to say anything about Guyad's odd behavior. Maybe it was her imagination, after all, and she didn't want to worry the queen, who had more important things on her mind.

CHAPTER 14

Rayah

Rayah sat alone in the medical ward during the night shift. Nothing else was happening at ten in the evening, so she lounged at a desk, reading a research paper on emergency medicine on her tablet. As usual, there were no patients, nor was there any other kind of work to occupy her mind. As she attempted to read, she mulled over what had taken place earlier that morning, when General Peterson announced to the entire group of soldiers in the palace that Queen Ellandra was six months pregnant.

Everyone had expressed joy at the news, but Guyad seemed interested in a strange way. He asked if the queen was pregnant with twins, and when General Peterson asked him why he suspected that, he simply stated that the queen was petite but looked rather large around the middle for someone only pregnant with one child. When General Peterson confirmed it was twins, Rayah could not help but notice the tangible excitement on Guyad's face. It wasn't, she recalled, a look of pure excitement for someone's good fortune. No, his face had expressed a more sinister motive, as if a secret suspicion of his had been confirmed. Her thoughts were interrupted when the double doors to the ward slid open. Kaled hesitantly entered.

"Hello, Captain," she said barely taking her eyes off

her tablet.

He looked around the room and asked, "Um, is anyone else here? Like Birchram or the doctor?"

"No, it's just me," she replied, putting her tablet down.

"Oh. Um, I guess I'll come back tomorrow." Now that she was looking at him, she could tell he had winced in pain when he spoke.

"Are you hurt?" she asked, concern brewing within her.

He closed his eyes and grunted in pain. "It'll be fine until tomorrow."

Rayah stood up from her desk and walked toward the door. "Don't be stubborn, Kaled. Come inside and let me take a look."

He gave a disheartened chuckle. "It would require you to touch me, and we both know how much you hate that thought. I promised my sister I would leave you alone and give you your space. It's fine, really. I'll just come back tomo–"

"I've already told you once not to question my professionalism. Now stop playing games and have a seat on this bed. Tell me what happened."

Kaled relented, walking slowly toward the bed and sitting down.

"How did you hurt yourself?" she asked.

"Odin and I were working on the submarine. I had thought I had disabled the propeller before starting the job, but I guess I didn't. Odin was inside the vehicle and turned it on. Thankfully he turned it off before the propellers gained any actual speed, but it got my arm pretty good."

"When did this happen? I thought your department

only worked the morning shift."

"It happened toward the end of the shift, but I thought I just banged it up. When the pain kept getting worse instead of better, I figured it was time to come in."

"But you're in uniform. Were you still working?"

"Yeah....I like to stay busy."

"Okay," she said. "Remove your tunic."

Kaled tried to unbutton his tunic, but every movement made him curse in pain.

"Here; let me help you." Rayah gently removed the close-fitting coat and saw him wince again. A small bit of blood stained the shoulder part of his black undershirt. "I'm going to take this off as well, but you might need to help me."

He nodded and moved his head to the side while she lifted his shirt to remove it. Now that he was barechested, she could see the damage to his shoulder and upper arm. She worked quietly on him, taking out her Diagnostica from the pouch that was fastened to her left thigh and running the small remote-sized device up and down his arm. Internal images of his body appeared on the large digital screen hanging on the wall behind his bed. Rayah saw how much damage the propeller had done to him and noted that the swelling had spread to his entire right shoulder and down to his bicep.

"You're lucky it didn't get your neck. You could have been killed."

He shrugged, not meeting her eyes.

"Hey. I'm serious," she reprimanded. "There's a small cut closer to your neck. This could have been drastically different. You need to make sure you do that lock-out, tag-out procedure before starting work on any dangerous electrical machinery. You know this."

Kaled didn't move. She put down the Diagnostica on the bed and gently moved his face so that he was looking at her. "Kal," she said tenderly, "just because you and I aren't in a good place, it doesn't mean I ever want any harm to come to you."

He nodded quietly and finally looked at her. They both froze, and Rayah found that she was unable to move, blink, or even take a breath. It had been ages since he'd sat shirtless with her standing before him. Maybe he was having the same thoughts, because she saw him swallow hard and then look away. Rayah pushed the sensual memories from her mind and focused instead on the task at hand.

"You need stitches," she said quietly. Her voice felt husky; she hoped Kaled didn't notice.

Rayah irrigated his wound and injected him with pain medicine and antibiotics. After stitching him up, she dressed the wound with bandages, using a protective gel to prevent them from sticking to the broken skin. All the while, she ensured her touch was as gentle as possible so that she didn't hurt him further...but she couldn't stop imagining what it would feel like to let her fingertips linger on his skin, and envisioned him shivering as goosebumps popped up on his arm...

"Does that feel better?" she whispered.

"Much," he whispered back. "Thank you."

"I want you to come back in a few days to get this looked at, so we can gauge if there has been any improvement. I work the night shift on Tuesdays and Thursdays. If you want to come at that time, fine, but if you feel more comfortable with someone else, that's fine too. Try not to get your bandages wet."

She picked up the tablet that was on his bed and started typing away at the screen. "You need to rest this shoulder. That means absolutely no working out or doing maintenance on any vehicles. You should be getting my orders in a few seconds; I've also emailed them to your commanding officer."

"Thanks," he said, rising from the bed. Almost instantly, his smartwatch pinged as the orders came through.

"My pleasure. Let me help you get dressed."

"Wow, you haven't said that to me in a while," he laughed.

She couldn't help smiling as well. "Yeah...this is a bit awkward, isn't it?"

"A bit, but it was nice just sitting here with you."

"I agree," she said with a smile.

As he left, Rayah wondered about the thoughts she had entertained earlier. She couldn't believe her mind had conjured up such inappropriate memories of a man she'd sworn never to get involved with ever again. She couldn't stop thinking about the way his shoulders sagged or how he averted his eyes when she pointed out the severity of his injuries. Did he not care about his own health?

Maybe she would need to make a concerted effort to be kinder to him, but doing so was no easy task. If she showed him any compassion at all, or dared to befriend him, it would lead to a colossal mess in the long run, a mess she would be left cleaning up by herself.

As Rayah pondered these things, the double doors opened once more. Of all people that may come to visit at this time of night, the queen was the least expected of them all. Yet there she stood, dressed in a beautiful three-piece outfit with elegant flat shoes.

"Hello, Captain," she said, looking around the room.

"Good evening, Your Majesty," said Rayah with a salute.

"Have you seen the doctor? Is he in?" asked Queen Ellandra, her eyes still darting to every corner of the medical ward.

"No, Your Majesty. He's off tonight."

In fact, thought Rayah, the doctor had been in a fantastic mood because he had a date that evening. When Rayah had asked for the woman's name, Dr. Kortez had smiled and told her to mind her business.

"Hmm," said the queen. "He was supposed to meet me here."

Just then, the doors opened again, and the doctor walked into the medical bay. He looked quite handsome in his dress pants and button-up shirt. It was evident he was prepared for a night out with a special woman.

"My queen," he said with a smile, "my apologies for making you wait. I was held up."

The doctor then turned and looked at Rayah. "Please excuse us. The Queen and I need some..." he trailed off, looking for the word.

"Privacy," added the queen. "We need some time alone. Can you please give us thirty or so minutes?"

****

Rayah stood outside with the rest of The Elite, waiting to get their morning workout started. The late spring weather brought forth beautiful aromatic flowers that made the already impressive garden even more stunning. She was glad to see that Kaled had finally returned to full health. He'd taken her up on the offer to be treated by her instead of anyone else on the medical team during his rehabilitation.

He'd visited her at the medical ward once every week for a month, and each time they were together, they were quiet, only speaking when necessary. She found the lack of words between them beneficial, for she was so consumed with her thoughts that she could barely manage to talk as it was. Kaled always chose to visit her when she was alone during the night shift; if anyone else had been present, they would surely have wondered aloud at the ever-present strange, tangible tension in the room. The last time he'd visited her was the night before, and she had massaged his shoulder with a healing cream now that his skin was intact. She'd given him a new tube of the cream and told him to put it on twice a day for a week.

Today was his first day back to working out with the group, though she suspected he'd been working out in his own apartment against her orders. Every time he removed his shirt for therapy, his obliques still seemed just as chiseled as they had before. She noticed him smiling at her while he stood talking with Tye and Bo, and when their eyes locked, he stepped away from his group and walked over to her.

"Hi," he said with a smile.

"Hey. How's your shoulder?"

"You're absolutely amazing," he said breathlessly. Then his eyes widened, and he backtracked. "I mean... the work that you do. You are an amazing nurse. My arm...it, um, it feels great."

She chuckled and reached for his hand. "It's okay. I know what you meant."

Rayah didn't register that she had taken hold of his hand. She was lost in his light green eyes and taken aback by how wonderful it felt to talk with him without the overwhelming desire to punch him in the gut. Butterflies fluttered in her stomach; she was certain she could stand like this all day without tiring of it.

"Did you apply the cream this morning?" asked Rayah.

"Um, I had some trouble massaging it in," he replied.

"Well, you can have O put it on for you. Or I could do it. You are my patient, after all. Just make sure, if you do come see me, that you do so at the medical ward, not my apartment. I don't want your girlfriend thinking that I'm doing anything behind her back."

"Actually, Rayah, about that –"

"Okay, kids," announced Aymes. "As promised, today, we are going to attempt to run three miles, but our goal is to go slow and keep an even pace so that you can focus on your breathing and form. You two will be up front and set the pace. Make sure it's something comfortable. This isn't a race."

Rayah let go of Kaled's hand and took a step back before anyone noticed what had happened...or before he got any ideas in his head.

"Never mind. I'll tell you later." With a smile, he left her side and reunited with his friends.

Evia and Ensin took their places at the front of the line, with Ameena directly behind them, taking off at an easy run as they'd been instructed. Aymes started toward the middle of the pack, but sped up slightly so that she and Rayah jogged alongside each other.

"What was that all about?" said Aymes quietly.

"What?"

"You and my brother. It looked like you two were about to kiss."

"What?" asked Rayah with alarm. "No. What makes you think that? Did he duo-com you? What was he saying?"

Aymes laughed, shaking her head. "He didn't say anything, but I felt a sense of euphoria all over him. Do you like him...in that way, I mean?"

"No. Honestly, we're just...I don't know...we're just trying to be friends again, I think. As you know, he hurt his shoulder, and I've been tending to his injuries."

"Mmhmm," grunted Aymes. "Yet he's only seeing *you* for his shoulder and not his roommate, who also happens to be a nurse. He only goes when you're alone during your night shift. Do you mean to tell me *nothing* is going on?"

"Nothing, my dear. I'm just tending to my patient. But like I mentioned earlier, I feel a closeness to him again, like we're starting to re-become friends, if that's a thing. It scares me to rekindle a friendship with him, but I honestly can't help myself."

"Okay, just checking. I don't want either of you getting hurt again, and I also don't want you to lead him on."

"He has a girlfriend, Aymes, and he's quite happy with her. Plus, I have this thing with Guyad."

"If my brother knew that was all a front so you could spy on this man, I think things would be different."

"Well," said Rayah with a smile, "good thing he doesn't know. I promise I'm not leading Kal on. I wouldn't do that to myself or him. I want to stop all the hate that's been in my heart for so long, and maybe patch things up so the four of us can be friends again. It would be nice to have that the same way we used to."

Up ahead, Rayah heard Ameena call out, "You've done one mile! Just two more to go, kids!"

Aymes sped up further to run alongside Ondraus, leaving Rayah to her multitude of conflicting thoughts. She looked behind her and saw that Kaled was rotating his shoulder as he jogged, but he smiled when he noticed her looking at him. Rayah needed to get her mind off him and away from this new dynamic between them.

When it was just Rayah and her own thoughts, everything had made sense inside her head, but when she'd tried to explain it to Aymes, she'd realized how confused she was. Rayah truly desired friendship with Kaled; no part of her wanted even to consider having another romantic relationship with him – a one-night stand to get him out of her system, maybe, but nothing more.

Eight minutes later, Ameena called out that they had completed two miles. Kaled sped up considerably so he could pull alongside the children.

"You're doing excellent," he assured them. "Just keep thinking about your breathing. In a breath, two, three, four, and exhale, two, three, four."

Both Ensin and his sister were huffing loudly, and Rayah recognized the look of someone close to giving up.

"Repeat with me," encouraged Kaled. He breathed in and out in a slightly exaggerated method, sucking in loudly and then pushing out the air through his mouth forcefully. "Slow down if you need to. I usually put on headphones when I'm running; the music keeps me focused on my breathing because of the beats."

Evia nodded. "How much further?"

"Just under a mile. You've already set a faster pace than the last time. You don't have to beat us; you just have to beat yourselves."

"I think what these kiddos need is a good cadence. We can call one, now that we're far from the palace and residential areas," said Bo with a large smile.

Kaled clapped him on the back of the shoulder. "Go for it, brother."

"In the morning sun
We all go for a run
It's good for our bones
Even if we groan
Show me what you got
Make your way to the top
It's good for the soul
So, we'll run till we're old"

Bo repeated the song with different verses while the rest of The Elite clapped in time and repeated the lines after him. The song had a good old rhythmic feeling, perfect for an acapella situation like this one.

"Man, I miss cadences," remarked Kaled as he continued to run next to the kids and Bo. "They really help, don't they?"

"Oh yeah, I've always loved them. My wife used to be in the military before we had kids. You should hear how that woman calls cadence. It's like someone singing to your soul. Hey, Kaled, before I forget, she said don't worry about bringing anything to the dinner tonight; just come."

"Are you sure? I feel like I'm imposing."

"We invited you, remember?"

Evia began to slow down considerably, dripping with sweat. "Must stop," she groaned.

"Does anyone have any water?" Kaled asked, turning to the rest of the group.

In a flash, Rayah was at the front of the line, passing a full water bottle with ice to Evia.

"Here you go, sweetie," she said. "Ensin, jog in place. If you stop, it's going to be much harder to start again." Rayah placed her fingers on the side of Evia's neck and looked at her watch as she did so. "Evia, you're fine, but you need to slow down a notch. We only have a quarter of a mile left, and if you want, we can switch between walking and jogging, okay?"

Evia nodded her head. "Yes, please. I'm sorry if I'm slowing everyone down."

"No, it's no problem at all. Besides, this is our cool-down day, so it's not a hard workout," said Rayah.

Ensin received the water bottle from his sister and drank the rest of the frigid liquid in a burst of large gulps.

"If this is a cool-down day," said Evia, walking as fast as her legs could carry her, "what does a real workout day look like?"

"Well," said Rayah, "we all have different strengths, but I usually run about five miles at a pace not much faster than this. I think my brother can do eight miles at this pace without breaking a sweat."

"Yeah," said Tye a few people back, "all of us are gearing up for a Perlieu run."

"How far is that?" asked Evia.

"About twenty-six miles," answered Rayah with a wink. "You'll never see me run for that long."

"Yeah," hollered Tye, "it was Kaled's idea. He's been running a lot lately, and then one thing led to another, and now we're all joining him at the annual Clivesdail Perlieu next month."

Rayah shot a look of disappointment to Kaled, who was already making a huge *I'm sorry* face.

"I didn't run the first two weeks, I promise," protested Kaled.

Bo came to his friend's rescue. "You're almost there, kids. How about one full sprint from here to that building over there. If you beat Kaled and me, you get a whole week off running."

"A whole week off?" repeated Ensin in disbelief.

"Yup, a whole week," confirmed Bo.

Kaled glanced at Rayah, who was watching him silently. "Let's do it," he said with a grin. "Just keep in mind, kids: I'm extremely competitive, and I don't plan to make this easy. I'm going to wipe the floor with you."

"On my count," said Bo. "One, two, three!"

The four of them were off. Ensin and Evia shot off like a cannon, pounding on the concrete running trail with their sneakers as they outran the adults who were trying to keep up.

"Faster; they're on your heels! Don't look back!" yelled Rayah.

As soon as the young twins touched the building with their fingers, they stopped and turned around to catch their breath, only to see that Rayah had lied. Rayah could barely see the kids from this distance in the dark. She caught up to Kaled and Bo, who had stood up straight with their hands on top of their heads, breathing in deeply.

"Woo-hoo! Did you see that?" exclaimed Rayah. She

jumped and gave Bo a high five before hugging him. She did the same with Kaled but stopped awkwardly while her arms were around the back of his neck. They stood there, in each other's arms for a second, still as statues, as if unable to move. Then, just as quickly, they dropped their hands and took a few steps away from each other.

****

The day sped by in a blur. Rayah had not meant to hug Kaled; she cursed herself repeatedly for her clumsy little show of affection. He couldn't possibly know that somewhere, deep down, she still felt something for him.

Rayah had considered eating her dinner at home instead of at the dining facility, but for some reason, she chose not to. She sat on a bench at the table near Ameena, Lina, Aymes, and Tru. They were all talking about how well the kids had run that morning. Rayah, on the other hand, was not paying attention. She absentmindedly ate her ice cream while staring off into the distance. It had been years since she'd relaxed in Kaled's arms, and for some stupid reason, he still had her wrapped around his little finger.

At some point, she realized that he had joined the male members of The Elite at the table. She smiled as she and Kaled made eye contact with each other. Some sick, twisted part of her didn't mind that he was staring. The hug, however brief, had felt amazing, and now a tantalizing chill ran up her spine as she dreamed of running her hands over his bare chest for that massage he needed. Was it a conflict of interest for her as a nurse?

After she'd chided him twice for questioning her professionalism, was she proving him right?

She would gladly set her professionalism to the side for a scandalous moment alone with him. The intimacy must have been his intention all along. Rayah had provided Kaled details on her availability, and he always chose to see her instead of any other available medical personnel. Of course, it was no surprise that he regretted what he'd done all those years ago. Kaled was craving her forgiveness; he wanted things to *somehow* return to normal. But did he still think of her in *that* way, too? Her throat got dry as those thoughts continued to take hold of her mind.

Then there was the matter with Guyad. She had been spending a lot of time with him lately. At first, she'd played coy, saying things like, "Hmm, I don't know; you seem like too much of a lady's man." She'd flirted with Guyad anyway to see if she could get any information out of him, but he was proving to be difficult. She was nearing a point at which she felt she had no choice but to start dating him...but what then? How in all of Vilmos would she date a guy that she had no intention of going to bed with?

Her thoughts swirled around and around as she continued to eat the last of her ice cream. Kaled was still looking at her, also seemingly lost in thought. The thought of getting up so that she could sit with him crossed her mind for a fraction of a second.

"Rayah." Hearing her name snapped her out of the strange catatonic state she had been in. Guyad was speaking.

"Hey," she said with a practiced smile.

He sat down beside her, too close to her, and asked,

"When are you going to say yes to me?"

Just then, Rayah noticed that Kaled got up and started to leave. Her friends at the table murmured to one another. As Kaled made his way through the crowd, a pretty young female soldier came up to him and reached for his hand.

"Hey, Captain Behr," said the soldier.

"Hi, Corporal Tivor; what's up?

"I was wondering: are you free this weekend? You can come over to my place and we can get to know each other if you like."

Rayah choked on a piece of the waffle cone she had been swallowing. *Wow, that was forward,* she thought to herself.

"Thanks, but I'm taken, actually," he said politely.

"Oh, what a shame. Well, if you get tired of traveling all the way across town to see that girl of yours, you know how to reach me."

Rayah felt a hand on her thigh. She looked and saw that Guyad was still there, sitting uncomfortably close to her. Somehow she'd forgotten about him.

"So?" he whispered in her ear. "Let me show you a good time."

Her smartwatch buzzed a few seconds later, and she read the message that was from Kaled.

Hey Rayah. I really appreciate all that you've done for me lately. You are amazing at what you do. I think it's best if I have someone else apply the cream on me instead. I wouldn't want your boyfriend thinking there was something between us. I'll catch you later.

Her heart ached momentarily as she read the text on her watch. She re-read the message twice before deleting it. Maybe she wanted more than just friendship with him, more than just a night alone in a bedroom, but she shook her head to rid herself of those thoughts. *No. I will never go down that road again.*

CHAPTER 15

Kaled

Blue skies and warm temperatures left no doubt in anyone's mind: the first week of summer had arrived. Kaled was still not dating anyone, although he got plenty of requests from ladies in the military and around town. His excuse remained the same: *I'm taken.* The statement wasn't far from the truth; though single, he couldn't spend any more emotion on some other girl. He focused a great deal of his energy on working out and meditating so that his mind was as far away from Rayah as possible. Things between the two of them had been amicable following his injury. Still, he needed to make sure he kept his distance so that his mind didn't fabricate any ludicrous possibility that they would get back together.

Ondraus had thrown a birthday party for Kaled, and all the guys from The Elite were present. Wilstead cooked the steaks to a perfect medium-rare, while Tye set up the entire room so they could all play hologram suite games at the same time. There were plenty of non-alcoholic drinks, and the overall vibe of the party was low-key and perfect.

After finding no ice in the freezer for his lukewarm seltzer water, Kaled took it upon himself to grab a bucket and go to the ice machine located on the building's second floor. He went up the stairs and noticed

Rayah leaving her apartment with a pair of heels on and a short miniskirt that showed off her athletic but wonderfully thick legs. Maybe, if he was fast enough, he could turn around and walk away without her noticing him. He tried to do just that but failed.

"Hey, Kal," she said in a friendly yet tentative tone.

He turned around and pretended as if he had not seen her a second earlier. "Oh, hey." He tried his best to keep his eyes focused on hers and not let them roam around her full-figured body.

"Happy early birthday. I heard from my brother that he was throwing you a party tonight. It's strange, isn't it, for him to plan the party on a weekday? But he mentioned you prefer to celebrate it that way."

"Yeah, ever since you and I...well, you know, anyways. I like to keep it separate from my sister's birthday. It just makes it easier for you and Ondraus to celebrate with her."

She walked a little closer to him until they stood six feet apart. Her smile didn't reach her eyes, yet they reflected the same awkwardness he felt within himself. "I had hoped things would be different this time around, especially now that we're getting along. I'd like us to try to be more than just civil with one another. Maybe we can even try to be friends. If you're still willing, that is."

"I'd like that very much," he said honestly. However, he didn't know how he could be friends with her again with all the physical history they shared. He had tried just being friends with her before, several years ago after their second breakup, but it had been torturous for him. Trying to live in that friend zone again could do more damage in the long run.

Rayah spoke, jolting him away from that inner

monologue. "So...am I going to see you at the actual birthday party Friday night? Everyone is going to be there. We've rented out a dance hall, and there will be plenty of your favorite alcoholic drinks. I even chose music for the playlist that I know you'll love."

Her offer sounded tempting for a fraction of a second, but he knew it would be best for the two of them if he declined. She must have really cut him out of her life completely if she was unaware that he couldn't drink alcohol anymore. There was so much about him that she didn't know. If he could have her to himself, he would go happily, but he was no fool; he knew she'd be busy with Guyad, and he couldn't stand watching that man with his hands all over her. "I'm not sure, Rayah."

"Kal, you've been working a lot lately. Every time I turn around, you're either working overtime or out for yet another run at ten in the evening. I don't know why you're always on the move, but you need some time to let loose, and what better place than the dance floor? Who knows, maybe you can save the last dance for me...that is if Veeta is okay with it."

"Who?"

"Your girlfriend."

"Oh, her. It's uh, Vellah."

"My apologies. Yes, her."

Kaled became silent. He didn't know if he should specify that he was single or leave matters as they were. He chose to change the subject. "I'm assuming Guyad will be at the party as well. Can he even keep up with you? No one dances quite like you do, if I remember correctly." He smiled as he attempted to keep his tone casual, trying not to give away his true intentions: checking out whether he had a chance of dancing with her all night as opposed to watching her with that other man.

"Hmm?" she asked, looking as if she hadn't heard him. "Oh, he's a terrible dancer. He tries, but he has no idea what he's doing. He thinks that as long as he twirls and dips me all night that he's dancing, when in reality, it just makes me nauseous. It's quite pathetic. Come to the party, Kal. Save me from having to dance with him the entire night. Besides, I didn't only have your sister in mind when I planned this thing."

That was all he needed for his birthday; to see the woman he loved dancing seductively with another man. Yeah, what a great way to celebrate another miserable year of existence. No thanks. Even sharing a few dances with Rayah wouldn't be worth that. "I'm sorry, Rayah. I, uh, already have plans. I'm going away for the weekend, Friday morning through Sunday night."

"Oh. I see." Disappointment shone in her eyes. She grew quiet for a second, searching his face before seeming to realize something. "Wait...are you not going because I'll be there?"

He didn't have the strength to meet her eyes. Instead, he looked down at his shoes for a second to compose his feelings, then raised his head and put on a practiced, forced smile. Honesty would be the best way to handle this. "I still have feelings for you, Rayah, and seeing you with Guyad isn't easy on me. I'm sorry, but I just can't stand there watching you dance with another man. Besides, I don't dance anymore."

He watched as her eyes filled with tears, and she bit her lip before silently nodding her head in understanding. Nearly a minute passed before she composed herself enough to say, "You used to be a great dancer."

"I used to be many things, Rayah." He thought of the ways he had hurt her over and over again. She looked so beautiful in that dress. It reminded him of that time on his eighteenth birthday when she had worn a cream-colored knee-length dress with a plunging neckline that clung off her shoulders and hugged her curves. He had felt like the luckiest man in all the world. That was a long time ago; she wasn't his now, and that outfit she wore wasn't meant for his eyes to undress. It was for someone else, and he felt the excruciating withdrawal, once more, of loving a woman he could never have again. He'd squandered every last one of his chances with her.

She walked closer to him and reached for his hand. "We had some good memories, Kal. There were times when you were quite amazing. I hope your girlfriend gets to enjoy that part of you. I know I did, and I'm sorry you feel this way. I truly am."

Kaled gently caressed the palm of her hand with his thumb. He wanted more but had no choice but to be content with this much. After an awkward pause, they both took the stairs to the first floor and walked down the hallway.

"Kal, I need to confess something to you. It's about –"

Just then, Guyad came into the corridor. "Hey, babe, I was calling you. Want to just hang out at my place tonight?" He closed the distance between them and didn't seem to pay attention to Kaled, who stood less than two feet from Rayah. Guyad kissed her on the lips while his hands traveled down past her waist.

Kaled didn't wait for Rayah to emerge from the onslaught of kisses that Guyad was laying on her. Instead, he quietly slipped away and walked to his apartment alone, forgetting all about the ice. Back inside, he tried to push that entire conversation out of his mind. There was no point dwelling on it or picking it apart to see if there might be hope that she secretly harbored feelings for him. By now, she was probably in Guyad's bed while Kaled sat, despondent, drinking water. After the party, once everyone had left for the night, Kaled thanked Ondraus for all the work he had put into it and made sure his friend knew that he sincerely appreciated all of the effort.

There wasn't much of a mess, but Kaled insisted on helping to clean it up anyway, hoping the action would keep his mind busy for a little while longer. After about an hour of cleaning and silence, he and Ondraus sat down to enjoy a cold soda and watch sports.

"You sure you don't want to come on Friday? My sister was kinda hoping you'd show up," said Ondraus, breaking the silence.

"O, we both know I'm not the best version of myself when Rayah's around. To be honest, I saw her earlier when I tried to get ice. We talked, and it was great, and she's amazing, but then Guyad came and kissed her right in front of me. Guess what was the first thing I did when I came back in? I tried looking for a beer. I was hoping someone would have ignored the house rule and brought some. If I go to that birthday party, where Rayah's already told me there will be alcohol, it will just turn into a huge colossal mess. I'm not going."

"Okay, I get it. I do. I didn't before, but...things are different now."

"You're in love with my sister, aren't you?"

"Yeah, dude. I think I'm falling for her. We haven't been together that long yet, but we've shared too many intimate moments to just go back to being friends as if nothing ever happened. I can get how hard it would be to see someone you love in another guy's arms. I'm sorry you're dealing with this, man. If I could ease the pain for you, I would."

Kaled gave a disheartened chuckle. "These girls, man. They'll either make you feel like you can soar into the sky or ruin you so badly you have to crawl your way out of alcoholism and depression...which sucks because I could really go for a shot of ranaq." Kaled finished his soda with one gulp. In his mind, he allowed the bubbly carbonated sensation to feel as if it were the burning, numbing sensation of hard liquor. He got up from the couch and went to his room, returning with a gift bag. "Aymes told me she'd be introducing you to Niklas on Friday before the party. Are you nervous?"

"Of course I'm nervous. What if I blow it?" asked Ondraus. "What if the kid doesn't like me? Or I say something stupid and Aymes rejects me or –"

"Dude, it's going to be okay," Kaled reassured his roommate. "My nephew Niklas is a sweet boy, and he's going to love you. He does bounce off the walls, though. If you think Evia and Ensin have a lot of energy when they're romping around the palace grounds after school, you have no idea what a toddler is like. Niklas does not tire of playing." Kaled reached into a bag. "Here. I got you this to bring it to him. It's a glow-in-the-dark ball. It's not high-tech, but he doesn't need much, other than someone to play with him. If you do this, I assure you, he will love you."

"Thanks, man. I really appreciate it."

****

Kaled had a dream of her; it was a stupid and destructive thing to do, but he couldn't control his brain when he was asleep, and his thoughts had gone to a place he'd been trying so desperately to keep under control. Before going to bed, he'd spent a wonderful, peace-filled day kayaking at Paramiyo National Park, an hour outside the city of Clivesdail. He must not have exhausted himself enough, because while lying outside in his sleeping bag, his over-imaginative mind had conjured up realistic images of him and Rayah together. The dream had been fantastic, but waking up to see that she wasn't beside him was heart-wrenching.

Bleary-eyed, Kaled looked at his smartwatch and realized it was still turned off from the night before. He had intentionally powered it down so that he wouldn't be tempted to look at all the messages from people wishing him a happy birthday or asking him why he wasn't at the party. He'd deleted his social media account months ago and was glad he did. He didn't need the temptation of looking up pictures of her at the party and lose himself in those beautiful amethyst eyes or those full, kissable lips or whatever form-hugging evening dress she would have worn.

Judging by the streaks of light peering over the dark horizon, Kaled assumed it was five in the morning, far too early for a hike. Instead, he turned over in his sleeping bag and got out his tablet to read a book. He had suffered this unrelenting dilemma of his heart before and survived it. All he needed was to continue keeping his destructive mind busy at all costs. He knew a trip away from the city of Clivesdail was necessary; he couldn't stand seeing Rayah make out with Guyad all over town.

Kaled had lost count of the number of times he'd spotted Rayah in the arms of that creep, his tongue halfway down her throat and his hands groping her as if they weren't out in public. Everywhere Kaled went, he was plagued by Rayah and Guyad's indiscreet displays of affection. Kaled wanted to remain invisible so he could keep his head down, get his work done, and be rid of this place once he'd succeeded in his mission to protect the royal twins.

By noon he had been hiking for several hours, enjoying the marvelous beauty of the park. It had many trails with rough terrain, leading up steep inclines to Mount Zur. Kaled covered the distance in an hour and a half, then took in a deep breath of fresh air and exhaled slowly as he stood on the mountaintop enjoying the view. From up high, he could see the vast wilderness, as well as the sparkling lake that beckoned him now that he'd finished working up such a sweat. He sat down and allowed the warm summer breeze to cool him off before closing his eyes to pray. He had learned this technique from his sponsor at the Monktuary several years ago. Kaled hated that he only pursued spiritual guidance when his spirit felt so quenched, but he was comforted to know that the All Creator accepted him as he was.

"I'm here again," he sighed with closed eyes. "I feel lost and out of control. Please guide me like a light tower guides a ship in the storm. Ease my pain and help me trust in you."

He stayed in his sitting position until both suns were at their highest point in the sky and the heat of the day bore down on him. The complete stillness of the afternoon quieted Kaled's self-destructive thoughts, working as a salve by providing a soothing comfort to his wretched soul. He'd needed a moment like this. Coming up here was the right decision. He felt at peace, strengthened to continue on his path of loneliness for a while longer. Though he didn't get an audible answer from the All Creator, he still felt heard and encouraged.

He began his descent down the mountain and chose a trail that would lead to the lake he had seen earlier, the same lake he'd kayaked across on the previous day. The forest was alive with birds chirping on tree branches or flying overhead with their wings spread wide. The massive park had an incredible isolating effect on Kaled. The large trees and mountains pierced the sky, making him feel incredibly small and reminding him that someone much greater than him existed and was fully in control. In the day and a half he'd been staying at the park, he had only seen a handful of people. His heart felt renewed and hopeful, exactly as he'd hoped.

After an hour of hiking, he arrived at the lake and stripped off his shirt, socks, and shoes, running up to the dock and somersaulting into the water. As he swam, he savored the cool water on his hot skin. Being submerged let him shut out the world for a while, and that was refreshing. After a while, he decided to head back to shore and stretched out on the grass, taking out his tablet to read the book he had started earlier that morning.

For some reason, Kaled had always resonated with books of poetry. Long ago, he'd written poems for Rayah. At first they had been awful, of course, earnest teenage ballads about love, dripping with melodrama.

After a while he'd started reading the classic Brennish poets – Arin Ezalen, Verak Ortez, Flori Nikan, and more. He found himself drawn to the style of Delvin Koh, who blended the romance of nature with romance of the heart in a way that Kaled had always felt in his own soul.

Koh's third collection, *A Song for the Dawn*, had long been Kaled's favorite, and he was two-thirds of the way through it when he heard a commotion by the dock. A man and a woman were kissing, maybe a little too much, and then the woman playfully pushed the guy into the water before jumping in after him. Kaled couldn't help but chuckle at the scene; it was something Rayah would have done to him back when they were together. The memory stung a bit, but it was also cathartic. He bent down to reading his book and was nearly halfway through the collection before he heard his name called out.

"Kal?" Rayah asked, her body and her swimsuit dripping water onto the ground.

He froze as soon as his eyes landed on her. The white bikini top clung to her breasts in a way that made them impossible to ignore. Had this been a different reality, he would have been here *with* her, perhaps sitting on this very shore eating berries, cheeses, and cured meat with a glass of the mint lemonade she always made during the warm summer months. If Guyad wasn't present and if Kaled thought he had a remote chance with her, he would have swooped her up in his arms and laid her out on the shore to remind her of what they had been missing.

Kaled's desires burned so hot that they overwhelmed him, and he broke out of his daydream and back to reality. He didn't know how long he had stared at Rayah in shock and longing. He hoped it was only a fraction of a second and that he had been able to keep a straight face the entire time.

Clearing his throat, Kaled looked away and broke from her spell. Anger and bitterness crashed across his mind as the desires dissipated. "You've got to be kidding me," he said quietly, shaking his head in disbelief. What a cruel joke that he'd gone an hour out of his way to be on his own – and most importantly, to be away from her – and yet here she was. Could there be any place in the entire nation of Brennen where Rayah and Guyad hadn't kissed? Why was it that Kaled couldn't escape her?

"Hey," he said a little louder, trying to avert his eyes from the very thing he had been dreaming about earlier that morning.

She knelt down on the grass beside him. "You were missed at the party last night. I was kinda hoping you were going to come, even if just for a moment."

Why did she have to say that? He knew she was being friendly, but it gave him false hope, which was the reason why his mind had invented that ridiculous dream of her. "I owe you a dance," he said, "so hold me to it, okay? But for now, I have to leave."

"What? Now?"

Kaled looked at her, and his eyes roamed. He knew they shouldn't, but he couldn't help it. His heart started raging inside his chest, and he felt like every nerve on his body was on end. He couldn't believe how much effort it took to appear calm and in control when he was everything but that. He looked out toward the lake and saw Guyad doing laps in the water, completely unaware that Rayah's ex-boyfriend was on the shore trying his best to fight the urge to kiss her.

Kaled got up and placed his tablet into his bag before picking up the other items near him on the grass. "Yeah, something came up. I'll be out of your way. Just give me a second." He moved quickly; he didn't want to be near her a moment longer than necessary. He offered a silent prayer: *Give me strength. Give me strength.*

"What came up? Is it something with the royal infants?"

"Um, no. A personal matter. I gotta run." He still didn't look up. Seeing her face was his weakness, and her being in a bikini made it exponentially worse. He grabbed a pair of sunglasses and put them on in case he found himself suddenly unable to hold back the tears of regret, anger, and unmet desires.

He turned and left the shore, making his way down the trail toward the camping grounds. A full two minutes had passed before he noticed that she was still behind him. "Are you okay?" she asked, in a voice somewhere between concerned and demanding.

"I'm fine," he said flatly, still not looking back.

"You don't sound okay. Why won't you look at me?"

"It's nothing, okay? Just go back to him." He tried desperately to keep his voice from breaking.

She reached out and grabbed his hand gently. Euphoria and pain shot through his entire body at the same time, and he stopped in his tracks. His heart was pounding, making it impossible to hear or think. He wanted to vanish. To his horror, she removed his sunglasses and looked into his misty eyes. He could tell she was trying to discern some meaning in them.

"Kal, what is going on?"

"I just need some space," he pleaded. "I do everything in my power to be anywhere you won't be, but you've been making it impossible. Every place I go, there you are. The gym, the cafeteria, the barracks, walking around town, the pool. Literally, every single place I go, there you are, and you're always in his arms, and his lips and hands are all over you."

He stopped talking for a while and closed his eyes, desperately trying to rid the image from his mind. "I came out here to be away from you, and even that was too much to ask. Why else would I spend my birthday weekend away from my friends, my mom, my nephew? I need to get away from you and Guyad. I need a break from all of this. Please, try to understand. Just go back to him and forget you saw me." He knew he came off angry and defensive, but she wasn't getting the message; she didn't know the misery he was living.

"Why do you think we're all the way over here?" she asked quietly. "So that we could be out of your way. I didn't know you were going to be here. I thought maybe you and Vellah would be at a hotel room in Clivesdail or something. It's not like I'm trying to shove my relationship in your face purposely."

"I know," he said, feeling exhausted. His mind was weary from fighting the urges he'd been battling since the moment Rayah had tended to his wound nearly a month ago. "Just get a room and stop groping each other in public like a pair of horny teenagers."

"That was low," she whispered in a tone mixed with sadness and anger.

He turned around as hot tears ran down his face, not wanting her to see him in this pathetic vulnerable state. His desire for her was crushing his soul beyond its limit, and he had to leave before he did something he would regret. "I'll just go so that you two can continue having fun. I'm not really in the mood for it anymore."

He didn't look back. Even as he turned to leave, he heard Rayah sniffling and knew that his words had cut her. Why must it be this way? *Good*, he thought to himself, *now I've made it easier for her to hate me. Great job, Kal.* Feeling drained of emotion, he went back to his campsite, packed up his tent, and drove home. He would just spend the rest of his weekend in his apartment playing video games and ordering delivery food so that he didn't have to step out into the cruel world for a few days.

CHAPTER 16

Kaled

"Mister Kaled!" exclaimed Evia as she opened the door to the Kortez family suite.

"Hey there!" Kaled walked inside, a bottle of soda in his hands as if it were fine wine. Only five weeks had passed since Kaled had that regrettable encounter with Rayah at the lake.

Alastair and Ensin were waiting near the door to greet him. "I was a little surprised that you accepted our invitation," said Alastair.

"Oh, well, your son mentioned free food, so I really could not decline such a tempting offer. Thank you for inviting me over."

"Certainly," Alastair said with a smile. "Dinner will be ready in about thirty minutes. Nerida is in the royal kitchen on the lower level of the palace. The cook's daughter is a classmate of our children and was kind enough to lend us some space in the kitchen. Nerida is making a family recipe, and it's one of my favorites."

Kaled was excited about spending time with Evia and Ensin and also thrilled by the prospect of a delicious home-cooked meal. While they waited for dinner, he went into the kids' bedroom and played holographic video games with them. The active games made for an intense workout; Kaled didn't remember the games being quite so vigorous when he was younger. Then again, Evia and Ensin were about to turn eleven, and it had been a long time since he was that age. After thirty minutes of fighting imaginary ogres with holographic swords, Kaled had worked up a good sweat. Before he was forced to admit that to the kids, the simulation room's door opened, and Nerida announced that dinner was ready and on the table.

The table was set with small packages, which seemed to be made from boiled banana leaves and tied with twine. When Kaled opened one, steam came out of the green package, carrying the smell of vegetables and meats that had been cooked inside a cornmeal exterior. Kaled had never tasted anything like this, and he helped himself to a tomato-based salsa that everyone else slathered over their food. As the five of them ate, they talked about everything imaginable: work, hologames, and the upcoming birthday party for Evia and Ensin. To his surprise, Kaled volunteered to help decorate. He'd never imagined himself a party planner, but here he was diving in. These kids brought out a side of him that he didn't know still existed.

After dinner, the kids wanted Kaled to play with them again, but Nerida and Alastair intervened, saying they wanted some adult conversation for a change. The children looked disappointed for exactly half a second until Nerida told them she'd arranged for them to play with some of their classmates for the rest of the evening.

"At what time do you have to leave?" asked Nerida after the kids had left with one of the palace guards.

"I have another hour before I'm going to my sister's place to watch over my nephew Niklas."

"Oh, that's sweet of you. I bet you're a fun uncle," said

Alastair.

"Thanks. I try to be fun, but really, I'm there to be a good male role model for the kid. Niklas doesn't have any other men in his life. His father left as soon as Aymes found out she was pregnant, and his grandfather – Aymes' and my dad – died several months before she got pregnant. But tonight, I do have an ulterior motive. I'm sleeping over at my sister's house to give her and Captain Jur some time alone and to give my mother a much-needed break from watching a two-year-old gremlin all the time. Then tomorrow, I'll take Niklas out for the entire day. I found a fun park in the city that I think he might like."

"That's nice. I'm sure Aymes appreciates having some alone time with Ondraus," commented Nerida.

"Actually, it's with the other Captain Jur. Rayah. The two of them are hanging out and having a girl's weekend, whatever that means," said Kaled.

They were all quiet for a few minutes before Nerida rose to clear the dinner table. "I can't thank you enough for volunteering to help decorate for the party. The kids are so excited."

"About that," said Kaled tentatively. "I won't be able to come to the actual party itself. I'll come beforehand to decorate and to help in any way I can, but I won't be attending."

"Oh, are you busy that evening?" asked Alastair.

"It's because Rayah will be there. It's best if we're not in the same room together."

"Wow, I didn't know you had anything against her. I've always thought she was a lovely young lady. Don't you two have to work together every day?"

"Work is one thing; we try to be professional at all

times. Actually, it's not that I have anything against her at all. It's the other way around. Besides, I don't like the person I become when I'm around her. I get really emotional. Plus, I was a real jerk to her recently. The least I can do is make sure I'm not around so that she can have a good time with a few friends."

"Seems like there's quite a story behind all that," said Nerida, bringing out a plate of small desserts and refilling Kaled's cup of soda.

"Trust me," said Kaled. "You don't want to hear it. It's an awful story, and it makes me look like the worst guy ever to live."

"We all have stories that don't paint us in the best light," said Alastair. "If you're willing to share, we're willing to listen. No judgments."

Kaled wondered whether it would be prudent to share his story or not. He had met with Alastair and Nerida before, but never in such an informal, relaxed setting as their living room after dinner. Maybe it would be safe to share only the highlights – or the lowlights, depending on how he thought of it – and nothing more personal than that. He let out a deep breath. Part of him longed for a stiff drink, but since that was not possible, he just dived into his story.

"I met Rayah in my second year at the Academy. I was thirteen, and she was twelve. Her brother Ondraus slept in the bunk bed underneath mine. He and I became instant best friends. Rayah and Aymes bunked together in the girls' dorm and were immediately inseparable. It wasn't long before Rayah and I became pals, too. That's how it started. Innocent, nothing but friends. Because our birthdays are only a month apart, our parents arranged for a joint two-week summer vacation every year.

"I started developing feelings for her when I was fifteen, and at my sixteenth birthday party, I asked her if she would be my girlfriend. When she accepted, it was one of the best moments of my life. The whole thing was pure young love; we stayed up late studying for exams, we laughed, we shared our first kiss. It was innocent and wonderful. She was an amazing girlfriend, and I think I was a pretty good boyfriend at the time.

"At the military academy, you get a coin when you graduate. I gave mine to Rayah. I was seventeen then, and even though we could have legally married at eighteen, we both knew our first few years in the military would be hard. We made a pact to get married at twenty-one, and we both agreed not to have sex until then. We knew dating after I graduated would be difficult due to the long distance; she still had another year left at school, and I was stationed two hours away at a training site to get my pilot's certification. Still, all was fine; we made it work. She and I saw each other once a month, and we were a happy couple. I truly thought I was ready to wait four years for her."

Kaled took out the smooth graduation coin from his pocket; it had become a sort of talisman, a sobering reminder of his wrongdoings. As he continued to speak, he pressed his thumb into the coin absentmindedly. "Almost a full year into our long-distance relationship, I started getting lonely. I felt a void each time Rayah and I had to part ways, and it started building within me until it turned into a giant chasm. I couldn't handle it anymore." Kaled's head drooped as he replayed one of his many significant failures.

"A few months after my eighteenth birthday, Rayah

came to my apartment to hang out. I left for one minute, and during that time, the woman I had been seeing on the side texted me. Rayah saw the message because I had accidentally left my phone on the couch."

Kaled looked at the ceiling and swallowed. Suddenly he didn't know what to do with his hands. "Rayah confronted me. I had to come clean about the fact that I had been sleeping with someone, and of course, Rayah broke up with me. She gave me back my coin, saying it no longer held any value to her. Somehow, she forgave me, and we remained friends. I deserved to be cast aside; instead, she showed me mercy. The thing about Rayah is that she is fiercely loyal."

He took a deep breath. Even all these years later, he still felt uncomfortable being the recipient of such undeserved grace. "Rayah's relentless compassion had redeemed me. It had pulled me up from the mire, and as a result, our friendship blossomed like never before. And we spent each summer vacation having fun under the sun or stuffing our faces with junk food and passing out from a sugar coma. There was always a small degree of flirting involved, but it was less than negligible; I knew we could never date again, and I told myself I was satisfied with our arrangement. One year, before I turned twenty-one, Rayah accidentally walked in on her boyfriend with another woman."

Kaled remembered the phone call; his heart had plummeted at seeing his dearest friend crying. A pang of conviction tore through him, knowing he had done the same thing to her. "Aymes and I both drove the two hours to console and support her. Aymes needed to leave early for a flight exam she had to pass, but I stayed." Kaled closed his eyes as he recalled Rayah's tearful question.

"Am I not beautiful enough? Why is it that every guy I've dated has cheated on me? What am I doing wrong?"

"I stayed with her throughout the night, providing a shoulder to cry on. We devoured a carton of ice cream together, watched a light-hearted movie, and eventually fell asleep in each other's arms. But when dawn broke, Rayah awoke as a new woman. She no longer wanted to wait till marriage, figuring it would be a while before the right guy showed up. We became lovers, and from that moment on, I was hooked."

He could almost taste her lips against his as he tried to continue with his story. "We didn't just become lovers; we became one soul. The passion between the two of us was electric, and I truly believed nothing could ever put out that fire. But after a while, the loneliness crept into me again. I tried to fight it with everything I had, but nothing worked.

"Life in the military isn't easy, and there were many times where our schedules conflicted and I only saw her once or twice that month. I started missing her body when she wasn't around. So after the seventh month, I called things off."

"I see," said Alastair compassionately. "Well, long-distance relationships are hard, especially at that young age."

But Alastair didn't know the extent of it. Kaled had dropped the news on Rayah out of the blue after he'd arrived home from a weekend away at her place. Rayah had answered the phone call expecting a *"Hi honey; I made it home"* conversation, not the serious one Kaled was about to lay on her. He could hear her on the other end of the phone call, stunned and on the verge of tears.

He didn't have the nerve to break up with her when he was at her place, though that had been the plan. Instead, he took advantage of the situation, pretending all was fine so that he could have another night with her before he called things off.

Kaled had told her he loved her on many occasions during their seven-month relationship, and he had done a fine job of showing her just how much she meant to him...by leaving her to date a woman who had caught his attention in his off-base apartment complex. In fact, the same woman would be visiting him as soon as he told her that things with Rayah were over.

If Alastair had known *how* Kaled broke up with Rayah, perhaps he wouldn't have been so understanding earlier, Kaled thought. If Nerida had known that Rayah had barely spoken a word on the phone while he tried to explain that he couldn't handle the long-distance thing, maybe she wouldn't be so compassionate toward him now. Kaled shook his head. It was hard reliving every manipulative and heartless thing he had done.

"We didn't talk for months after that, but we were part of a group text chat with our siblings, and I managed to convince myself that everything was fine enough between us. Of course, I know better now. I know I did wrong, but at the time, I honestly thought I'd done the right and honorable thing by telling her how I felt. I thought I was the good guy because at least I didn't cheat on her that time. I didn't hear from her much until my sister, and I visited Rayah and Ondraus for the Winter Solstice holiday.

"I barely had any time alone with her," continued Kaled. "Instead, she danced mostly with Aymes and with other guys who had come to the party, including one named Sy. Even though I had the last dance of the night with her, I could already tell her mind was on somebody else. She said we could still be friends, but this time she laid down some ground rules. The damage had been done, and our friendship was more like an acquaintance than anything else."

He took a long drink from his soda, looking to see how Nerida and Alaistair were reacting to his story. He'd expected to see judgment and accusation, since he knew he didn't come off looking like the good guy. However, they were both watching silently, with gentle understanding on their faces.

"That summer, Rayah invited Sy to join our annual family vacation. The two of them were inseparable, and worst of all, I could tell Rayah had fallen in love. She had moved on, and I, on the other hand, felt more alone than ever before. I kept to myself during that vacation. I hooked up with some other woman during that time, but it did nothing to rid my mind of Rayah."

Kaled noticed Nerida on the edge of her seat, visibly tense, which would have made him smile if not for the seriousness of the event he was about to describe. "I wasn't prepared for how that messed me up. Seeing her with another man really crushed me. I smiled through it all and somehow survived that terrible vacation. My father died a few months after that, and the tradition of combined family vacations ended. We never had another one. Rayah and her entire family came to the funeral, and it felt good to hold her hand during the service. She was such a good and sincere friend...and that's when it happened. I think that's when I truly fell in love with her, but by then, it was far too late. I'd had my chances, and I'd blown them all.

"A few months later, a mutual friend told me that Sy was planning to propose to Rayah. When I heard that, something in me completely shattered. At that point I had already started drinking, though it wasn't as bad as it would eventually become. I jumped from woman to woman, trying to find love. I wanted something as beautiful as what I had once shared with Rayah, but no one came close. She consumed my every thought. I was stuck in the self-made prison where I had been living the past year."

Kaled continued in a pleading tone that surprised even him. "I needed healing. I drove to her place with the intention of severing our friendship once and for all. Being her friend, even from a distance, was killing me."

As Kaled recounted his story for Nerida and Alastair, he was fully immersed and remembered every single detail and word said during that fateful night...

****

Two Years Ago

Kaled knocked on the door. He had practiced his speech multiple times during the two-hour drive and readied himself for the most difficult thing he would ever have to do.

"Kal, what a surprise! You didn't say you were coming!" greeted Rayah excitedly.

The surprise was mutual, thought Kaled. He had known Rayah for nearly eight years, and in all that time, she'd never looked the way she did now. The rich mixture of curly purple and turquoise hair had been replaced with straight, dazzling silver. She had lost weight in all the wrong places; her luscious curves were gone, and she wore makeup even though he could count on his hand the times he's ever seen her with makeup on. Kaled found himself shocked at how vastly different she appeared. Had she done all this just to please a guy?

"Hi," he managed to say after swallowing the lump in this throat.

Rayah peered behind Kaled. "Where's Aymes?"

"It's just me."

"Oh. Um, we've talked about this, Kal," Rayah whispered tentatively. "That was one of our rules, remember? You and I shouldn't be in the same room alone, not after all that's happened between us."

"I know, but I promise this will be quick. Besides, I don't want an audience."

Rayah opened the door further and allowed Kaled to come into her apartment. She purposefully, he noted, planted herself several feet away from him. "Is everything okay?"

Kaled ignored the question; he *needed* to ensure that all hope of getting back with Rayah was completely gone. "I hear things between you and Sy are going well."

Her demeanor changed. Kaled watched in dismay as her eyes twinkled and a blanket of joy and euphoria enveloped her. "Yes," she said dreamily. "Honestly, Kal, I think he's the one. You haven't taken the time to get to know him, and I understand why, but oh! You would love him! Ondraus and Sy hang out all the time; mom and dad love him. He's wonderful. I'm head over heels for him," she swooned.

Good, he thought bitterly, *this will make it easier for*

me to leave her once and for all. "That makes me so happy to hear," lied Kaled, though he cringed at the way the words wavered. He wanted to come off as strong, and most of all as a supportive friend. Instead, his voice had betrayed him.

Rayah caught on immediately. "What's wrong, Kal? Why are you here? In the past year that I've dated Sy, you never once asked me about my relationship with him." She eyed him suspiciously.

"You'll be happy to know the feeling is mutual. Sy loves you, Rayah; I heard that he plans to propose soon." Again, Kaled attempted to smile, but his face wouldn't comply. His lips quivered, and he could feel a powerful rush of tears at the brink of pushing through his misty eyes.

Rayah bounced with excitement, but just as quickly noticed Kaled had not joined in on the celebration. "Kal," she said, the tenderness in her voice shattering him, "why haven't you answered my question? Why are you here?" Rayah walked closer to him, her eyes searching his. "Tell me," she pleaded.

"I love you," he said finally. The words just tumbled out of his mouth. He had planned to say them after a long, romantic speech about how Rayah was always the one for him. Instead, his brain backfired and shot straight to the point.

She laughed, a musical sound that filled the whole room. "Funny one, Kal. You almost got me."

He stood silently once more. That was how badly he'd hurt Rayah over and over again, he realized: now that he was confessing his love, it came off like a childish prank. "I'm not joking," he whispered.

Rayah shook her head in disbelief. "Don't do this

right now, Kal. Please." She turned away from him and faced the opposite corner of her small apartment.

He approached her and put his hand on the back of her shoulder. "I'm sorry," he said, still unable to raise his voice above a whisper. "I'm sorry it took me so long to mean it, and I know my timing is awful. But please believe me. I love you."

She shook her head again and didn't turn around. "How dare you? Do you have any idea how long it took me to heal after you broke my heart?" He couldn't see her eyes but could hear the quiver in her voice. "Do you have any idea what I went through? I *waited* for you. I waited, hoping you'd come to your senses and return. You dated other women, quickly replacing me, while I sat here trying to put myself back together again." Her tone was restrained and mournful, like she was trying very hard to control her voice so that tears didn't come out.

He walked around and faced her, tilting her chin with his finger so their eyes met. "I never replaced you. That's impossible." Even as he said it, he could hear her scoff, her eyes unreadable.

"You've said that you loved me in the past," she scolded. "You said it multiple times, and yet you walked out on me for another woman. Sherice. I will never forget that name."

"How did you–"

"How did I know? It's a small world, Kal, and an even smaller military. I had friends who lived in that apartment complex, and they talked. You didn't even wait an entire day after our breakup. As soon as you hung up with me, you got with her. After a weekend spent in *my* bed and in *my* arms, you dropped it all to be with her.

How dare you say you love me? You have no idea what that word means." Anger and bitterness mixed in her misty eyes. She wasn't the type of woman who yelled; instead, her words came out in a punctuated, icy tone.

"You're right. I didn't know how to cope with being apart, and it..." Kaled sighed, looking down for a moment. "It's all my fault, and I'm sorry you found out through someone else."

"I'm going to say yes to him when he proposes," she said firmly.

"I know." Tears began to well in his eyes, and he hated himself for it. He turned away and wiped off the tears in frustration, then turned back to face her. "I...I came to say goodbye."

She stood there, confused, her eyes searching for some meaning that would explain the words he had just said.

"My life has been a sham this past year. I wanted a relationship in the same area code as me, but no girl has compared to you. I know you said we could never go back to dating, but I just can't get over you. I've tried to. I've tried standing here on the sidelines being happy for you and Sy, but I just can't. I'm in love with you, and seeing the two of you together while at the same time I'm dying to kiss you and be near you, it's... it's..."

"What are you trying to say, Kal?"

"It's painfully exhausting. I want you, and..." Tears began to creep out of his eyes again. "It's excruciating to see you with someone else. I know you've moved on. And I don't blame you, okay? I really, honestly am happy that you've found someone who can love you properly. I wish I would have grown up a little sooner, but I didn't. But Rayah, I can't live my life watching you with that other man. I need to leave you once and for all."

Now it was her turn to wipe at tears. With a strained voice, she reached out for Kaled's hand, forcing him to look her in the eyes. "We've been friends since the moment we met. Don't throw that away. Why would you do this?"

"Because I'll always want you. And if I had my way, I'd kiss you right now and make you forget all about him." He shook his head and started to walk away, "I wish you two the best."

He made it to the door and turned the knob, so close to never seeing her again. Rayah was still facing him, sobbing silently yet doing her best to be strong, trying to accept her new reality somehow but torn over losing one of her closest friends. "Please don't do this."

"I love you, Rayah, and I think the best way to honor that is by walking out one last time so that you and Sy don't ever have to think about me."

She shook her head. "I need you in my life. Please, don't walk out on me again."

He was no stranger to making wrong decisions with Rayah, but this one would be the most catastrophic of all. He walked back toward her and wrapped his arms around her. This time she had him. His defensive wall broke down, and so did his restraint. He wiped away the tears on her face and kissed the top of her head. Breathing in her scent brought back all of the beautiful memories they had shared, only for him to be reminded that he was going to sever that connection forever as soon as he gained the strength to leave her embrace.

He ran the side of his hand along her face, trying to get one last touch, one last memory he could hold on to, but noticed she was fighting a similar struggle. Instead of pulling away, she leaned into his caressing hand and closed her eyes, letting out a shudder.

There was only one way he could read that body language. He leaned in and kissed her. Perhaps he expected her to slap him across the face or push him away from her in disgust. But instead, to his delight, she pulled him in closer and kissed him passionately. His lips pressed against hers and then traveled down her neck. His hands caressed her body, desiring more but having the sense to be content with this kiss. Did this mean she was taking him back and kicking Sy to the curb? He didn't know, nor did he care at the moment. Her lips were reviving him with every succulent kiss, driving him deeper and deeper into the madness that sometimes was called love.

"Say yes to me," he said between breaths. He could feel Rayah's hands on his chest, her touch sending electric pulses throughout his body.

"We should stop," she said breathlessly, pulling away just a little but staying close enough to remain in his grasp, inches away from his lips. She shook her head as if not knowing what to do. "I love him, Kal. We need to stop."

But he didn't. He should have; he knew that now, but he couldn't think clearly in the heat of the moment and continued kissing Rayah. When she didn't stop him, his hands traveled down and gripped her thighs. That was the exact moment the door opened.

"Rayah?" Sy stood frozen at the threshold of the doorway, his mouth agape in horror.

"Sy!" Rayah quickly tore away from Kaled and ran toward her boyfriend. "It's not what it looks like. Please, try to believe me. We were just saying goodbye." Panic laced Rayah's words.

"Goodbye? If that's how you say goodbye, how do you say hello?" Sy pulled out a small velvet box from his pocket. "I thought I made you happy. You said that you loved me. I...I was going to propose tonight at dinner. Why? How long has this been going on?" Tears sprung from Sy's eyes.

"Never. I promise. Please, I know how this looks. He was here to end our friendship, and I don't know, he kissed me and..." She looked like she was drowning, thrashing around, trying desperately to stay afloat, yet knowing full well, it was a losing battle. Not once, though, did she look toward Kaled, who just stood there with his arms to his side, feeling lost.

Sy didn't move. He stood limply like a blade of grass, the weight of his grief visibly pulling him down. "Why would you ruin us like this?" he whispered. "I loved you."

Kaled interjected. "I'm sorry, Sy. She's right, though; it's my fault. I came to end our friendship and –"

"No. You don't get to talk. What do you take me for? Kal, isn't it? You're the guy that broke her heart years ago, and here you are again, except this time ruining my life along with hers. Screw you both."

For a moment, Kaled wished the tall, lean man crumbling before him could be muscular and threatening instead. A punch to the nose or gut would be a small price to pay for the terrible, inexcusable, irredeemable damage Kaled had just inflicted on Rayah's life. But to his dismay, Sy was a gentleman who had been in the way of Kaled's terrible choices.

This wasn't right, Kaled thought. Rayah had been in

Sy's position before, had been cheated on more than once, and each time she'd forgiven. There had to be forgiveness for her too, didn't there? Yet at the moment when she needed grace, the exact same grace she'd so willingly given to others, it wasn't there for her...

"Sy, wait, please!" begged Rayah.

"We're over. I don't want to see your face or hear from you ever again. You two deserve each other."

Kaled recognized the expression Sy wore at that moment: a broken man who had just had all of his hopes and dreams pulled out from under him. Kaled had been wearing it himself just a few minutes before. Sy's face contorted into a grimace as he turned away, slamming the door shut behind him. Rayah crumpled to the floor, sobbing uncontrollably. It was heartbreaking to see her like this, and Kaled wasn't sure if he should speak up or not. So he stood there a few moments longer in silence until finally, she stood up.

"Rayah, I'm sorry."

"I told you to stop," she said softly between sobs.

"I know, but..."

"I told you I loved him and that I was going to choose him, but you kept kissing me anyway...even after I asked you to stop."

He nodded his head, "I know, but I couldn't help it. You were –" He felt the end coming, and he was getting desperate.

"Don't," she said, shaking her head. "It's over. The friendship, everything. You came to say your goodbye, and you burned everything down in the process. You came, you conquered; now leave. Why is it that you are so bent on always hurting me? I've learned my lesson now, so goodbye."

Kaled wanted to plead further, but his words were stuck in his throat, and all that came out were more tears and the shame of what he had done. He walked toward the door with his head down. "Please forgive me," he croaked.

CHAPTER 17

Kaled

"I visited Rayah in her apartment intending to break up our friendship so that she and Sy could have their happy-ever-after. Instead, I let my emotions get the best of me, and I kissed her. Unfortunately, Sy walked in at that very moment, and as you can imagine, it was catastrophic. Sy broke up with Rayah, and Rayah, rightfully so, didn't ever want to see me again. And that's how it all went down," finished Kaled. It surprised him how much it hurt to tell a story he had played numerous times in his head over the past few years.

"That was the last time I saw her until that day at the Winter Games, two years later. Though at this point, it's been two and a half years since the incident. I sent her multiple messages, emails, video chat requests. I desperately tried talking to Ondraus, but she had instructed him not to talk about me. She changed her number. She cut me out of her life, and I only got worse from there. I hit rock bottom, slept around, hoping to numb the pain. It didn't help. I turned to alcohol, and of course, the pain was right there waiting for me as soon as the buzz wore off. My sister Aymes finally forced me to get help. There's a Twin Monktuary several hours from here; my sister dragged me there, and we stayed for a full two months until I got sober. She probably saved my life. I don't know what would have become of me if she hadn't intervened."

Kaled looked at the faces of his audience. Their eyes were huge, but not in a judgmental way; more like they were feeling the weight of his odyssey. "After I got sober, I thought I should try to get into a healthy relationship with a woman. I had hoped that I was finally over Rayah and could move on with my life, but nothing made me satisfied. After a few failed attempts, I concluded that love wasn't an option for me."

"I've dated a few women since then but have always been upfront with my intentions. I let them all know the relationship would be purely physical with no love or emotions in the way, and they were okay with that. I'm not saying my dating life had a happy ending or that I found it in any way fulfilling, but it did at least numb the pain and make living without Rayah's love or friendship somewhat bearable. But when I saw Rayah again, it felt like all the work I had done to get over her was for nothing. So now, I just stay busy. I have nearly no downtime. If I keep my mind occupied, it helps to push away thoughts of her."

Seeing her again had reopened that wound he had labored so hard to mend. It felt like being out on his tiny kayak when a giant powerboat went racing by; there he was, minding his own business, when suddenly he was being hurled back and forth by forces beyond his control. This was uncharted water for him, and he had to live with his shame and her scorn from dusk to dawn.

He'd survived telling the story of his great fall, and after a proper goodbye to Alastair and Nerida, Kaled made his way to Aymes' apartment in the city of Clivesdail. He arrived a little earlier than he'd expected but hoped that Rayah and Aymes were already gone. As his luck would have it, however, they were not.

Rayah was sitting with Niklas on her lap; the boy giggled wildly while she blew raspberries on his neck. This wasn't the first time Kaled had volunteered to watch Niklas so that Aymes and Rayah could go hang out, but until now, they had always orchestrated it so that he and Rayah never saw each other during the hand-off. His heart fluttered when his eyes landed on her and saw her laughing and enjoying herself.

He missed seeing the fun, light-hearted side of Rayah; it was good to know that part of her personality remained intact even despite all the walls he'd seen her put up. Their encounter at the lake, plus the re-telling of the incident to the Kortez family, made seeing her now more painful than it would have been on any typical night. As soon as Niklas heard the door open, he looked up and leaped off Rayah, running toward Kaled with his arms wide open.

"Kal-Kal!" he said, jumping up and down. Kaled smiled down at his nephew, picking him up and giving him a huge hug. From the corner of his eye, he could see Rayah watching him too, but he couldn't read her face.

Aymes came out of the kitchen, with their mother Edina following behind. "Oh, hey bro," Aymes said as she walked up to him and gave him a quick hug. "Um...we are on our way out. Thanks again for coming to watch him for me."

"Of course," said Kaled with a smile and still holding his energetic nephew.

"Come on, Niklas," said Aymes. "It's time for bed. You're up way past your bedtime, young man. Sorry, Kal. I tried to get him down earlier, but he was excited to see you and wanted to stay up. He's really thrilled about tomorrow."

Kaled nodded, then looked at his nephew and said, "Hey, bud, you gotta go to bed, alright? That way, you have enough energy to play tomorrow. I found a really nice park I want to take you to."

"Okay, Kal-Kal." Niklas ran toward his bedroom, and Kaled almost laughed at his sister's expression when she witnessed how easy it was to put her son to bed.

"Okay, Ma," said Aymes. "I'll be back late tonight, maybe past midnight. We're just going out dancing. Bye."

Aymes kissed her mother and waved at her brother. Rayah also kissed and hugged Edina goodbye but made no eye contact with Kaled as she left the apartment with Aymes. Only then did Kaled realize Rayah hadn't spoken a word since he entered.

As soon as they were gone, Kaled exhaled loudly, feeling his mother's eyes on him. The two of them walked to the kitchen, and he went by the fridge to get a drink. To his left was a locked glass liquor cabinet, with seven glass bottles of alcohol displayed proudly inside. Aymes had received each bottle from their father after her greatest accomplishments. One, from the Heroes Vinyard, celebrated Aymes' coming of age at her eighteenth birthday. Another had been given when she passed her flight exam. Each bottle had a special significance to Aymes.

Kaled, on the other hand, had drunk all of his bottles ages ago during the height of his alcoholism. He no longer had a visible monument to his past triumphs; instead, he had squandered them and devalued the sacredness of his father's gift.

Kaled stared at the cabinet for a while, wanting

something to numb his pain. His emotions were raw, and he knew a call to his sponsor should happen before he did something stupid. Kaled grabbed a pitcher of a lavender-colored liquid with mint leaves in the fridge. He poured himself a glass and could instantly tell it was Rayah's classic lemonade. Kaled took a sip, allowing the bitter-sweet drink to go down his parched throat and savoring its flavor. The glass was the closest thing to her touch that he would experience ever again. He sat down, rubbing the bridge of his nose and closing his eyes for a while. His mother, Edina, sat down with him and took his hand.

"I'm sorry, son. I would have messaged you had I known you were already on your way home."

"I appreciate that, mom. I just wish I could get over her, you know? She's clearly doing just fine, and I'm here still stuck in the past, like the idiot that I am. I wish I were like most guys. Why am I the only one who gets all weird and emotional? It seems like other guys just move on to the next thing, and that's it. Why am I the way that I am?" He hung his head and stared at the table for a few seconds, feeling like the most useless man alive. What was the point of having emotions anyway?

"Your father was a lot like you when he was younger," Edina said after a short pause. Kaled looked up at her and arched an eyebrow. He had never heard of this before. "Oh, don't look at me like that, son. Where do you think you got your love for poetry? Ryzen always wore his feelings on his sleeve. Sure, you didn't see it much. By the time you were born, he was already a married man and a father of twins, but you should have met him in his younger years. Ryzen was always in tune with his emotions. And yes, there were times when he let them get out of hand until he learned to control them better. But that's what made your father so special to me."

"Yeah, but dad was also a smart and honorable man. I doubt he ever messed up his one chance at true love the way I did."

"You keep saying you'll never find love again, and I think it's your attitude that's standing in the way. Also, I wouldn't be so sure about Rayah being content. She might be able to fool you, my son, but she can't fool me. I can read in between the lines. She is not happy."

"No, mom. You weren't there at the lake last month, I was vile, and I think I made her cry."

"Look, I don't know what the All Creator has in store for you." Edina took her son's hand in hers and gazed imploringly into his eyes. "Yes, you messed things up with Rayah, and you already know that. Learn from it! Grow. Change. Stop living in the past and torturing yourself with this insane idea of not being able to love again. If you are open to it, it will come. But when that time arrives, my son – look at me when I'm speaking to you, Kaled – when that time comes, you need to man up."

Tears sprang from Edina's eyes as she continued to drive home her point. "You said yourself that your father was a man of honor. He was a good man and will be forever missed. You share his name, Kaled Ryzen Behr, and his blood courses through your veins. The next time love presents itself to you, you take it, and you make a commitment as a man that you will stay. You stay even when things get hard, Kaled. Life will always have ups and downs. Things can't always be easy. Regardless, you must stay. Do not ever put a woman through the torment you dished out to poor Rayah time and time again."

Edina sighed heavily; her eyes still wet and pleading for him to understand. "I had such high hopes for the two of you. I thought surely you would get married, and instead, you let your hormones get in the way of happiness and dull your good sense."

Kaled could barely look at his mother. He wasn't open to the idea of loving again. He'd spent all his love on one woman, and he was empty; his capacity to love another had run dry. "Mom, that will never happen for me. I'm not worthy of it, anyway."

"You're right," said his mother, now getting up from the chair. "You aren't worthy. None of us are. Love is a gift, and when it's presented to you, you don't just throw such a gift away. Learn from your mistakes and rise above." She kissed him on the top of his head. "I'm going to bed now. I have a busy day with some friends tomorrow. Thanks again for taking care of Niklas for us. Go to bed, and please, for the love of all that is good, think about what I have said."

She left the kitchen and made her way down the hallway to her bedroom while Kaled stayed a moment longer, mulling over the harsh words she had given him. His mother had been incredibly supportive during his journey to sobriety and had also been an unwavering tower of support even through the worst of his mistakes. Now, however, she spoke in a way that cut through all the fluff and got straight to the heart of the matter.

Kaled wanted to believe her, wanted to believe there would be a day where he could learn to love again, but that felt physically impossible. If it weren't with Rayah, there would never be a point. Maybe his mother's advice was something he could give to his nephew several years down the line and save the poor boy some unnecessary heartache. He would warn Niklas about pursuing passions that led nowhere and would tell him to hold on to true love no matter what. For Kaled, it was far too late.

Kaled drank the rest of the lemonade, the same lemonade he had enjoyed for years in his youth, back when he was in Rayah's good graces. As he got up from the table, his phone pinged with a message from Vellah. She wanted to see him next month. He agreed.

****

"Kaled!" yelled Aymes as she shook him awake.

A strange sensation sat on Kaled, like a debilitating low after a euphoric high. His eyes flickered open only to find himself lying in a pool of his own vomit with an empty bottle of alcohol at his side. He could smell the rich scent of renaq, the most potent drink in all of Brennen. It had always been his favorite. Kaled sat up quickly, only to be rewarded with a throbbing headache and a miserable look of disappointment on his sister's face. He readied himself for the deluge of questions and accusations she would lay into him.

"How could you, Kal?" sobbed Aymes. "You were sober for so long; why did you pick up that bottle?"

"What do you mean why?" he snapped back, closing one eye against the brilliant light streaming in the window. Wasn't it obvious? He loathed himself and couldn't stop thinking about the way he'd ruined, yet again, his friendship with Rayah. The desire to reach for a drink had stayed with him constantly since he'd first become addicted years ago. Couldn't his sister understand how impossibly exhausting it was to fight such temptation non-stop? His entire existence, since his miserable downfall, had been spent treading water and fighting the waves of self-loathing that threatened to engulf him. He would have to remove his sobriety tattoos from his arm; he'd spent a year and a half of fighting his inner demons, and they'd finally overpowered him.

The door opened, and Ondraus rushed in. "Bro..." he muttered as soon as he laid eyes on Kaled, who was still on the floor, too dizzy and nauseous to stand. "We have to get you cleaned up right away. General Peterson is on his way, and he's furious. I think he plans to cut you out of The Elite."

The gravity of the situation wasn't lost on Kaled. If he had to leave the team, so would Aymes. The two of them would get redeployed somewhere else, probably far from Clivesdail, and that would mean Aymes and Ondraus would have to break up or endure a long-distance relationship – which was precisely what had ruined Kaled and Rayah's bond. The thought of his sister paying for his selfish neglect sobered him instantly, and he stood up. He must have been more hung over than he thought, however, because the room spun and everything went dark.

Kaled's eyes flashed open. He felt disoriented. Sweat covered his entire body, and the thunderous crashing of his heart against his chest made it impossible to hear in the eerily dark room. Where was he? Where had Aymes and Ondraus gone? He waited impatiently for his eyes to adjust and noticed a small child sleeping soundly in a separate bed nearby: Niklas. Why had Aymes put her son to bed next to an inebriated failure like Kaled?

Kaled fumbled out of bed, accidentally stepping on a toy Niklas had forgotten to put away. He ran toward the kitchen and punched the light switch on. Fear gripped him as he approached the glass liquor cabinet. Even from a distance, he could tell with relief that it was locked. Seven. He counted again to be sure. Yes. All seven bottles were there untouched, taunting him.

The drinking, the vomit, the headache, the shame – he'd had the nightmare again. Every single time, it felt real. By now, he should have been able to recognize it as a dream, he thought, but his heart was slamming against his sternum, and his legs were shaking underneath him. He only knew one thing that would calm him down when his mind and body got like this, and it was staring at him from the other side of that glass.

"Kal?" asked Aymes from behind. She must have entered the apartment without him noticing. "You okay? You're sweating."

She stopped talking and followed his gaze, then gasped and grabbed his wrist. Somehow Kaled knew that she understood what had snapped him awake at half-past two in the morning.

"I need to get some fresh air," he said, turning to face his sister.

"Kal, please don't. You're scaring me. At least let me come with you," she pleaded.

He placed his hand on hers for a moment and summoned up a smile. "I'm fine. Please, just trust me." He'd lied. He was the furthest thing from fine.

Kaled took his keys, smartphone, and ID but purposefully left his wallet in the apartment. He wandered, like a leaf in the wind, with no destination in mind. The vivid nightmare continued to haunt him; it had felt so real. Kaled pulled up his shirt sleeve and ran a finger over his sobriety tattoos. They were each in the shape of a crescent moon; he had one for every six months, three in total, with the first two paired together to complete a circle. He couldn't throw away all of that hard work, but then again, his throat and every fiber in his body called out for the drink.

The thought of alcohol allured him, even as he continued walking with no ill intention in mind. Without planning to do so, he ended up in front of a club, probably the same club Aymes and Rayah had visited earlier that night. The bouncer eyed him; what was a man in pajamas doing in front of a night club? Could the bouncer see the desperation in Kaled's eyes? Patrons stumbled out of the establishment, and one, in particular, called his name.

"Captain Behr," called Corporal Tivor. "Fancy meeting you here."

Corporal Jes Tivor worked with Guyad in security, though Kaled suspected she shared more than just an office with the man. Jes's breasts nearly overflowed her top, and she was a slight breeze away from showing the whole world the goods under her scandalously short skirt. In one hand she held her pair of heels, and in the other a bottle of rum. As she took a swig of the drink, some of the precious liquid escaped her lips and spilled onto her chest. Kaled's throat tightened as he took in her form, his eyes lingering on her chest. He had come out seeking fresh air with the hopes of extinguishing his desire for a drink; instead, he now faced two temptations.

"Hi," he said while taking a few steps back, trying

desperately to make his escape before he gave in to his desires.

Jes approached him. "Wanna go back to my place?"

"How much have you had to drink?" he asked. There was no way he could enjoy himself if he thought he was taking advantage of a woman who was too far gone to consent.

"This is my first sip," Jes told him, holding up the bottle. "I was the driver, but all my friends went home with other people." She took another step toward him, her huge eyes looking up into his. "It'd be a shame if I was the only one who didn't get to leave with a date after I was such a good girl all night long."

She reached out for his hand, and like an idiot, he stopped walking, letting her draw a few steps closer until they were mere inches from each other. How long had it been since he'd had sex? Too long. Far too long. Jes ran her finger up his arm, sending goosebumps all over his body. Her lips parted seductively. If he couldn't have Rayah or the drink he so desperately needed, what would be the harm in going to bed with Jes? Maybe being celibate so long had clouded his mind; Jes could relieve him. She could make things better.

"Come on," she whispered, "I'll make it worth your while."

Kaled merely nodded. His desire to stay clear away from alcohol drove him in a new direction. He welcomed any distraction to get away from the call of the drink.

"But first," he ordered, "you have to leave the bottle."

"Done."

Even though Jes had only taken a sip or two of the rum, Kaled still insisted on driving the hovercar. Jes kissed the side of his neck, whispering things into his ear that dissolved his senses. Kaled wanted to explore her entire body with his hands and lips, but a voice in his head screamed at him indignantly.

What are you doing? Stop.

Kaled pushed the thoughts away. He wanted this. He needed this. He deserved this.

Finally, after what felt like an eternity, they arrived at the barracks. "I'm on the second floor," she said, trying to kiss his lips.

"Not here."

He didn't know why, but he jerked his face out of the way before her lips met his. Maybe, somewhere in the back of his mind, he felt guilt and didn't want his dalliance displayed for anyone to see. Jes hopped onto his back, wrapping her legs around his waist. She nibbled on his ear as he trotted up the stairs, holding her thighs firmly. They made it to her apartment, and he didn't bother waiting for her to lead him to the bedroom. Instead, he pressed her against the wall.

"Are you playing hard to get?" asked Jes as she removed his shirt.

Stop, Kal. You are seeking peace, and this is not the way. Stop.

"Hmm?" Her words snapped him out of his thoughts. That blasted voice, or conscience, or maybe it was the All Creator himself, continued to bombard his brain.

"You haven't kissed me yet," said Jes.

Kaled's hands were moments away from undoing her skirt's zipper. To his astonishment, he stopped. He couldn't move forward. He didn't owe Rayah anything. He couldn't possibly have been cheating on her since they hadn't been a couple in years, but it still felt wrong, almost as if he were cheating on himself.

"I'm sorry, Jes. I can't. I'm in love with someone else. This isn't right." Kaled stepped away from her and grabbed his keys. The sooner he left, the better.

"I'm not asking you to love me," she said, unfazed.

The comment made him chuckle. "I know. I'm sorry for leading you on and wasting your time. I'll just grab a cab home. Take care."

As he stepped out of her apartment, Rayah, of all people, walked into the hallway. For a moment, they both stood frozen, staring at each other. Jes opened the door.

"Hey Kal, you forgot your shirt."

Mortified, he turned around to grab his shirt from Jes, mouthing a silent thank-you. In that fraction of a second, Rayah left. What a fine mess this night had been, thought Kaled. He left the building and sat on a bench outside the barracks; he wasn't ready to go home.

The thought of grabbing a drink still tortured him, so he remained rooted to the bench to prevent himself from committing such a stupid mistake. Instead, he tilted his head back to look at the stars. The sight of the vast night sky and the All Creator's grandeur normally set him at ease; he hoped tonight would be no different.

He found, to his surprise, that memories of Rayah flashed before his eyes. Rayah's first camping trip with him at the academy, where she almost got lost during the land navigation course. The time they accidentally fell asleep on the beach when he was eighteen, and their love still had a hint of innocence. The magical passionate night on the balcony of a cabin nestled in the mountains. All of the beautiful memories swelled within his chest, and for a fleeting moment, he didn't feel like a complete failure. Love and friendship had always made him soar above the clouds.

Every time he entertained the good, the bad always crashed into him, demanding that he drown his regret at the bottom of a bottle. Kaled's heart became heavy with images of him betraying Rayah's trust, squandering their friendship, cheating on her, and leaving her for another woman. He had wronged Rayah time after time, and when she'd finally had enough and cut him out of her life, Kaled found the abandonment unbearable to live with.

"No," he reminded himself, "you have to stop thinking of her, Kal. It'll ruin you. Enough is enough."

Instead, he thought of someone else; his father, Ryzen. Maybe that was where he'd gotten his love for the stars in the first place. His father always took him and Aymes on camping trips, and Kaled had come to enjoy the ritual of stargazing in the wilderness.

He missed his father with all his heart. Kaled's life had ripped apart at the seams, and he wondered if having his father would have helped avoid all of the stupid decisions he'd made since Ryzen's death. Thinking of his father felt cathartic, but it made Kaled ache to see him again. Deep down in his core, Kaled suspected his father's untimely departure was the catalyst for all his other sorrows. Kaled had not known how to deal with his emotions after his father's death, nor had he handled his feelings well after his catastrophic breakup with Rayah. Now, as a consolation prize, he had to live with a vice that could easily destroy everything he held dear in his life.

With a heavy sigh, he pulled out his mobile phone

and removed the wireless earbuds from the chamber. "Call Duo-Com Master Andrei Iyoshi," he said into the night. Kaled cringed as he saw the time; it was a little after three in the morning. He wondered if his sponsor would wake at such an early hour.

"Kaled Behr," came the groggy voice of Master Iyoshi. "To what do I owe the pleasure of this call?"

"I'm struggling," Kaled managed to say through the massive lump in this throat. He unleashed the full story, detailing how he had come close to succumbing to his desire for a drink and even to sleeping with someone just to drown out the noise. After he'd finished his monologue, he felt drained and empty of emotion.

Even over the comm line, he could hear the attentiveness in Master Iyoshi's voice. "Thank you for telling me all of this, Kaled. Now, I must ask, have you been attending your meetings?"

"I've missed the last few," confessed Kaled. The irony was not lost on Kaled; at the crucial moment he needed the meetings the most, he had intentionally failed to attend them.

"You're looking for peace, Kaled," Andrei said gently. "The only way to make peace with Rayah is to make peace within yourself. Take care of this now, or the nightmare you suffered can become a reality."

Kaled had dreaded this moment; he fully understood the meaning behind Andrei's words. Kaled needed to complete the final step in his sobriety program. A crucial step in the healing process consisted of making amends with people he'd hurt. Kaled had been successful in doing so with friends and family, but had not been able to face Rayah at any point. Now, however, he knew he needed to reach out to her. It didn't matter if she forgave him, Kaled reminded himself. Casting this last stone of apology into the grand ocean of acceptance was something that needed to happen tonight.

"I know, Master Iyoshi, but I'm scared. What if she doesn't forgive me?"

"She may not, and that is still okay. From the beginning, you have learned that you can only control your own reactions, not anyone else's. Perhaps Rayah will forgive you and perhaps she will not. That is out of your hands. But don't let that truth stop you from trying."

"Master Iyoshi, will you please read to me from the sacred text?" asked Kaled as he continued to look up at the vast sky.

"Of course; it would be my pleasure." The older man cleared his throat and then continued in a firm and authoritative voice. *"The All Creator is faithful and sovereign; he will not allow you to be tempted beyond your ability. He shall always provide a means of escape when temptation comes knocking on your door so that you may be able to decline its call.*

"Rejoice, even in your time of suffering, and know that it will yield endurance. Your mourning will turn to hope. The All Creator has poured his love into our hearts, and he will never abandon us."

Silence lingered for a minute while Kaled took the time to absorb and internalize the comforting words. Even if Rayah did not forgive him, which was a reasonable possibility, Kaled could count on one constant: an All Creator who loved him even with all of his imperfections.

"Thank you," said Kaled. "I appreciate it. I feel better now."

"Do you need me to stay on the line until you get

home?" asked Master Iyoshi.

"I'm not going straight home," Kaled answered. "I'm going to stay out here and meditate for a while."

He heard a chuckle over the phone. "You always did think best when you were outdoors. I'll call you in the morning to be sure you arrived safely."

Kaled ended the call with his sponsor but remained on the bench a moment longer. He wondered if he should see Rayah now or wait until tomorrow. He chuckled out loud; she had explicitly warned him against calling her for any reason other than work. He was about to break that rule. A light on the second floor of the barracks caught his eye. For no reason at all, he stared at it as he pondered when best to bother Rayah with his apology. Part of him still felt inadequate; he knew he had to face Rayah, but most importantly, he needed to face himself.

Speak truth into your life, said the voice in his head.

"I can't," whispered Kaled. "There is no good in me, not even a drop. I detest myself."

Try.

Kaled breathed out forcefully, brought his hands to his head, and massaged his temples. He racked his brain for any good thing to say, yet even when a positive thought popped up, he felt too ashamed to tell it to himself.

"I'm a half-decent brother," he said.

And...? persisted the voice.

"I'm a half-decent uncle."

There is more.

"There is nothing else. I have nothing, and I am nothing."

Kaled continued watching the light on the second

floor. He couldn't see into the window, but the small orb of light gave him hope for some reason.

You are so much more than the things you spoke, Kaled. You know it's true.

"It doesn't feel like that right now," he mumbled back. "Please help me, All Creator. I am drowning in my pain, and I can't stand it much longer. I know that you say you love me and that you won't ever leave me, but sometimes it's hard to accept that."

You are loved, Kaled Ryzen Behr, and my love for you is unconditional. When you can't trust in yourself, trust in me, for I am forever, I am constant, and the love I provide is pure. You can rest in me when you lack strength.

Peace. It had finally come, and it washed over Kaled, cleansing him of all his impurities and imperfections. "Thank you, All Creator," he said out loud.

"Were you talking to yourself?" asked Rayah.

Shocked to hear her voice, he ripped his eyes from that light in the window and saw Rayah standing beside him. Kaled sprang from his seat and stared at her.

"Um, I guess I was kinda praying out loud."

Rayah laughed good-naturedly. "Were you thanking the All Creator for hot sex with Corporal Tivor?"

Her bluntness caught him off guard, and he chuckled as well. "That would be a very strange prayer."

"Then what are you doing out here alone at this unholy hour?" she asked, her voice more serious.

"I needed to clear my head. Rayah, I was such a jerk to you at the park, and I can't stop thinking about it."

Rayah nodded her head slightly. "Kaled, being a jerk? Shocking."

Kaled cringed at her sarcastic tone. "I deserve that. I went out there to be by myself and didn't expect to see you. I know you were trying to be a good friend. Instead, I responded by treating you terribly. For that, I'm sorry."

She watched him silently for a few seconds, mulling over his words. "Thank you, Kal," she said. "That means a lot."

"There's more," he continued. "I've been battling my own demons for a while now. After losing my father, then losing you, I found myself lost as well. I never meant to take advantage of your kindness and the love and friendship you always provided me, and I am truly sorry for all the hurt I've caused throughout the years. But I want you to know that I'm trying very hard to be a better man. It's too late for us, but maybe with some hard work, I can shine a little light in this dark world. I don't expect you to forgive me. I own up to what I did, and there's no excuse for my behavior."

Rayah took a step toward Kaled as if she planned to hug him. His imagination must have been in overdrive, though, because no hug came. Instead, she ran her hands down the sides of her legs. "Of course, I forgive you. Kal. You are so important to me, more than you will ever know. And you're right; it's too late for us. I wish that weren't the case, but there's no way around it. But I can love you as a friend if you'll have me."

Kaled couldn't believe the capacity of Rayah's heart. How was it possible that the woman he had hurt the most was capable of forgiving him again? "I would love that very much."

Rayah smiled. "Good. I should get going, though. It's late, and Guyad and I have plans in a few hours."

"That's great," lied Kaled in what he assumed was a believable encouraging tone.

"You sure you're okay out here?" she asked.

"Yeah, just enjoying the stars."

She bade him farewell, and he watched as she walked across the lawn to the front doors of the barracks. Once there, she paused outside the door, glancing over her shoulder and watching him for a moment before heading in. Five minutes later, the light on the second floor switched off.

After Rayah bade him a good night, he walked toward the street to call a cab. A great sadness pierced his heart, but Kaled knew instinctively; it came from a different source. He tried duo-comming his sister the entire ride home but couldn't get through to her. When he entered the apartment, Kaled noticed the kitchen light still on and heard murmuring. He approached the kitchen and saw his mother and sister sitting at the table, holding hands and praying.

"Please," said his mother, Edina, "please protect him, All Creator. Don't let him fall."

Kaled's heart lurched to a stop at the sight of his sister and mother pleading for his safety and sobriety. He smelled a mixture of alcohols hanging in the air, which made him look toward the liquor cabinet. All seven bottles were turned upside down, the amber liquids draining into the sink. One single bottle of renaq alone could cost over two hundred nayen.

"My son!" exclaimed Edina noticing Kaled standing in the kitchen.

She and Aymes ran to him, embracing him fiercely. Their arms felt like protective wings, covering him from the elements of the harsh world around him.

"Hi, mom," he croaked.

"Thanks to the All Creator, you are home," said Edina

as her tears soaked his face.

"Did you?" asked Aymes, her voice shaking. "I could feel your struggle. It was intense."

Kaled shook his head. "No. I didn't get a drink. I wanted to, but was able to fight off the temptation. Sis, I'm sorry about the..." he pointed at the sink.

"I saw you eyeing them earlier," said Aymes as fresh tears sprang into her eyes. "It scared me," she added with a whisper. "I promise never to store that stuff in my home again."

"But that was dad's gift to you before he passed."

Aymes waved her hands. "It doesn't matter. If dad knew his gift would be a stumbling block, he would have done the same thing."

After another round of hugs and prayers, Kaled made his way back to his bed. There, young Niklas lay sleeping, blissfully unaware of the battle his uncle had just fought. Making amends with Rayah provided him a sense of peace. Did he still long for a stiff drink? Yes. He supposed he would always want a drink for the rest of his life, but at least he wasn't desperate for it. At least he could dismiss the desire. And as far as his other needs...he would just have to deal with those in a healthier way. A ten-mile run might do the trick. Finally, at long last, he fell asleep.

CHAPTER 18

Rayah

Rayah looked at herself in the mirror and tugged down on her dress. *Hmm, too short. It's not that type of party.* She rummaged through her closet once more and found a pastel-colored dress with a lovely floral pattern, then looked at herself in the mirror and smiled at the reflection staring back at her. Satisfied, she added cream-colored heels to complete the outfit. She had spent an eternity on her hair, too. Rayah typically kept her hair pulled back in a tight bun or braids when in uniform. Wearing her hair down in its natural curly state wasn't practical in her day-to-day routine unless she was going out. Today, however, felt like the right opportunity to do just that. Her thick purple and turquoise curls were perfectly coiled and had just the right amount of volume.

She checked the time on her smartwatch and saw she had another fifteen minutes before she needed to leave. She had planned to arrive well ahead of time to help Nerida and Alistair decorate the party venue, but unfortunately, a whole group of soldiers had come just as she was hoping to leave the medical ward. They'd been conducting a land navigation course on foot and not realized they were all in a field of poisonous Granada Baum Vines, which gave them all a ferocious red bumpy rash all over their bodies. She'd treated them all as efficiently as possible and had still managed to leave on time, just not as early as she'd wanted.

A week ago, Rayah and Ondraus had celebrated their twenty-fourth birthday; unsurprisingly, Kaled did not come to the party. He did, however, visit Rayah at work to present her with a gift and a personalized card. Rayah knew their friendship would be more awkward than it had in the past; Kaled had changed, and so had she. Regardless, she had spent much of the evening scanning the crowd, hoping he would show up. For some reason, it was still important to her to know that he was happy, and she found herself hurting on his behalf when he kept withdrawing from the people he loved.

Rayah stepped outside of the barracks and saw Kaled and Vellah together, about fifteen feet away and apparently unaware that she was close enough to overhear their conversation. *That's odd,* thought Rayah. *I thought he was with Corporal Tivor.*

Kaled and Vellah stood facing each other while holding hands. "You're amazing," Vellah said breathlessly. "I can't believe you pulled all of that off. The candle-lit dinner, the live band, the view, and the horse-drawn carriage. All of it was absolutely breathtaking." Vellah sighed dreamily.

"I aim to please," Kaled responded with a smile. "Call me when you get home."

"I will." Vellah hopped into a cab and waved goodbye while Kaled watched the vehicle soar into the air.

Kaled turned around, finally noticing Rayah. "Oh, hello," he said.

"Hi," she replied. She'd been making her way toward the sidewalk to wait for her own cab, half hoping to escape undetected.

Even after that park bench talk, it still felt strange to start up a conversation with Kaled. She and Ondraus had gone out for coffee with Aymes and Kaled several times in the weeks following Kaled's pre-dawn apology. Rayah knew she and Kaled would never share the same level of friendship that they once had, nor did she think it would have been smart to try. She wouldn't be able to survive another train-wreck of a complicated relationship where romantic feelings could muddy matters.

"If you're waiting for a lift, it may be a while. Vellah's ride took forever to get here," Kaled warned.

Rayah looked at her phone and noticed, with a bit of panic, that her ride had not yet confirmed a pickup time. It could be another twenty minutes before the cab arrived. "Looks like you might be right. Ugh, I'm going to be late."

"Want me to give you a ride?" offered Kaled.

"I thought you weren't going to the party. But yes, I'd love a ride."

"Oh, I'm not going, but I don't mind taking you there."

"Why don't you come? It could be fun. You never let loose and have fun anymore."

"I don't know, Rayah. Maybe it's not a good idea. We just became friends again, and I don't want to mess anything up."

Rayah understood his hesitation and appreciated his candor and thoughtfulness. "Kal, we're not going to be in my apartment alone. Nothing is going to happen," she assured him. "It's a party with lots of people. You're already dressed nicely; you might as well come and hang out. Now that Vellah is gone, I know you don't have anything else to occupy your evening."

"Okay, let's do this," Kaled agreed.

When they entered his hovercar, Kaled pressed on a touchscreen display that seemed to scan his eyes. After a couple of seconds, the screen turned green, and a text appeared saying: "Drive safely."

Rayah had never seen such a device before and couldn't comprehend why Kaled would have it in his vehicle. She also noted that Kaled did not punch in the coordinates for the party venue and instead chose to steer the hovercar manually.

"Why are you driving instead of letting it do it for you?" she asked.

"Oh, I guess it's just a force of habit. I like to be in control when I drive. I didn't mention it earlier, but that's a lovely dress you have on. It looks cheerful."

"Cheerful?" Rayah couldn't help but laugh at his description.

"What? I couldn't think of a better word," he defended himself, pretending not to laugh.

A few minutes into their drive, he received a call, which he put on the main screen.

"Hey Kaled," Vellah's cheerful face appeared on the display.

"Hey, I know you haven't gotten to Belvue yet. To what do I owe the pleasure of your call?"

"You're silly; you know that? Oh, is someone there with you?"

Rayah felt her face go hot. *Great.* Now Vellah was going to think that Rayah and Kaled had a secret thing together and -

"Yup, you've heard of my friend Rayah," said Kaled nonchalantly.

"Oh yes, though we haven't been properly introduced. Nice to finally meet you."

"Likewise," said Rayah feeling utterly uncomfortable.

"Kal, dear, when you get back to your apartment, can you please check to see if I left my make-up purse in your bedroom? I can't find it anywhere. It's the one you bought me last time you came to visit."

"Ah yes, the pricey one. I'll check if it's there. I'll send it by priority courier if it is."

"You're a doll. Thank you. Okay, I gotta go! Bye!"

The call ended, and the rest of the ride to the venue became awkwardly quiet. Rayah peered out the window to look at the gorgeous, bustling city of Clivesdail. Many large cities in Brennen had skylines packed with tall, sleek buildings, as well as robust transport systems to take the population from one place to another. Clivesdail alone had ten million residents, and the city's clean and beautiful appearance had been planned and developed over centuries by Brennen's best civil engineers. Outside the urban areas, large pockets of the country still looked the way they had centuries ago; cottages, dirt roads, and expansive farmlands were common.

Rayah saw Kaled's reflection on the passenger window and caught a glimpse of him checking her out. For a moment, she enjoyed knowing his eyes had been on her body; she liked knowing, in a sick and twisted way, that he still found her attractive. But then she remembered the sweet way he and Vellah had just been talking minutes ago, causing Rayah's desire for his attention to vanish. Thankfully, his eyes didn't linger, and before she knew it, they had arrived at the party venue.

"Oh, shoot!" Rayah exclaimed as she frantically

looked in her purse.

"What?" asked Kaled.

"I left their present in my other purse! Oh, this is embarrassing to walk into a party empty-handed."

"Well, you are in luck," answered Kaled. He opened up the trunk of his car and took out two wrapped boxes. "I was going to give the kids their gifts tomorrow, but we can do it now. And..." Kaled took out a pen from his back pocket and wrote Rayah's name on the packages. "They can be from the both of us."

His thoughtfulness shouldn't have shocked Rayah, but it did. "Kal, you are so sweet. Thank you. I promise I'll write your name on mine as soon as I get home."

"What are friends for?" he asked as he handed her one of the gifts.

As soon as Rayah walked in, she was amazed to see how the place had fully transformed. Simple beige walls had been replaced by shimmering streamers and decorations. A hologram stage featuring popular musical group Bayfront Band occupied a corner of the room while strobe lights livened up the atmosphere.

Within seconds, Rayah and Kaled were excitedly greeted by Evia and Ensin, who came rushing to them.

"You both made it!" Ensin exclaimed happily. "Ooh, a present for me! What is it?"

"Seriously, Ensin," said his sister with an eye-roll, "you have to wait. Thank you guys for coming to our party! I thought you weren't going to make it, Kal."

"Well," answered Kaled, "Rayah is quite persuasive."

"Kids, put the gifts on the table and let our guests breathe, please," said Nerida as she approached them. The kids disappeared into the crowd and Nerida turned back toward Kaled and Rayah, holding a clear cup of a dark blue fruity drink. "Hi, you two. Thank you for coming. I'm a little surprised to see you here, Kaled."

"Yeah, Rayah convinced me to come," Kaled answered back.

"Well, that's a good thing if you ask me. Our children love both of you very much, and it wouldn't be a party if either of you were missing." Nerida's warm smile spoke to the beauty of friendship and camaraderie they had all experienced in such a short time.

Rayah elbowed Kaled. "That's sweet of you to say. You see, Kal, can you imagine if you would have left these kids hanging? Nerida, I love what you did with the place. It really came together. I'm so sorry I couldn't come and help earlier; things got crazy at the clinic."

"Oh, it's okay, love. Kaled came and helped set everything up. It was his idea to do the hologram Bayfront Band; I would never have thought of that. Would you like some Azule Punch?"

"Sure," said Rayah. Then, looking at Kaled, she added, "you didn't tell me you were here earlier helping with the decorating. I thought you were with Vellah all day."

"I'm a man of many talents," answered Kaled with a smile. "Besides, you never asked."

"That was really sweet of you," said Rayah. Kaled truly was full of surprises, some good and some bad.

"Hi, Kaled. Care to dance?"

Rayah turned to see an older, lean woman with a kind face, who Rayah recognized as the gardener's wife.

"Of course, Mrs. Jardine. How is your daughter enjoying the party so far?"

The older lady whisked Kaled away, and Rayah found herself staring in his direction. She nearly jumped when

Nerida approached her from behind with the cup of Azule Punch. The tart drink made Rayah's lips pucker; she couldn't understand how Ensin and Evia consumed anything made out of azule berries all the time. Perhaps it was an acquired taste.

"I'm surprised your date is dancing with another woman," teased Nerida.

"Hmm?" It took Rayah a few seconds to process what Nerida had said. "Oh, Kal? No, he's not my date. We're just friends. Well...trying to be. It's a bit complicated."

"Love usually is a bit complicated," said Nerida.

"Me? Love Kal? No, thank you. Been there, done that. That ship sailed long ago."

"Did it, though?" Nerida arched her eyebrow and smiled.

"Nerida, even if I wanted to, I could never go back to him. You have no idea how he's hurt me."

"I've heard his side of the story. All of it, I think; he didn't seem to leave anything out. He's done some awful stuff to you, which he feels terrible about. You obviously have a great deal of mercy and maturity if you'd consider being his friend after all that's transpired between the two of you."

"Thank you." Rayah sighed. "I don't know if I have much of a choice. Living without his friendship is like wandering in a desert; it's not much of an existence. In a way, he completes me like no one else can. But to want him in any way other than friendship? That's a hard no." Rayah didn't care if he wrote her sonnets every day for the rest of his life or if he came crawling back on his hands and knees for another chance at her; she would *never* consider dating him again.

"It's a pity," Rayah continued, "because Kaled truly

is a good man. He knows how to make a woman feel special and loved. I actually still have one of the poems he wrote me when we dated at the Academy. And the note on my birthday card last week was so sweet and kind. But he's always had one flaw, which is that he can't always control his, uh...urges. I know he's never intentionally betrayed my trust, but it still doesn't excuse his behavior. If it weren't for his infidelity, he and I would have married. And the thing that hurts the most is, I honestly believe we would have been happy. Look at him," said Rayah pointing toward the dance floor. Kaled was dancing comically with both Evia and Ensin, who laughed so hard they could barely stand up. "He would have made a great father. He's so much more to me than just a great kisser; he was the love of my life. No one ever came close to that. Well, maybe Sy, but...now I'm not so sure."

"Do you think," Nerida asked gently, "there's a possibility that he's changed?"

"That's the problem. I always want to believe that he's changed, and then I constantly get burned. I've given him more chances than he deserves. The All Creator knows I was never granted such grace when I needed it most."

"I will pray that you find a good man who will treat you right and genuinely love you as you've never experienced before. And if, by any chance, you find yourself falling for Kaled again, pay attention to his actions and not his words."

"Thank you, Nerida," said Rayah while pushing back tears. The last thing she needed was to feel emotional while at a party.

Rayah danced with different partners throughout

the evening: Alastair, members of The Elite, Dr. Kortez, and even Mr. Jardine. The only friend she had not danced with was Kaled. Both of them stayed on opposite sides of the dance floor, every so often glancing at one another and sharing a smile from afar.

Until that point, all the music had been energetic and heavy with synthetic sounds. Now that the evening was winding to a close, though, a slow, sweet song played from the speakers. *The Rose of Eternity.* Instantly, Rayah froze on the spot as memories flooded her senses. She had first danced to this song with Kaled at his coming of age party. Years later, when she gave herself to him, it had been this song that played silently through the wireless sitting on the bed.

The song was far too sacred for her to dance with anyone else but Kaled. Rayah left the dance floor and took a seat by the drinks table. She watched as Nerida and Alastair danced closely, very much in love; she saw Ondraus with Niklas on his shoulders and Aymes wrapping her arms around his waist, the three of them dancing slowly to the precious song. Rayah assumed Kaled might not be as sentimental as she, yet when she scanned the crowd to look for him, she saw him standing alone with his eyes closed and his hands in his pockets.

Rayah stood up, wiping away a stray tear that had escaped. Aymes walked over and placed an arm around Rayah's shoulder.

"Hey, friend," said Aymes quietly.

"Hey," Rayah tried to make her voice sound happy as if nothing were amiss.

"How are you doing?" asked Aymes.

"Fine," Rayah answered. "This new dynamic your

brother and I have is going to take some getting used to. I thought our friendship was less vibrant after he cheated on me to get with Sherice and before the incident with Sy. But wow, it just all feels awkward."

"I don't want to dish out any excuses on his behalf," Aymes said, "because honestly, I know he did you wrong many times. But, trust me, he's been through a lot. It's not my story to tell; eventually, he must share it with you when he's ready. All I can say is that the distance you feel between the two of you is very much on purpose."

"I figured as much. Like I said, it will take some time to get used to. How's *my* brother treating you?"

Aymes swooned, grabbing hold of Rayah's hand. "Why did I wait so long to date your brother?" she asked. "I mean, he's amazing. He's so good with Niklas, and wow, he's such a great kisser."

"First of all, boundaries," said Rayah, pretending to be grossed out yet unable to hide her smile. "But yeah, I told you years ago that he liked you."

The smile on Aymes' face faded as a sobering thought surfaced. "After Niklas' father and I split, my dating life was practically non-existent. I tried getting to know a few guys, but everything changes when you're a mother. You can't bring just anyone home and introduce them to your child. To be honest, I stopped believing I could ever find love again and that if I did, the person would flee the other way as soon as they found out I had a son. Your brother has made me feel like love is possible. It almost feels too good to be true." Aymes' eyes sparkled as she visibly swooned over the thought of Ondraus.

"Well, it is true," encouraged Rayah, placing her

hands on Aymes' shoulder. "Plus, the three of you make quite the adorable trio."

Aymes looked over her shoulder and caught a glimpse of Ondraus and Niklas stomping around and roaring like huge prehistoric monsters. She chuckled lightly. "Or maybe I gained another child. Not really sure."

Rayah watched her brother and Niklas silently. She felt a painful ache in her heart and quickly wiped the tears that had begun to form before anyone at the party had a chance to notice. "What you three have is so beautiful. You have no idea how badly I want children of my own."

Aymes squeezed Rayah's hand. "Our first night at the palace, you told me you didn't place too much faith in relationships anymore. Yet anytime we sit down to watch a movie, you always choose a romantic comedy. Just last week, when you let me scroll through your e-book library, it was obvious you like two genres. One is medical dramas and the other is romance. I think you still believe in true love, Rayah." Aymes turned to face her friend, who silently held back tears. Perhaps Rayah's statue-like appearance would have fooled anyone else, but Aymes knew her too well.

"Maybe I do," whispered Rayah. Her voice was strained as she spoke, but aside from that, she knew her face was void of the turmoil she felt. "But it feels like a naive, unattainable dream. I don't find it easy to trust in men right now, but I've been working on it the last few months. It's such a long process."

"I know a thing or two about that," affirmed Aymes. She grabbed two cups of soda from the drinks table. "To all the guys that have hurt us," she announced, and then blew a loud raspberry.

"I can definitely drink to that," laughed Rayah, adding her own raspberry.

"Hi, Rayah and Aymes," interrupted Evia. "I made these bracelets for everyone as a party gift."

"These are beautiful," Rayah said as she received the bead bracelet. "Thank you. It's just like yours. How thoughtful."

"Yeah! They're moon bracelets, and they shimmer in the dark and in the sunlight. I like fashion accessories," Evia said joyfully. Suddenly the girl's face contorted with pain and confusion. "Something's wrong."

"Are you okay?" asked Aymes in alarm, catching Evia just in time before she collapsed to the floor.

From across the room, Kaled screamed out, "Ensin!" Rayah looked and saw that Ensin, too, was on the ground and groaning in pain. The room erupted with alarmed voices, loudest of all Nerida and Alistair, who were running to their children's side.

Dr. Kortez scrambled to his nephew. "We need to get them to the medical ward now! I drove my Uni and it only seats one, but I'll meet you all there!"

"Does anyone have any mind blockers?" asked Rayah. "I think they're suffering from a connection."

"Please don't let it be another Gaoled!" pleaded Nerida.

I'm calling Guyad, said Rayah through duo-com.

She felt Ondraus' agreement, and then he rushed to Evia with a small white tablet in his hand. "Here; put this under your tongue. It's going to block the pain," Ondraus told her.

Rayah had already gotten Guyad on the phone. "I need you to check on Queen Ellandra. Something might be wrong with her babies."

"What would make you think that? Besides, the Queen is asleep; I don't want –"

"Check on her NOW!" yelled Rayah authoritatively.

She ended the call and looked for her brother, who was now crouching near Ensin, providing him with a pain-blocking tablet as well. Ensin looked pale; his face covered in sweat, and his eyes were closed as he continued to writhe in pain.

"My brother left to grab his car," said Aymes. "Let's start moving the kids outside."

We have a ride. Come on. Let's get the kids and go, said Rayah through duo-com. "Bo," she said out loud, "can you help me with Evia?"

In an instant, Bo grabbed Evia and followed Ondraus and Rayah out the door toward Kaled's hovercar. Rayah sat in the front passenger seat so Ondraus could be in the back with both kids, who were slumped against him.

Kaled grabbed Rayah's and Ondraus' hands and closed his eyes to pray. "All Creator, please protect the queen, her babies, and these two kids we love very much. In your name, we ask these things humbly." He let go of their hands and warned, "Hold on."

The hovercar lifted into the air and surged away toward the palace.

Guyad

Guyad shook his head and cursed. If he got in trouble because his girlfriend had a "feeling" about the queen's well-being, then Guyad was going to have some strong words. Regardless, he ran up the four flights of stairs and up to the tower to the royal suite. The guard on duty stepped to the side and greeted Guyad with a nod. Guyad knocked hard on the door.

"I must come in and check on Queen Ellandra." His heart pounded violently; he would never do something so unprofessional on his own. He winced at the thought of how strange and inconvenient this was for them.

The king opened the door, wearing a pair of satin boxers.

"What's the meaning of this, Sergeant Lurca?" demanded King Tarrington.

"Your Majesty, I know it's late, but I need to check on the queen." He came in and saw Queen Ellandra on the bed, fast asleep. He placed his hand on her forehead and then crouched down beside her, "Are you feeling well? Captain Jur thinks something may be wrong." Guyad then looked at the king. "She feels really hot. Captain Jur wants to check her. I don't know; she must have some medical surveillance on the queen."

The king nodded, so Guyad removed her covers and cursed loudly. The queen was lying in a puddle of blood. "We need to move her now! I don't have time to wait for a stretcher." Guyad put his muscular arms underneath the queen and lifted her out of bed in one smooth movement.

"Make way!" he yelled as he jogged with the queen in his arms.

He tried not to show it, but he was absolutely terrified. What if something terrible happened to the queen or the royal babies? He couldn't let that happen. Her blood covered his arms and torso, but he didn't care; the only important thing right now was for her to get seen immediately. Hopefully, with a miracle, they would survive whatever terrible thing was happening.

The king followed closely behind, praying out loud.

Finally, they reached the medical ward's automatic double doors and saw that Dr. Kortez himself was just arriving.

"Your Majesty!" the doctor exclaimed in alarm. "Lurca, lay her on that bed! Zendo," he called out to the nurse who was on duty, "get out the sonogram!"

Guyad gently lay her on the bed and stepped away, feeling terribly hopeless and helpless. His usual rough exterior was stripped away momentarily as he slumped into a chair in the hallway and began to cry.

He hoped no one would see him in this emotional state. A moment later, the king joined him, pacing the hallway. Guyad wiped the tears from his face and stood up. A few moments later, Rayah came bursting into the hall from a far staircase, followed by Kaled and Ondraus, who were holding Evia and Ensin in their arms.

"Sergeant Lurca!" exclaimed Rayah upon seeing the blood all over his uniform.

"The queen," he stammered, "something's wrong with her babies. I...I carried her over here."

Rayah closed her eyes, and a few tears escaped. She recovered quickly, nodding her head and then walking up to him as she kissed him on his cheek, not caring about military decorum. "Thank you." She then looked at the king. "Your Majesty, we're going to do everything in our power to protect your babies."

Rayah

Rayah rushed into the medical ward, followed by her brother, Kaled, and the two young Kortez twins. "Dr. Kortez, what's our status?"

"Scrub in," replied the doctor. "We need to do emergency surgery. These babies are coming out right now or else we'll lose them. How are those two?" he asked, nodding at his niece and nephew, who were now taking a seat on the beds while Kaled stayed with them.

"My brother gave them a mind blocker, and it seems to be doing the job. Captain Behr, will you look after them?" Rayah asked Kaled as she and Ondraus reached into the linen cart and pulled out a clean pair of scrubs. She saw Kaled nod, and then she disappeared into a closet to change out of her dress.

Now she was baffled about Guyad. He had looked distraught about this whole ordeal and had done something that was quite frankly heroic. Had she been entirely wrong about him? It wouldn't be the first time she had totally misjudged a guy...

She and her brother entered the surgical room where Dr. Kortez and Lieutenant Zendo were waiting. Rayah grabbed a towel while her brother prepared two small cribs. Dr. Kortez was already in position, holding a small object that would use a laser to cut through the queen's abdomen so he could remove the babies.

"I can't regulate her heart rate," said the worried doctor, turning to Ondraus, who was closest to the medication cart. "Give her fifty units of Derilium and get ready for baby number one."

Rayah watched his hands reach deeply into the queen's abdominal cavity. With an expert tug, he was able to pull a little girl from out of the womb.

Rayah received the baby, who had not yet cried. Instead of having bright blue skin, the newborn girl was pale and grayish. Rayah had never seen anything like that before, not even in the medical textbooks.

"Come on, sweetie. Breathe." Rayah placed the little

girl in the crib, turning on the incubator lights and grabbing a tool to suck out the mucus in the infant's throat. Finally, the baby cried, but her skin color remained unchanged. A moment later, Ondraus was holding the other infant. The worst might be over, but none of the patients were out of the woods. All three still had an erratic heartbeat, and the kids were still gray...

"Closing her up," said the doctor, while Zendo passed him towels and different tools. After a short while, Dr. Kortez left the queen's bedside and stared at her vitals on the monitor. Then he began to pace. "I have to think," he said, massaging the bridge of his ridged nose. "Rayah and Ondraus, take a blood sample from the infants; Zendo, do the same for the queen."

Once Dr. Kortez had the tubes of blood, he inserted them into a small analyzer, which quickly provided the results on a digital screen that he read, murmuring to himself. Rayah couldn't read the doctor's face, but he seemed stunned and perplexed.

"Zendo, get the Kortez twins prepped into proper attire to come into this surgical room."

"Doctor?" asked Ondraus as soon as Zendo was out of earshot. "Do you know what's wrong?"

"I have a suspicion, and I'm about to test my theory. Please start an IV line on the infants." A few minutes later, Zendo and Kaled came back, pushing both kids in wheelchairs. "Thank you. Please wait outside. I'll call you when we're done."

Rayah didn't understand why the doctor had dismissed Lieutenant Zendo when the medical ward clearly had enough sick patients to warrant extra helping hands. But no answer was forthcoming. The doctor breathed in deeply and started the transfusion to the infants first. To Rayah's surprise, the blood was not a dark purple. Instead, it appeared red.

"Doctor, the blood –" interjected Rayah in alarm.

"I know. Just do it."

Once the babies had received their unit of blood, it was the queen's turn. Along with her babies, she had a cannula providing extra oxygen into her body and was now resting peacefully. All three monitors had stopped beeping madly and had slowed to a normal rhythm. When the last of the transfusion was completed, the doctor sat on a chair and breathed out slowly. Perhaps sensing that Rayah would unleash a flurry of questions, he spoke before she had such an opportunity.

"My niece and nephew are different from you and me. In all my years of medicine, I've never seen anyone like them. My brother and Nerida are not the birth parents; they found the children one day near a pond. After searching weeks for the parents, they concluded the infants must have been abandoned, and made the decision to adopt them. Their skin is not naturally blue; it's a strange sickly light brown color, like an undercooked pheasant. You now know as much as I do. I'm sorry, but I hope you can understand why I would have kept this a secret. Now please, help me clean this up. I can't let Zendo know about the color of their blood."

CHAPTER 19

Rayah

Rayah felt like her head hadn't stopped spinning since the moment Evia and Ensin collapsed at the party. The royal twins, Luna and Saule, had been through a harrowing birth the previous week, which would have ended drastically different had it not been for three things: the strange connection the Kortez twins had with the babies, the doctor's quick medical thinking, and the decisive intervention of Guyad Lurca. Rayah still didn't know what to think of the knowledge-bomb that Dr. Kortez had dropped on her at the time of the life-saving blood transfusion.

The Kortez twins, Ensin and Evia, were not like ordinary beings from the planet of Vilmos. No one knew where they'd come from, but they were most likely from another world. Rayah didn't get a chance to see with her own eyes what their natural skin color looked like, since the children were on a strict diet of azule berries that kept their skin blue. Their markings weren't natural, either, but painted on by their mother. Though Rayah had many questions about the Kortez twins, the doctor and the children's adoptive parents did not know any more information than what they'd already shared with her. Rayah's thirst for knowledge was left unquenched.

At the moment, though, Rayah was in Guyad's bedroom, watching him with concern as he lay on his bed with a terrible headache. She provided him a glass of water and a small pain-blocker tablet. "You should have called me sooner," she scolded.

"It's just a headache, no big deal," he scoffed dismissively.

"No big deal? I saw you walk face-first into the barracks main entrance because you were in so much pain you weren't even paying attention to where you were going." She stood up and closed all his blinds, then removed his boots and unbuckled his belt.

"Feel free to hop on," he said, attempting a devilish grin but quickly wincing in pain.

She redirected the conversation immediately like she usually did when they were alone. "How about you be a good boy and go to sleep? I'll play with your hair."

That seemed to do the trick. Guyad lay his head on a pillow and became visibly relaxed as she ran her fingers through his hair. Dealing with Guyad's relentless hormones had turned into a full-time job, but Rayah had found, through trial and error, that his demeanor changed whenever she calmed him with this method. With Guyad's defenses down, she could glean information from him.

"How was your trip last night?" Rayah asked him.

His eyes were closed, and he responded as if in a hypnotic state. "It was good. I went to see my father."

She began massaging his temples and then the inner part of his brow, applying pressure to relieve his pain. "I thought what you did with the queen the other week was amazing."

"I tend to be amazing," he said smugly. "What thing exactly?"

"When you carried her to the medical ward. Good thing you're so big and strong."

His eyes opened, and he looked at her in confusion. "I did what?"

Her fingers stopped, and then she looked down into his eyes. "You don't remember?"

"Things have been blurry lately. I must not be getting enough sleep because I'm forgetting stuff. I remember now, kinda."

He closed his eyes again and exhaled. Rayah continued working on his hair as she became increasingly convinced that something was wrong. The more she got to know Guyad, the more she understood what made him tick. He was a regular guy who loved two things: his job and satisfying his physical urges. However, he'd become increasingly more forgetful over the past few weeks, to the point that Rayah wondered if anyone else had noticed. There were also times when his disposition completely shifted, not like a mood change, but a complete personality change.

One time last week, Rayah had stayed up all night at the medical ward watching over the infants, the Kortez twins, and the queen. At the end of her shift, Ondraus had relieved her. On her way home, she'd bumped into Guyad, and he had seemed overly concerned over the well-being of the queen and her children. His monologue had started in a typical Guyad way as he droned on and on about how lucky the queen had been that he'd gotten to her on time and was strong enough to transport her to the medical ward. Rayah waited patiently as he rambled, letting Guyad's ego shine through in its usual manner. He suddenly stopped talking, and his face became expressionless, his eyes blank.

He'd turned to leave toward the palace even though he had just come from there.

"Babe, where are you going?" she had asked, confused.

"None of your damn business," he'd snarled.

Rayah had sensed that Guyad wasn't himself. Though she was taken aback by his brash comment, she'd decided to test her theory further. "Darling, come; let's go to the bedroom. Forget about work."

He answered in the way she had dreaded: he'd declined. The following day, however, when she asked him about it, he had not remembered the conversation at all, nor did he remember her indecent proposal.

As she played with his hair now, dread for his well-being filled her. If Rayah didn't figure out how he fit into all this and how to protect the royal twins, someone would end up hurt. A part of her felt terrible that she was using him to get information, but this was possibly a life-or-death situation. What else could she do?

Instead of enjoying Guyad's presence, Rayah found herself thinking of someone else's touch: Kaled. Last week Kaled had taken her hand for a quick prayer. The gesture shouldn't have been world-shattering, but try as she might, she couldn't get it out of her mind. She knew things were complicated between the two of them, and dating him was not a possibility, but there were plenty of times where she wanted to set their insipid friendship aside for a few lust-filled hours. A knock on the door brought her out of her inappropriate daydream.

"Can you get that, babe?" groaned Guyad.

"Sure."

Rayah made her way to the door and opened it,

shocked to find Kaled facing her. They both looked at each other in confusion for a few seconds, but Kaled recovered first.

"We're all being summoned to the palace," he said.

"How did you know I would be here?" she asked, surprised.

"I didn't. I was looking for Guyad since he wasn't answering his messages. I can now see why." Kaled's remark wasn't in an angry or sarcastic tone; it was flat and matter-of-fact. He smiled, but the expression didn't reach his eyes. Without another word, he walked away.

Fifteen minutes later, Rayah and Guyad met with The Elite and other palace staff in a large conference room. General Peterson and King Tarrington were deep in a conversation at the head of a long table. Rayah recognized General Peterson's son, Captain Yosef Peterson, picking out a water bottle from the refreshment table.

General Peterson opened the meeting. "An hour ago, we received word that Rancor has escaped from the high-security prison where he has been incarcerated for the last twenty-six years."

"Can we trust the source?" asked the king.

"Unfortunately, yes. All of the guards are dead, and no one even knew of the escape until just this morning during shift change. Looks like all those men and women were poisoned to death. This hasn't made the news yet, but I suspect it will in the next few hours. They'll want the public's help in catching him."

Rayah's heart thrummed madly against her chest. Could this be the reason for the prophecy? Never in a million years would she have guessed that Rancor would be involved. Though she hadn't even been born by the time he was put in jail, she had grown up hearing his name as part of a creepy fairy tale that was used to get kids to sleep on time.

"Go to bed, Rayah," her mother would warn, "or Rancor will find you and take you." There were even songs made about him, which children sang in an eerie tone whenever they wanted to scare their friends during a sleepover, as if singing his song would make him appear out of nowhere. Everyone in the kingdom of Brennen and all the surrounding countries knew about the infamous Rancor.

Brings back some creepy childhood memories, huh, sis? asked Ondraus through duo-com.

Yeah, agreed, Rayah. *Do you think he's the one who the kids described from their dream world?*

He would have fit the description if he were twenty-six years younger. Those burn marks on his palms are courtesy of General Peterson, Ondraus pointed out.

If not Rancor, who else could it be? Rayah didn't know anyone else who matched that description as closely as Rancor did, and now all of a sudden, he'd broken free from an impenetrable prison. For someone who looked exactly like Rancor to show up in the Gaoled of two kids who'd never met him, just in time for the real Rancor to escape prison a few weeks later... Rayah wasn't sure she could believe in that kind of coincidence. She scanned the room and saw that Guyad was just as alarmed as everyone else.

Kaled looked like he was in the middle of a duo-com conversation with his sister. He must have felt Rayah's eyes on him, because he looked up and smiled when he saw her. For some reason, she couldn't look away. It felt as if the entire room dissolved, and all that remained was him and her alone.

For some reason, her mind chose that moment to revisit an early memory from her first week at the Academy. She was homesick and crying on the lawn by the training field. She'd thought she was out there all alone, but a handsome young boy had been finishing his homework under the warm sun when he spotted her. He'd introduced himself as Kal and then sat with her until his joyful, easygoing attitude eased her sadness. Before he'd left, the thirteen-year-old boy asked if he could hug her. Now, at twenty-four, all Rayah wanted was the comforting hug Kaled had given her ages ago.

"Can we count on the King of Susa to take care of this situation? Do we know if he's got his best men and women out there to track him down and bring him to justice?" asked Captain Peterson.

"I'm sorry, Captain, but I think that doubtful," replied Ondraus.

"What makes you say that?" asked King Tarrington.

"Your Highness," said Rayah, "my brother and I served at Benal. We spent the entire two years at that post dealing with refugees who were leaving Susa because they were dying of hunger and persecution in their own country. We spent countless hours with refugees who needed medical intervention. Each of them spoke ill of King Aljan."

"A lot of them," added Ondraus, "said that King Aljan was never the same after his father died, and that he seems...disconnected, almost robotic at times. That's the main reason why that country is such a mess. They've been on the brink of civil war for years, so I don't think he's going to spend much of his time or resources on trying to track down Rancor."

Guyad slammed his fist on the table. "Well, then, we

must be ready. We'll increase security here at the palace, tell local authorities to do the same thing, and put up a strict curfew so no children are out by themselves at all, especially after the first sunset around eighteen hundred hours."

"Excellent, Sergeant Lurca," said General Peterson. "Please make that happen."

"Certainly." Guyad straightened his back, tapping on the screen of his tablet and glancing over at Rayah.

Rayah smiled back encouragingly and thought, *This is the real Guyad. He likes to feel important. He enjoys his career because he's excellent at it, and he likes for others to know.* She could see his ego spilling over as he reveled in receiving praise from his leader. That said, she had a sinking feeling that Guyad's odd behavior and the escape of evil mastermind Rancor had something to do with one another.

As of now, no one knew exactly when all of the prison guards were killed or when Rancor escaped. The previous night, Guyad had returned after supposedly been visiting his father. Being off base was not cause for suspicion, of course, but on top of Guyad's odd mood swings and not remembering essential things like *how he'd saved the queen's life by carrying her to the medical ward*, it was all just too much to overlook.

But how would General Peterson react if she went to him with her theory? She could already picture how that conversation would go: "I wasn't sure if he was being manipulated, so I offered him sex, and he declined. I mean, hello, have you seen my body?" Rayah wondered if she could convince Guyad to be seen at the medical ward. Erratic behavior and memory loss could be signs of a severe problem, possibly even a brain tumor. She didn't know how yet, but she knew she needed to take action, whether telling General Peterson of her suspicions or running tests on Guyad. It seemed like the pieces to a puzzle were swirling in front of her face, and she couldn't see how they fit together. But she needed to figure it out – and fast.

CHAPTER 20

Ondraus

Ondraus took a deep breath while he watched his sister shake her head in disagreement.

"No, I don't like this one bit," she protested. "They're kids, for the All Creator's sake."

"Rayah," said Ondraus calmly, "we have our marching orders. General Peterson and Captain Peterson have already said what must be done, and we need to carry it out."

"O, one thing was to have those kids train with us when we worked out. Okay, I could understand that. There was value in teaching them how to run in case the need arose. But this? Teach them how to fight? They just turned eleven! We didn't even hold our first Nemi until we were sixteen. This is ridiculous."

"Rayah," he warned, "if we don't train them, we put them at risk for not knowing how to protect themselves. They must learn. I don't like it either, but shit just got real. We need to prepare for the worst."

She tapped her foot on the grass as she wiped a tear that had escaped her eyes. "Fine," she said after a minute of silence. "But you tell them. I have to change out of this sweaty, dirty shirt. I feel so gross right now."

Ondraus chuckled as his sister left to grab her bag. He jogged back to the palace to visit Evia, Ensin, and young Jerah Peterson in class. When he came upon the door, he looked through the small glass window and watched the children as they sat silently, taking notes on their tablets. At the same time, the teacher discussed the importance of knowing how to do arithmetic without the use of technology.

Ondraus' watch told him that only a few minutes remained before class ended, so he stood in the corridor, scrolling through the news feed on his phone to kill some time. He heard someone whispering in the room down the hall and decided to check it out, since he thought the rest of the floor would be unoccupied.

He was disgusted but not surprised by what he saw: Guyad with another woman in his arms, and if Ondraus had to guess, it was probably that redhead who had hit on Kaled a few months back. The two were sloppily making out, and Guyad was clearly in the process of undoing his trouser zipper before Ondraus decided to do them a favor of locking the door and closing it quietly behind him.

He hated that his sister was going out with that creep. If she had indeed been dating Guyad, Ondraus would have stormed in and punched him in the face, but this was not an ordinary situation, and the whole thing left him feeling at a loss. Part of him wanted to stand up for his sister, while the other part of him knew he couldn't without blowing her cover – and then everything she'd endured over the past few months would be wasted. He shook his head in bewilderment and walked down the corridor once again until he arrived at the classroom door.

Thankfully, General Peterson had already spoken to Nerida and Alastair about the added training their children would be undergoing. Had they taken it in stride or oppose it the way Rayah had done only moments ago?

Ondraus didn't like the general's decision either, but he did see the value in teaching the kids how to protect themselves. Wouldn't it be better than the alternative? What if they were in danger, and no one else was around to protect them?

At three o'clock, the class let out, and the door opened. Ondraus waved to Evia, Ensin, and Jerah Peterson. "Hey, guys, we've been trying to contact you all morning, but we realized you're not allowed to have your phones on in class. However, from now on, you must have your phones on at all times, including when you are in bed or in class. We need to make sure you're able to contact us at any moment, and vice versa. Something's come up, and we need to start teaching you a few more things, starting today."

"What's wrong?" asked Evia with a look of worry on her face.

Ondraus didn't respond right away; he didn't know how he would deliver the news without sounding scary. Looking at all three children, he asked, "Have you ever heard of a man named Rancor?"

"Yes," said Jerah. "There's a rumor he's the one that took Mr. Yemley's son a long time ago."

Ondraus nodded his head. "Correct, although there's still some uncertainty about that. At any rate, Rancor has escaped prison, and we want to be more proactive. That's all. Starting today, after class, the three of you will meet with us at the obstacle field course by the training grounds at Primeda Fortress. We'll run there each time, not jogging but running, and that also means no recess after class, at least for the time being."

A look of fear and suspicion was written on each of their faces. They weren't too young for this kind of responsibility; the Kortez twins were now eleven, and Jerah Peterson was fifteen. Jerah had been singled out because his father and grandfather were military and had trained him from a young age. Who better to help the Kortez twins through this transition than a classmate?

"Jerah," said Ondraus, "we need your assistance to keep these two under your watch and to aid them as we teach them a few offensive and defensive maneuvers."

"Yes, sir."

"Thank you. Here, I've brought you all a change of clothes, plus a bottle of water and a snack. Eat and drink now, and then find a restroom to change into the workout clothes. You can store your stuff in your backpack. You have five minutes."

Five minutes later, with workout clothes on and snacks eaten, the children were beginning their stretches. Ondraus noticed how Jerah looked at the Kortez twins when they stretched their hamstrings. Jerah didn't say anything, but Ondraus could read the confusion on his face.

"Okay," declared Ondraus, "we're going to drive over to Primeda Fortress, just five miles from here. When we get there, I want you to put on your backpacks and run around the lake, which equals exactly one mile."

"You want us to run with our backpacks on?" Asked Ensin. "Won't that be harder?"

"Yes, it will be harder," admitted Ondraus, not flinching but feeling the gravity of what he was asking them. The four of them hopped into a hovercar and took the short but pleasant drive to the fortress.

"I've worked at many military fortresses throughout my career," said Ondraus, "and this is by far my favorite."

Ondraus enjoyed looking at Primeda Fortress from above. Unlike many of the buildings in Clivesdail that were sleek, shiny, and tall, the fortress was squat and made of a beautiful rough stone. In addition to state-of-the-art technology and infrastructure, it also hosted one of the largest training grounds in all of Brennen.

Once they touched down on a landing pad, the four of them set off for their run. "There's the lake," Ondraus said, pointing. "We're running, but not sprinting. Keep a steady pace; focus on your breathing. Let's go."

"Ondraus," said Ensin after a short while, "can you tell us more about this Rancor guy? Why does it matter that he escaped prison? Are you allowed to say?"

Ondraus huffed out while he ran steadily beside the children. "I don't know if your parents would like me to tell you the story."

"Please, Captain Jur," pleaded Jerah. "All I know is that my grandfather is the reason why Rancor has those burn marks on his hands, but no one talks about how all that happened. According to my grandfather, my dad used to have nightmares about Rancor when he was younger, which I guess is why they don't like to discuss it much."

"I don't know where Rancor came from, nor does anyone know what his motives were. It's like he just woke up one day, mad at everyone, and decided that they should all should pay some sort of price. He was a mass murderer. According to the reports I've read, Rancor has killed over forty people. Most of those were at a village outside Clarcona, a coastal city in Susa, but he also attacked a number of people in Brennen as well. There's a rumor, and that's all it is, that he even kidnapped children. If you ask around, you'll see many children went missing a little over twenty-six years ago. Their bodies were never found, which means no closure for those parents."

"Do you think that's what happened to Mr. Yemley's kid?" asked Evia with concern.

"Who knows? He was out playing with his brother, and only one of the two came back in. According to the police reports, Brett tried to fend off whoever the abductor was, and he tried to explain what he saw and where the person had gone, but he wasn't as verbal then as he is now."

"That's terrible," murmured Evia.

"Yes, it is and was terrible," said Ondraus. "Pick up the pace, Evia; you're slowing down too much. I'm sorry that I'm so tough on you, but I need you all to take this very seriously. Come on, just a little further."

Ondraus hated this. Though he wasn't as open with his emotions as his friend Kaled, he still felt terrible about introducing these children to more serious matters. He'd grown up with the stories of Rancor; he too had awakened in a cold sweat from nightmares as a child.

Since the meeting three days ago when General Peterson and the king called them all together to discuss Rancor's escape, he and the rest of The Elite had gone back to research the history. Ondraus and his sister had drawn the unfortunate task of pulling up the autopsy reports and becoming acquainted with Rancor's unique killing style. All the information revealed that Rancor was a deranged psychopath with no value for anyone's life. Oddly enough, no death appeared to be correlated with the others. They all seemed like random acts, but the way he killed was precise and full of anger. There was a reason why he inflicted such pain, but Rancor had never shared it with anyone.

Ondraus and the kids finally arrived at the training grounds. The Elite had made the Kortez twins run to this location before on multiple occasions, and Ondraus was proud to see that they did manage to cover the whole distance without getting too winded, despite the heat of the midday summer sun. Incredibly, Guyad was there talking to Rayah, his hand on her arm while she giggled as if she appreciated his attention. For a moment, Ondraus entertained a vivid and satisfying mental image of slamming that two-timing cheat against the wall and punching him in the face until he'd had enough, but reminded himself that his sister was playing Guyad all along. Their relationship was fake, he reminded himself.

"Hi, kids," said Rayah after waving Guyad goodbye.

Ondraus almost laughed out loud as he noticed his sister's relieved face when Guyad finally left. Even her shoulders seemed to relax more. Behind her was Kaled, who, as always, tried to appear unbothered by her affection toward another man. The poor guy didn't know how not to seem obvious.

Evia and Ensin ran up to Rayah and hugged her. "Hi!" they chorused.

Captain Yosef Peterson, Jerah's dad, stood among The Elite, but he was not in a workout uniform like the rest of the group. "Hello, father," greeted Jerah as he stood to his full height. "Hello, Captain Jur."

Captain Peterson nodded his own greeting. "Good

afternoon, son, children. I know Captain Jur gave you a quick explanation about what will be taking place. Jerah, from now on, you'll be training with these two. Your class schedule will be cut in half. I haven't spoken to Mr. Pilmen yet, but this is coming from above, so it will be approved. Jerah, this group of soldiers will be helping your friends reach your advanced level of training, and I want you to assist them, because these soldiers will also be busy with other tasks that General Peterson has for them. No one else in this entire compound knows or cares about these kids as much as this group of soldiers and you. That's where you come in. You're still a minor, and you remember how hard it was to train at such a young age. Surely if anyone here is qualified to help guide them, it's you."

"Yes, father," said Jerah with a solemn nod. "May I ask a question, sir?"

"Go ahead, son."

"Why do they need to be trained up? Don't we have plenty of soldiers here and within a short flying distance from nearby cities? Plus, not to be rude to my friends, but why do they specifically need to be trained and not the other children from our class?"

"Excellent observations, son. Unfortunately, all I can say at this time is that if something bad were to happen to the king and queen's babies, these two would most likely be the best chance and hope for them."

Jerah opened his mouth to ask a question, but closed it again before anything came out, as if remembering that it was not his place to interrogate an officer. Even though he clearly wanted to know more, he had the discipline to accept the duty he had been charged with. Captain Peterson departed, leaving only the children, and The Elite on the training grounds.

"This is an obstacle course," began Kaled after everyone had settled down. "You will start here, climb up that rope, then proceed to the monkey bars, low crawl in the mud under that barbed wire, and scale that six-foot wall before jumping down and running to the finish line." Kaled then turned to face Bo, who held several backpacks. "You will do this all while wearing five-pound bags."

"Yikes," said Ensin. "Am I to assume that is supposed to mimic an infant's weight?"

"That is correct," answered Kaled with a curt nod and strained face. He, too, did not appear to like what they were asking the children to do. "Those babies won't stay that small forever. They'll eventually gain weight, so we'll be adding mass to your bags as you get stronger and more capable. I will run the course first to demonstrate how it should look. Keep in mind, you will be timed. We kept things pretty easy since it's your first experience doing something like this." He pointed to Evia and Ensin. "Jerah, please feel free to help them as they go. You, too, will be wearing a bag."

"Yes, Captain," said Jerah, smiling back.

Ondraus took out his smartwatch and told Kaled that the timer had started. Kaled picked up a significantly heavier bag and climbed up the rope quickly.

"Captain Behr, you're supposed to show them how *they* would be able to climb it," called Rayah, who stood next to Evia.

"You think he's being a show-off?" asked Evia.

Rayah chuckled for half a second. "No, Kal isn't a show-off. He's just really athletic and competitive."

Ondraus noticed that Rayah had responded without

taking her eyes off Kaled.

"Yeah, let me try that again." Kaled worked his way down half the rope and then jumped to the ground. He glanced at Rayah before smiling at the kids. "To get started climbing a rope, there's a bit of a trick," he announced as he instructed them how to loop part of the rope around their foot so they could use it to push off. He climbed the entire rope that way and then continued with the rest of the course. When he was finished, sloppy and muddy, he went straight for Aymes, who did her best to flee, trying not to get hugged. Unable to escape, she ran right behind Rayah and placed her arms around her in a giant protective hug.

"I know you won't even dare," said Aymes with a grin and then placed her chin on the back of Rayah's shoulder. Kaled had been running and had to stop quickly to not crash into Rayah. He stood there, just five inches from her, frozen in place.

Rayah smiled playfully. She could deny it all she wanted, thought Ondraus, but his sister still had feelings for Kaled. Their story wasn't over just yet.

Ondraus then called for the kids to come up to the starting line of the course. Climbing the rope proved to be nearly impossible for Evia and Ensin. Jerah slithered up easily; he wasn't as quick as Kaled, but he still made it look effortless. Ensin managed to climb the rope eventually with a little help from Ondraus, but Evia lacked the upper body strength and could not defeat the first obstacle no matter how hard she tried.

"It's okay, Evia. You did your best, and that's what matters. Go on ahead to the next obstacle. We'll train you up the way we did with the running," encouraged Ondraus.

The children traversed the monkey bars with ease, and they all seemed to enjoy the muddy low crawl. When Kaled had scaled the wall, he did so completely alone. Jerah had told Ensin to go up the wall first, promising that Evia and Jerah would give him a boost up. Then Ensin held out his hand while Jerah helped from below, and Evia could easily go up the wall. Last was Jerah. He told Evia and Ensin that he would run toward the wall and that he would need them to pull him up, and they did just that.

The final exercise was the run. Ondraus yelled, "Run as fast as you can, as fast as you possibly can!"

Evia and Ensin looked at Ondraus with a devious smile. Finally, this was something they could do better than anyone else. Though the three kids had started the run simultaneously, the young twins passed Jerah in a matter of seconds. The twins sprinted to the finish line, where Rayah and the rest of the Elite were cheering them on. Ondraus didn't catch up to them until a full two minutes later, but his heart was full of pride at seeing them excel in their element.

Rayah

Rayah watched with pride as Evia and Ensin raced toward the finish line at an incredible speed, which left poor Jerah far behind. She knew they weren't up to a ten- or twenty-mile run yet, but they were unstoppable over short distances. She didn't like that she and the rest of The Elite had asked these two children to train as if they were joining the military. The kids didn't know it yet, but they'd be learning how to handle a weapon as soon as Captain Peterson thought it was prudent to do so. All of this was going on, whether anyone liked it or not, because these poor children happened to have the ability to connect with the royal infants. Had it not been for Evia and Ensin, those babies surely would have died the night they were born.

The mid-day summer sun beat down on the training grounds. Rayah's uniform clung to her body uncomfortably as beads of sweat kept dripping from her hair down her cheeks. She sought refuge from the heat under the shade of a beautiful, large Naran tree. Dazzling orange leaves filled the branches, giving off a wonderful citrus scent whenever the breeze hit it just right.

Even as she stood there watching Jerah finally catch up to the twins, with everyone around celebrating their completion of the course, she couldn't help but look over at Kaled. He picked up Ensin and gave the boy a tight muddy hug, which only made Ensin laugh hysterically.

Kaled, the version Rayah had grown up loving, was a playful and easygoing guy. At times, it was jarring to see how much he had changed; then again, she had changed a lot too. Back when they were together, they had loved one another so deeply that it brought a true richness to her life. When they separated, it created a chasm, not only in their relationship but in her self-image, and she suspected the same happened to him as well.

"Okay," said Bo, once Kaled stopped trying to chase after the children with hands full of mud to throw at them. "We're almost through for the day. Before we dismiss, though, we're going to introduce you to hand-to-hand combat."

Rayah noticed the eyes of both Ensin and Evia widen in surprise. "For now, we're just going to teach you the concept," continued Bo, "and show a few ways to block an opponent. Then we'll have one of The Elite demonstrate."

Bo instructed his sister Lina to come up front. He showed the children how to block a punch, how to kick someone properly, and how hard to punch back. Rayah knew from experience that it was all about body mechanics and ensuring every muscle was properly engaged to give the most significant hit to the opponent. The Elite had already been working on hand-to-hand combat all morning and afternoon. Rayah was exhausted from so much training in one single day and appreciated watching someone teach for once.

"I'm going to pick Kaled to be the assailant. Besides, I figure no one wants to get his muddy hands on them anyway," Bo laughed. "Now, who will volunteer?"

"I think Rayah should volunteer," said Aymes with a grin.

Rayah shot her a look. Behind Aymes, she heard Ensin add, "Aymes is acting as his wingman," to his sister Evia.

"I'm good, thanks," said Rayah, not wanting to be in the position to be so physically close to Kaled.

"I don't know, Rayah," said Aymes, "I've seen you fight with everyone here all day except for my brother. I think we've all been waiting for your chance to knock that silly grin off his muddy face."

Rayah didn't think this was a good idea. She watched as Kaled jokingly flicked mud onto his sister for that last comment she made. "I rather not," she said in another attempt to buck this off to someone else.

"If you're that worried about the mud, he can take off his shirt. Go ahead, Kal; take it off and get ready to fight," said Bo.

Rayah could tell that Bo had a slight smile on his face; it appeared that everyone wanted to see her squirm. Kaled took off his shirt. Sunlight poured through the trees at the edge of the shaded field, giving a hypnotic glow to the cerulean skin of his lean, muscular body. Removing the shirt was definitely a bad idea. Rayah tried to unglue her eyes from his torso. She began to sweat, and her breathing quickened slightly as he approached her.

"Sorry," he said. "I promise I didn't ask my sister to do that."

Rayah was too focused on his body to register what he had said, and she had suddenly gone thirsty. Regardless of how she felt, though, she was determined not to let him win. If the group wanted a fight, then she'd give them a fight. She looked into Kaled's light green eyes and smiled at the thought of pinning him to the ground. "Give it your best shot, Captain Behr."

Bo gave the signal, and it was Kaled who attempted to strike first. His hand sliced through the air and came within inches of hitting her face before she blocked it with her forearm and ducked to land a kick to his thigh. He fell backward, but quickly sprang back just in time to jab toward her abdomen, which she barely escaped by taking a swift step backward. She smiled for a half second, just enough to egg him on. He grinned back and came charging at her. His hands wrapped tightly around her neck, and Rayah instantly spun free by twisting his wrists. She kicked high, but he caught her foot and she fell on her back. She writhed, doing her best to prevent him from pinning her down, but each time she tried to get up, he stopped it with the forward pressure he applied to her.

"After this," whispered Kaled in Rayah's ear, "I'll teach you how to get up when an attacker has you down. But for now," he added with a sinister grin, "you're all mine, Captain Jur."

Kaled had Rayah completely pinned to the ground; his hands gripped hers as he forced her into submission. She wanted to knock that cocky grin off his face, but couldn't help enjoying the view of his taut muscular arms as he worked to keep her from counteracting his advances. She'd seen him in this position before, shirtless and sweating above her, and the memory fogged her brain.

She was momentarily transported to a time and place where she was really his. Rayah lost herself in his eyes and gripped both his shoulders exactly like she had done countless times before in private under entirely different circumstances. She closed her eyes for a fraction of a second and imagined his lips on hers, quivering at the thought.

CHAPTER 21

Kaled

Kaled was dying to kiss her. He knew he had seen that exact look in her eyes before; they beckoned him to dive deep into his desires and allow himself to feel the very thing he had been trying in vain to extinguish within him for months.

"Okay," called Aymes from a few feet away, "let's go ahead and conclude our lesson for today. Come on, kids; nothing to see here."

As soon as Rayah heard Aymes' voice, she seemed to break out of a spell. Her eyes refocused, and she quickly tapped Kaled on the arm. "Get off. Excuse me," she said, not facing any of the amused-looking Elite soldiers. "I need to grab a drink of water."

Had Kaled known that her water bottle was stored near a tree, he might not have followed her as she walked briskly away, but he knew he felt something and had to follow his gut even if it backfired.

"Rayah, hold on," called Kaled as he tried to catch up to her. She didn't stop, so when he got close, he reached for her hand. When she finally did face him, he could see that her eyes were wet and red as if she had just been crying. "What was that?" he asked quietly, hoping against all hope that she would kiss him.

"Nothing," she replied. "Please let me go."

With his free hand, he wiped a tear from her eyes.

He moved closer until they were barely an inch apart. His hands cradled her face. "Talk to me," he pleaded in a whisper.

She hesitated. "There's nothing to discuss." The sadness in her tone wrapped its fingers around his heart. Rayah cupped his hand before gently breaking away from him. It was as if she had not wanted to leave, but felt compelled to do so at the same time. He continued after her as she turned to walk away.

"There's loads to discuss!" He could feel himself at the brink of yelling, demanding an answer because he couldn't help how in-the-dark he felt. "Don't deny there was something there. I saw it in your eyes, Rayah. For a moment, I thought you were going to kiss me. Tell me you felt something. Anything."

Kaled had suspected for some time that Rayah felt more than she led on. The stolen glances they'd shared throughout the previous weeks reminded him of the innocent crush they'd had before they first started dating years ago: friends, longing for more, and on the brink of something beautiful. Unfortunately for him, she knew how to guard her feelings better than he ever could. He feared she would walk away without giving him a straightforward answer.

"Kal, you know full well that I don't see you that way now. I can't. Not after what happened between us." She might have been better at hiding her emotions, but couldn't conceal her lip quivering.

There. He had his answer. "Don't lie to me, Rayah. I know what I saw," pleaded Kaled.

"What you saw earlier was just your imagination. Please try to understand that you and I can never happen again. There's nothing there."

"Oh," Kaled said quietly. His heart shattered. He couldn't help the way his lip trembled, or how his eyes stung as the realization dawned on him; his overactive imagination had conjured up a vision of his heart's greatest desire. How could he be so stupid?

"Wow. That looked...so real." He sighed, hung his head low and turned to walk away. Sooner or later his mind would need to discern dream versus reality because finding out like this, from her lips, was far too painful an experience.

"I'm sorry, Kal. Truly, I am." Rayah's words came in a whisper so low it could have been the murmuring of the wind itself.

"It's fine," he muttered. Shouldn't he be used to this feeling of devastation by now?

Kaled needed to leave before he could no longer hold back the waterfall of tears that threatened to burst out of him. He took a sharp right out of the training grounds and toward the lake. That trail had always been a popular place for soldiers to exercise, and Kaled spotted dozens of people jogging around the perimeter of the water or resting under large shade trees to escape the sweltering heat. Kaled sat on the grass near the lake's sandy shore, grabbing handfuls of sand and letting them trickle out of his fingers while he stared out at the crystalline, tranquil water. Overhead, a large bird with a bill that looked like a sword came barreling down at lightning speed, spearing a fish in one attempt.

Finally alone, he didn't try to stop the tears that streamed down his cheeks relentlessly. Every time he wiped his face, it was wet again almost instantly. In the past, moments of weakness like this would have made him crave the taste of alcohol, and Kaled found himself surprised to note that the craving was absent. No desire other than peace and quiet stirred within him. He could not believe his lapse in judgment and discarded any hope that Rayah may have been lying. She felt nothing romantic toward him. Nothing.

Kaled sensed a shadow out of the corner of his eye and knew instantly that Rayah had followed him to this spot. Couldn't she just leave him alone? He couldn't let her see him in this emotional state.

"I don't want to leave things like this between us," said Rayah.

Rayah's voice sounded fragile, as if *she* were the one on the brink of falling apart. Kaled didn't want to see her. A cacophony of conflicting feelings surged within him, as part of him felt heartbroken and needed a moment of reprieve while the other part held only anger and confusion.

"Kal," Rayah attempted again, "I'm sorry if I led you on."

"There's nothing to apologize for," he said without looking up, wiping his moist face impatiently. "I misinterpreted what I saw. I should have known better." Kaled could feel the nerve endings on the palms of his hands aching to reach out and hold her, but that was a sensation they would need to get used to. His hands would ache for the rest of his life and they would never know the warmth of her skin against his again.

"I feel terrible," continued Rayah. "Is there anything I can do to –"

"Actually," cut in Kaled as he stood up and wiped his hands on his pants, "there is something. Please, do yourself and the rest of us a favor and stop dating Guyad."

Perhaps the disgust in his voice came through, because Rayah looked wounded. "Who I date has absolutely nothing to do with you."

"Look, I know it's not my place to talk about who you date. I get it. But do you honestly have to date *that* guy? Rayah, you're too good for him. He's been cheating on you since day one, and if you can't see that –"

"Please, quiet down before you make a scene," she warned.

He turned to face her, his eyes pleading for her to listen to reason. "I can't just stand by and watch history repeat itself. You're one of my best friends, Rayah, and I don't want to see you get hurt again!" Kaled's loud voice caught the attention of a group of soldiers running nearby.

"I don't know what you're talking about. Everything between him and me is fine. You're letting your feelings for me cloud your judgment," Rayah said delicately.

"Maybe I am," Kaled agreed bitterly. "It's like Sy all over again, isn't it? You've dated Guyad for a few months, and here I am again, the biggest fool trying to intervene. Earlier, when we were sparring, I thought…"

He stopped; he couldn't bring himself to repeat it. He already felt like an idiot and didn't need to add more attention to his foolish heart. "I know I'm out of the picture. It's not about me anymore. But Guyad? Really? He's such a low –"

"Kal, seriously, you need to quiet down," she warned him again.

"I can't, I just –"

Rayah yanked his hand hard and pulled him into the nearest empty room, which turned out to be a small supply closet loaded with military grade non-perishable foods.

"You're going to blow my cover," she hissed.

"What are you talking about?" asked Kaled, completely stunned by her remark.

"I've been spying on Guyad. Seriously, Kal. Do you honestly think I would date that arrogant ass if I didn't have a perfectly good reason?"

"Wait...what? I'm lost. I saw you the night we first arrived at the palace. You couldn't take your eyes off of him."

Rayah nodded a concession. "Yes, "I'll admit, I was attracted to him when we first met. But it didn't take long for me to realize what a sleaze-ball he is. After that, I tried to keep things friendly."

"That's quite the definition for friendly," he quipped in disbelief.

She ignored him. "Then one day he came to me asking a lot of questions about the queen. It was the same day you walked in on us dancing in the medical bay."

Kaled remembered that day in painfully explicit detail. He nodded stupidly, trying to understand why the woman he loved was dating a guy for some reason that still didn't make sense.

"After that meeting, I asked my brother and General Peterson to stay behind, so I could talk to them about what Guyad had said. That's when General Peterson said we should keep an eye on him. It started that way. The first night I was out with him at Yemley's was nothing more than two friends getting together, but the more suspicious I got, the more I felt I had to change my tactics to gather more intel. So after a while I decided to start dating him."

"It's been months," Kaled said at last.

"Yes, I'm quite aware." He could hear the strain in her voice.

"You've dated a guy you don't like for five months. How do you even do that?" The revulsion in Kaled's voice came out loud and clear.

"Easy: you fake it. I tried telling you this before your birthday, but I didn't get the chance. Plus, it hasn't been five months; it's been more like two."

She spoke so matter-of-factly, as if her lips, her touch, meant nothing and could be squandered away with just anyone for something else other than love. He couldn't comprehend how she was capable of that.

He shook his head skeptically. "It doesn't look fake to me."

Her eyes looked as if they were burning coals. She stared him down until Kaled felt the heat of her exasperation. "I never said it was easy," she replied coldly.

"Guyad is one lucky bastard if you ask me," spat Kaled.

"Good thing no one asked you," Rayah said indignantly. It seemed to him that she was just barely managing to keep her composure. Kaled could tell his words had wounded her and he regretted it instantly. "How dare you judge my motives? I'm not the one screwing around with two different people at the same time. You are such a hypocrite, Kaled."

"I'm not screwing around with anyone, let alone two people at the same time."

"Why are you denying it?" she pressed. "I saw you with Corporal Tivor and then Veeta, or whatever her name is, a few weeks later. One woman is never enough for you. You always want more. There's no reason to hide the truth. I'm not your girlfriend, it's not like you are going to hurt *my* feelings with your infidelity."

Her accusations stung him. She still thought him capable of such heinous acts. Kaled had grown during their two-year time apart, but she had not been around to see his true repentance for his previous transgressions.

"I broke things off with Vellah over five months ago," Kaled told her, "the same night I saw you with Guyad at Yemley's. And as far as Corporal Tivor is concerned, yes, I was at her place to get laid. But I didn't go through with it. I didn't even kiss her. You can ask her yourself if you want. I've been single and celibate for the last five months. Believe it or not, I've learned a bit of self-control in the last few years."

The news must have surprised Rayah, because she stood silently for a second, her eyes searching for proof. "Five months? That can't be right. Vellah was in your apartment a few weeks ago. I explicitly remember her saying she left her makeup purse in your *bedroom*. She was going on about the romantic dinner and carriage ride you set up."

"Did you also happen to see the gold wedding earring she wore?

Rayah's jaw dropped. No sound came out of her mouth. She stared at Kaled, bewildered.

"After I broke up with her, I set her up with a buddy of mine named Zerod, who I knew she would hit it off with. Actually, you saw Zerod at the Winter Games. He and his sister hung out with Vellah and me for an hour after the competition. Vellah came to Clivesdail because she wanted a romantic setting to propose to him, and I volunteered to help plan the event. She got dressed in my bedroom the night before while I gave him a tour of the city."

Silence. Kaled could hear the occasional squawking of birds outside while Rayah stood utterly speechless. Finally, she found her voice and said, "Wow. I can't even begin to express how sorry I am for thinking –"

Kaled grunted out a sigh. "It's fine. I know my reputation ruins your image of me."

"Still, Kal, I feel horrible for accusing you. But why are you single? Kal there's no reason to –"

He cut her off again, wanting to end the conversation before she continued with her multitude of accusations and questions. "It's no secret that I'm still in love with you. I can't be in a relationship with anyone else as long as you're around. It's pitiful, I know. Can we just drop this? I'm not really in the mood to flesh out my failed relationships."

Kaled opened the door of the supply closet to let her out. Maybe she would get the hint. But no, just as Rayah was about to step over the threshold, she stopped and looked at Kaled's extended arm. She ran a finger over his tattoos.

"Is that what I think it is?" she asked, a hint of fear in her tone.

"Yes," confirmed Kaled. He let go of the door to cover his tattoos with his hand. In a perfect world, he would have shared this piece of himself when the time was right, not in a dingy supply closet, when he wasn't sure if he and Rayah were fighting or making up. Kaled was left feeling extremely exposed. "I started drinking when my father died, but it wasn't until that regrettable night in your apartment two and a half years ago that I spun out of control and became an alcoholic."

A flood of tears streamed out of Rayah's eyes, splashing onto the wooden floor. Her reaction surprised him. "Oh Kal, I didn't know. That must have been terrible." Rayah took his hand. "Had I known...I...I would have come, I..."

Why was she always so compassionate? Kaled sucked in a deep breath, fighting to control his feelings. Would she have put her ire to the side to come to his aid when he needed her the most? Two and a half years ago, she had made it clear that he was never to speak with her again. She had cut herself from his life, changed her number, and blocked him on social media. He had been too ashamed and drowning in his sorrow to reach out to her. Would she have come?

He shook his head, "You hated me, Rayah. You say you would have come, but –"

"I would have come, despite the anger I felt at the time. I couldn't just let you suffer alone, Kal. Even after all you'd done. No one deserves that..."

Kaled closed his eyes as her words washed over him. A memory flashed before his eyes: his company commander issuing an ultimatum. *You'd better shape up, Lieutenant Behr. You either get sober or you're out of the Royal Army.*

"Thank you," he said through the lump in his throat. "It was a rough year for my family. We were all still mourning my father's death. Aymes was pregnant and her boyfriend didn't stick around. Still, they tried to get me help, but I was a mess. I felt like I had lost so much and could barely keep my head above water. It wasn't until after my commander threatened to get me dishonorably discharged that I finally agreed to an intervention. Niklas was three months old when Aymes and I left for the Monktuary; we were there for two months. I've been sober since."

Kaled continued. "I never expected to see you again. I've been terrified of crashing down just like I did before." He shook his head in frustration and cursed softly. "You have no idea the misery I've been living in since we've been here. It's so hard being near you but not with you. It's like knowing I could swim up to get air but being pushed underwater each time I try to come up to the surface."

He loathed himself and hated being so vulnerable and utterly pathetic. No other woman ever got under his skin as Rayah did. She had somehow unlocked a part of him and taken a piece that made him malfunction anytime she was nearby. He was tired; if he could, he would rip out his own heart and set fire to his feelings. Let them burn down. Let it all be damned.

"I needed you," he confessed through gritted teeth. "I was lost and cast aside. But I deserved *all of it*. Sometimes I wonder if you ever truly loved me, because you moved on and I haven't. Regardless, I'm hopelessly and helplessly devoted to you. If I could turn back time, I would. I would never have kissed you, and I would have saved both of us a world of hurt."

He exhaled as the gravity of those words sunk in. As hard as it was to say, he meant it. Kaled would have preferred living a dull, gray life of no emotion at all as opposed to having true love in his grasp and then seeing it burst into flames before his eyes.

"At the very least," Kaled croaked, "I would have said my piece on that fateful night and left before I had the opportunity to mess things up. Rayah, I never intended to hurt you. All I had wanted to do was bow out of your life and let you enjoy it to the fullest."

"I know," she whispered.

Tears formed in her eyes once more. He couldn't bear to see her cry. He knew, when it came to her, that his emotions shoved him out of the way and climbed into the driver's seat. He hated that about himself, but couldn't ever force himself to be different.

He figured he had said enough. There was no point in going further. He nodded his head slowly, tried to smile, and walked toward the door. There was still one more thing to say, but this time he was a little older and a little wiser; he wouldn't turn back to face her like the last time. He would just say it and walk away, then go back to living as a mere shadow, an acquaintance in her life. He knew too well how to play that role, and he would wait patiently until this mission regarding the royal infants was complete. He could start over and try to survive in a hollow, loveless relationship with some other woman down the line.

"I got one thing right, though," he said slowly with his hand on the doorknob. "I never stopped loving you." He hung his head with a sigh; the weight of those words crushing him. "I'm thankful you've forgiven me and we're still friends, but I must confess being near you makes my life a million times harder. I'll always want you, and you will never feel the same. I wouldn't wish this crucible on my biggest enemy." He opened the door to leave.

At the last possible second, she reached for his hand. "I'm not done talking," she murmured. Tears were still wet on her cheeks, her eyes puffy.

"I don't have anything else to give or say. I'm dead inside, empty. Just let me go with the little dignity I have left, *please*." His voice was flat, almost emotionless.

A bottomless pit sank in his stomach. He had just uncovered every wound and poured salt all over them. His emotions were drained, and there was nothing he wanted more than to shove his bleeding heart further down so he could pretend once again that he was fine and could go on like this.

"No. You don't get to walk away." She closed the door and stood in front of it so that he had no choice but to face her and listen to whatever she would say. By the look of her stance, she was going to rip a whole new world of hurt into him. He barely had the strength to brace himself.

"How dare you say that I never loved you? How dare you even question that? It's insulting." She wiped a few tears angrily. "*You* broke my heart, Kaled Ryzen Behr. You cheated on me and still, even after *that* I forgave you! You were weak, and your need for physical intimacy became more important than your commitment to me. I was faithful to you, but you always chose another woman as long as they were in the same city because you couldn't handle the distance. We could have had it all, but instead, you ruined us."

Rayah began to sob as she spoke in between ragged breaths. "Every time you walked away, every time you chose to be with someone else instead of me for *convenience's* sake, it showed me that I wasn't worth the work. I wasn't worth the sacrifice. Sy, on the other hand...he was wonderful. He treated me like I truly mattered, like I was the only one in the world for him. And *then*, after you broke my heart, and I'd finally gotten to a place where it's mended, *you* came back into my life to declare your love for me."

"I know. I–"

"I'm still talking." She walked up to him, putting her index finger on his chest accusingly. "And then you do the one thing I couldn't resist. I had thought that after so long, I would be able to dismiss your touch, but apparently not." She shook her head and looked up for a moment. "As soon as you held me and kissed me, I came undone. I don't know why, but I can't say no to you." The last phrase left her lips with a tone of resentment and bitterness.

As she said it, Kaled moved closer to her and placed one hand on her waist and the other on her face. He could hear his mind screaming at him not to approach her, not to be seduced by a woman who was off-limits. *A friend. She's just a friend.* But he couldn't obey the wisdom of those words. Instead, he told himself that all he wanted was to hold and comfort her for a moment and nothing else. She closed her eyes, as if she were trying to keep her willpower while still giving in to whatever spell he had over her.

"I loved him," she shuddered.

Kaled winced; he hated hearing that. He let both hands drop by his side. Once again, he felt like a grand fool.

"He wanted the same things I did. I wanted to get married; I wanted children. You came and destroyed it all – my dream, and me.

He lowered his head and nodded in understanding. "I know. I was there," he whispered. "I'm sorry."

"And now this. You're back in my life, and we've got this strange dynamic happening all over again. Do you think this is easy on me? We used to be lovers and now we're friends trying to get over all of the trauma that's happened between the two of us. It's hard!"

"I'm sorry I destroyed everything; I wish I would have been a better man, but –"

She put her finger on his lips, and then removed it as if being burned by the heat emanating from them. He would give anything at a chance to kiss her once again. "Don't you remember the rest? Are you forgetting what happened?" She searched his eyes, and then after a moment, said, "I kissed you back."

Kaled tilted his head. He knew, or at least thought he knew, that she had kissed him back. How did any of this change what transpired?

"Dammit, Kal, don't you get it? Had I just said 'no,' you would have left, and all would have been fine. But that's not what happened. I kissed you, because when you touch me, I can't control myself. I needed you and wanted you." She bit her lip; her eyes lingered on his, and then his bare chest, for a fraction of a second too long.

Kaled could have been stupid enough to read her body language and fantasize that she was at last desiring him. But he refused to allow himself such inappropriate thoughts. He couldn't trust his perception on this whole ordeal. He longed to kiss her luscious lips, to relive a moment of passion with her, but that was his past. His future held no such prospects.

But Rayah wasn't done. "I'm angry with myself and what I abandoned by giving in to my desire for you with that kiss. I lost Sy because your touch rekindled something in me that I thought I had extinguished long ago with all the tears I had shed. And I have this burden of shame and guilt that I carry with me, everywhere I go," she whimpered.

She was visibly trying to keep herself together as her

tears fell, but Kaled could tell that she was finally letting go of something that had been weighing her down for years. He envisioned fragments of her hard exterior crashing to the ground as she unveiled her truth, and his heart broke even further than it had been. He didn't know it was possible, but here he was on the verge of unraveling even further. He had no idea how his actions had affected her. All this time, she was fighting her demons, a hardship his carelessness had caused. Kaled determined in his heart and mind to offer whatever he could to make things right by her.

"What can I do to lighten your burden, so you're free from whatever shame or guilt you carry and be healed and have a chance to pursue all you desire? I wanted marriage and children too, but without you, there's no point. Like I said earlier, I've come to terms with it."

He felt a strange transformation in himself starting to occur. Though he wanted her with every fiber in his being, he wanted her to experience happiness more than anything else. "But I'll hold your hand and do whatever it takes, whatever is in my power, to shine the little light I have left in me, onto you," he added compassionately.

He held her hand and made sure he didn't cry. He needed to be strong for her. After all he'd put her through, it was the least he could do, and besides, his feelings and personal desires mattered not. He was determined to continue burying them deeper and deeper until nothing remained in him but an empty shell.

He began speaking truth into her life, something he'd learned long ago when he tried to heal by reading the sacred religious texts. They said that speaking truth and encouragement to someone was like breathing new life into their lungs. Kaled had witnessed that himself, when Master Iyoshi had read the texts to him that night on the park bench. Maybe, just maybe, he could do the same for Rayah.

"You're a good woman. An excellent soldier. A great friend to my sister. A wonderful mentor to Evia and Ensin. Beautiful. Caring. Bold. Strong. Brave. Smart. A fantastic nurse. Compassionate. Fiercely loyal." This was too easy for him. He had spent all his adult life loving her; he had nothing but uplifting words to give.

"Whenever you need to be reminded of who you are, you can come to me, and I'll do so freely. And during the times when you don't, I'll be on the sidelines cheering you on silently."

Her head was buried in his chest, the place she'd always rested it during the days when everything was happier and simpler. He stroked the back of her neck and breathed in, trying to regulate his heartbeat and feelings. At last, he gently kissed the top of her head and smiled when she finally looked up. Her face was still wet, but she seemed at peace now, at least for the time being.

"Thank you," she said at last. "I needed that."

"Me too," he replied. She was all that he wanted. Having her in his arms, though euphoric, would do him more damage than good. He needed to leave before his brain dared to think there was hope for the two of them to get back together. Though it pained him to do so, he released her. "I should go. It's easier on me if we keep our distance."

CHAPTER 22

Rayah

"Rayah?" asked an exhausted-looking Kaled upon opening the door. He held a moaning Niklas in his arms, and puffy dark circles under Kaled's eyes revealed the saga he had endured the last two nights.

"Hi. Can I come in?"

"Sure, but um, Aymes isn't here. She and O are –"

"I'm here now, Aymes," said Rayah pointing to the wireless earbud in her ear. "Let me check Niklas out, and I'll give you a call back as soon as I can."

Rayah removed the device from her ear and placed it in a small compartment in her smartwatch. "I'm sorry for cutting you off, Kal. Your sister called me saying that Niklas is sick. How are you?"

"I'm fine, just really tired. Little man, on the other hand, is having a rough go of it."

"Hey honey," said Rayah to Niklas while she stroked his hair and gave him a quick kiss on the top of his head.

"I frowed up," said the boy with a whimper.

"Yeah, all over my shirt," added Kaled with a half-smile.

Rayah instructed Kaled to sit down on the sofa so she could examine Niklas. From her bag, she took out a set of tools and began with checking Niklas' temperature. "When was the last time you gave him a fever reducer?"

Kaled rubbed his eyes and yawned. "An hour ago."

Rayah nodded and proceeded to check Niklas's eyes, nose, and throat. Then she had Kal remove the child's diaper so she could check for a rash. As she worked on Niklas, she couldn't help but look at Kaled as well. Rayah worried he too might get sick if he didn't get sleep soon and let his body's natural defenses do their job.

"Is it cold in here, or is it just me?" asked Kaled as he put the diaper on his nephew.

Rayah was in the process of taking out a rapid Tomoq test from her satchel when Kaled had asked the question. She retrieved the thermometer and scanned his forehead. "Kal, you're burning up. I'm going to have to test you for Tomoq as well."

"Is that what you think Niklas has?"

"Yes, I think so. Niklas seems to have the trifecta. He has an ear infection, he's teething, and he might have a bad case of Tomoq brewing in his throat. Thankfully, some antibiotics and good sleep can help make our little man feel better."

Both Niklas and Kaled tested positive for Tomoq. Rayah sent the results to Dr. Kortez, and within minutes she received a notification that their prescriptions would be ready for delivery.

"I'm going to call your sister now," said Rayah, though she wasn't sure if Kaled heard her. Niklas was on Kaled's chest, fitfully sleeping while Kaled rested on the couch with his eyes closed.

"Hey Aymes, your son has Tomoq, and so does Kaled."

"Oh, no!" Aymes exclaimed. "Maybe we should cut our mini-vacation short. We're only two hours away; we can start heading home now."

"I don't think that will be necessary. I've already ordered their prescriptions, and I'll stay over so that Kaled can get some rest. He looks like a hot mess."

Still on the phone with Aymes, Rayah wandered into the kitchen and found a large box of take-out in the trash can. Likewise, every shelf in the fridge held fresh ingredients and fruits and cheeses, but no completed meals. "How's your mom?" asked Rayah as she took out a large pot and began to fill it with water.

"She's great. I just got a picture message from her. She's with your mom and dad at that beach club we used to go to back in the day."

"Oh, is that where they ran off to?" asked Rayah, amused. "Oh, wait. I just got a similar photo from my mom, except it looks like they're getting ready to go on a sunset boat tour. Oh, to be young."

Aymes laughed heartily at Rayah's remark. "Hey, thanks for coming over and taking care of them. I really appreciate it. I owe you one."

"It's my pleasure. You know I love him very much."

"Him who?" asked Aymes.

"Funny, funny," said Rayah, rolling her eyes. "I meant I love your son. Don't *you* be getting any ideas. I'll see you in two days. Send O my love."

Thirty minutes later, the doorbell rang, and Rayah signed for the prescriptions Dr. Kortez had ordered. She retrieved the syringe that came in the package, dispensed the medication, and walked over to the couch.

"Hey sweetie, I've got your meds," she said, sitting down beside Kaled.

Kaled watched as Rayah stroked Niklas' chin to wake him. As soon as Niklas opened his mouth, Rayah pushed the syringe's plunger down, quick as lightning. She felt

Kaled's eyes on her and wondered what was on his mind.

"Your turn," she said to Kaled, taking out a blister package of pills. "I assume I don't have to coax your mouth open?"

Kaled's face flushed at her comment. "I think I can manage," he said with a smile.

Rayah took out one pill from the blister and handed it to Kaled along with a cup of water. "I'm going to put Niklas to bed; I suggest you sleep as well," said Rayah as she took the young boy in her arms. "Also, don't forget to take the fever reducer. I left it on the kitchen counter."

"Thanks." Kaled got up and followed her to the bedroom. "I'll go prepare him a cup of milk."

"Maybe we can give him that later. He's still a little warm, and fever plus milk usually results in curdled vomit. But some juice would be lovely. Thanks."

"Oh," said Kaled. "I wish I would have known that before. It explains a lot. Juice it is."

Niklas' bedroom had one twin-sized bed with railings, as well as a mattress on the floor where Kaled slept. Unsurprisingly, Kaled's mattress was neatly made despite him not feeling well. A night light illuminated the ceiling with patterns of stars, faraway planets, and nebulas. Rayah put a clean pair of pajamas on Niklas and gave him the cup Kaled had offered; the young boy fell asleep within seconds.

Rayah heard the shower running as she crossed through the hallway toward the kitchen. She took off the lid from the simmering pot and stirred the contents as a wonderful aroma wafted into the air. *It's a shame*, thought Rayah, *that I can't pour some cooking wine into this stew.* Instinctively, she looked at the liquor cabinet behind her and noticed it was empty. She wondered if Kaled's recent struggle with sobriety had anything to do with that.

"What is that amazing smell?" asked Kaled as he entered the kitchen a few minutes later.

"Oh, hey. It's ensopado stew. It's actually a Susain dish, but I learned to make it when I was stationed in Benal. We would make it for the refugees and..."

The words got lost in her throat. Kaled had approached the stove and stood elbow to elbow with her. He leaned over the pot and took a whiff, an enthusiastic groan escaping his lips. Rayah caught the scent of his shampoo and was overcome with the desire to bury herself in his arms and sniff his hair.

"Can I have a bowl?" asked Kaled as his eyes drifted toward hers.

"Of course. Do you think I made this whole batch for Niklas? He eats like a bitty mouse."

They both chuckled. The atmosphere changed slightly; Rayah could feel the shift. The room grew silent. Needing some distance between them, she backed into the kitchen counter, but doing so only made it easier for her to appreciate his muscular frame. Kaled said something; she was sure of it because she saw his lips move, but her brain wouldn't translate the message. Instead, to Rayah's astonishment, he moved toward her, stopping a mere inch or two from her face. He reached into the cabinet above her and retrieved a bowl, his eyes on hers the entire time. For a fleeting moment, she thought he was going to kiss her.

"Um, let me serve you," she added quickly, taking the bowl from his hands.

Rayah could feel heat rising within her and needed to keep her mind busy before it entertained such a wild thought. She silently thanked the All Creator that Kaled was sick and contagious. Even if she wanted to kiss him, and she most definitely didn't, it could not happen. Rayah took out a ripe ginaio fruit and a glass of juice to go along with the stew.

"This is so good. I didn't notice till now how bad my throat hurt, and this hot soup is soothing the pain. I need the recipe," Kaled said as he ate.

Rayah enjoyed watching the look of joyful satisfaction on his face. "Believe it or not," she said, "there is no recipe. It's a pinch of this and pinch of that until it all comes together, as if the spirits of my ancestors are saying, *that's enough, child.* I would just have to show you."

"Deal. Hey, in all seriousness, thanks for coming. I should have called you myself, but I didn't want to bother you."

"Kal," she said softly, taking his hand, "I hope you know how important you are to me. Even though things will never be the same between us, I still care about you. And besides, I love Niklas as if he were my nephew, and who knows...maybe one day he will be." Noticing the look of shock on his face, she quickly added, "Through Ondraus, of course."

"Oh, right. Ondraus," Kaled added as an afterthought. "Still, I'm very grateful. I'm sorry if I ruined any plans you had with your boyfriend."

"My boyfriend? Really, Kal? You know that's just a technicality. I'm using him for information."

Kaled opened his mouth, but closed it quickly. Rayah was certain he had something he wanted to say, but he chose silence instead. He took another heaping spoonful of stew and ate it, closing his eyes.

"True," he said, breaking the short silence. Kaled stood up and placed his dirty dish in the dishwasher, then looked back at Rayah. "Um, maybe I should do as you suggested earlier and take that nap before Niklas wakes up."

"Good idea. I'll be here if you need me."

"Oh...you're staying over?"

"Yes. I guess I forgot to mention it to you, but I already told Aymes. I'll just sleep in her bed. Don't worry if Niklas wakes up in the middle of the night. I'll take care of him. You go sleep. You've earned it."

"Thanks. Before I go, I just want to say one more thing. You matter to me too. Thanks for being a friend, even when I'm difficult to get along with."

He ducked in as if he planned to hug her, but seemed to change his mind, waving goodbye instead. Kaled disappeared out of the kitchen and left Rayah alone with her thoughts. She poured herself a cup of coffee and sat by the large window in the kitchen. The second sun dipped toward the horizon, painting the sky in brilliant swaths of pinks and blues. The clouds, rich with color and puffy, reminded her of cotton candy. She always loved the sunsets in Brennen; they reminded her that the All Creator not only loved his people but enjoyed bestowing beauty for them to see.

An entire month had passed since Rayah and Kaled's mutual confession in that cramped supply closet. During that time, Kaled had kept away as much as possible, only nodding to her from a respectful distance. Rayah knew his actions were deliberate; he was trying to protect himself from his romantic feelings toward her. The smallest thing could shatter his resolve: a touch, an embrace, even a poorly aimed smile. Now, as Rayah sat alone in Aymes' kitchen, she couldn't stop thinking about him. She had told Kaled she didn't see him in a romantic light anymore, but was that a lie?

If he pressed his lips against hers, she didn't know if she could deny herself the short burst of bliss that would wash over her. Kaled, however, had been a complete gentleman each time he could have pressed for more. Though the thought quite obviously kept crossing his mind, he'd restrained himself in the supply closet and just now in the kitchen.

It appeared as if Kaled had done a lot of growing up without her noticing.

In an effort to protect her mind and heart, Rayah had treated Kaled like nothing more than a ghost and failed to notice how he'd evolved. Kaled, the guy who gave up a chance at true love to have a partner in bed because he could not deal with a long-distance relationship, had been single nearly the entire time they'd been at the palace. When he told her the news of his celibacy, she'd almost fainted.

She, on the other hand, was stuck in a fake relationship. With Guyad, she had no real intimacy, joy, understanding, or moments of stillness. Only the pursuit of lust existed in his hungry eyes. She'd never truly connected with her previous boyfriend, Odin; the relationship fizzled out before they could make it to the bedroom. Maybe that was why she couldn't get Kaled out of her mind; her body was screaming for affection and intimacy, and she was locking on to the familiar face that had at one time provided those things so well.

No, she had not lied to him that day in the supply closet, even though it pained her to realize that. Just as he had come to terms with the idea that nothing could ever happen between them, she had too. At the end of the day, her heart did not trust him, plain and simple. Desiring him was another matter altogether. She closed her eyes and swallowed hard; just thinking of him that way made her ache.

He'd hurt her one too many times, and it had taken ages for her to heal from each crack in her self-image. Whole years had passed when she wondered if all she meant to him was physical attraction and nothing more. Rayah's therapist had helped her come a long way, and Rayah had no intention of throwing away all of that hard work.

If Rayah had been enough for him, if she had truly been enough, he would have been able to deal with a long-distance relationship. Maybe that had caused the most pain all along. Not the night in her apartment when Sy walked in on them, but the fact that Kaled continuously devalued her by leaving her side to be with someone else who was more conveniently located. When Rayah finally found some measure of happiness, Kaled came back into her life, confessing that he'd supposedly loved her all along. He kept behaving like a child, walking away from a toy and then getting upset when someone else picked it up. Rayah was no toy.

Rayah desperately wanted to cast all the blame on him. She wanted to hurl all of her hurt on the man who had dished it out in the first place. However, to her surprise, she'd learned that she had harmed him too. The old cheerful Kaled was gone and only showed his face around Evia, Ensin, and Niklas. Her anger, disdain, and neglect had peeled away all of his beautiful complexities. The man she had fallen in love with was gone, leaving in his place a man equally as wounded as she, trying to brave the world with a straight face as if nothing was amiss.

Still, no matter how she tried, she couldn't get him out of her mind. Her nights were tortured by the thought of him lying beside her like he used to do long ago. She was desperate for his touch. If she thought that both of them could set their feelings aside and just give in to their lustful desires without anyone getting hurt again, she would do it in an instant. But that was not their reality. He wore his emotions on his sleeves, and she knew that he wouldn't be able to handle a one-night stand. His emotions, she reminded herself, were what made dating him a wonderful, unforgettable experience. He knew how to express love on a deep, passionate level that connected her soul with his. No other man she'd dated had ever been capable of that. Passion or not, he could not be trusted.

Rayah felt like she'd been given no choice but to stop loving him long ago, and had sworn to herself that she would never fall for him again. She loved him as a friend, but no more. Yes, she wanted a commitment and a forever love, but that could not happen with Kaled, at least not the version of him that always left when things turned hard. Maybe there was some hope of getting back together with him, but it would be harder than anything they'd ever done. Could they possibly be up to the task? If she came to him with this proposal, would he see the value and take her up on this outrageous idea, or would he dismiss her as he had done in the past?

Rayah finished her coffee and tried her best to push thoughts of Kaled out of her mind. Instead, she focused her attention on a medical publication that she had intended to read the previous week on her tablet. Night fell as she immersed herself in an article about new advancements in the treatment of hypothermia patients, including some intriguing approaches that could help save lives in the future.

She heard Niklas in the other room and went to check on him. The smell caught her off guard. *More vomit.* She picked him up and brought a spare pajama and diaper to the bathroom, working silently so as not to wake up Kaled, who snored lightly. As she filled the tub with warm water, she debated whether to wash the soiled linen now or wait till the morning. Rayah didn't want to run the chance of the foul smell waking Kaled, so she chose the latter.

Once Niklas was bathed, she wrapped him in a towel and took him to Aymes' bedroom, and dressed him. "I'll be right back," she whispered. Rayah crept toward Niklas' bedroom but noticed the light was already on.

"Oh Kal, I'm sorry if I woke you. I tried being quiet," she said apologetically.

"No, you're fine. I'm just a light sleeper."

"I remember," she said with a pang of longing.

"Shoot, I forgot to do the laundry. We don't have any clean linens," said Kaled after rummaging the hallway closet. "I'll run the laundry now, but Niklas won't be able to sleep in his bed in the meantime."

"That's fine. He'll just sleep with me," said Rayah as she helped Kaled start the laundry.

Once the soiled linen was in the wash, Rayah got in bed with Niklas, who whined quietly. "I want Kal-Kal," he cried.

"Kal," called Rayah, "he wants you instead. Here, let's

switch places."

Kaled entered Aymes' room and yawned. "Okay, buddy. Uncle Kal-Kal is here. Let's go night night."

"I want Aunty Ray-Ray," cried Niklas. Tears flowed from his large, tired eyes. "Peese."

"Which one do you want, honey?" asked Rayah, feeling at a loss.

"I wanna boff."

"What do you say Kal?" asked Rayah. I don't mind sharing a bed with both of you, but just want to make sure you feel comfortable with the idea.

"It's fine," replied Kaled, already getting into bed. "I'm too tired to think of a different solution."

****

Rayah felt a warmth coursing through her body like the sunlight that poured into the bedroom. She refused to open her eyes; instead, she closed them tighter and snuggled deeper into her warm blanket cocoon. With time, she became marginally more aware of her surroundings. A strong but peaceful heartbeat echoed in her ears and drowned out the hum of the air conditioner and morning songbirds. This incredible sense of security felt familiar somehow, but she couldn't place her finger on it. Finally, after much deliberation, she opened her eyes.

The vision before her was like a dream; in fact, it *had* to be a dream. Rayah had fallen asleep with her head on Kaled's chest, and his arm was wrapped protectively around her neck and shoulder. *Is this real?* She wasn't sure. If it was a dream, what harm would there be in laying here enjoying it further? If it were not a dream, however, she would need to get up immediately.

Rayah lifted her head and heard Kaled moan sleepily. His eyes flickered open, and the look of surprise on his face told her this was most certainly not a dream. Suddenly embarrassed, Rayah sat up in bed and swallowed hard.

"Kal, I'm sorry. I don't know what happened, I–"

"There's no need to apologize, Rayah," he said with a half-smile. "Do you know where Niklas is?"

Almost as if on cue, Niklas's voice came from the hallway, asking his mother for breakfast. Aymes must have cut her vacation short. Rayah and Kaled remained on the bed, frozen, neither knowing what to do next.

"Um," said Rayah warily, "I hope this doesn't make this strange between us. We can't have blurred lines if you know what I mean."

Kaled smiled kindly. "Things are already strange between us, and I suspect they always will be. You've made it *painfully* clear that you don't feel anything romantic, and we can never get back together. Last month, I went off the handle because I imagined you wanted me. Trust me when I say I don't ever want to make that mistake again. You only want friendship, but I want everything. It just is what it is."

He reached for her hand and squeezed it. "I understand you only came to nurse us back to health. You're a kind and compassionate woman, Rayah, those things are in your nature. But I also understand that after today, you'll go to work and then spend the evening with Guyad. This," he said, pointing to the bed, "was just a one-off. You'll go back to him, and I'll go back to avoiding you at all costs and loving you from afar."

"I don't like that arrangement," confessed Rayah.

The feel of his hand made her yearn for a deeper connection.

"It's the only way," he countered. "Trust me. I am constantly thinking and talking about you. I annoy myself to the fullest, and I know it annoys Aymes and Ondraus."

Rayah dropped her head, feeling defeated. Her heart and body were at a crossroads; one needed a friend while the other desired a lover. She couldn't have both, not with Kaled. "I need you in my life, not in the shadows or the sidelines. Front and center. You are a part of me, Kaled."

"And you are a part of me. But I can't. It's torture, Rayah. Please don't ask this of me. You should probably get going. I'm sure Guyad is wondering where you are and wouldn't appreciate that you and I have shared a bed."

"That would be quite hypocritical of him," said Rayah, her hand still in Kaled's. "He's been cheating on me with so many different women I've lost count."

"I don't understand him. I would do anything in my power to have you in my arms again, to kiss you, make love to you, and he, on the other hand, has you and messes around with other women. I would move mountains for a chance at you."

Rayah cocked her head, completely puzzled by Kaled's remark. "Need I remind you of your past? You cheated on me."

Kaled closed his eyes and lowered his head. "Yes, but I learned my lesson. I cheated on you when I was eighteen, but I never did it again. Not to you, not to anyone," he said with conviction.

"Please Kaled, don't lie to me. We are so past that. It's

okay. I'm not your girl anymore; you should be able to just tell me the truth."

"It is the truth," he said evenly while gazing into her eyes.

"Kal," said Rayah in a tone that sounded like a scolding, "I know for a fact that a woman was in your bedroom the night you called things off with me. Sherice. Name ring a bell? I had friends tell me she was constantly visiting your apartment."

Kaled cocked his head to the side. "I never got with Sherice until after you and I broke up." He sighed and held her hand a little tighter. "Is that what you've been thinking all this time? How could I dare cheat on you again after you graciously gave me a second chance? I know I didn't break up with you in the most honorable way, but that's because I couldn't face you."

"But–"

"Yes, she pursued me constantly. That's why she always came over. At first, it was easy to tell her to stay away, but as the months passed, I got lonely for affection and attention. My friendship with Sherice evolved into something else; I wanted sex, but I made that clear to her that it couldn't happen until after my breakup with you."

Rayah was struck dumb with this news. "All this time, I thought...I was *positive*..."

"It doesn't change anything, though, does it?" asked Kaled with a hint of hope in his tone.

At first, Rayah didn't know how to answer. She searched her heart and mind, hoping that perhaps his revelation did change things. Maybe she could allow herself to love him not only as a friend but as a man. She felt herself inching toward the edge of possibility when painful memories flooded her senses. Images of herself crying for nights on end because of the hurt he had caused made her pause.

"Maybe a little," she confessed, "but not enough."

"I figured," said Kaled. His eyes appeared glassy, and his voice strained. "I have to live with the consequences."

"For what it's worth," said Rayah, "I've missed this. Laying here talking with you, waking up in your arms...I've forgotten how warm you are."

Kaled smiled. "It could be the fever. And your hands are still freezing like always."

"I know!" she agreed. "Cold hands are not a good thing when you have to deal with patients. I don't know why they're always ice cold."

Kaled took both of her hands in his, instantly warming them. "You'll always be my ice queen."

"Kal?"

"Hmm?"

"Can you just hold me for now? I could really use a hug."

"Of course, whatever you need."

Rayah scooted toward him and laid her head on his pillow, facing him. Kaled wrapped his arm around her and rested his chin on the top of her head. All of the men Rayah had ever dated or slept with flashed before her eyes. None, she realized with a pang of longing, compared to the way Kaled held her. Everything about him just seemed right somehow: his muscular arms, the strong and fierce beating of his heart, the warmth that radiated from him, and even the way her head and body fit perfectly in his embrace. All of it made him special above all other men.

"I love you, Kaled," whispered Rayah as she breathed in the calming, masculine scent of his soap. Once again, she quietly thanked the All Creator that Kaled was sick and contagious. No kissing allowed. Having a fever, chills, and a burning throat might be worth it, though.

"I love you too, Rayah. With all of my heart."

Somewhere, in the distance, Rayah heard Kaled's name called out. Before she had the opportunity to discern the voice, the bedroom door flung open.

"Kal, breakfast is –"

"Mom!" exclaimed Kaled, shooting up in bed.

"I –" stuttered Edina, "I'm so sorry for interrupting." She closed the door immediately and hollered, "Breakfast is ready in case you two worked up an appetite."

Kaled got out of bed, his face flushed with embarrassment. "I'm sorry, Rayah. I'll be sure to let her know nothing happened. I don't want her thinking there's hope for us either. She's just as bad as I am."

Rayah simply nodded her head. Her mind swirled with many emotions, questions, and raging hormones. She tried not to pay attention to how his shirt fit perfectly across his chest, nor let herself imagine taking off the shirt for a better look. It would be best, thought Rayah, to leave without breakfast and avoid everyone's suspicious faces in the apartment. She felt the blurred lines between friendship and intimacy, which she could not allow to happen.

CHAPTER 23

Rayah

"Get up, Rayah, and fight me!" Kaled bellowed.

Sweat streamed from Rayah's forehead as she took a deep breath and got into a proper fighting stance. They had been at this for fifteen or twenty minutes, which might as well have been forever for Rayah, and her muscles screamed for a break. Rayah pushed through her exhaustion; after all, she needed this. A month ago, Kaled had bested her during hand-to-hand combat; she'd taken him up on his offer to teach her his technique. Ondraus and Aymes watched from the bleachers, each rooting for their sibling. Rayah had laughed when they told her they didn't want to miss this particular face-off.

Rayah barreled toward Kaled and swung for his face. He barely had time to block the punch before Rayah quickly jabbed him in the side of his ribs. She spun and swept her leg toward Kaled's ankle, causing him to stagger backward. With a somersault, she popped back up and launched an uppercut, catching his chin.

"Man, you are fast," said Kaled.

"I told you!" hollered Ondraus.

Kaled stomped his bare foot on the padded flooring and grinned mischievously. "What I might lack in speed, I make up for in strength. Come at me, woman; try to drop me."

Rayah brought up her right leg, pivoted with her left, and attempted to kick him hard in the head. Kaled caught her leg in mid-air and pushed her backward, causing her to fall on the floor. Instantly she rolled backward, springing to her feet once more, and struck his chest repeatedly with the heel of her hand. Kaled couldn't block every strike; her speed got the best of him. Rayah performed another leg sweep, this time, he fell onto the floor, and within a split second, she was on him.

"Finally," Rayah said breathlessly while pressing her palms against his chest to keep him pinned to the floor, "you're all mine."

Kaled arched an eyebrow.

"Get your mind out of the gutter, Captain Behr," said Rayah slapping his shoulder playfully.

"Oh, so I'm back to Captain Behr now. I see."

His eyes twinkled, and Rayah couldn't rip away from the magnetism of his gaze. The room seemed to fizzle out of existence; only she and Kaled remained. Rayah felt his hand on her waist; the sensation of his deliberate touch made her skin come alive.

"You've caught on? When you annoy me, I call you by your rank."

"Stop fraternizing with the enemy!" yelled Ondraus while Aymes cackled in delight.

"I've definitely noticed," he replied with a smile. "Perhaps there is something *you* haven't noticed."

"Oh yeah, what's that?" She asked.

Right as she finished her sentence, Kaled applied pressure on her hip and flipped her over. "Don't ever let your guard down." Kaled mounted her and gripped both of her wrists. "Buck me off!"

For the past twenty minutes, they had fought, dropping one or the other with equal success. Kaled had helped perfect her technique to prevent getting pushed to the ground, but she had so far not been able to effectively get out from under him each time. Technically speaking, she knew exactly what steps to take to get him off her; the problem was putting her plan into action. In this position, Kaled had great leverage over her. If he were a bad guy, he could easily hurt her or take advantage of her.

"Come on! Like I taught you," Kaled taunted as he continued to press his full weight into her. "Plant both feet and do the bridge."

Rayah did as he instructed; she pushed her hips up while slicing her arms down to her side. The quick movement worked! Kaled collapsed onto her, but she wasn't out of the clear just yet; his weight still pressed down on her. She wrapped her arms around his chest to prop herself up further, and then, in one fluid movement, she grabbed his arm while pivoting her hips and flipping him onto his back.

"Finish him off this time!" yelled Ondraus.

Rayah brought down her forearm and lightly struck Kaled on the face, then landed her elbow on his abdomen.

"You did it!" said Kaled while lying in his defeated position. Rayah reveled in the pride his compliment carried.

"About time," she answered with a smile. "I gotta say, the view is great from up here. I'm victorious!"

"Go ahead and enjoy the victory. Next time, I won't be offering my play-by-play instructions."

"Okay, but say that's like a month from now. It's

going to take that long for my muscles and bruises to recover."

Aymes interjected. "You see, this is why I didn't invite Niklas. Are either of you planning to get up, or should we book you a room somewhere? Actually, Ondraus, let's go ahead and give them some privacy. They look like they're about to make out." Aymes and Ondraus walked out of the training room while chuckling silently, leaving Rayah and Kaled alone.

Rayah's face became flushed. It wasn't until Aymes had mentioned it that Rayah realized she was still straddling Kaled. Now that they weren't actively fighting, it dawned on her how intimately inappropriate this may appear. Embarrassed, Rayah stood up, grabbed a bottle of water, and began drinking deeply from it.

"Ignore my sister," said Kaled as he picked up his own bottle. "She likes to instigate. She knows we're just friends, but that *clearly* doesn't stop her from trying to annoy me."

Rayah laughed uncomfortably. *Was there any truth to Aymes' comments?* If it had been any other partner, Rayah would have gotten up immediately after the training session was over.

"Are you this tough on Aymes?" Rayah asked Kaled, trying to divert the conversation.

"Yes. Turns out, Aymes and I like kicking each other's butt a little too much. Our previous duty station, Harloq, had a fort-wide competition last year, and Aymes and I finished one and two." A slight grin turned up the corner of Kaled's mouth. "I won't ask you to guess which of us was the *one*."

"Wow, good for you. I feel honored having a champion teach me."

"Ha-ha," laughed Kaled sarcastically. "But in all seriousness, though, I am happy you took me up on my offer and that you did so well. It's always good to learn new ways to defend yourself."

"Thank you. I do appreciate it," said Rayah, taking his hand. She didn't know why she had reached for Kaled's hand, but couldn't seem to bring herself to let go either.

Kaled turned toward her, a look of longing on his face. All Rayah could think about now was the taste and feel of his lips against hers. She took a step closer toward him and wrapped both her arms around the nape of his neck. He breathed in deeply, closing his eyes, but his hands remained by his sides. Rayah rested her head on his chest; she could hear his heart thundering loudly. After what felt like a lifetime, he placed his arms around her waist and pulled her closer to him. Their foreheads met, and then their noses until finally, she brushed her cheek against his. Whatever self-restraint she had practiced these last six months faded away with every heartbeat.

This is it. I can't wait any longer. Just as Rayah had finally made up her mind to kiss Kaled, her smartwatch began to buzz.

"...And that would be your boyfriend," said Kaled in a strained tone. He took several steps back; the breaking of their embrace felt like severing a part of her soul.

"Kal, it's just a technicality. He's not really my boyfriend. You know that."

"Rayah, if you are making out with him and having sex with him, he's your boyfriend."

The smartwatch continued to buzz. Kaled had already gathered his things. "It's not like that, Kal," she called out.

"I'll see you around, Rayah." Kaled had tried to smile, but it was obvious to her that he had walked away devastated...and he wasn't the only one.

****

Rayah had spent the entire day dreading her evening with Guyad. Most of the time, she wondered if being in a *relationship* with him was worth the trouble. Gleaning information from him took immense amounts of patience and cunning. Even with all the effort that Rayah had poured into her side mission, she'd fallen short on useful intel. Maybe she should just give up, she thought.

She had uncovered new information; how useful it would prove, however, remained unknown. A month ago, right after the meeting in which it was discovered that Rancor had escaped, she had met with Guyad at a hot tub to try once more to get information from him. She found out that his mother died when he was young and that his father made many stupid decisions to keep food on the table once he was left with the full responsibility of raising a son. Guyad had said he visited his father every single month for the past several years, and when she asked if he ever tired of it, had said, "He's the only family that I've got. Besides, my past is what pushed me to get into the military, and I have a pretty great life if I can say so myself."

Keeping Guyad focused on anything other than her body forced Rayah to be creative. She purposefully turned a blind eye when other women pursued him or when he'd comment, "She's cute," as they passed an attractive female followed by, "Of course I don't mind if you check her out."

For tonight's dinner, Rayah had cooked up a large steak dinner with his favorite side dishes, which she hoped would fill him up and get him in the mood to relax with a movie instead of anything else. She was wrong.

Rayah and Guyad were currently on the couch; she was straddling him, and his hands were on her thighs as he kissed her neck. Though they were both fully clothed, she felt dirty and desperately wanted to climb off. She couldn't continue with this ridiculous charade. Rayah chided herself as she allowed Guyad to touch her when all she could think about was someone else's touch: Kaled.

"You're a tease; you know that?"

"Mmhmm," she agreed, pretending to moan with pleasure as his hands continued to grope her. His clothes were thick with perfume from the last woman he'd been with, and Rayah suppressed a violent cough.

"Come on. Stop playing games, and let's take this to the bedroom." He tugged on her blouse and started to undo her buttons.

Looking for yet another excuse, she asked, "Don't you have a meeting in a few minutes? Who was it with? It's not with another woman, is it?"

He looked at her with his usual cocky but devilish grin. "Many women want me, babe, so who am I to say no?"

The fact that he didn't even bother apologizing or even hide the truth in her statement was laughable. That was how highly he thought of himself. In his mind, he was irresistible, and she should count herself lucky to be the object of his lustful pursuit. Although Rayah found this sort of behavior and way of thinking detestable, that didn't necessarily make him guilty of treason. For the safety of the royal infants, she pressed on and remained unfazed while she ran her fingers through his hair, hoping he would give her a straight answer. She arched an eyebrow.

"I'm meeting with a buddy of mine, a *dude*, and we're just gonna get drinks and catch up at Yemley's shop."

"Yemley's Yummylicious Shoppe," she corrected.

"You're Yummylicious," he added with a hungry smile.

Rayah stood up but gave him an encouraging grin. "All this kissing is making me thirsty. I'll be right back."

"No matter what I do, I can't seduce you," he said, both annoyed and intrigued.

"I think you like the challenge," she called out from the kitchen with as much flirtation as she could muster. In truth, she was growing very tired of this game.

"That might be the case, but I'm starting to lose my patience."

She stood in the kitchen and looked around for a bottle opener; she desperately needed some *liquid encouragement* to deal with this guy. When she opened his utility drawer, she noticed a wrinkled piece of paper that she had first seen nearly six months before. Her hand shook as she picked it up and glanced at the note, afraid of what it might say. There was no denying it was the very same piece of paper General Peterson had read from on the first night he had invited them to the palace months ago. On that night, General Peterson had revealed the Kortez twins' story and the eerie chant they'd repeated time and time again while in a coma in the medical ward.

"What are you reading?" asked Guyad, confused as he stood in the kitchen's threshold.

"I don't know; you tell me." She did her best to keep her voice curious and free from accusation.

He took the piece of paper from her and read it. "That's a strange thing to write. Where did you get that? From one of those new books you've been reading lately?"

She looked at him in bewilderment. He seemed confused about the paper, as if he genuinely had no idea where it had come from. Guyad was many things, but a good actor was not one of them. Unfortunately for him, he had no roommate, so he was almost certainly the only one who would have put this paper in his kitchen drawer. She took the paper back from him.

"Who exactly are you meeting with later?" she asked.

"A friend of mine. I thought I told you."

"No. I meant a name."

"What, are you jealous?"

She took in a deep breath, placed her hands on both of his shoulders, and gripped them tightly. Of course, the moron thought she was ready to go to bed with him, when in reality she was screaming on the inside, yelling, *Wake up! Lives are at stake. Tell me what you know before it's too late.* His ability to remain focused on getting in between the sheets with her was unparalleled.

"Maybe I should go with you to this meeting," said Rayah. As much as she hated herself for doing it, she pulled him closer to her and bit her lip, trying to seduce him. "After that, you and I can spend some time together in your bedroom. You're right; I'm getting tired of making you wait."

"Finally," he said as he leaned in to kiss her parted lips. He thrust his pelvis hard against hers with her back against the kitchen counter. Yet as he was about to kiss her, his eyes changed dramatically. They went from that euphoric look at the prospect of intimacy to a blank, dead stare that somehow was also filled with pure evil. He gripped her hand hard, like a vice. "Who are you?" he asked in a voice that was definitely not Guyad's.

"Babe?" she said, trying to remain calm and in control, although she was terrified.

O, you better get in here! I need help, now! she screamed through duo-com.

Are you hurt? Where are you? I'm at Aymes' place.

I'm in Guyad's apartment. Send the closest person here now; the pin code is 5378. Tell them to come armed and with a tranquilizer hypo-spray. Now!

Her head was full of every curse word she knew. What had she gotten herself into? How was she going to fend off this massive man on her own without trying to kill him? And what had happened, anyway? It sounded like he'd been taken over somehow, or maybe he had some kind of mental disorder, split personalities or –

"I said, who are you? Where did you get that?" Guyad ripped the piece of paper from her hand. "You've been trying to get to him, haven't you? Well, it's too late!" He picked her up easily and threw her across the small kitchen, her body slamming hard against the wall. Rayah's head instantly throbbed, and she felt a trickle of blood running down her hair. She knew her brother had felt her reaction, and even now, Ondraus was screaming through duo-com, demanding details and telling her someone was on the way.

"Who are you?" repeated the strange voice as Guyad ran toward her in an attempt to attack her once more.

Rayah sprang up in time to get out of the way as he barreled right past her and collided with the wall. She dropped into a defensive stance, ready for his incoming assault, then blocked blow after attempted blow with her forearms as he kept coming at her. She punched him in the stomach, and when he faltered in pain, she landed a hard kick to his head.

The kick must not have been hard enough, though, because he lurched forward and reached for her throat. Quickly, Rayah lowered her chin so that her neck wasn't as exposed, then reached over his extended hands and grabbed one of his wrists. With the heel of her free hand, she thrust toward his nose and simultaneously kneed his groin. She heard the sickening crunch of his nose and tried to run out of the kitchen, but he grabbed her hair from behind.

Rayah fell to the floor, scrambling to sit up. Guyad hovered over her, the weight of his body making it impossible for her to get on her feet. Her mind raced as it went through the catalog of self-defense moves and landed on the one Kaled had recently taught her. In one motion, she planted one hand firmly on the floor beside her, placed a stiff arm on his chest, her left foot outside of his leg, her right foot behind her, and sprang to her feet. Her body ached from the strain, and help was yet to arrive. If she were going to survive her encounter with a deranged Guyad, she would have to push through the pain and the anxiety in her mind. She punched him again in the nose.

"You bitch," grunted Guyad. He charged at her and slammed Rayah against the wall again, the force of which almost knocked her out. As her eyes blinked back to refocus, she noticed his massive hands coming toward her neck once more. Rayah tried to block him, but it was too late. He had grabbed hold of her with a vise-like grip. She tried in vain to loosen his grasp on her throat, but she was losing oxygen and lacked the strength to do anything.

Mercifully, the apartment door swung open with a loud crash, and in rushed Kaled, pointing a Nemi straight at Guyad's chest.

Tell him to put it on stun mode, she told her brother through duo-com, hoping that Ondraus would relay the message to Aymes, and somehow, she would pass the message on to Kaled on time. She had tried to say it out loud herself but found it impossible to speak. She felt sure that Guyad was moments away from crushing her windpipe.

"No way," grunted Kaled defiantly.

As soon as Kaled spoke, Guyad looked behind him and, in doing so, accidentally loosened his grip on Rayah's throat.

"Trust me, Kal," she pleaded hoarsely, wrenching Guyad away from her and landing a hard punch in his chest, which only made him go off balance for a fraction of a second before he charged at her again.

Kaled fired, and the Nemi's energy beam created an orb around Guyad's chest. Instantly Guyad went down. Rayah rushed to him and grasped the collar of his shirt menacingly.

"Who are you? What have you done with Guyad?" she yelled. In a fraction of a second, Kaled was beside her, his weapon still pointed at Guyad's chest in case he got up.

"I'm your biggest nightmare, and you won't live to tell the tale," spat Guyad in an eerie, evil voice. His eyes weren't their usual dark purple; instead, they appeared light gray, cold, and full of malice. The hatred this man emitted with just his eyes was enough to make Rayah shudder. She would do everything in her power to make sure he couldn't deliver on his threat.

"How are you controlling him? Let him go!"

The man that embodied Guyad laughed in a way that appeared as if venom were coming out of his sick mouth. "Over *his* dead body."

Suddenly, Guyad's eyes went back to a dark purple, and he gasped. "Rayah, I can't fight him! It's Rancor!"

This moment of seizing back control – if that was what had happened – instantly took its toll on Guyad. His eyes were fully dilated, and he looked exhausted as if he'd been struggling with all his might against Rancor. "He's trying to kill the babies; we have to stop him!" pleaded Guyad.

"Should I shoot him?" asked Kaled, not sure how to handle what he was witnessing.

"He's..." Guyad was losing his battle with Rancor. His eyes were flickering open and closed as the battle within him raged. "He's projecting, he –"

His eyes changed again, and instantly he cocked his head back and head-butted Rayah, using the opportunity to get up and go for Kaled instead. Guyad knocked the Nemi out of Kaled's hands and then attempted to punch him in the stomach, but Kaled slid out of the way in time. Both men dived for the weapon while Rayah ran to her purse to get her electronic cuffs.

In the short time it took her to retrieve them, Kaled had put Guyad in a headlock, compressing his arms down as hard as he could, but Guyad fought back and would soon overpower Kaled.

"Where's the hypo-spray?" demanded Rayah.

"Left front pocket," Kaled said, gesturing to his pants with his head.

Of course, it is, she said to herself. She reached into his pocket and saw that Kaled cast his eyes to the ceiling while she did so. She grasped the spray, pressing the device against Guyad's neck. Instantly Guyad crumpled to the ground. Rayah and Kaled both bent down; he moved Guyad's body face down, and she engaged the electronic cuffs and put them on Guyad's wrists. As soon as she was done, she took a few steps back. When she did, everything that had happened in just a matter of minutes bombarded her senses, and she let out a sob.

Kaled rushed to her with an urgent look of concern in his eyes. "You're bleeding," he said as he gently placed his hands on hers. "I'm sorry, I tried to get here as fast as I could, but –"

"You came; that's all that matters now," she croaked back. She was utterly spent, her body weak. She'd been dancing near fire for so long, trying to draw information from Guyad, and she'd so nearly been burned.

"Of course, I came. How couldn't I?" He pulled her in close and hugged her. She kissed him on his cheek, then buried her head in his chest to hide in the warmth of his embrace and lose herself in the steady beating of his heart.

CHAPTER 24

Rayah

The unlocked door swung open and Tru and Tye Ryder came bursting in with their Nemis drawn. Once they saw Kaled and Rayah embracing and Guyad handcuffed and unconscious on the floor, they turned off their Nemis and walked over to their friends.

Rayah kissed Kaled on the cheek again and said, "Thank you," and then broke free from his embrace to quickly tell Tye and Tru what had occurred. "Do you have something that can scan to see if he has a device on him or something? How is he being controlled?"

"I might have something, but it's in our I.T. office," said Tye. "In the meantime, let me call in the ambulance to get him taken to the medical ward, and we'll look at him there. Your brother called; he's still several minutes out."

Rayah shook her head. "I need security guards all over Guyad. We can't risk him getting loose and going anywhere near the babies. Whatever he has in mind, he was willing to kill Kal and me both to carry out his plan. Tell General Peterson and the rest of The Elite to meet us in the conference room; we have much to discuss."

A few minutes after arriving at the palace, Ondraus and Aymes ran into the medical ward, and they both rushed toward Rayah. Ondraus took his sister's head, cupped it gently, kissed her on the top of her head, and then wrapped her in a massive hug. Then he turned his attention on Kaled and hugged him too as he said, "Thank you for getting there on time." She didn't often see her brother this way; fear had not yet erased itself from his face.

"Has the doctor seen your head yet?" he asked. "I felt all of it, and I think you might have a concussion." She could tell her brother was still spooked.

"I'm fine," she assured him, "and yes, Birchram just used the dermal healer on me, and I'm as good as new aside from the throbbing headache. He's gonna check me for a concussion in a few minutes."

After the medical exam, she and the rest of The Elite met in the conference room. General Peterson entered a few moments later after ensuring that Guyad was well guarded and handcuffed to the bed's railing. He walked directly to her and said, "You gave us quite the scare, soldier. Thanks to the All Creator that you are safe." He clapped her on the shoulder and then looked at the room of soldiers that were standing before him.

"A few months ago," began General Peterson, "Captain Rayah Jur had an encounter with Sergeant Guyad Lurca that had left her uneasy as to his loyalty to the crown. She met with her brother and me, and we discussed the issue and decided that keeping an eye on Sergeant Lurca would be best. Well, tonight, it seems that she was able to find valuable information, which resulted in a dangerous altercation. Captain Jur, please fill the group in with your findings."

Rayah provided a quick summary of everything. She told them why she began dating Guyad and how she found out he visited his father once a month in jail, and earlier that night, she discovered it was the same prison where Rancor had been serving his sentence before he escaped. She described his countless headaches and times that periods of his day were forgotten blurs and had even had Dr. Kortez check him out, but the results had been inconclusive. Finally, she told them all that Guyad had made an appointment to meet up with someone at Yemley's Shoppe for drinks, but that he wouldn't share the name of his contact.

"Whatever is going to happen," she concluded, "is going to happen soon. I think we need to be on high alert, and we need to find out what is going on with Sergeant Lurca and how he is being manipulated. Whenever he comes to, he has to fight to stay in control, and he's losing that battle."

After the meeting, General Peterson left and told his son, Captain Yosef Peterson, to start briefing all of the palace guards to be at maximum alertness until further notice. The Ryder twins went to the medical ward to scan Guyad for any devices that might have been manipulating him. Lina called Yemley's Yummylicious Shoppe to see if there had been anyone waiting at the shop for a while in an attempt to meet up with Guyad. Bo contacted the prison to see if they could talk to Guyad's father. Ameena and Wilstead went back to the barracks to grab everyone's go-bags and any other necessities, since the group had now been tasked with staying at the palace barracks. Ondraus and Aymes went to visit Evia, Ensin, and their parents to let them know what happened and to be on the alert, and to make sure their phones were on at all times.

Upon Ondraus' repeated requests through duo-com, Rayah went back to the medical ward so that Birchram could continue to use the dermal healer on all of the bruises that were starting to show on her neck and wrists. Unfortunately, both Birchram and the doctor were busy with Guyad, who was beginning to wake up and became increasingly violent.

"Here, let me," said Kaled with his hand out.

Rayah passed him the dermal healer and walked up close to him, lifting her head slightly so that their eyes met while he gently ran the device up and down her neck. His free hand rested on her hip as he continued to slowly, gently take his time with her. The way he held her and watched her at this moment was such a strong contrast compared to how other guys had ever held her. Kaled's tender touch reminded her of the friendship and bond they'd shared. Rayah desperately wanted to trust him with her heart again.

"I found something," said Tye after his scanner began making a loud, repetitive beeping sound. "It's in his eye, but I can barely see it."

Rayah and Kaled approached the bed where the Ryder twins, Birchram, and the doctor were standing.

Guyad began to laugh hysterically, "if you pull out our connection, you kill him, and I'll still be free to roam and destroy all that you hold dear. I am everywhere."

"What if he's telling the truth?" asked Tye.

"I've never encountered anything like this before," said the doctor, perplexed.

"I have," announced Kaled. "I've been doing a lot of reading in my free time." he glanced at Rayah. Immediately she inferred that he had meant that it was yet another hobby he'd picked up to get his mind off her. "And yes, I've seen this technology exists; it was in an issue of the Brennen Technology Insider. But it's supposed to still be in the testing phase, and it's not for public use. Whoever got their hands on this must have stolen it or paid lots of money; this was no easy, one-person, inside job."

"Very good," said Rancor in Guyad's body.

"I need to talk to Guyad; how can we make that happen? We need to find out what he knows," said Rayah to the group.

"When I stunned him with the Nemi, he came to for about a minute. Should we try that again?" asked Kaled.

They all agreed and took a step back while Kaled aimed the small handheld weapon at Guyad's chest and pulled the trigger. Instantly, Guyad took in a deep breath, as if he had resurfaced from being underwater for too long. He looked frantically at Rayah.

"It was supposed to be tonight. I've been trying to fight him all along, but I'm not aware of anything when I come out from his control. There's an accomplice; I don't remember who. The details are blurry, but he plans to destroy the babies so that he can rise to power. He's not here; he's hidden somewhere. If you encounter him, you won't survive; he's a projection. Please, take the device out! I can't have him keep using me like this!" He had spoken in a hurried slur to get everything out before Rancor took over again.

"You might die," said Rayah. "I'm not sure it won't kill you."

"He's already killed me. I've been doing things with my hands but not with my mind. He's destroyed everything I hold dear – my country, my king. Don't allow him to take away my honor. I can feel his rage and persistence. If you let him stay inside of me, he will break me free and kill you all the first chance he gets." It was roughly sixty seconds before his eyes turned gray and evil again. The man who had been pleading for the safety of the crown and his honor had left.

"That was wild," said Tru, stepping back as Rancor had started to thrash against his cuffs.

Guyad's warning was proven correct almost immediately. Rancor had full control of Guyad's body, evident by the blood trickling from his wrists as he continued to attempt to release himself from the bed.

Bo and Lina walked into the medical ward. They informed the group that Guyad's dad died a little under a month ago. For some reason, Guyad hadn't attended the funeral. Lina reported her findings: no one had sat alone at Yemley's the entire night, and since it was so late, there weren't that many people in the shop in the first place.

A call to General Peterson concluded that he did not want to disengage the probe in Guyad's eye for the time being. They would keep him in a medically induced coma until they could explore other opportunities. One by one, The Elite dispersed and made their way to their new sleeping accommodations inside the palace, which comprised two rooms, one for the men and one for the women. Rayah looked forward to sharing a room with Aymes for a change. She had roomed with Tru this whole time while Lina and Ameena had lived together from the get-go. But as everyone bade their goodnights, she pulled Kaled to the side and asked if she could speak with him privately.

"You're not going to lock me up in a supply closet, are you?" he asked jokingly as they walked outside toward the palace garden.

"Don't tempt me," she teased.

The twinkling lights throughout the garden gave the place a magical ambiance. Rayah could smell the flowers' delicate scent as she and Kaled continued to walk closely together. They found a marble bench, and she asked him to sit with her for a while. The two of them grew quiet, but she took his hand in hers and squeezed it as she looked out at the trees, whose branches swayed gently with the night summer breeze. Rayah was contemplating whether or not to tell him how she felt and what she wanted.

A month ago, he'd left her wanting more as he walked out of the supply closet, and she had barely been able to think of anything else since then. In fact, she had secretly wanted him for several months, but hadn't given serious thought to pursuing her passions because she felt it would only lead to another heartbreak. Was he more than just an irresistible itch she needed to scratch? She didn't want to embark on a purely physical journey with him; she could do that with anybody, and had proved it to herself while dating Guyad. If all she wanted was sex, she'd had plentiful opportunities with a willing partner who was arguably the most handsome man in the palace.

It was clear to her that she wanted more than just sex; she wanted *forever*. For years, she'd tried to convince herself that she didn't believe in true love, that there was no such thing as meant-to-be. Maybe true love didn't exist, but Rayah was sure of one thing: she wanted a guy who valued her for more than just her body. She needed someone she could trust, who would cherish her and stay even when things got hard. It appeared that Kaled has done a lot of growing up lately, but was it enough for her to get over her reservations and attempt a fresh start with him?

"Wow, you did it," he said, without as much enthusiasm as she had expected. "You were able to get vital intel. Good job. Hey...I'm sorry for leaving after our training session yesterday. I, um, didn't want to intrude while you were on your phone call."

"Thanks," she said quietly. "I feel that I owe you an explanation about my relationship with Guyad."

"No, please don't. It's not necessary. I can picture it just fine, thank you."

"He and I never did anything other than kiss," she said gently.

"Don't take this the wrong way, but how is that remotely possible?" asked Kaled while looking her up and down, taking in her body with his eyes.

"I was very strategic," she replied with a half-smile.

"Thank you for telling me. I appreciate it." He exhaled slowly. "It was driving me mad."

"I also owe you a big apology."

"For what?"

She gave a one-note laugh and shook her head. "You're sweet. I owe you an apology for everything. I spent so many years mad at you; I didn't realize I was equally at fault. So much time was wasted on hating myself and carrying my pain and hurt that I didn't even think about yours, nor did I care. I was wicked, and it was unfair to you. I had no right to treat you the way I did." She could feel her eyes getting misty. "I'm so sorry, Kal."

He wiped a tear from her face. "It's okay, Sunshine."

"Mmm," she hummed while resting her head on his chest. "I haven't heard that in forever." She fell silent for a while and then whispered, "I've missed you terribly."

"Me too," he added as he kissed the top of her head.

They sat there, quiet in each other's arms for a full minute, before she stood and pulled him up by the hand. She placed one of her palms on his chest and breathed in deeply. He lowered his head and brushed his lips against hers for a fraction of a tantalizing second. "I want you," she said finally.

He needed no further invitation. He gripped her waist with both of his hands, pulled her closer, and started kissing her neck. Feeling him against her body, she began to discard her radical thoughts of testing him with her abstinence. His lips had a way of undoing her resolve; his desire for her was intoxicating, and all she wanted to do was give into those sensual advances and have her way with him.

At long last, their lips met. All their years of separation vanished instantly; it felt as magical as their first kiss. The experience was surreal; she had *never* imagined nestling against him again. She could feel electric energy passing from his lips to hers, and the floor underneath her seemed to disappear. As he devoured her, he lifted her off her feet, and she wrapped her legs around his waist. She ran her fingers through his hair but kept her lips on his. It had started as a slow, gentle kiss, but it had quickly become the type of kiss that turned up the heat. Rayah let him lead, allowing him the time to savor every succulent moment. She bit his lip playfully and then closed her eyes as his hands gripped her tighter, and his lips traveled down her neck, the whiskers of his facial stubble giving her goosebumps as he nuzzled her.

Kaled walked quickly, a man on a mission, to the gardener's cramped utility closet and wrenched the door open with one hand as he ran his other hand up and down her torso. He closed the door impatiently and leaned her back against the wall inside the small room.

"Let me love you," he replied.

"Mmm," Rayah purred. Her mind and heart were at a crossroads. With every kiss he lay upon her, she could feel the walls in her resolute mind come crashing down; the wave of emotions that had been pent up for the past few months rushed at her, demanding release. She could feel his desire for her like hot coals on her skin; how could she possibly say no to him? She loved him and didn't want him just for now, but forever. Their hearts still required a lot of mending if they were going to make things work. She was convinced now more than ever that she had to press pause.

"If I do this tonight," she said breathlessly, "it'll only be a momentary night of pleasure."

This made him stop. His hands were no longer groping her curves. He eased her to her feet but kept his arms around her waist, swallowing hard.

"Oh. I'm not sure if I'm okay with that," Kaled whispered sadly.

She pulled away slightly from him so she could see him better. "Neither am I. I want all of you, Kaled, not just your touch. I'm afraid that if we have sex now, it might ruin things. We've spent so much time apart that I barely know you anymore."

Kaled nodded. He gazed into her eyes and said, "I'm the same man you fell in love with...just a little broken."

"We're both broken, Kal," said Rayah. "I'm still carrying a lot of my insecurities and trying to work on my self-image. I've been seeing a counselor for the last several months. Two broken people shouldn't jump into a relationship."

"So what does this mean?" he asked.

"I guess what I'm saying is that we need to start over. Our friendship has to go back to being deep and genuine, although I feel we've been trending down that path already. We need to talk, laugh together, work together, heal together. We need to date the way we did back at the Academy...back when we were innocent."

"Babe, we lost our innocence long ago," he said with a smirk, his arms still wrapped around her, making it hard for her to think straight.

His remark made her laugh, and she hit him playfully on the shoulder. "Date me," she said. "Date me without us having to retreat to the bedroom. I need to get to know you again. My heart needs to learn to trust you again. When the time is right, I'll be fully yours."

He looked into her eyes. "You don't trust me?" he asked her.

Rayah looked away. She didn't want to hurt his feelings. "I want to trust you," she said as tears began to well in her eyes. "It's not easy, Kal. You wounded me many times. Maybe not like some married men do to their wives and leave them for a mistress, but..." She couldn't continue her thought.

"But it feels like that?

She nodded her head slowly and closed her eyes as she tried to blink back the tears.

"I've changed, Rayah, and I know you know that here." He pointed at her forehead first, then paused and pointed at her heart: "But I need to convince you here. I've given you many reasons to believe that I'm capable of leaving you for another woman. I've paid the price of my selfish behavior, and I know what it feels like to be at my lowest point." His eyes revealed the regret he had been carrying for years.

"I'm afraid you'll walk out on me again," Rayah told him, her lip quivering. "I love you. The very moment I met you, I knew I wanted to be with you. But then you cheated on me and didn't have the decency to tell me about it until after I found out. Later, after dating you again, you left me for Sherice. You might have loved me, Kal, but you loved sex more, and I always came in second."

Rayah let out a long, slow breath. "Even during all this time when we've been apart, I've loved you; I just desperately wanted to erase that part of me. I promised myself long ago that I wouldn't fall for you again because I knew I wouldn't survive another breakup. But now everything feels like it's changed, and what if that change is good? What if we have another chance at something real? If so, I don't want to mess this up."

"I don't want to mess it up either," confessed Kaled. He pulled out a small object from his pocket and got down on one knee.

"Kal, what are you doing?" Rayah asked, alarmed.

"I'll do whatever it takes to have you in my arms again. You're right; I want it all; I don't just want one night. So..." he presented her with his graduation coin and took a deep breath.

"I, Kaled Ryzen Behr, am making an oath of commitment, my word as a man and as someone who wants to love you more than just skin deep. I will date you and will not pressure you into anything. I propose we wait until marriage. Long ago, that was our goal. In the meantime, there will be highs and lows, and I want to be able to prove to you that when tested through the fire, you'll see my love for you is pure as gold. It's unwavering. I will not hurt you or take advantage of you again."

Rayah was dumbstruck. For a moment, she just stood motionless. He was still on one knee, and her mouth still hung open. "You would do that?"

"I give you my word," he said firmly.

"But...what if it's years?"

She thought he would change his mind at that, but instead, to her surprise, he answered, "Even if death comes first, I'd prefer to die knowing you and I loved each other and that I've kept my honor in your eyes, rather than squander it away on one night of pleasure."

She took the graduation coin from his hand and closed her fingers on it. He stood up, and she rewarded him with the most passionate, sensual kiss they had ever shared.

"We should stop before I lose control," he said in between breaths.

Reluctantly Rayah agreed, and they let go of one another. The two of them were like magnets being forced to pull apart; stepping away from him at that moment felt unnatural, even painful. She had high hopes, however, that saying no at the moment meant saying yes to something better for them in the future.

They walked silently toward the barracks, their arms interlocked, and her head resting on his broad shoulder. She missed strolling like this. Something as simple as walking with someone she cared deeply for could bring forth such contentment that it breathed new life into her lungs. When they reached the door to her room, she took his hand in hers. "I promise I won't string you along. Trust me when I say I want this badly."

"So do I. I promise never to be your source of pain again." He pulled her hips closer to him and finished speaking in a whisper, "I'll bring you light, joy..." He lost his words as she kissed his lips again, unable to help herself.

"And excitement," she added with a grin.

Once she kissed him goodnight, she walked into the bedroom, her head in the clouds, and found Aymes, Tru, Lina, and Ameena giggling childishly.

"Finally," said Aymes with a snicker. "Now, we won't have to pay admission for any steamy hand-to-hand combat training sessions." She hugged Rayah and then hopped into her bed and went to sleep.

CHAPTER 25

Ondraus

Ondraus found this new dynamic of living with all the guys in the palace quite amusing. It had only been a week, but already the five men had resorted to playing childish pranks with one another, mostly since Kaled was now in such a better mood. Ondraus was sure the women in the room across the hall could hear all the ridiculous laughter and shenanigans occurring on the other side of the door. Bunking together felt the same as it had back when they were at the academy, though only Kaled and Ondraus had shared that experience.

This morning was no different; Tye had already placed shaving cream on Bo's open palm as he slept like a rock and then subsequently awakened with a feather to his face, resulting in a face full of shaving cream. The men had also tried swallowing mouthfuls of cinnamon, which proved to be impossible and sent puffs of brown clouds from their mouths as they coughed uncontrollably.

Tonight, though the pranks had been temporarily paused. The men were currently playing cards and listening to music, enjoying a moment to themselves after another grueling day of work. Both General and Captain Peterson had been pushing them to train as often as possible and to ensure all of the royal army was at their fittest shape for combat as well. The palace remained on maximum alert, which meant more soldiers pulling guard at night. A mandatory buddy system had also been implemented; no one was allowed to go anywhere alone.

Ondraus visited Aymes as much as possible, and together they would video chat with her son Niklas, who seemed to like Ondraus as much as Ondraus liked him. As the men played cards, though, he grew quiet.

"So...do you?" asked Kaled.

Ondraus suddenly realized that Kaled must have been talking to him. "Say that again?"

"I asked, do you have a five?"

Ondraus looked down at the cards in his hands, but purposely shot Kaled a look to make it appear he was hiding something. "Nope."

Kaled grinned and took the bait. He pushed forward the pile of potato crisps they were bargaining with. "I'm calling your bluff," he said with a smirk.

"I fold," said Wilstead, who snacked on some tinned meat even though dinner had only been an hour before. Bo was on the other end of the table, already out of the game, absently scrolling through his library of e-books to find a bedtime story he could read to his daughters on their nightly video call.

Tye looked at Kaled and Ondraus, and after a few seconds, he folded too. It wasn't just a pile of potato crisps on the line. The grand prize, by unanimous agreement, was a full day off from training. It might have been Ondraus' imagination, but he felt like the guys competed harder for that prize than they would have for money.

"I'm going to take your sister out on a stroll by the cliffs and have a picnic there and totally make out with her the entire day when I win," said Kaled as he eyed his opponent. "Show me your cards."

"Well, if you're going to play that game," said Ondraus, shaking with laughter, "I am not on a restriction like you are. So when I win, just fashion a guess as to what your sister and I will be doing on our day off."

"GROSS! Come on, dude, that's my sister we're talking about. You didn't have to go that far." He leaned over his chair and pretended to dry heave. Bo and Tye fanned him with the cards on the table as if reviving him.

The time came to show their cards, and Ondraus' hand won. "Enjoy the crisps, men, for my true prize awaits!" exclaimed Ondraus in an exaggerated tone of victory with a fist pump in the air.

"Excuse me?" said Aymes, who stood leaning on the door frame.

Ondraus ran up to her and lifted her into his arms. "Hey babe," he greeted her with a kiss. "Never mind that. How does a stroll and a picnic near the cliffs sound?"

"Seriously, O?" exclaimed Kaled, throwing a pillow at Ondraus. "Don't believe his charm, sis; that was my idea for a date with Rayah."

Ondraus laughed heartily and kissed Aymes, who was still off the floor and in his arms. After the passionate hello, he eased her onto the ground.

"A picnic sounds wonderful, honey, even if it was my brother's idea," she assured him.

The rest of the ladies entered the room. Rayah came in with a satin cap in her hands, and Lina followed with a layer of night cream on her face. Ameena brought in a large bottle of wine and fetched all of the wine glasses from the storage area near Wilstead's locker. Tru held a mending kit, and Aymes took out a comb that had been in her back pajama pants pocket. She and Rayah walked over to Ondraus' bed; Rayah sat on the floor, and Aymes, directly behind her on the bed, took out the comb and started working on Rayah's thick purple curls. Tru sat next to Wilstead and began to mend a patch on his uniform that had torn earlier that day when he was working. Wilstead repaid her by removing her socks and massaging her tired feet.

"Let's get this meeting started, shall we? I have guard duty for four hours tonight, and I'm already exhausted," said Aymes as she started to part Rayah's hair into sections so she could braid it.

"Yes, good point," agreed Wilstead.

This nightly debriefing had become their ritual over the past week. General Peterson, wanting to prepare for the absolute worst-case scenario, had instructed each Elite member to work on side projects that would allow the queen, king, and children to escape at a moment's notice if the need arises.

"I'll go first," said Wilstead. "My sister and I have been purchasing plenty of dry food items, reserving a small quantity of the queen's breast milk, and having all of that shipped to the Greensboro Fortress. We've also changed the queen's diet slightly and removed broquil, which gave her babies gas, and substituted karifol instead, which has the same type of dense nutrients she needs but with none of the side effects. We're supposed to start a hydroponics bay at the fortress and are sending packages of seeds there as well."

Ondraus looked at his sister and noticed her eyes were closed while she enjoyed Aymes' gentle but nimble fingers in her hair. "Rayah and I just purchased several more medical kits and equipped them on all of our Ready Vehicles. The inventory for these products was sent to you all by sonic mail earlier this afternoon. These include hypo-sprays, sterile surgical instruments, dermal healers, and vials of medicine, along with instructions on how to dose properly. There are also sonic filters to make any water potable. These filters," he said, reaching into a bag by his bed and passing out a small thimble-sized item, "must be kept in your canteens at all times. We also gave the Kortez twins and the royal infants an extensive round of immunizations. Next week, we have scheduled to start teaching advanced life-saving courses to you all and then to the troops."

"General Peterson," added Rayah, "would like for us to train regular volunteer civilians as well. He said to offer it as a free class that can count as extra credit in all school grades and as community service for those who need it."

"I think he's going a little overboard with his ideas on this. I mean, civilians wouldn't be called to fight or to be medics; that's the whole point of the military. We have troops everywhere," said Ondraus.

"Actually, bro, it was my idea," said Rayah, turning a little red from embarrassment.

You know me; I over-plan, she said through duo-com.

Ondraus laughed out loud at his sister's innate ability to take a task and go a step further.

Aymes spoke up next. "Kal and I have been adding a few adjustments to the Ready Vehicles. Just yesterday, we fixed the cloaking device on one of our airships and added the fortress and Marez Cave to the nav waypoints. Only our team, the royal family, General Peterson, and the Kortez family have access, which is done by a retinal scan. No one else can use those vehicles, so keep that in mind."

Aymes then tapped Rayah on the shoulder and said, "My turn now." Rayah looked up and smiled, and Aymes kissed her on the forehead.

"Thanks. That felt amazing, and you always do such a great job on my hair."

"My pleasure, sistah," Aymes said, and they both switched places. Rayah sat on the bed with Aymes on the floor by her feet, and Rayah started massaging her shoulders. Aymes closed her eyes and leaned forward. "Oh, yeah. That's the spot."

Ondraus watched the two of them. They had always been affectionate toward each other. The fact that the two women had reunited again warmed his heart. He appreciated that the woman he loved was also such great friends with his one and only sister. He chanced a look at Kaled, who took a seat near Aymes.

"Nuh-uh, bro. You wait your turn," said Aymes, shoving him away with her foot as Rayah burst into laughter.

Ameena brought forth the filled wine glasses, passing them to everyone except for Aymes, who had to work later that night, and Kaled. Instead, the Behr twins were handed glasses of carbonated water with crushed mint leaves and fresh berries. Aymes took a sip and tilted her head back. "Wow, Ameena, that's delicious. Thanks for thinking of me."

"Of course," said Ameena as she took a sip from her glass of wine. Ameena and her brother Wilstead were the youngest members of The Elite, at twenty-two years old, but no one else could compare to their knowledge of foods and cooking. The running joke was that if the palace's food ever ran out, they could take the group's boots and make a five-star meal.

"My brother and I have been studying the city's underground infrastructure," Lina said, "and have mapped the quickest way out of the city without being noticed. We've also made plans on how to equip the Greensboro Fortress with more safety features. It was abandoned for many years, so most of its systems were running on obsolete technology. We now have sensors that will alert us if anyone is near, and we've been testing their range capability. We've also been working on plans to equip both the palace and Primeda Fortress for an attack. We've stocked more Nemis and have staff carrying them around even while inside instead of keeping them in the ammunition locker. We've also started some work on the submarine dock entrance and the helipad. We've been swamped, so we've tasked soldiers to help us as well."

"Last but certainly not least," said Tye, "we've been working with Evia and Ensin on their sign language. So far, they can do over fifty different signs. General Peterson wants us to start teaching you all as well. So, here's one to learn for tonight." He made an obscene gesture and was rewarded with a hit in the face from a flying pillow.

"Disgusting, bro," said Tru. "This is the actual sign for tonight." She maneuvered her fingers in the air and said, "It's the order to attack."

"Thanks, Tru," said Rayah, who was now flexing her fingers as she practiced the sign. "I've also been spending time with Evia, Ensin, Nerida, the queen, and the babies. Nerida has been teaching us a lot about infant care."

Aymes had moved to sit beside Ondraus with her hand on his lap. "What needs to happen is you all coming over and taking turns babysitting my son," she declared. "Niklas is a handful, and he's just one boy. I can only imagine what raising twins will be like. I know my brother and I were a handful."

"It's not a bad idea, sis," agreed Kaled. "I'm sure our mom would appreciate the time off from watching Niklas, especially since we're stuck here until who knows when. As soon as this High Alert is lifted, we should do that."

Ondraus could see the smile creep onto Rayah's face as she nudged Kaled and said, "I haven't even seen your awesome uncle skills yet, but when I've hung out with Niklas, he's always told me that you are the best uncle ever. I can't wait until this lockdown is over and we can leave the palace grounds."

"Have you guys been able to talk to Guyad since the incident last week?" asked Bo.

"Kinda," said Rayah. "Doctor Kortez brought him out of the medically induced coma earlier tonight, and he was just as crazy and evil as last week. He keeps shifting from Guyad's purple eyes to Rancor's gray eyes, and whenever Rancor takes over, he just hurts Guyad. He's broken his wrist already from trying to rip out of his shackles. Whenever it's Guyad, he keeps trying to warn us about Rancor's body and saying that he's some sort of projection. I don't know if he means a hologram or what. I mean, a hologram wouldn't be able to do much damage, would it?"

"I don't know, Rayah," responded Tru. "Holograms are normally passive; they're just projections of light, meaning you can walk right through them. We also know that solid holograms exist. However, there's a theoretical type of hologram called a photonic, which is both passive and solid and can change its matter density at will. If Rancor is a photonic or something like it, he could inflict an unimaginable amount of pain and destruction. We couldn't apprehend him or even shoot him because he could phase out of his solid state. To defeat a photonic, we'd have to hack into its system, which means finding the physical computer that was running the program."

"That's a valid point," said her brother Tye. "I hate when you're right. Maybe we should do some research on holographic technologies and see what we can learn."

That concluded their session. Ondraus noticed Rayah taking Kaled by the hand and stealthily leading him outside, probably to a cramped utility closet, as if Ondraus didn't already know that was their favorite makeout spot.

"How much longer before you go on guard shift?" Ondraus asked Aymes, wondering if he had enough time to hang out with his lady before she had to leave for work.

"Hmm...we have enough time to talk a romantic stroll to the utility closet," she said with a wink.

"It's already taken," he said as he took her hand. "How about enough time for a dance?"

"I'd love that."

CHAPTER 26

Aymes

Aymes was ready for her midnight-to-four shift...well, as *ready* as someone could be for doing guard duty when any reasonable person would rather be asleep. She walked toward the courtyard with Rayah, who was kind enough to volunteer as her mandatory walking buddy.

"It's such a beautiful night," Aymes said as she looked up at the brilliant stars that dressed the night sky in a glamorous glow.

"It sure is," responded Rayah. "I can't believe they haven't let you go see your son yet."

Aymes sighed in frustration. "It's annoying. I get that the High Alert is important and we have to be careful, but this is a little ridiculous. I miss my son, and watching him through a holo-chat is not enough for me. My mother always tells me how he's constantly asking why I'm not home and when I'll get to see him again." She looked at her friend. "This is so hard on me. I've never been away from him this long."

Rayah held Aymes's hand and squeezed it. "I'm happy you have your mom."

"Me too. This would be impossible without her. I'm not married like Bo is. I don't just have my son's good-for-nothing father at my disposal. He's off somewhere with his new trophy wife and pretending he doesn't have a child of his own to help support, and honestly, I'm too tired at this point to keep fighting him on it. Part of me wants him to be part of Niklas's life. I mean, a kid needs their father. The other part of me feels indifferent. Besides..."

"Mmhmm, go ahead and say it," said Rayah with a nudge.

"Besides, your brother...he's so good with Niklas. I don't know; I don't want to get ahead of myself. I can't afford to dream of a future like that. But it does remind me that good men are out there. I don't know about Tye and Wilstead, but Bo, my brother, and O are fantastic with kids. Have you seen the way they act with Evia and Ensin? Even with little Luna and Saule, they are just so mindful of them."

Aymes let out a dreamy sigh. She had been with Ondraus for six months now, and it somehow seemed like five seconds, as if the time had flown by; she already couldn't imagine life without him. She still couldn't understand why she'd never dated him years ago. She'd known he liked her, but Aymes always felt he was too young for her, and she liked her men mature. Then again, her plan hadn't worked out so well with Niklas's supposedly mature father.

Aymes' ex-boyfriend wasn't interested in being tied down with a family and jumped ship as soon as he learned of her pregnancy. She often tried to tell him that he could still be in the child's life, even if not with her, but he wanted none of it. Being in the military as a single mother was very hard, and there was nowhere near enough support. Thankfully, she had her mother and her brother.

Aymes considered herself blessed to have a brother

who was kind, sensitive, and playful. How many nights had Kaled stayed up bottle-feeding Niklas so that Aymes and her mother could get some sleep? Ondraus was also stepping up, and she could tell that her son liked him a lot. Aymes was very selective of who she dated after she had her son, and had never physically introduced her child to any of her men because she felt there was no future with any of them. That all changed with Ondraus.

"To be honest," said Rayah once they finally reached the courtyard, "I think he loves you. Like head over heels, would propose if he felt it weren't too early and freak you out, type of love you."

Aymes turned to look at her friend and smiled. "If he asked, I would say yes, in a heartbeat. You don't let go of a good man."

The two friends hugged, and the soldier who had been on duty now walked Rayah back to the palace. For the twentieth time, Aymes checked her mobile device, her smartwatch, and her Nemi sidearm. At least there was a nice cool summer night's breeze to keep her awake as she stood outside alone with her thoughts. Three hours passed without a single sound other than the crickets making their usual night song; she spent her time closely examining her surroundings, but nothing made a single peep. Suddenly, she received an urgent message through her smartwatch. The screen strobed with amber light, which meant Evia or Ensin was calling her. Her heart stopped as she answered.

"Something's wrong! I think someone took Luna and Saule!"

Her world stopped, froze, and then quickly started with a succession of commands and actions that she tried to juggle single-handedly. She duo-commed her brother.

Kal, the babies are gone. Call Belfast and see if he's still guarding their door. Then meet me at Fleet.

She called General Peterson and his son. She scanned the grounds, the sky – nothing. Maybe this was all a mistake? She couldn't run the risk of doubting Evia and Ensin.

Ondraus

He awoke with a start. Someone was shaking him and the whole room seemed abuzz with chaos. As he rubbed the sleep from his eyes, he saw Kaled running to turn on the lights and yelling that the kids were gone. In a flash Kaled was gone, running over to the girl's quarters and shouting the same thing before sprinting out of the building with his Nemi in hand.

Ondraus slipped on his shoes and ran up the stairs, three steps at a time, his lungs and heart heaving. He attempted to call Belfast as he climbed the fifteen flights of stairs to the royal chambers, but the phone rang and rang without answer. He deliberately chose not to take the elevator as it was notoriously slow, and he didn't have the time to wait around. As he sprinted, he yelled out loud to alert any royal guard who might happen to hear his voice.

"Belfast, check on the royal babies! Belfast! BELFAST, ANSWER DAMMIT!"

Another soldier seemed to be just ahead of him as he climbed the stairs to the fifteenth floor. By the time Ondraus caught up, he saw Belfast slumped on the floor. The other soldier, Corporal Zuri, confirmed that Belfast was dead. Things had just gone from scary to deadly, and both men pulled out their weapons. Ondraus reached for the door, but it was locked.

"I've got you covered," said Corporal Zuri as he aimed his Nemi at the door.

"Wait!" Ondraus shouted, suddenly remembering he had the highest security clearance aside from General Peterson. He used his thumbprint, and the cipher lock on the door clicked, giving him access. Ondraus rushed in and punched the lights on, revealing a man dressed in all black with his weapon aimed directly at Ondraus' chest. Before the intruder could fire, Corporal Zuri shoved Ondraus out of the way, shooting three times and dropping the attacker to the floor.

Ondraus sprang onto his feet and mouthed *thanks* to his comrade.

"Stay where you are," he yelled authoritatively to the shocked king and queen. "Corporal Zuri and I have to secure the room and make sure no one else is in here."

"What is going on? Who was that?" yelled the king in fright and confusion as he sat up in bed, trembling.

"I don't know. The Kortez twins believe your children may be missing." Ondraus sprinted frantically toward the nursery. He found the infants' caregiver dead on the floor, both cribs empty. "They're not here!"

"The room is secure," announced Corporal Zuri. He helped the queen up from the bed.

Queen Ellandra let out a scream upon seeing the dead woman, then broke into hysterical sobs as the four of them searched the room as quickly and efficiently as possible.

The babies aren't here, said Ondraus to his sister through duo-com.

Ondraus felt compelled to rip the room apart if necessary. Where could the babies possibly have gone? Who had taken them? How had Belfast and the nanny been murdered without anyone hearing anything? He stood still for a moment, trying to gather his thoughts, before his sister broke in on duo-com. *Are there any secret passageways? Are any windows open?*

He ran toward the window in the nursery, and though it was closed, he noticed a pair of fingerprints on the glass. "When was the last time you opened this window?" he said while opening it and taking a look outside.

"Over a month ago," replied the queen in a frantic shrill voice. He could feel her pacing behind him on the verge of a complete breakdown, which would be completely natural. He, on the other hand, had to keep his cool, though he just realized he was in nothing but a pair of unlaced sneakers and his boxers.

He ran yet again through the chanted vision Evia and Ensin had uttered months ago: *He comes at night, by flight to strike.* Could this be it? He had been looking down at the ocean and down by the palace grounds, but now looked up. Something was barely visible; it must have had a cloaking device, but the cloak effect always rippled slightly when the hidden object passed in front of a bright light like the sun or the moon.

He called Aymes. "I think I see an airship. It's about twenty miles out, northwest, heading toward the sea. I bet you the kids are on it. We need to get going now."

"Meet me on the balcony. Get your Glyden Suit on as soon as you get in."

He sprinted out of the nursery toward the balcony in the king's and queen's room, noticing as he did that they were following him. "We're going after them, Your

Majesty; I think that was the kids in an airship. General Peterson has the entire palace looking for them as well."

O, we're all getting into the airships now. It'll take us a minute to reach you. We don't have visual on Rancor's airship, do you?

I did a minute or so ago; I think it's cloaked.

The king interrupted his duo-com with Rayah. "I'm going with you."

"Your Majesty, I –"

"If you're wondering whether or not I can handle myself out there, need I remind you that I grew up with Captain Yosef Peterson? Those are my children we're talking about."

"Apologies, Your Majesty." The airship arrived at the balcony and a mechanical-looking rope was let down. The king put up his hand, and the rope automatically wrapped itself around his forearm, zipping him up into the belly of the ship.

A few seconds later, Ondraus zipped up as well, leaving the crying queen in his wake. As soon as he was inside the ship, he ran to a small closet and pulled out a skin-tight Glyden Suit that came with a self-retracting helmet equipped with a digital screen and audio.

"Captain Ondraus Jur is online," came Aymes' voice over the helmet.

"We need a visual on that airship," Captain Yosef Peterson ordered.

"Working on it, sir. Just a few more seconds," said Tru Ryder.

Ondraus saw his sister sitting down as she put on a pair of flight boots. He walked up to her and sat to do the same. He also saw Kaled walking around the ship's

Utility Deck, inspecting everyone's Glyden Suits.

"Let me check you," said Kaled, now standing in front of Rayah and Ondraus. Rayah got up, and Kaled had her lift her arms to see if the propelling system would automatically engage. It did, leaving her suspended in mid-air. "Arms down," he instructed. Instantly, she floated to the floor. He then followed the same process with Ondraus, completed a checklist on his tablet, and then disappeared to the Command Pit.

"We've got visual; please stand by," said Aymes.

After a minute, both General Elden Peterson and Captain Yosef Peterson walked out of the Command Pit. They were surprised to see the king had made it onto the ship but did not address him immediately.

It was the younger Peterson who spoke. "Captain Aymes has visual on the assailant's airship, and Captain Kaled has locked onto its coordinates. We're running cloaked so that we remain undetected. We have the full specs on that type of airship, and they are being sent to you right now." Yosef swiped at the digital image projected on his forearm, and within half a second, Ondraus saw the detailed drawings appear on his helmet's heads-up display.

His sister wasn't duo-comming him, and he knew why. When she got nervous before a mission, she tended to go through every single possible scenario in her head, rambling over and over. She must have decided to save her brother from the torture by not including him in her unraveling thoughts. He held her hand and gave it a reaffirming squeeze. It had been a while since he and his sister had put their lives on the line in service to their country, and now the stakes felt like they couldn't be higher.

DAWN OF THE ELITE

The rescue of the king and queen's children was no simple task. If The Elite failed, it would not only be a national disaster, but something more that Ondraus couldn't put his finger on. Why was Rancor so obsessed with Luna and Saule? Why was he so interested in these infants that he was willing to pull such a complicated heist? What could be so important?

Captain Peterson continued talking. "The plan is as follows. Use your Glyden Suit and quietly land on the deck of their airship. You should be able to see it through your helmet's screen with the modifications Lieutenants Tye and Tru Ryder just made moments ago. We are still scanning their ship, and it may be another five minutes before we have a reading on how many lives are on board, but we can't wait until we have that. We must move before they detect us."

The room remained silent as Captain Peterson continued. "Keep your wits about you; you have been approved to use deadly force against anyone you meet once you can confirm that the children are on board. You must confirm that first. Lieutenant Tru Ryder will remain on board to work communications and technology, but her brother Lieutenant Tye will drop down with you. You'll enter through here and proceed down the stairs to the belly of their ship. We're picking up heat signatures there, so that room is probably your best bet. We are mobilizing a backup team now, but it might be a while before they are ready to touch down."

The quick pep-talk and game plan surprised Ondraus. He had noticed the same thing with General Peterson as well. Perhaps both men appreciated quick details and did not like droning on with unnecessary talk. He'd never had a commander speak so briefly, and he appreciated it. Kaled emerged again, this time wearing magnetic boots to help keep him from flying out of the doors once they opened.

General and Captain Peterson, along with the king, left the Utility Deck and retreated to the Command Pit located upstairs. Kaled made sure everyone with a Glyden Suit held onto a safety chain by the ceiling. As soon as he engaged the door, a deafening rush of night wind came in. It was only possible to hear Kaled through the helmet.

"Bo, you go first, and then Tye and Lina. Wilstead and Ameena are next, then O, and last is Rayah. Guys, keep in mind that Tye doesn't have his sister with him, but he'll be able to communicate with her up here, and if anything is important, she'll share it with you all in your helmets," said Kaled.

Kaled slapped Bo's shoulder to signify it was time to go. He spaced each of The Elite by ten seconds so they all had a staggered entry time. As they neared the end of the line, Ondraus saw Kaled tell Rayah to be safe, punctuating the benediction with a pat on her the helmet. With Ondraus, Kaled gave him a fist bump and said, "Be safe, brother."

Ondraus leaped out of the belly of the airship and instantly dropped fifty feet. He kept his arms tucked to his sides so that he could glide toward the assailants' ship smoothly like a rocket. Adrenaline pounded through him as the wind rushed past his body; if not for the fact that this was a rescue mission, he would have hollered in delight. He saw the airship thirty feet away and lifted his arms to engage the propulsion, slowing down so that he could land safely on the deck.

The airship Ondraus had just been on was smaller

and sleek, made for tactical and rescue type missions, whereas the one he had just landed on was a Mariner Class airship. Mariner airships were much larger and looked like regular cargo boats that just happened to have the ability to fly. He saw his sister land on the opposite side of the deck but couldn't spot any of his other Elite comrades.

Sis, do you see any of our guys?

Bo's on my left, she answered back, *and I think someone is to the right of you, crouching down.*

Ondraus squinted his eyes to see better, which engaged the helmet's heat signature function. The audio of the helmet came alive.

"This is Captain Peterson. I see all of you. There are five unknown persons in the middle and toward the helm of the ship."

The small colorful figures appeared on Ondraus' heads-up display. He leaned in closer to gauge whether or not he could hear the unknown contacts talking.

"I don't see anything," said a man who was looking out into the sky using binoculars.

"Neither do I. I can't wait till we dock at Susa; this Rancor guy gives me the creeps."

"Same. I don't like this one bit."

"Rancor is pretty nasty, but I wonder if Imicem is just as bad," said the one on the left, pulling up his trousers, which had been sagging below his thin waist.

"I overheard him talking to the investors while I was putting away the fishing nets earlier," said the other. "Rancor is running the show and calling the shots, but Imicem has been doing all the actual work."

"What do you mean?" asked the other, taking his eyes off the dark sky and facing his friend.

"He's the one who lured Guyad, overpowered him, and implanted the device into his eye. He said he regretted having to do it, but it was for the greater good. Besides, we know he's the one that went inside and stole the babies, and I bet he had to kill some people in order to do it."

"Poor babies. Had I known we were stealing babies instead of money, I wouldn't have signed up for this," said the man with the small waist.

Ondraus felt conflicted. They were definitely on the right ship, and they had the approval to use deadly force, but these two men were not the typical 'bad guy' persona. He asked his sister for her thoughts, and she agreed: if possible, he'd try not to kill the men.

Tru's voice came through the helmet. "Hey guys, Tye says he heard the conversation between the two men standing closest to the helm. When you attack, don't use deadly force. Just tie them up. Tye says he's going to go first and recommends that Ondraus, who's on the left of him, go at the same time."

Now, at least, Ondraus knew who was crouching down to his right. He noticed Tye give the *attack* hand signal, and they both leaped out of their hiding locations. In moments, they'd silently subdued the two men with rear choke holds. Tru announced to the group that two enemies were down, and they still had three more armed men on the deck that so far, had no idea they were being ambushed.

Guess I'm next, said Rayah through duo-com. She did not leap out the way Ondraus and Tye had done; instead, she crept quietly until she was behind her target, then choked him out the same way as her comrades had. Ameena and Wilstead took down the other two men while Bo and Lina waited silently, too far away from the initial action to do anything other than watch. In moments the group had bound the assailants' wrists with electronic shackles and searched their pockets for radios and weapons. They confiscated all weapons and turned off all the radios, throwing everything overboard. Bo and Wilstead moved the bodies behind crates on one end of the ship so that no one would find them easily.

So far, so good, said Ondraus.

Yep. Now for the lower decks where Rancor might be hurting the kids. You weren't there, O; that man is evil and strong. He almost killed me the last time I faced him.

That was in Guyad's body. Plus, this time, you're not alone. We're going to make sure he never hurts anyone again.

Ondraus was sure this would be an easy mission. They had the element of surprise and had already taken care of five men without being detected. The ship was large, but not large enough to hide many people below. Ondraus and the others crept down the aluminum stairs and into the dark hallway below decks.

A light flickered, and a rotting fish smell wafted up from somewhere. The Elite paired off two by two while Tye led up front. His eyes would be their ears; whatever he saw would be reported to his sister, who would then relay it back to them through the helmets. Two armed guards were standing fifteen feet away but had not yet noticed the oncoming group of soldiers. Tye took out his Nemi and shot one in the chest, and Rayah shot the other at precisely the same time to prevent any potential calls for backup.

Tru's voice came through the helmet again. "The

door to the right leads to a room that is showing twenty people inside. That might be where the babies are. So far, I see no one else on the way nor coming up behind you."

CHAPTER 27

Rayah

Throughout Rayah's military career, she and her brother had always relied on communicating seamlessly through duo-com. Never had she been in a predicament like this one where stealth was a matter of life and death. The mission had gone seamlessly so far, but Rayah was well aware that everything could change at the flip of a switch.

Tye signaled the team to stop where they were to come up with a plan. "I'll make this quick," he whispered. "The scan shows twenty people. Most of them seemed to be surrounding this person here, and I bet that's our guy, Rancor. If he's there, we stand a good chance the babies are there with him, and if not, we'll be able to force him to tell us where they are. I see two people standing by the door, and they could be facing the door or the center of the room. There's just no way to know. I'll go first."

Rayah interjected. "If Guyad was right about the whole *Rancor is a projection* thing, we're going to need you to disrupt that, and I'm sure none of us know how to work your gadgets."

"Yeah, good point," Tye agreed. "Wilstead, you and Ameena go first. Hang low and listen first at the door just in case. If you're able to be quiet and take them down like we did the guys upstairs, great. If there's no way to be stealthy about it, then we'll all pile in and get the party started that way. Rayah and Lina, you two are quick on your feet; get those babies, and then get out as fast as possible. We'll try to take care of the fighting. Remember, those kids are our only objective. If we can deal with Rancor, great, but the mission is to recover the royal twins. Let's get in position."

Wilstead and his sister Ameena led the group down the hallway and placed their ears on the door to see if they could listen. If they didn't have to use their Glyden Suits, they would have been able to bring a backpack full of useful tools with them, but the suits required everyone to travel light. Ameena made herself flat with the floor and peered in the small gap underneath. She popped herself up, opened the door silently, and crept in quickly with her brother trailing immediately behind her.

They'd left the door open, and Rayah held her breath as she watched through the crack. Ameena and Wilstead positioned themselves behind the two men closest to the door. With a quick fluid movement, the twins snapped the guards' necks, and the men dropped limply. The bodies were rapidly pulled into the hallway and stripped of their uniforms, which Ameena and Wilstead put on and then took positions by the door as if they were the guards who'd been there all along.

A visual feed appeared on Rayah's helmet screen.

"Smart move, Ameena," said Tru. "Thanks for positioning your helmet directly toward all the action."

A tall, young man around his thirties with shoulder-length dark purple hair stood over Luna and Saule with his palms up, as if trying to conjure something. His hands had scorch marks on them. It was definitely

Rancor. His eyes were closed, and he chanted something Rayah could not decipher. A glowing crystal hung around his neck. Fifteen men, all in expensive tailored suits, stood around the room, transfixed by Rancor.

"We gotta move now," said Rayah quietly to the rest of the group in the hallway. They all nodded in agreement. Whatever Rancor was doing, it wasn't good, and they needed to stop him.

Bo and Ondraus came in first, firing at Rancor. Somehow they both missed – or their shots phased through him. Either way, they'd lost the element of surprise.

"Kill them," ordered Rancor. "I must complete the process." He closed his eyes again and lifted his hands; the children, during the second that Rancor had broken his concentration, had begun to cry, but as soon as he closed his eyes, the children were magically subdued and became quiet again.

The men in suits drew Nemis and aimed at The Elite. Rayah fired first, killing one man on the spot before she had to duck from incoming weapons fire. Energy beams were flying everywhere now, crisscrossing the room like laser lights at a nightclub, and there was no way she could just freely run to the children without getting herself killed in the process. She looked at Lina, who seemed to be having the same thoughts.

O, cover us; we're making a run for them, said Rayah.
I got your backs. Go.

Rayah started running as fast as she could toward the babies and got within a foot of them before she was knocked to her feet by a protective orb of energy that surrounded them and Rancor. Someone attempted a shot at her, but she rolled out of the way in time and popped back onto her feet, tripping her attacker with a leg hook. He fell, and she stomped hard on his windpipe. She chanced a look around the room and saw only two men left; Ondraus and Tye were taking care of through a series of punches to the face, leaving them bloody and unconscious.

Lina kicked one of the guards hard in the face before her brother Bo finished the man off with a shot. Together they ran toward the babies, slamming into the protective orb just as Rayah had done. Lina and Rayah aimed their Nemis at Rancor, who finally looked up; his eyes appeared red with rage. As soon as his concentration broke, the orb dissipated, and the babies began to cry again. Rayah shot Rancor in the chest, but the beam passed through without harming him – he *was* a photonic!

Lina ran toward the infants and picked them both up, but Rancor knocked her to the floor. Rayah swooped in to catch the babies before they hit the ground, immediately sprinting back toward the door. Bo charged toward Rancor but somehow ran *through* him, smashing into the wall with a crunch as blood spewed from his nose.

"Why isn't he dying?" yelled Ondraus with frustration, firing his Nemi over and over again at Rancor while Rayah and Lina fled with the babies. Rancor raised his hand, and the door to the room slammed shut and locked with a deafening click.

"Not one of you will leave this room with your life," said Rancor menacingly. "You have no idea who you are dealing with."

Rancor rushed toward Bo, picking him up with one hand and slamming Bo's head hard against the wall once more. Lina and Rayah ran to a corner where

Tye was crouched behind some fish crates. Lina stayed there, shielding the infants with her body, while Tye opened up a small laptop and began typing away at the screen with rapid fury.

Back in the center of the room, Ondraus jumped on Rancor's back and punched his head without making any dent whatsoever. There was absolutely nothing they could do to harm this evil man. Rancor casually strolled toward Tye and the infants, deliberately ignoring The Elite's hopeless attempts to stop him. Rayah stepped in front of him, knowing her slender body could not stop a man with such infinite strength.

Rancor stopped and smiled in a sickly manner as if oil were dripping from the sides of his greedy mouth. "I remember you," he said with an edge of desire. He lifted Rayah by the neck with one hand and slammed her against the wall. "I should have killed you earlier when I had the chance...but then again, I also like to play with my dinner." He picked her up again and forced her face toward his, kissing her hard. She pushed away in disgust and spat in his face. "Feisty. I like that."

"Get away from my sister, you deranged psychopath!" yelled Ondraus, rushing back in. Rancor threw an elbow toward him, but Ondraus dodged it in time and tried to land a return punch. Yet again, nothing seemed to hurt Rancor.

"Get on with it, Tye!" yelled Ameena, who stood with her weapon aimed at Rancor.

Rayah heard a commotion outside the door. She couldn't tell if it was their backup or more evil men she and her worn-out team had to fight. Rancor let go of Rayah and asked, "What is he trying to do with that computer?"

Rayah needed a distraction – something, anything. "You wanna play, come get me," she said with a rasp; her throat burned like she'd swallowed lava. She wondered if such a stupid phrase could get his attention.

Rancor looked back at her and smiled his evil, greedy smile, the same smile she'd seen on Guyad's face so many times.

Grateful to get his attention off of Tye, she blurted out the first thing that came to her mind. "First, tell me: why are you doing this? Let Guyad go; he's no good to you anyway. You've already won."

"You really think me that stupid, little girl?" said Rancor with a laugh. He pulled out his own Nemi and shot it at Wilstead, who fell instantly. Ondraus sprinted over and, after placing his ear to Wilstead's chest, began doing chest compressions on him. "I need Guyad," Rancor added. "I still have a mission for him."

"What could it possibly be?" she asked.

"Nah, ah, ah. I don't think so. I know there are plenty of people listening in. If you are listening to this, General Peterson, you have a decision to make. You either kill Guyad or wait and see what I have in store for you all through him. He can't help but do my bidding." He looked around the room and shot Ameena in the leg, and she grunted in pain. "Where's that handsome young fellow who came to your rescue last time you and I met? Hmm? Watching this, maybe? He has a thing for you, doesn't he? It sure is a shame you won't live to see him again. At the very least, I could take you with me, control your mind and body. Yes, that sounds more pleasant than death, doesn't it?"

Rayah spat in his face again, which made him laugh. He threw her to the ground once more and said, "No matter. I have my eye on someone else anyway." He rose his Nemi and aimed it at Lina, but Rayah kicked the Nemi out of his hand, then scooped it off the ground and fired at him, doing no damage as usual. She tossed the gun to her brother and jumped out of the way before Rancor could punch her in the stomach. The evil man attacked her with fury burning in his eyes; Ondraus and Bo jumped into the fight as well, with Lina right behind them. They continued this exhausting fight, blow after blow, not having any effect at all.

Rancor grabbed Rayah once again, yanking a knife off the nearby table and holding it up to Rayah's neck. He twisted her arms behind her and pressed the blade hard against her skin, which made some blood trickle out.

"I'm tired of this," snarled Rancor. "It ends now. You are much too fast for me, and I cannot be killed. I have many things to do. Hand over the babies or I begin to kill you all one by one, starting with this one." He licked her face and looked directly at Ondraus. "She's your sister, isn't she? Oh yes, I can tell she is. I think I'll enjoy your reaction when I kill her."

"Got it!" yelled Tye, and a moment later, Rancor was no more. His knife clattered onto the floor.

Ondraus ran to his sister and held her. He pressed his hand on her neck, ripped off a piece of burlap from a desk, and pressed that on her skin to help stop the bleeding. "Let's go, sis," he said out loud.

Ameena and Lina picked up the infants, waiting as the rest of the group pried the doors open and burst out into the hall. To Rayah's relief, they ran directly into their reinforcements. King Tarrington, in a pair of tactical pants and a black shirt, stood in front of them with eight other men, including Captain Peterson, Birchram and Zendo. He ran to his children and cradled them both in his arms.

"Thank you, from the bottom of my heart. Thank you for your excellent work," the king said.

Captain Peterson added, "Well done. We fought off a few other men and have apprehended the pilot as well. Sergeant Odin Skyler is piloting this airship back to the palace as we speak."

Birchram and Zendo helped Wilstead and Ameena onto stretchers, leaving Ondraus to properly dress Rayah's wound with an adhesive patch. Rayah tried to help Ondraus treat the others, but he forced her to rest; the last thing they needed right now was to have her rip that neck wound any wider. She watched as Ondraus applied Sanar Ointment onto Bo's face to help with the bleeding, pain, and swelling. Captain Peterson led the group back up to the main deck; everyone still had their weapons drawn in case there were any more bad guys.

"Your Majesty," said Captain Peterson, "we're all happy the babies are safe, but we need to get them strapped in and ready to move out. I'd prefer it if we use Captain Lina Xulu. She's great with a Nemi, and she's also fast in case we need to leave in a hurry."

The king agreed, and he helped Lina put on the child carrying harness onto her chest and back before strapping his infants onto the device. The king must have read Lina's perplexed look, because he added, "I'm the only one who knows how to work this blasted harness," with a slight chuckle.

"Hold on," said Tru through the helmets. "I see another heat signature, just one person, and they are on their way to the main deck as well but from the other end."

Rayah cursed under her breath. "You've got to be kidding me."

The able-bodied soldiers ran upstairs, leaving Wilstead, Ameena, Birchram, and Zendo downstairs, waiting for the all-clear, along with Lina, who had the babies safely strapped onto her. The king ran up the stairs as well, but Rayah and Ondraus stood in front of him, shielding him with their weapons drawn as the rest of The Elite, Captain Peterson, and the other men searched the deck for the unknown person.

"We lost his heat signature," said Tru. "He must have a device to block our scans."

Of course, he does, said Rayah through duo-com.

Rayah kept her eyes peeled and strained her ears for any sudden sounds. She scanned the area in front of her but couldn't see anyone outside of the group she was with. Then, from behind, she heard a scuffling of feet and turned around to see a man in black wearing a helmet that covered his face. The man had an arm around the king's neck and held a small pulsing orb in his other hand.

He's got a bomb on this ship, doesn't he? asked Ondraus.
Sure looks like it, responded Rayah.

Rayah's mind raced; she went over every possible scenario for how this could play out. The detonator looked like it was armed, and therefore only he would know how to turn it off, or they would all die. The longer they stayed up here talking, the closer they all came to a messy end.

"My quarrel is not with any of you," said the man with the obscured face. "Just with the king." His voice sounded synthesized, almost robotic.

"Drop the weapon, or we'll shoot," said Ondraus authoritatively.

I have a clean shot, duo-commed Rayah.

"Who are you?" demanded King Tarrington.

"I am the one who will bring forth justice and give you a taste of your own medicine."

"What are you talking about? What have I done? Again I ask, who are you? Give me a name!" asked the king, irritated, and confused.

"You can call me Imicem. There are many like me seeking justice; I'm just the only one willing to claim it. We are wasting time. In five minutes, this place will blow up unless I stop it, and I'm not stopping it until I have free passage off this ship."

"So," said Ondraus trying to buy his sister some time, "all you want is a clean getaway. No desire to kill anyone unnecessarily?"

"Correct."

"You seem like a decent fellow; why are you hanging out with evil men like Rancor?" asked Ondraus.

"He made an offer I could not resist."

GO NOW, yelled Rayah through duo-com.

Rayah shot at the man's chest, which made him stumble back for a fraction of a second. That was enough time for the king to wrench himself from the man's grasp and step away. Imicem was still alive; he must have been wearing a pulse-vest like Wilstead's. Another shot, however, might do the trick. Ondraus barreled into the assailant and took him down easily, landing a few nose-crunching punches to the face. The detonator flew out of the man's hands, and Tye ran toward it, scanning it with a handheld device before punching keys onto a digital screen. Ondraus got up, reaching for some electronic cuffs when the man pulled out a knife from his pants pocket and jabbed it deep into Ondraus' side.

Rayah watched in horror as her brother's eyes widened from pain and shock. His blood seeped through his uniform as he clutched his side and dropped to his knees. "No!" she screamed, tensing to run to his aid.

Before she could move, Imicem pulled out a small device, the size of a pair of dice, and dropped it. As soon as it hit the floor, a deafening screech and blinding light obliterated Rayah's senses.

CHAPTER 28

Rayah

Rayah had never been more disoriented. The searing light felt like it had scorched her pupils, and she couldn't open her eyes without screaming in pain – not that she could hear herself with her ears still ringing so intensely.

I can't stop the bleeding, said Ondraus through duo-com.

Fear gripped Rayah like a vise. Her brother's internal voice sounded weak. She called loudly, "Ondraus was stabbed and is bleeding. Hurry; he needs help, and I can't see him." Before she had finished saying her sentence, she heard something overhead, like a quickly descending line. Instinctively she tilted her head toward the night sky but could not open her eyes.

"Folks, this is Captain Behr," said Kaled. Rayah could hear his voice right next to her as he touched down onto the deck. "I'm taking the wounded and the infants first. Please stand by." Then, much quieter so only Rayah could hear him, he added, "I've got Birchram here with me; he can see since he was belowdecks when the Diversion Cube hit. He's patching up your brother right now. I have to make several trips, but I'll be back for you."

Before he left her side, he gave her hand an encouraging squeeze. Just when Rayah thought she could relax and there was no longer any present danger, she heard Tye scream, "I still haven't defused the detonator!"

"Kal! Get Tru down here now, or we're all dead!" yelled Rayah. She didn't know if he was within earshot or back in the airship unloading the first batch of priority patients.

"Already here," said Tru.

Finally, the pain in Rayah's eyes began to ebb away, and she noticed Tru was on the deck working on the device.

"Can't we just throw it overboard?" Lina asked, rubbing her eyes.

"No," replied Odin through the headset embedded in the helmets. "We're over the city now; the results could be catastrophic. I'm trying to steer us toward the water, but it might take longer than five minutes. These Mariner Class airships aren't built for speed."

"You next," said Kaled to Rayah. He had returned to the airship and started placing a harness around her waist quickly. The rope ascended as soon as he tugged on it, making a fast whirring sound as it zipped Rayah up into the belly of the rescue ship. Once she was up there, she found General Peterson, of all people, unclipping her and sending the mechanized rope back down.

"Your brother is over there," said General Peterson, pointing a finger toward the medical room. He wore a worried expression and was working quickly, committed to getting his entire team and his only son back onto the ship before it was too late.

Rayah acknowledged General Peterson with a nod and then walked toward the rear of the ship to a small room with clear walls. She pressed a button on her suit that made her helmet retract automatically and tuck itself into a thin compartment in the Glyden Suit's collar. She walked in and saw that her brother was giving her the thumbs up.

How much time do you think we have? asked Ondraus through duo-com.

I don't know. Maybe a minute, at most. I'm scared, O.

The thought of losing any number of soldiers still left on that airship was terrifying, but her biggest concern was her beloved Kaled. She didn't know what she would do if he didn't get back.

Me too, sis. Let's hope Tru can disarm it in time.

"They got it!" yelled General Peterson. "Tru and Tye were able to stop the bomb." His relieved expression said it all. His shoulders relaxed, and when his son arrived safely back on the airship, the general gave him a big hug.

Last onto the airship was Kaled. When he emerged, Rayah rushed to the doors and unclipped him. She pressed the button so the doors would close and then wrapped her arms around him and kissed him.

"I was afraid I'd lose you." She tightened her embrace and exhaled deeply.

"How are you?" asked Kaled. He touched her neck gingerly, and she winced in pain.

"A little sore everywhere. We took quite the beating down there, but I'll be fine. O is fine too." She rested her head on his chest for a few seconds and closed her eyes so that she could shut out the world. He kissed the top of her head and rubbed her back while their bodies swayed gently to the rocking of the airship's movement.

A few minutes later, they arrived at one of the palace's landing pads, where Dr. Perry Kortez, the entire

Kortez family, and Queen Ellandra were waiting for the team. As soon as the doors to the sleek airship opened up, the queen ran in. She was still in her nightgown and looked as if she had been a hysterical mess for the past hour.

"Is everyone safe? Please say everyone is okay," the queen pleaded. She saw her husband, the king, who was holding the infants in his arms. She kissed her babies and took them both, instantly crying with relief. "How is the rest of the team?"

"They were all very brave. Some were injured, but nothing serious," answered Birchram.

"Praise the All Creator," murmured the queen.

The group disembarked and made their way back into the palace. Several of them went to the medical ward, including the infants, for a thorough workup to ensure that whatever spell Rancor was trying to cast on them had no lasting effects.

"Once again," said King Tarrington to Evia and Ensin Kortez, who were following the group back to the palace, "you two have saved my children. I don't know why you have this connection with them, but I am forever grateful."

Back at the medical ward, Dr. Kortez, Birchram, and Zendo were busy working on their patients. Zendo placed the infants into a small crib-like patient bed and hooked them both up to monitors, taking some blood samples as well. Dr. Kortez worked on Wilstead, who had taken a Nemi shot to the chest. Severe third-degree burns covered Wilstead's torso, and the shock to his system was so bad that he needed to be sedated. Birchram worked on Bo, who had suffered severe head trauma from the constant collisions to the wall during his encounter with Rancor. Birchram gave him medication for the swelling and pain and asked Lina to apply the dermal healer.

Rayah worked on her brother. She checked his dressing to see if the bleeding had subsided. Relief washed over her when she noted the knife wound was no longer bleeding profusely. Next, she cleaned him up, added a fresh dressing, grabbed their Diagnostica, and scanned him for any additional tears or internal bleeding they may have missed. Finally she worked on Ameena, who had severe burns from the Nemi shot to her leg. Rayah looked up every few minutes to make sure Guyad was still in his coma.

"Rayah, how's your pain? You've been taking quite a few beatings lately," asked Dr. Kortez.

"Pretty terrible. Every part of my body hurts, and I have a wicked migraine."

"Here, I'm prescribing you some Ezeck, five-milligram dose. You can take one every six hours." He handed her a small bottle with the capsules and then walked away to review Wilstead's status.

General Peterson gave the next round of orders. "Now that we have all these other patients here, I think it would be best if we move Guyad to the holding cell in the east wing basement. We'll have the six men from Rancor's airship taken there as soon as the medical team is done evaluating them. I want them questioned tonight. I've already messaged our new head of security, Sergeant Moyacan, to bring an escort team here, and they are on their way. We'll need to set up medical equipment there to monitor Guyad's vital signs. Doctor Kortez, if you could take care of that now, it would be appreciated. Tomorrow morning we'll transport Guyad to the high-security prison in the city. They have a medical ward there as well."

It had been forty-five minutes since The Elite had all arrived at the palace before Rayah finally sat down. The doctor had said he would run additional tests the following day, but for now he felt confident that the infants were okay and could go to bed with their parents. One by one, the soldiers retired to their sleeping quarters with the agreement that they would meet for a proper debriefing in the afternoon. Aymes was the last straggler; after hugging and kissing Ondraus and saying goodnight to the others, she too went downstairs for the night.

Zendo was on as the third shift duty nurse and would be staying with the patients. He worked silently at a computer while his five patients slept quietly. The only other people in the medical bay were Kaled and the four guards filling out transfer paperwork before moving Guyad to the basement holding cell for the night. Kaled could have gone to sleep when the others did, but Rayah could tell he had no intention of leaving her side until she was safe in her bed. She'd been planning to use the dermal healer on her neck, but Kaled intervened, taking her hand before she had the chance. Instantly she was reminded of the night when Guyad had attacked her; Kaled had used the dermal healer on her neck that night as well.

Kaled hadn't spoken at all after getting off the airship. He just stood by her side; if he wasn't speaking to his sister through duo-com, then he was saying nothing at all. She gazed into his eyes as he passed the dermal healing device up and down her skin; the natural markings on the sides of her neck shimmered an iridescent color as the device ran over them again and again. Kaled was quiet, yet his eyes were doing all the talking; his gentle touch on her skin as he ran his finger up her arm and down again was warm and inviting. When he finished, she rested her head on his chest and breathed in deeply.

From behind, she heard some movement; Kaled let go of her and looked past her shoulder, toward where Guyad lay on his medical bed. Rayah approached Guyad carefully and read his vital signs. He was still in his coma. Maybe she and Kaled had misheard; it must have been Bo or Ameena who made the noise.

"Good night, Zendo; thanks for everything. Catch you later," said Rayah.

"Good night, guys. Enjoy your rest; you both earned it."

The palace was absolutely still. Only the sound of Kaled and Rayah's footfalls could be heard throughout the peacefully quiet building. Though exhausted, Rayah wondered if she would get any sleep after such an eventful night.

"Do you think they'll let us go back to sleeping in our normal apartments after this?" asked Rayah. "This whole *sleeping with four other women* thing is great but doesn't allow for much privacy." She winked at him and then took his hand in hers and kissed it.

"That would be nice," said Kaled, "but I'm not sure, Rayah. I tried following that masked guy. I was keeping my eye on him in case he decided to escape, but his light flash blinded our equipment. Rancor is still at large, and now we know there's an accomplice. Plus, I have a theory."

"Tell me. I have one too, and I wonder if we're thinking the same thing."

"His voice sounded robotic, didn't it?"

"That's exactly what I was thinking," agreed Rayah. "Why try to hide your voice unless..." She didn't want to finish her thought.

"Unless we would recognize the voice," said Kaled.

Rayah nodded solemnly. "Exactly."

"Are you going to take those pills the doctor prescribed you?"

"Zero chance, Kal. You know I don't take narcotics unless I have to. That stuff is super addictive. But I'll keep it in my go-bag just in case the pain does get out of hand."

Sis, call security now –

O? What's up? asked Rayah through duo-com, but there was no answer.

Suddenly, her smartwatch illuminated with a distress message. "Security, we have a level one –" The audio cut off; it was Ameena's voice.

Rayah stared wide-eyed at Kaled; they both took out their Nemis and ran back up the steps and down the hallway they had just walked through. Rayah had a sinking suspicion about what was happening, and she was desperately hoping she was wrong. Perhaps Kaled had the same thought, because he ran full speed beside her. It was as if they both knew where to go: back to the medical ward.

"Ameena, we heard a distress call. Was that you? Can you check on Guyad, please? Ameena? Do you copy?"

Rayah's attempt at calling Ameena confirmed her fears that Guyad had awakened. She was already envisioning whatever trick that chained man had up his sleeves. A trail of blood led from the hallway toward the medical ward and up toward the royal suite tower. At the end of it was Guyad, and he walked with strange jerking movements.

Guyad's wrist was freshly amputated and a piece of gauze had been wrapped haphazardly around it to staunch the blood flow. He climbed the main stairs, shooting every royal guard in his way. In a matter of seconds, Rancor – through Guyad – had unleashed pure evil in the palace. He may not have successfully kidnapped the infants earlier, but if Rayah and Kaled didn't act fast enough, Rancor might still meet his objective.

Rayah looked at Kaled. "Duo-com your sister and tell her to go and check on my brother and the other patients. Tell her to come armed and to bring the others."

"Already on it."

Both Rayah and Kaled shot Guyad. They landed direct hits, but he did not fall. The futile shots reminded Rayah of her useless attempts to shoot Rancor earlier; this made no sense. Guyad was a regular man of flesh and blood, possessed, but not a photonic. But maybe that was the answer. Rancor, not being the actual host of the body, could not feel the damage inflicted. Rayah shot again and again. Guyad continued to trudge up the stairs, and as royal palace guards attempted to stop him, he just shot them dead.

"We have an emergency, security level one threat. Everyone stay in your bedrooms, lock the doors. Repeat, do not come out of your bedrooms!" The voice came from the royal guardsmen on the third floor next to the Kortez family suite.

Rayah and Kaled ran up the stairs and continued shooting. It hurt her to see the physical, irreparable damage they were doing to Guyad's body because of the evil man who had taken over his mind and actions. Parts of Guyad's uniform were melted to his chest due to the weapons fire he had sustained. His face and pants had blood smeared on them from his bleeding, amputated hand.

"Help," said Guyad in a guttural plea. "Help me! I can't stop him. I've been trying, and I can't stop him!" He gasped for air as his broken body took yet another step toward the objective Rancor forced upon him.

Rayah knew that the blasts they were laying on Guyad should have been lethal. No one could sustain that much gunfire and still live. Yet here he was, pleading for aid while the man possessing him continued to climb the stairs toward the king and queen's suite. General Peterson came out of his room and also started shooting. He was wearing only a pair of boxers and was running up the stairs as fast as possible so that he could be at the king's and queen's door to help the royal guards who would be defending their country's leader.

"HELP!" screamed Guyad again. "Please don't let me do this! I cannot kill our king and queen. STOP ME! PLEASE!" he yelled in desperation as tears flowed freely down his face.

"The device in his eye. I bet that's what he means. That's what we have to do," said Rayah as she and Kaled closed in on the distance between them and Guyad.

"How? How can we do that? He'll get us all killed. Plus, I don't have anything to pull that out with!" said Kaled.

Guyad stopped his ascent and held onto a support column in a desperate attempt to force himself to stay in place. Witnessing Guyad fighting back so valiantly was remarkable. Guyad's face showed no pain or mercy whenever Rancor took control. Yet, whenever Guyad fought back to command his own body, his face contorted with anguish; he felt everything. The fact that Guyad could fight against Rancor, despite the intense pain, was a testament to his loyalty to the crown.

"We need tweezers and restraints," said Rayah through her smartwatch.

She saw General Peterson run into the queen and king's suite. She hoped he was looking for the items she had just requested; if not, they would all be dead in a matter of minutes. Finally, Rayah and Kaled caught up with Guyad, who had wrenched himself away from the support column and was only a few feet away from the king and queen's suite.

General Peterson and the king came out from the suite with tweezers, a pair of handcuffs with a fluffy pink lining, and a set of bed sheets. The king and the other royal guard had their weapons drawn at Guyad, who was now only three feet away.

"PLEASE HELP ME! DON'T LET ME KILL HIM! WHATEVER YOU DO, DON'T LET ME KILL MY KING!"

"Guyad!" yelled Rayah. She was directly behind him, and he stopped. His eyes turned to their usual purple color for a moment. "I'm going to try and remove the device, but you need to fight him off a little longer!"

Guyad whimpered just before his eyes turned stone gray again. Now that Kaled had a cleaner shot, he fired at Guyad's hand, and Guyad's Nemi fell to the floor. General Peterson sprinted in, kicking the Nemi down the hallway. Kaled tackled Guyad and knocked him to the ground while the king, the royal guard, and General Peterson all piled on top of him, placing the handcuffs on his ankles and then wrapping strips of bedsheet around his hands and feet to bind him further. Rayah grabbed the tweezers and sat on top of Guyad's chest, leaning one arm on his face to keep him from moving. She plucked out the device, and instantly, Guyad stopped struggling.

Guyad shuddered, and a tear fell from his eye. "Thank you," he croaked. "Can I...have a drink? I'm in...a lot of pain." He struggled to speak; his words came out in a raspy, guttural tone.

Quickly the royal guard went into the king's suite. Rayah took Guyad's trembling hand. He was dying. The pain inflicted upon him was finally taking its deadly toll, and he only had minutes left. She couldn't stop the tears from wetting her cheeks; even Kaled kneeled beside them and gripped Guyad's shoulder.

The king placed his hand on Guyad's forehead. "All Creator, please ease the pain of this brave soldier. Take him to the place of rest."

"The babies? Are they okay?" Guyad asked in a voice so low it was barely a whisper.

"You helped save them, Guyad," said Rayah. "If it weren't for your tip about Rancor being photonic, we would not have survived. You helped save all of us. Your dad would have been so proud of you."

The royal guard came back out with the queen, holding a bottle of renaq and several shot glasses. Queen Ellandra gasped at the bloody scene before her as she saw the mangled soldiers who Guyad had killed. The king poured amber liquid into each glass, and one was filled with water for Kaled.

Rayah took the glass and downed the alcohol in one gulp. The heat of the drink burned her throat and almost instantly started to make her feel numb. The queen knelt and brought the glass to Guyad's lips, and he drank deeply. With what little strength remained, he smiled his thanks to the queen.

"Please...forgive me," he said weakly in between fits of coughing up blood.

The king responded by kissing him on the forehead. "You are, by far, the bravest man I have ever had the honor to witness." The king's affirmation brought comfort to Guyad, and he smiled and closed his eyes before drawing his last, ragged breath. "For king and country." He exhaled and was gone.

"For king and country," echoed the small group that surrounded him.

Rayah burst into sobs. Why did it have to end like this? Guyad was a good and brave soldier. She kissed his forehead and then cried in Kaled's arms on the floor. She was vaguely aware that the rest of The Elite and other guards had finally shown up at some point during the altercation. They were all standing still with their heads bowed.

General Peterson stood up and spoke into his smartwatch, and his voice echoed in all of the other small smartwatches from the men and women below. "We need to move his body and check for any survivors. The medical ward has a small morgue."

O, are you okay? Please answer. Rayah was desperate to hear from her brother.

He stabbed me again in the same spot. Aymes is here trying to patch me up. I've never seen so many dead bodies in one place before, sis. Are you okay? Where are you?

Guyad is dead. We had to pull the controlling device from his eye. The royal family is safe, but there are a few more dead here in the main hall.

The queen retreated to her suite; the king, however, followed the soldiers down the stairs. General Peterson stopped for a moment to check in on the Kortez family, who were shaken up but otherwise fine. Rayah couldn't help counting the dead palace guards as she and the others continued on their way – three, four, five.

Finally they approached the hallway that led to the medical ward. Soldiers were going back and forth, carrying dead bodies to the morgue. When Rayah finally reached the room, she saw Dr. Kortez; he had blood all over his pajamas as he tried to save a soldier who was coding. Rayah instantly approached the mayhem, and only then did she realize the coding soldier was Ameena.

In a daze, Rayah looked around the room and found the stretcher where Guyad had been earlier that evening. His bloody amputated hand was on the floor. He must have physically pried himself out of that shackle with immense force. Guyad may not have initially felt the excruciating pain from his hand while Rancor forced his body into submission, but he certainly felt it whenever his own mind was present.

Zendo's body, a scalpel still protruding from his throat, had been laid with the others in a row on the far side of the room. Ondraus, clutching his newly re-injured side, was talking Aymes through the process of treating a soldier who had suffered minor burns to his abdomen.

"I should help," said Rayah absently. She felt numb; the chaos and gore of this living nightmare had drained her of emotion. How could any of this be real? Their triumphant rescue of the babies might as well have been years ago.

Kaled agreed and began helping the wounded as well. The king, pajamas soaked with blood, moved bodies and prayed with the suffering. Thankfully, no further harm had come to Wilstead or Bo, who were still sound asleep through their heavily medicated states. The rest of The Elite worked tirelessly for over two hours until the first-morning sun started to peek out over the horizon.

"How are we doing on supplies?" asked General Peterson, weary-eyed.

"Fine, sir. We'd been adding to our inventory and we were prepared for an attack, but we'll need to order more tomorrow," said Dr. Kortez.

"Good. I'll call the city morgue. They should be open by now anyway. I'll also have my son work on getting additional soldiers. We'll need nine more and a nanny." He looked away for a moment and shook his head. "Poor man did the unthinkable, and he wasn't even in control of his actions. What a terrible way to go."

They'd lost fifteen souls that night, including Guyad, Belfast, the nanny, and all six men from Rancor's airship. They'd never even had the chance to question the prisoners. Dr. Kortez had to force Rayah out of the medical ward after dawn broke. He and Birchram were going to stay; all the patients were stable but would need to be moved to Lexel Hospital, ten minutes away.

Rayah and the remaining Elite staggered back to their quarters. She kissed Kaled goodnight and went to the bathroom to shower. Rayah watched as all of the blood washed off her skin and went down the drain, then she staggered to bed and lay down, sniffling as tears began to wet her cheeks.

"I can't sleep," said Tru.

"Same," said Lina.

Rayah could see them all even though the lights were off. She nodded her head and wiped away a few tears. "Neither can I. It's just been one long, terrible night."

Aymes jumped down from her top bunk and tapped Rayah so that she would scoot over. Aymes got into the bed with her. "We don't need to do this alone," she said while quietly sniffling back her tears. "We lost a lot of good men and women today. I can't stop seeing their faces."

"I feel," added Lina, "like I'll never be able to wash off all that blood. There was just so much."

From a distance, Rayah saw Tru get into bed with Lina as well. They clung to each other like a life preserver. The night had ended in carnage and a sense of dread; when would Rancor attack again?

"That feeling will stick with you for a while," warned Rayah quietly. Her throat felt constricted as a sob threatened to escape her lips.

Rayah had seen more death, probably more than the rest of them combined, in her time as a trauma nurse. It came with the territory. Yet this attack felt unlike any she had experienced. Rayah had seen piles of bodies before, and pools of blood...and she'd felt the overwhelming guilt of second-guessing herself. Could it have all been avoided had they dealt with Guyad sooner? It could have. Rayah knew that thought would haunt her for years.

When she finally put her head back down, she snuggled against her friend and tried to copy Aymes' breathing rhythm. She learned that trick long ago and it usually worked to calm her nerves. She didn't know how long she lay awake before she finally drifted off to sleep.

CHAPTER 29

Kaled

Kaled slipped into bed with Rayah, draped his arm over her body, and closed his eyes. He breathed in the scent of her shampoo as he eased himself back to sleep again after being awakened by his sister Aymes. Roughly two hours passed before he felt Rayah stir. She turned onto her side and looked surprised to see him on her bed.

"Hey, babe," she yawned. "I thought I went to bed with the *other* Captain Behr."

"You did," he chuckled. "My sister went to start working on the airship and wanted me to stay here with you. She left about two hours ago." He shimmied his body closer to hers and kissed her lips.

"Mmm, this is a great way to wake up." She placed a hand on his shoulder and kissed him back passionately. Then, as if remembering that she wasn't in a private room, she looked around to see if any of the other women were watching.

"It's just you and me," he said, stroking her hair. "Tru and Lina are at Lexel hospital visiting Ameena, Bo, and Wilstead. Ondraus was released from the medical ward and went up to spend some time with Luna and Saule; I wouldn't be surprised if they have one of us Elite or at least a royal guard physically inside the nursery with them at all times."

"Yeah, I wouldn't blame them," she said sadly.

Kaled saw the pain in her eyes. He wiped a tear from her face and kissed her forehead. "How you feeling, babe?"

"I feel like a Wooly Bear has run over me." Rayah sat up and winced as she moved. "I'm also furious at this whole thing, and I have so many questions. I can't help but wonder what would have happened if we'd removed the device from Guyad's eye sooner. He was a good soldier; he didn't deserve this."

Tears sprang from Rayah's eyes as she let out a muffled sob. Kaled kissed her head and tried to comfort her the best he could. Rancor and that unidentified man were still out, and their whereabouts were unknown. Baby Luna and Saule would not be considered safe until those two madmen were apprehended.

Rayah lifted her head and wiped her tears. "What time is it?" she asked.

"Noon."

"I could have slept longer; that was only five and a half hours."

"Yeah, same. Hopefully, we'll all get a better night's sleep tonight. We have that debriefing in another hour. Do you want to keep relaxing here, or do you want to get up and ready to face the day? I can get you a cup of coffee," offered Kaled. He traced his finger up and down her arm and smiled as goosebumps appeared.

"Mmm, I can think of an activity I'd much prefer to engage in," said Rayah, leaning in and planting a kiss on his lips. "We're alone..."

A surge of erotic desire coursed through his veins as his lips met Rayah's. He had spent years yearning for her body, her touch, and the intimacy they once shared.

Now, to his surprise, all of that was his for the taking. He watched with delight as she climbed on top of him. Lust and desperation gleamed in her eyes, the meaning of which he understood instantly. Perhaps his eyes told the same story; he knew they both needed to make love after the traumatic night they had just survived. A moment in each other's arms would provide respite from the tragic images engraved in his mind. He grabbed hold of her thighs and lost himself in her beauty and in the delicate touch of her skin.

Somewhere, in the back of his mind, a voice yelled for his attention, but he was consumed by the moment. The voice grew louder and louder, gnawing away at his brain, demanding he listen. Rayah's hands were on her nightshirt; she was seconds away from removing it. Kaled placed his hand on hers and sighed in resignation.

"We should stop," he said reluctantly as the thoughts continued to bombard his senses. "I made a promise to you."

"I know," she muttered, "but...I need you. Let's just forget that whole thing. Say yes to me," she purred.

Rayah's lips seduced him with every kiss she lay on him. The weight of her body made every nerve inside him tingle in response. The idea of saying no to her made him feel foolish; how could Kaled reject the woman he desired with all his being? He watched as her hair danced in front of her face, almost hypnotizing him. His mind and body stood at a crossroads.

If he succumbed to his desires now, would she still trust him with her heart later? How could he prove not only to her but also to himself that he was a changed man if he failed his first test of loyalty? For years he had walked out on her, taking the easy road to satisfy his needs. If he broke his promise *again*, he could lose her forever. Kaled's heart crashed against his chest, panic rising in him at the thought of ruining his own life and hers. Saying no now would mean saying yes to a bigger and brighter future. He knew what he had to do.

"Come on, babe; let's get up and grab some coffee," he said finally with much difficulty. She stopped and observed him, trying to read his face.

"You're really serious about this promise, aren't you?" she asked.

"Yes. I am. I know it may sound silly, but it's important to me that you know I am a man of my word."

"It's not silly," replied Rayah, sighing while a look of shame and disappointment crept into her misty eyes. "I'm sorry I got carried away." Reluctantly, she climbed off him and sat up on the bed with her head tilted down, her face unreadable.

Fearing he had hurt her feelings, Kaled took her hand and began apologizing. Rayah, however, stopped him. "No, darling; you're right," she assured him. Though her words agreed with his decision, it was clear she would have preferred to continue. "I love you, and I was using this as an excuse to drown…everything." Rayah grew quiet and closed her eyes. "So many people died, and it's all my fault," she whispered as she wiped a tear from her cheek.

"Something tells me," Kaled said quietly, "that we'll all carry that burden for a long time." He wiped the tears from her face and then stood up and extended his hand. "Come on, let's go get that coffee. I think we earned it."

✳✳✳✳

A week had passed since fifteen people died in Rancor's attack on the palace. The bodies of the six men from Rancor's ship were sent to Susa for a traditional Susite burial, which in Kaled's opinion was a better fate than they deserved. Regardless, something far more beautiful was in store for the nine members of the royal staff who had been killed.

Kaled, The Elite, nearly all the palace workers, and several hundred citizens of Clivesdail attended a special memorial service at The Heroes Vineyard, located thirty minutes south of The Heart of Clivesdail.

Massive vines loaded with big, juicy grapes filled the majestic Heroes Vineyard. Kaled saw the expert farmers pruning vines and placing harvested grapes in large wooden barrels. Some distance to the north, a soldier marched deliberately back and forth on a raised platform beside a marble monument. No matter the season, weather, or time of day, a soldier always kept up that march, the clack of their boots echoing through the vineyard.

Whenever someone died a heroic death in the line of duty or while trying to protect someone from coming to harm, the body was laid to rest in this vineyard. The Heroes Vineyard was open for all, military and civilian alike, who had laid down their lives for someone else. That kind of sacrifice was said to be the greatest testament of pure love and bravery. Citizens from all over Brennen would make the journey to this location to bury their heroic loved ones.

The grapes were used to make a ceremonial wine, which was drunk at these memorial services in memory of all that these honorable men and women had sacrificed. It was also the first alcoholic drink everyone from Brennen drank when they turned eighteen and became official adults. Kaled vividly remembered his father uncorking a wine bottle from the Heroes Vineyard on his and Aymes' eighteenth birthday. The bottle had a gold label, which Kaled had stared at in wonder. The party guests sang a traditional song to him and his twin sister, the lyrics of which encouraged them to be strong, faithful, and brave. When his lips had touched the sweet but dry drink, he'd felt filled with bravery and love *For King and Country*. Every young man and woman partook of this tradition when coming of age.

Now, many years later, he was finally visiting the Heroes Vineyard, although he wished the circumstances could have been different. He and the rest of the group were dressed in bright, shimmering gold-colored clothing. The gold represented the rising of the spirit to meet with the All Creator at the true vineyard in the sky. At first, a furious debate had raged about whether Guyad would be allowed to rest his bones in the Heroes Vineyard. Some of the court officials were adamant that Guyad had broken his code of honor and had killed fellow countrymen and women in cold blood. The king himself, along with Rayah, Kaled, and General Peterson, had fought against this.

Rayah had made her case to the court officials. *You were not there to see the battle he was fighting. He's the main reason many of us are even alive. Had he not been such a strong, brave, and honorable soldier, we would all have been killed. Provide him his due honor; don't make his sacrifice be in vain. We owe him that much.* After all of their testimonials, the court officials granted Guyad the highest honors, dressed him in the most expensive linen, and anointed him with oils.

Kaled walked alongside his sister, behind Rayah and Ondraus. The vibrant green vineyard had rows wide enough to allow mourners to pass through in pairs. As they walked, several musicians at the front and the back of the long line played their string and wind instruments. The music warmed Kaled's heart and brought back memories of his two-month convalescence at the Twin Monktuary. The musicians played a contemplative yet encouraging song derived from the old religious texts. Some folks hummed along to the melodic tune, while others sang it quietly, and all the voices together combined to create something rich and majestic. Kaled reached out for his sister's hand, and he began singing along.

"Soar high, beloved;
Reach the heavens and rejoice.
We know we'll see you again..."

As he walked and sang, he looked at the picture-placards that lined the path. Each placard had the name of the individual, their birth and death dates, and a summary of their heroic deeds. He wondered how many Elite or other army members would end up here before Rancor was brought to justice.

Rayah's shoulders trembled as she cried silently. Though Kaled couldn't see the tears from his position, he knew the emotional burden she carried and how heavily it weighed on her heart. He hated that she blamed herself for not realizing sooner that Guyad had been possessed. Even with the threat Rancor had provided, none of them could have known that the monster within Guyad would awaken and wreak so much destruction despite being in a medically induced coma. Over the past week, Kaled had attempted to reassure Rayah that none of what transpired was her fault, but it was evident she still felt responsible. Everything could have ended differently had they removed the manipulation device from Guyad's eye sooner. The senseless deaths, the multiple soldiers wounded, and the lasting trauma and guilt borne by the survivors could have been completely avoided.

Finally, after walking for nearly twenty minutes, the funeral procession arrived at a clearing. Farmers in their ceremonial clothes gathered around the grave site, as did the men and women leading the service. All the bodies had been dressed in their uniforms and laid on a bed of rose petals. Guyad's body rested among them, wrapped in a blanket of bright gold and purple. Kaled felt grateful for that, preferring to remember Guyad as a handsome and brave soldier rather than seeing the horrific injuries he'd sustained on that final night.

One by one, King Tarrington Branaugh and General Elden Peterson took turns speaking of each person and their accomplishments, their honor, and their sacrifice. Each time they finished speaking of a person, the funeral employees pressed a button, descending the body seven feet into the ground.

"Lieutenant Carston Zendo," said General Peterson, "came from the city of Tolkeiny. He had always wanted to be in the medical field, and was only three months away from being promoted to Captain. His service to his country and his fellow brethren was something he never took lightly. Under Dr. Perry Kortez, Lieutenant Zendo helped in saving over thirty lives in his short career. He leaves behind a mother, father, and younger brother. His last moments on this planet were spent trying to protect his patients and stop Rancor. Lieutenant Zendo, you will be missed." General Peterson ended by saluting, the cue for the funeral attendants to lower the platform into the ground.

Last was Guyad. King Tarrington approached the covered body and rested his hand on the area that would have been Guyad's forehead. "Sergeant Guyad Lurca was a dedicated soldier who was known for his professionalism and heroics. His career is punctuated with many awards for his dedicated service. Had it not been for him, we wouldn't have known that Rancor was back. Not many of you know the exact circumstances of his death, but suffice to say that he died as he lived, a loyal servant to this country. Our team of soldiers has a lot of work to do, but we will find the evil men responsible for this bloodbath, and we will bring them to justice. You may rest, young man. You will be remembered for your strength, honor, and bravery. Go and be with the All Creator, who welcomes you to his great vineyard."

King Tarrington ended the eulogy with a salute. The musicians played an uplifting tune that reminded Kaled of springtime. He and the rest of the attendees in uniform saluted while non-military folks placed their hands over their hearts, and all hummed along to the beautiful song rising above the crowd. Sunlight gleamed elegantly on Guyad's wrapped body, giving it an ethereal quality as it descended. Kaled felt strange mourning Guyad's death; he'd spent his entire time at the palace loathing the man only to find out he never truly knew Guyad at all.

Funeral attendants pressed the buttons that began

laying mounds of dirt on each grave, which was the signal for the farmers to come and open small golden boxes next to each grave site. King Tarrington, General Peterson, and close family members reached into the boxes, pulling out grape seeds and placing them over the bodies. Soon new vines would grow, bringing life and joy from this moment of sorrow.

Guyad had no family members present, so the king and General Peterson performed the duty for him. When all the seeds had been planted, a nearby cage opened and dozens of butterflies flew out, their blue and yellow and orange wings bright against the brilliant sky. Rayah's hand squeezed Kaled's just a bit more tightly as the butterflies flew away, and he glanced sideways to see her smiling at them. King Tarrington said a final prayer to close the ceremony. Now the nightmare was over and the healing could begin.

CHAPTER 30

Rayah

A *Heron*-class airship hurtled toward Clarcona, a coastal city in Susa, with Rayah and the rest of The Elite inside. Three and a half months had passed after Guyad's death, but this was not their first mission since that fateful night. The king and General Peterson had not wanted them to search for Rancor straight away, insisting instead that Bo, Ameena, and Wilstead properly heal from their extensive injuries and spend time with their families. In the meantime, at the palace, everyone continued to restock on supplies and make additional modifications to their airship.

Mastering sign language had become an essential objective for all Elite members. They knew the outcome on the night when Rancor first attacked would have been very different if Tye and Tru had not been communicating back and forth with the group. Silent communication was critical, and next time there might not be one twin in a secure location relaying orders over their headsets.

The Elite had gone on six other missions since the night of the attempted kidnapping, and each mission only brought about a minuscule amount of information. They'd captured foot soldiers who knew next to nothing, and retrieved "secret" documents with information The Elite already knew. General Peterson had also sent out some of his most experienced soldiers from throughout Brennen to search and be on the lookout for Rancor, but they had also not turned up anything.

Heron-class airships could hold up to twenty people on two decks. The lower Utility Deck had an open space design with a small one-bed medical room on the far starboard corner, benches attached to the walls, and a storage compartment for Glyden Suits. An aft cargo hold held an inflatable speed boat and five sleek two-person land vehicles called Zoomers. On the far end of the Utility Deck stood a set of doors to allow soldiers to jump out of the airship during rescue missions.

The Elite currently sat on the upper Tactical Deck, equipped with reclining leather chairs, sofas, and tables lined with high-security laptops. At the fore of the Tactical Deck was the Command Pit, a small room where the pilot would steer the ship and access the navigation and weapons systems. Kaled piloted the airship while the rest of The Elite lounged on comfortable leather chairs on the top deck, enjoying mugs of hot coffee.

The group discussed the Winter Solstice holiday that had occurred two nights ago. Aymes was asleep with her head in Rayah's lap; she had complained of a stomach ache earlier and needed a moment of rest. Rayah was pretty sure Aymes had dozed off nearly forty-five minutes before, but had kept playing with her hair anyway. Like anyone else in the military, Aymes had the fascinating ability to go to sleep literally anywhere and in nearly any position.

"How did you guys spend your Winter Solstice?" asked Wilstead.

"Oh, we had a fabulous time," responded Rayah. Her heart still felt full and overjoyed from the much needed time off they'd been granted. "For the first time in nearly four years, both Behr and Jur families were under one roof. We rented a bed and breakfast in The Heart of Clivesdail, and it had a massive kitchen and backyard with a romantic little garden. It was simple, but it was beautiful."

Rayah had enjoyed spending time with everyone. The sight of Rayah and Kaled back together again had surprised their parents; Rayah smiled when she recalled the looks on their faces. Still, when she reassured them that she and Kaled had done a lot of soul searching, growing up, and apologizing for their past behaviors, they'd needed no further explanation.

It had also been fascinating to witness how Ondraus had introduced Niklas to his parents. Ondraus had been nervous all week and had imagined that his parents were going to give him an earful about the hardship of dating a woman with baggage, but that didn't occur. They received the young boy into their arms as if Niklas were their own grandson, and had spent the afternoon playing and doting on him.

"Yeah, it was pretty cool to hang out together," said Ondraus. "We roasted a giant pig, and my mom made her famous elderberry pie. Believe it or not, Mr. Yemley went door to door the day before the holiday and gave away small batches of Choco Moo Brew; he says he loves drinking it during the cooler months and wanted to deliver it to all the homes in a one-block radius from his shop," said Ondraus.

"Hey, yes! We saw Mr. Yemley, too," replied Lina. "He's such a nice guy, isn't he?"

"Hold on, let's go back to the bed and breakfast," interjected Tye. "I know you and Aymes shared a room," he said, pointing at Ondraus, "but what about you, Rayah? Did you share a room with Kal?"

"Okay, that's my cue to leave." Ondraus didn't pause for a second; he stood and left to see Kaled in the Command Pit.

"Yes, share the dirt, Rayah," Lina urged, leaning in. "I've meant to ask the same question."

"Yes," confirmed Rayah with what she hoped was a straight face. "We shared a room."

"Two beds?" asked Ameena.

"One medium-sized bed," answered Rayah, but she could feel herself blushing.

Rayah didn't mind dishing out details to her girlfriends, but it felt strange with the guys around. She and Kaled had slept on the same bed and kissed a *lot*, but that was as far as they'd gone. Instead, the two had spent most of the night talking. They'd discussed their previous relationships and what they had learned about themselves. They spoke of his journey through alcoholism and how Aymes got him to seek help before it got too out of hand. Rayah promised she would never drink in front of him after that.

Both Rayah and Kaled understood they would need to get to know each other beyond flesh on flesh to make their relationship work. Lust alone wasn't going to build a relationship that would stand the test of time. After they'd talked themselves out with discussions of their past and future, she had laid her head on his chest and listened to his steady heartbeat as she ran her fingers through his short hair. Rayah had fallen asleep next to Kaled dozens of times in the past, but it was even more refreshing to wake up beside him the next morning with their clothes still on and their promise to each other still intact.

Kaled had been the source of such intense heartache in the past. Rayah knew the only way to protect herself this time around was to take things slowly and not immediately fall head over heels for him. Her goal, however, proved more challenging than she'd imagined possible. Kaled had truly transformed into an amazing man, and the more time she spent with him, the more convinced she became. In her younger days, she'd felt what she thought was true love for Kaled, but her heart burned now with something far more profound, richer, and soul-binding.

"Alright, give it up, Wilstead. You owe me some money," said Tye triumphantly.

"Hold your horses," said Wilstead with a wave, "she didn't say if they –"

Rayah interrupted. "Kaled was a perfect gentleman."

Tye choked on the coffee he had been drinking. "Rayah, I'm sorry to say this, but he's going to get tired of waiting around," said Tye. "I'm just speaking up for the guy, okay? Men have needs, and if you deny him, he's going to go to someone else that can satisfy him. That's just the way it is."

She hated that mentality with a passion; how was it any excuse for a guy to leave? If a woman left a guy because she wasn't getting enough action, she would be called some very nasty names. Tye's statement had wounded her. In reality, Kaled *was* the type of man who needed physical interaction during a relationship. That was the very reason he had left her high and dry before. There was a measure of truth in Tye's words, and she would be lying if she didn't acknowledge that she repeatedly feared the same thing.

Rayah had been working relentlessly on her self-image. She strived to believe that she was more than *a good time in bed*. Repairing how she saw herself and her value would be crucial before she could embark on a serious, long-lasting relationship. Yet, here was Tye, who'd never had a relationship last longer than two months, talking about how she needed to open her legs or else a man would leave her. Rayah opened her mouth to give a retort, but Aymes, who she could have sworn was asleep, sat up and beat her to it.

"Kaled won't leave Rayah," Aymes said matter-of-factly. "For several reasons. One, he's in love with her. Two, he gave his word. That may not mean much to you, Tye, but it means everything to Kal. Three, he's a changed man. I was there for all of the ups and downs. I was there when he was battling his demons, and I can swear he has no intention of going back there again. Four, if he screws this up, I will personally beat his ass so hard he will be unrecognizable."

"Besides," Rayah added, "what makes you think women don't have these same strong natural urges? Do you honestly think it's only men? That is old, outdated information. Women enjoy and want sex just as much as men. The fact that some women can control themselves better than some guys is a different thing altogether, and that just has to do with maturity and self-control. Nothing more. If a guy can't go without sex when he's dating someone, that's on him."

"Wow, Tye, you're such an idiot sometimes," said his sister Tru.

"It's mutual abstinence," corrected Bo. "Rayah, I'm

rooting for you guys. I couldn't go that long without sex if I were dating someone, but I understand why you guys have chosen to do so. Thankfully, I'm married and don't have to worry about any of that anymore." Bo had started his encouragement with a sincere face but ended with a smile that showed how grateful he was to be married.

But Rayah wasn't done. "I want to make something very clear to you, Tye. Whatever amount of fun, wonderful, satisfying sex you *think* you have with the women you date pales in comparison to what I have in store for Kal. You don't know firsthand my stamina, flexibility, and ingenuity; you have no clue what I am capable of. I can assure you he will be rewarded for his loyalty and commitment once we are finally joined. I know how to please him on a level that you will never get to experience with any of your little playthings. So no, there's no need to feel bad for him or look out for him. He knows full well what is on the table. If he wants it, he knows what he needs to do."

An awkward silence fell upon the room. Rayah surveyed the stunned faces, wondering if she had gone too far in her defense. Even among a group as close as The Elite, intimate details like that might have been considered over the line.

Aymes chuckled and gave Rayah a high five. "Really disturbing hearing that about my brother, but yes, girl, know your worth and own it."

"She's a hundred percent right, Tye." That was Kaled's voice on the intercom. He must have heard the entire dialog and was now sounding off to share his feedback. "I know *exactly* what's at stake, and I'm in it for the long haul."

Tye looked at Rayah for a moment before conceding with a gracious smile. "Alright. Point taken. My apologies." Rayah smiled back and accepted the gesture with a nod.

Wilstead tried to change the subject. "Did anyone else notice how strange the king looked when he announced the holiday on the tele-screen? Was it just me or did he look like he was faking his enthusiasm?"

"It was definitely faked," Ameena said. "I don't know if I would have noticed before working at the palace, though, but now that I know him so much more, yeah, I can tell that was his fake diplomacy face."

"I bet it has something to do with the queen," said Bo. "When was the last time any of us saw her?"

"Good point," added Wilstead. "She wasn't even on the tele-screen like she is every year during the Winter Solstice address."

Rayah purposely averted her eyes from the conversation. She had her own theories but preferred not to share them with the group.

Yeah, the queen is probably messing around with Dr. Kortez and she's too embarrassed to show her face in public, said Rayah through duo-com.

Cool it, sis, admonished her brother. *Unless you have actual proof, you can't think that of our queen and the doctor.*

How else can you explain the random times she comes to visit on the third shift? asked Rayah. *Even when he's not supposed to be working, he'll come to meet with her for twenty minutes or so. It's sketchy. And, each time they've done this, they've asked you and me to leave.*

Think about it, said Ondraus. *If they were having an affair, why would they do it at the palace and not his place? I think you're letting your imagination run away with you.*

I was right about Guyad, Rayah added.

Yes, but you dated him and got to know him on a whole new level. Our queen would never do such a thing.

Fine, Rayah conceded. *I'll give it a rest.*

"I bet the twins are taking up more of her time than she expected," Lina volunteered. "And she's never liked cold weather, so I bet that's part of it, too."

"I think," added Tru, "the king knows there's a big chance that Rancor will come and start some trouble on a national level. That's why he made this Winter Solstice into this grand spectacle. It's never been celebrated like this before. If dark times do come, it will be good to have a happy memory to cling on to."

Rayah got up just as Ondraus came back into the room. She walked past her brother, into the Command Pit, and locked the door. Kaled was sitting in a leather chair that had navigation controls on panels beside him. He turned and saw the closed door and beckoned her over with his hands. She straddled him and wrapped her hands around the nape of his neck. She loved sitting in this position; it felt intimate.

"Thank you for what you said earlier over the intercom," she said.

"Of course, darling. I meant every word."

Knowing her worth was something Rayah had been working on for quite some time, but seeing it validated in the eyes and actions of the man she loved was another thing entirely. She thanked the All Creator that Kaled was in her life again, and she vowed to show him that he, too, was worth waiting for.

CHAPTER 31

Ondraus

Ondraus had never been to Clarcona before, but his mother and father used to go there all the time when they were dating. According to his parents' stories, Clarcona was known for its beauty. Back then, tourists had lounged on clean sandy beaches as merchants wandered among the palm trees selling freshly caught fish and handmade seashell necklaces. Lovebirds flocked to the city not just from all over Susa but from the surrounding nations as well.

That was no longer the case. Clarcona had a dreary atmosphere; even the trees seemed to lean to one side, too tired or ashamed to stand up straight. Green, murky ocean water crashed against broken beer bottles and piles of garbage, which littered the beach as far as Ondraus' eyes could see. Instead of bungalows or huts selling artisanal items, the seafront was home to huge, hulking towers, most of them half-abandoned during construction. The whole place was a big gray, dusty wasteland.

The Heron landed on the top of an abandoned parking garage. Kaled turned on the stealth mode so no one could see the airship without specialized equipment. The team convened around the large meeting table on the ship's Tactical Deck; Kaled and Rayah joined them. They went over the plan for what felt like the thirtieth time. They discussed the scant intel they had gleaned from the events that had taken place thus far. The men on Rancor's ship had probably hailed from Susa, based on their accents, and the water-resistant footwear they wore suggested they were familiar with life at sea. Unfortunately, finding the specific coastal city they were from had proven to be near impossible.

The Elite also went through the limited information they'd been able to gather from the facial recognition program Tru had run on the fifteen wealthy men gathered around Rancor in the airship. Ondraus had noticed that all of the men were extremely well dressed in fine suits; if they were there with Rancor, it was probably because they thought he had something up his sleeve that could help them get richer. Tru had discovered they were all wealthy through different means; some were investors, while others had regular day jobs as lawyers or mayors. Hundreds of questions still lingered, though. How had these people found out about Rancor's plan? Had any of them helped him escape from prison? How many other wealthy and influential people might still be backing Rancor? The Elite had been ordered to disperse in teams of two to get as much information as possible.

"Hey guys," said Kaled, "how about we go in teams of two, but not with our sibling?"

"That's a terrible idea," said Wilstead. "Duo-comming is literally the only reason why we're here as The Elite." The rest of the group nodded their heads and agreed with Wilstead.

"Hear me out," interjected Kaled. "You all saw how instrumental it was for Tru and Tye to communicate with all of us. If it weren't for them, we'd have had a much harder time rescuing those kids. We might have more situations like that. Besides, there's this strange gut feeling I have. It almost feels like a warning. We should break into non-sibling teams."

Aymes observed Kaled. She had tilted her head slightly and grew quiet for a moment considering his words. "Okay, he might have a point," she added.

Ondraus felt his smartwatch vibrate, and when he looked at the touch screen, he noticed he only had one bar of signal instead of the usual five. "Anyone else here have bad reception?"

"My connection is really weak," Wilsted said, tapping his watch as if that would improve things. "If we don't have signal, separating the twin pairs is an even better idea, right? Duo-com might be the only way for us to get in touch with each other."

"Well then, it's settled," said Aymes with finality. "Since that's the case, I choose O."

The rest of the group looked at each other and then started quickly blurting out who they wanted to be paired with. Ondraus was especially interested in one particular mission site, which he and Aymes would be canvassing together. Ever since the strange encounter with a mysterious man named Mr. Imicem, Ondraus and his over-thinking sister had yearned to discover the man's true identity. According to their intel, Mr. Imicem had offered a job on his airship to a man named Aslowe, who'd been killed in The Elite's assault.

Once they were all teamed up, Kaled led everyone in prayer before going downstairs. Aymes unlocked the aft cargo hold and tapped a touch screen to operate a mechanized lift. A whirring sound filled the area as the slowly rotating lift produced a Zoomer for each team of two.

Until now, Ondraus had not shared a one-on-one mission with Aymes. Being a duo-com certified twin had always guaranteed that he and his sister would work side by side. He feared the unforeseen consequences that might pop up from being paired with his girlfriend instead of Rayah. Thankfully, he and Aymes could communicate silently through sign language if the need arose, though duo-com was still vastly superior.

As Ondraus pondered this new dynamic, another thought presented itself. Perhaps he and Aymes had the upper hand. Unlike everyone else, the two of them had been dating for several months. During their relationship, there had been multiple times when they had shared glances across a room and somehow inferred what the other meant. He might not be able to read her thoughts the way he could with Rayah, but he could certainly read her face and body language. Besides, a few extra hours of having Aymes to himself, even while working, could be fun.

None of the teams were in their official work uniforms. They wore street clothes appropriate to the place they were visiting, which also meant some of them had to do a wardrobe swap when the team partners got switched up at the last minute. He and Aymes were dressed in long brown pants made of a nylon and cotton blend, along with a long-sleeved coat, a hat, and steel-toed boots. Ondraus' smartwatch showed five in the afternoon, and he could see boats making their way back to docks, where fishermen and merchants worked on unloading their cargo.

"How's your stomach?" he asked Aymes.

"Much better. I don't know if it was the tuna I had for lunch or my brother's horrible driving that set me off."

"Ha! He does tend to drive a lot faster," said Ondraus.

"You say faster. I say crazy."

They blended in easily; no one so much as looked at them. Ondraus swaggered confidently up the dock and approached an empty boat slip, deliberately looking at his watch several times before he spoke to Aymes loud enough so the men in the nearby slip could hear him.

"They're late," said Ondraus.

"Either that or they gave us the wrong location," added Aymes, looking annoyed. She spat on the dock and slouched.

Ondraus stifled a laugh. "I hope he wasn't pulling our chain. It's not like we don't need the money."

"Who you guys waiting for?" asked a man with a scruffy beard.

"He goes by Imicem. Anyone heard of him before? He told us he had a job for us, but I'm wondering if he's even showing up."

"Imicem? I never saw no Imicem, but I did hear of him. My friend Aslowe took a job a few months back with some guy named Imicem, and he came back in a coffin. I think you're better off not meeting that guy; he sounds like trouble," said the scruffy man.

Ondraus didn't show it, but he felt that this mission was another bust. He might try a few other spots, but he had been hoping that these docks, where the five men had first been hired, would be a hot spot. Just as he was about to tell Aymes that they should go, someone spoke up.

"You're at the wrong dock," said a younger man with a terrible attempt at a beard that appeared to be more like sparse patches of whiskers on his youthful face. He was tall and slim, though Ondraus assumed he was thin due to circumstance and not choice or genetics. The young man carried a basket full of fish guts while a cigarette hung loosely on his chapped lips. His clothes looked to be secondhand; they had a weathered look just like the dilapidated city of Clarcona. "Look, I agree with Erwin here. Don't go looking for those guys. They're trouble."

"What dock is it?" asked Aymes. For a moment, she had stopped slouching, and something as simple as that caught the young guy's eye. He watched her and stood perfectly still.

"It'll cost you, pretty lady," he said with a charming boyish wink.

"I don't think so," interrupted Ondraus. "Come on; he doesn't know."

"Oh, I know exactly where they are," said the young man. "It's just twenty minutes from here. If you were to hurry, you'd catch up to them before they all go on their fancy little meeting in the open sea. I heard them talking about it earlier this morning when I was dropping off my sister for work. They set out later this evening."

"Where is it?" asked Ondraus, already knowing this boy was going to want something in return. He just hoped it wasn't Aymes, or they would have to leave without the vital intel. He didn't like how the young man was looking at Aymes; it wasn't a sinister look, but it still made him feel uneasy and unwilling to barter.

"I'll tell you in exchange for a kiss, from her that is..." the young man's voice quaked as he stated his terms.

"You can forget it," spat Ondraus.

"Deal," interjected Aymes. Ondraus was ready to

put his foot down; there was no way he would allow his girlfriend to kiss some stranger just for information that might not even be worthwhile. "What's your name?"

"Helix," said the young man with an edge of nervousness. He swallowed hard and shoved his hands in his loose pants pockets to keep them from fidgeting. "I want a real kiss, by the way, not some tight lip peck on the cheek, and I want his shoes. We look like we're the same size, and I could go for a new pair that ain't all tore up."

Aymes approached Helix, and Ondraus reached out for her hand to stop her. She just smiled and said, "Best start taking off your boots, dear."

She went to the young man, who appeared to be barely eighteen. "Put that cigarette out first," she demanded. Helix stomped it out eagerly. Clearly, he thought Aymes was in charge. She looked at him politely and took his hands so that he could wrap them around her waist. "Have you ever been kissed before?" she asked. He shook his head. Aymes winked at Ondraus, who watched frozen in horror.

After a full minute or two of non-stop kissing, an eternity for Ondraus, Aymes pulled away. Exhilaration shone on Helix's youthful face, his eyes wide in wonder.

"Not bad for your first time," she said with a smile. "A little tip, though: lose the cigarette. No girl wants to make out with an ashtray. Plus, it doesn't make you any more manly; your job is manly enough, I can assure you."

"Thanks," said Helix, his ears turning red from the compliment. He gave Aymes the exact address and told her what the boat looked like. He also mentioned that he wasn't seriously going to take boots from a stranger, but Ondraus insisted since the young man's shoes were in a pitiful state of disarray, as evidenced by the tape strategically wrapped around them.

Ondraus raised an eyebrow at Aymes as they left the dock area. "Wow, you and my sister sure have no problem kissing random guys for work-related missions."

"Well, we got the information we needed. Plus, I didn't see you offering to make out with him."

"Yeah, but –"

"Besides," Aymes cut him off, "I'm tired of going on mission after fruitless mission. So far, everything has been a dead end, and frankly, I'm bored. If I'm going to be away from my son, I want to have a tangible reason for it. I wasn't going to leave without that information. Even if it amounts to nothing, which it probably will, I still needed to give it a try. Plus, it was his first kiss. How sweet is that?"

"He was lying. The boy looks like he's eighteen; surely he's kissed plenty of girls by now."

"Not to sound like that person, darling, but I've kissed many, *many* guys in my day. I know the difference between a guy who is experienced and not. Believe me, he had never kissed anyone besides his momma, and probably a pillow when no one was watching."

As they walked toward the parking lot to hop on their Zoomer, Aymes stopped suddenly and clutched her stomach. "I think I'm gonna be sick."

Ondraus scooped up her hair and kept it away from her face while vomit erupted out of her mouth. As soon as she finished, he placed his hand on her forehead and looked into her eyes. "Are you not feeling well, my love? We can follow up on that lead some other day. Come on, let's get you to the Heron."

"Thanks, darling," said Aymes. "I'm feeling much better now. Man, remind me not to have the tuna next time. It really did a number on me." She wiped her mouth with a small rag she had in her pocket and sat behind Ondraus on the Zoomer. As he drove, she kept her hands wrapped around him, resting her head on his back.

Twenty minutes later, they arrived at a marina full of large and elegant boats. They immediately spotted the ship they'd come looking for. The name *Caprisor* was written in bright cursive letters on the back of the massive vessel, which appeared to be far more sophisticated than the airship they had attacked a few months back. Aymes and Ondraus looked around and noticed there wasn't anyone else in the area. They sneaked onto *Caprisor* and found a small lifeboat attached to the exterior railing, which seemed as good a place as any to hide. This was where being with Rayah would have come in handy; they could at least have made small talk through duo-com. As it was, he and Aymes were stuck in silence – and he couldn't even do any of the usual things he might have wanted to do with her in a small, dark room.

After about an hour of sitting at the dock, the ship set off into the open sea. At that point, the captain of the boat announced they would be going into the air. So *Caprisor* was an airship, too, thought Ondraus. That would greatly complicate the task of escaping if they were discovered.

Ondraus checked his smartwatch: still no signal bars. He showed Aymes, and she showed him hers, which was similarly useless. Maybe they were too far away from the city to get a proper signal. The sky was turning dark, and the first sun had set before a group of men walked to the main deck, stopping twenty or thirty feet from Ondraus' hiding spot.

"Rancor will be pleased when we report our numbers and deployment date," said a man with a long hooked nose as he walked in front of a group of ten others. Ondraus sneaked a peek and saw the men sit down at a bench with a long table. A young lady dressed in heels and a service uniform came by and took their drink orders. Though the boat was large, it looked to Ondraus like the type that was rented out for personal affairs rather than a public cruise ship.

"Yes, well, Rancor must deliver what he has promised," said a man with a large stomach. "I must say, my investors are not pleased at all. They were told they would have access to a new energy source, unlike those energy stones, and would be able to control the market. So far, all we have are a few dead colleagues."

"A small price to pay *if* this all works out," protested the first man.

A distinguished gentleman, dressed in fine white clothing, stared at the female server hungrily before chiming in. "I'm all for it. Look what he's done to the kingdom of Susa. Before, all the energy sources were reasonably priced, and now that he's been controlling the king for several years, we've gotten so rich I barely know what to do with myself. To think we can expand to Brennen as well? All we need are those damn babies, and then we're off to make some money."

"But why does he need those babies?" asked the corpulent man. "Imicem has explained it, but I swear I still don't understand. I don't want to sound stupid in front of them. They don't look the type to want to repeat themselves more than once."

It was clear to Ondraus that only the men speaking to each other were the actual investors. The others were guards, standing on the deck ready to pounce on any interlopers.

The man dressed in white took out a cigar and had the female server light it for him. "Their essence," he explained, "will give him the strength to come back fully. He's only partially here. Don't ask me what that means; I have no clue. But the babies will break that divide and give him back his youth and strength. After that, he'll give us the knowledge on how to harness the power of the energy crystals with his new formula, and we'll cut off all the nationally protected energy crystal growers throughout our region. We've already taken over most of Susa's power sources. Imicem says he has an idea where Marez Cave is, though he needs more time to be sure, and once we find it and kill off all its house members, we'll be the only available source."

"We'll become rich beyond our wildest dreams," added the man with the long hooked nose. "Our army is almost in place. They're ready to head out in the next few days, and we'll take over Brennen. They won't see any of it coming. They think they only have to worry about Rancor. How wrong they are."

The light of the setting sun reflected off of Ondraus' smartwatch, and one of the bodyguards noticed it immediately.

"Identify yourself! Come out with your hands up, or we'll shoot."

CHAPTER 32

Aymes

Aymes couldn't believe their bad luck. The muscular bodyguard had a Nemi pointed straight at them, and she and Ondraus were in too odd a space to try and fight back at the moment. They only had two choices: jump out of the lifeboat and plummet into the icy ocean from this height or do as the man said and come out with their hands up.

She and Ondraus did as they were told. She didn't know about Ondraus, but she was furious that they'd gotten stuck in this position without the ability to duo-com. *Fine idea, bro!* she thought angrily. If she had to be stuck out here with no signal bars, she'd rather have had her brother with her. For all she knew, Kaled and Rayah were probably back at the airship making out, and here she and Ondraus were about to fight their way out of a bad situation.

The man gripped Aymes' hand hard, pulling her off the lifeboat and onto the airship deck. He pressed the weapon's muzzle against the side of her head while his other hand gripped her waist. "Make a bad move, buddy, and your pretty girlfriend here is dead," he warned Ondraus.

"Maurick," said the man with the long hooked nose to a nearby bodyguard, "tell the captain to put our ship on stealth mode. Things might get messy with our uninvited guests, and we don't want any witnesses."

"We're just two fishermen," blubbered Ondraus. "Please, sir, I don't have much money, and I saw this boat and thought it was a nice place to take my girl to gaze at the stars. That's all. I didn't know anyone would be on it." He looked down, drawing attention to his ratty shoes.

Ondraus sounded convincing, stuttering uncertainly exactly as a peasant fisherman would have. Aymes knew she had to follow his lead and play it cool for as long as she could. Level-headedness might be the difference between life and death.

"How much do you think those two stowaways heard?" asked the man in the rich white clothing.

"Hard to say, sir. The lifeboat is close. I heard everything clearly, and they were only a few feet away from me."

"Kill them. Actually, kill the man and leave the girl. Have her get cleaned up and then take her to my room."

Aymes surveyed her surroundings quickly. The other guards were facing them but had not pulled out their weapons yet. Apparently, she and Ondraus didn't look threatening. Ondraus hadn't reacted with a military or combative stance just yet. He looked shocked and continued pleading their innocence. Aymes watched her boyfriend and saw that he quickly made the sign to attack.

That was all she needed. Ondraus continued with his theatrics, and Aymes quickly slammed her free hand on the guard's forearm, knocking the Nemi out of his hand. In an instant, Ondraus took out his weapon and shot the man dead in one quick tap of the trigger. Aymes knew more weapons fire would start now that the other guards were on the alert. She ran forward, grabbing the fallen Nemi and opening fire. One guard shot her in the shoulder, and she could feel her skin sizzle in pain.

Aymes spun and aimed her weapon at her attacker, but Ondraus beat her to it. With two shots in the chest, the man crumpled to the floor, dead.

"Maurick!" yelled one of the investors from under a table. "Call for backup, you idiot!"

Before Maurick could honor the request, Aymes shot him in the groin and barely had time to watch him fall to his knees, writhing in pain. A large man lunged toward her, slamming her to the ground. Aymes watched in distress as her Nemi clattered onto the floor out of her reach. Mercifully, Ondraus kicked the weapon toward her just as he ducked in time to avoid a powerful blow to the face. With a fraction of a second to spare, Aymes shot her attacker in the face.

Just as she sprang to her feet, Ondraus hurled himself toward a new attacker. The two collided in a flurry of limbs, and Ondraus' Nemi flew overboard.

"Aymes, behind you!" yelled Ondraus, his shout punctuated by the shattering of bone as he punched his attacker hard in the face.

Aymes didn't respond in time. A bleeding hand covered her mouth; a Nemi jabbed deep into her spine. In one swift, powerful movement, she stomped hard on her assailant's foot and slammed the back of her head to his forehead. Her attack caught him off guard, and he loosened his grip on the weapon long enough for Aymes to turn around.

"You bitch," he growled as he brought his hand toward his bloody nose.

Aymes wasted no time. She aimed and fired her weapon, killing him on the spot. In the moment it took her to catch her breath, she noticed Ondraus drop to the floor, clutching his stomach. Aymes realized in horror that Ondraus still had no weapon to defend himself with. She ducked as an energy beam hit the wall above her head and quickly grabbed the Nemi from the attacker she'd just killed.

"O!" she yelled and tossed the weapon to him.

A wave of new bodyguards flooded the deck. *Get up, O,* she thought in desperation. She watched as his eyes flickered open, and he summoned the strength to stand up, though it was clear he was badly injured. To her right, a man barreled toward her, but she was ready for him. She kicked out her foot to set a trip, sending the large man hurtling to the ground. Before he had the time to turn over and shoot, she landed on his back and placed her hands on the sides of his head, snapping his neck with one quick movement.

Behind her, a man grunted in pain. Was it Ondraus? When she turned to look, she saw one of the guards fall backward; Ondraus had shot the assailant to protect Aymes. Ondraus' moment of chivalry didn't come without a personal cost; he received a blow to the head from an oncoming attacker. She desperately wanted to run to her boyfriend's aid but couldn't. A man had picked her up from behind and slammed her hard onto the ground. For a moment, all went dark.

Aymes shook her head. There was absolutely no time to dwell on the effects of a concussion. Mercifully, her eyes re-adjusted, and she jabbed the man by the throat, instantly making him gasp for air. The man, however, didn't slow. His large mass of a body loomed over her like a tree, and he picked her up once again. Aymes attempted to kick and punch her way out of his grasp, but it was useless. He was on his way toward the railing, no doubt to cast her overboard. She writhed violently and then plunged her teeth into the side of his neck in one final attempt to save herself.

A strangled yell pierced the air as the man loosened his grip on Aymes. She took advantage, wrenching herself free from his grasp. Aymes landed on the deck, her eyes darting back and forth as she tried to find a weapon. None were nearby. She kicked the large tree-man hard in the groin. When he fell, she made sure to stomp on his trachea, and a muffled wet gurgle told her that he would be no more threat.

Aymes surveyed the deck in dismay. Though she and Ondraus had killed over ten men already, more streamed from the doors. Her body was exhausted and she knew Ondraus felt the same. Aymes called out to her brother through duo-com.

Kal, we need help now! Whatever you are doing, stop it and come find us. We're on the airship Caprisor, and we've been out at sea for about an hour or more. Bring heavy weapons. Get everyone here. Ondraus can't last much longer, and neither can I.

We're on our way! responded Kaled. *I've been trying to contact you; I thought I felt some pain on your end. What is going on?*

There's no time. I need to concentrate. Just come find us.

Twenty men had reached the deck by now. Aymes took in a deep breath as she and Ondraus dropped into a combative stance. Out of the corner of her eye, she noticed he looked nervous. His usual charming smile had disappeared and he'd gone silent as he surveyed what they were up against. She felt scared too. This group was far too large for them to handle on their own, yet they had no choice but to give their all.

Another man came charging at Aymes. She ran straight at the wall, taking two steps up it to flip herself over and land behind him. She snapped his neck with a hard but quick turn of his face that made a sickening crack sound. Ondraus moved closer to her. They stood back to back, fighting off men who surged out of every possible entrance to the top deck. Ondraus seemed to have caught his second wind, throwing blow after blow. She could hear the swish of the air as his arms landed yet another painful jab, punch, or chop.

Aymes saw two men rushing at her. She killed one with her Nemi, but the other shot her in the shoulder, the same one that was already burning in pain. A yell of agony escaped her lips as she felt her layers of skin crackling and sizzling. If she didn't get medical attention soon, she could lose all function to her arm. Ondraus spun toward the man who had fired on Aymes and delivered a ferocious kick to the groin. Though the man fell to his knees in pain, he raised his weapon and shot Ondraus three times in the chest. Aymes watched in horror as the man she loved slumped to the floor. The attacker grabbed Ondraus, picking him up like a rag doll and throwing him overboard.

There was not a second to react. Aymes knew beyond a shadow of a doubt that if he were still alive, he would drown in a matter of seconds. If he were already dead, she knew she would regret not retrieving his body so she could give him a proper burial at the Heroes Vineyard. She shot the assailant in the back five times and quickly jumped out of the airship, plummeting into the ocean like a stone.

She braced herself for impact. She knew the impact from that height would hurt, and she was right. The crash into the water felt like landing face-first on a sidewalk after falling out of a fifth-story building. The freezing water attacked her with the ferocity of a million knives stabbing at her repeatedly. As soon as she surfaced, she tried to suck in a breath, but her body shivered so violently that she almost couldn't do it.

Aymes couldn't see Ondraus anywhere. He was gone. Holding her breath, she looked underwater and thought she saw a body floating facedown. She summoned all the energy reserves she had left and swam to the figure, saying a prayer the entire time. "Please be alive. All Creator, please let him be alive." She reached him and lifted his head to find his eyes closed. She checked his pulse, but her fingers were too cold to feel anything. Regardless, it was clear he was not breathing.

Maybe he swallowed too much water, she surmised. She swam behind him and placed her arms around the bottom of his navel, giving a sudden jerk toward her. This was a maneuver that Ondraus had taught her many months ago when he found out she was a mother, a procedure commonly used to help a choking person. *You need to know what to do in case of a medical emergency,* he had warned. She only hoped this was the right move to make at this moment; Aymes wasn't sure if this technique was only for food obstruction or could be used in a drowning event like this one.

Ondraus' eyes flickered open as water shot out of his mouth. He breathed in deeply, clutching at his chest. "You jumped," he said weakly.

"Of course I jumped!" she responded. He looked terribly weak. Whatever pain lingered in her arm, lungs, and skin had momentarily faded away. All that mattered was Ondraus. His head drooped, and she tried to keep him facing up so that he didn't drown. She was no doctor but could tell he was in bad shape. His breathing sounded ragged, and he couldn't seem to keep his eyes open or his head stable.

"O, tell me where it hurts."

"I have a headache," he murmured through chattering teeth. "And my chest hurts a lot."

She wished he would have said something medical, something that she could relay to Rayah when the rescue came, but she was losing him, and keeping him above water was becoming increasingly difficult with her injured arm.

She remembered a random thing from her final year at the military academy during a class on how to survive in open waters. While she held Ondraus' head up, she kicked off her shoes. She then helped Ondraus turn over to float on his back to take off her pants. She made a square knot on one end near the bottom of the pant legs. She then grabbed her pants by the waist and swung them over her head to capture as much air as possible. She screamed through gritted teeth as her injured arm protested in agony. It took her two attempts, but she finally made a flotation device out of the pants-balloon. She secured it around Ondraus' neck and then took off his shoes and pants to do the same.

What is going on? asked Kaled. *I've been trying to duo-com you for an entire fifteen minutes. We're about twenty minutes out. Rayah is on the floor, in the fetal position, practically unresponsive from the pain but won't let me give her a mind blocker pill because she's worried sick about her brother. And I'm –*

If you don't hurry, Ondraus and I are going to die. We don't have twenty minutes. Get your ass over here. We're in the middle of the ocean, and it's fucking freezing. We've been shot multiple times. Give Rayah the mental blocker. Shove it down her throat if you need to because Ondraus and I both will need immediate medical attention. He's complained of a headache and chest ache.

It was impossibly hard to communicate. Every word she said to her brother took precious energy from her. She tried her best to block out the pain, focusing all of her attention on treading water while holding on to her flotation device and simultaneously keeping Ondraus' head above the waves. He had turned a sickly pale blue color, and his head rested on her good shoulder.

"Babe," he said weakly, "I love you, and I want you to know that you've made me the happiest man in all of Vilmos. These last few months have been the best of my life."

Aymes knew what this was; he was giving her his dying words. She wouldn't have it. No, he couldn't die today. "Darling, reserve your strength; they're on their way. Kal said he'd be here in twenty minutes."

"We both know I don't have twenty minutes." Somehow, in the middle of his terrible pain, he smiled. "In my bag on the airship is your earring. I've been trying to find the right time to propose." He took in a sharp breath, and Aymes could see she was losing him.

She held on to him so he wouldn't slip away from their makeshift float. He grew quiet, and his eyes closed. For a moment, she thought he was gone, but she placed her fingers on his neck and felt a weak pulse. She, too, felt like she was fading away. It must have been the intensely cold water that sapped her strength, not the damage to her arm. She was afraid of closing her eyes; what if she fell asleep and never woke up? What if Ondraus slipped out of her grasp and sank? *No,* she thought with intense resolution. *I'm not giving up that easy.*

Aymes kicked her feet to keep her circulation going. She had no idea how long someone could be submerged in water this cold, and was afraid that this might be the end for both of them. The minutes crept by, and her stupid smartwatch still had no signal and couldn't give her the time. Meanwhile, the sky continued to grow darker. She continued kicking her legs with the little energy she had left. *Stay awake and fight,* she kept urging herself.

Off in the distance, she saw an airship cut through the sky at an incredible speed. That must be her brother driving the airship like he'd stolen it, as usual. He was coming in fast, almost too fast, straight toward Aymes and Ondraus. Aymes had never attempted an emergency water rescue, and she knew her brother had never done one either; if he screwed up, he would kill everyone in the airship. She braced herself for a deafening splash, but Kaled had set down on the water with only a small wave that lurched over her and Ondraus' head for a split second. She looked to her left and saw the emergency doors to the airship already open. Tye and Bo stood there in wetsuits, ready to rescue them. Aymes stopped fighting. Help had come.

CHAPTER 33

Rayah

From a distance, Rayah could see her brother and Aymes in the open water. She knew the ocean temperature was almost freezing, and she was prepared to treat hypothermic injuries. Rayah looked at Tru, who stood on the Utility Deck near the emergency doors, wringing her hands nervously and casting glances at a bloody patch of gauze on Rayah's forearm. After Aymes had duo-commed with Kaled about their current predicament in the waters and the severity of their conditions, Rayah knew she would have to provide emergency medical care to both of them. Unfortunately, she would not have a doctor, fellow nurses, nor even wireless communications to help her. With no other choice available, she'd dragged Tru to the small medical bay and gave her a crash course on how to provide an IV and use a dermal healer.

Rayah could feel the flutter of an anxiety attack about to surface in her chest. Though she had experience as a trauma nurse when she was stationed in Benal, it was a completely different matter to try and save both her brother and her closest friend. Rayah closed her eyes to steady her nerves. Her best would have to be good enough.

Kaled spoke through the intercom system. "You got this, babe. I know you do."

He had sensed her need for encouragement despite their distance. "Thanks," she replied. Rayah sucked in a deep breath as she watched Tye and Bo press a button on the digital keypad by the emergency doors. The two men climbed into a life raft with a powered line. Behind them stood Lina and Wilstead, who stayed on the airship to help bring the life raft in.

Tye and Bo quickly zipped out of the emergency doors and steered themselves toward Aymes and Ondraus. Rayah looked up at the visual feed that came in. She already guessed the injuries her brother had sustained since she'd felt his thoughts over duo-com. Her brother appeared dead, but she knew he wasn't. Even though her mind couldn't connect with his at the moment, she could still sense him.

The video screen showed Tye and Bo pulling Aymes and Ondraus onto the life raft. Lina and Wilstead pressed another button on the screen, activating a winch to haul the raft back in. As soon as the raft was secure and Aymes' and Ondraus' wet clothes had been removed, both of them were covered with shock-sheet blankets designed to treat hypothermia. Bo and Wilstead lifted Ondraus and carried him to the one-bed medical bay where Rayah waited impatiently. Tru ran into the med bay and grabbed the dermal healer, heart rate monitor ring, and IV kit with a prepped bag of lactated ringers at four milliliters per kilogram that Rayah had left out for her.

"I'll walk you through it," said Rayah.

Rayah made sure not to show how anxious she felt so that Tru could lean on her for support. Tru nodded her head and mouthed thanks before leaving the med bay and kneeling beside Aymes' life raft. Rayah glanced at the video screen, holding her breath when she saw the injuries to Aymes' shoulder and arm. Ondraus lay motionless before her, his pulse weak. Both of them needed immediate care, but there was only one of her. How was she supposed to decide?

She tried calling Dr. Kortez, but he hadn't answered and she *knew* she had a bar of signal. He was probably committing any number of sins with the queen, thought Rayah bitterly. Left with no other choice, Rayah split her mind in two, one part to walk Tru through Aymes' injuries and the other to save her brother, whose condition was critical. She decided the first thing needed was to warm up their core temperature.

She talked Tru through the exact steps she'd be performing on Ondraus. "Tru, we need to heat them up. Get out the IV kit and clip on the wireless endothermic warmer to the IV line. Now find a vein and then clean it with the alcohol pad."

Warming them was crucial. Both Ondraus and Aymes had been in the freezing water a lot longer than Rayah would have liked, and they were dangerously close to dying from that alone. The endothermic IV warmer would raise their temperatures from the inside out, and the lactated ringers would help their bodies hydrate and heal the ferocious burns caused by the Nemi shots.

Rayah had already finished hooking Ondraus to an IV before she finished her instructions to Tru. While she waited for Tru to find a vein, she ran the trauma priority care list through her mind. Rayah looked up at the screen and watched as Tru fumbled for the needle and tried to find a viable vein on Aymes' forearm. Rayah wished she could do this for her, since it would save time, but Ondraus would most likely not make it off that table alive if Rayah left his side for a moment. Tru would have to complete this task herself. That bloody gauze was still stuck to Rayah's forearm; hopefully, Tru would do a better job than she'd done the first time Rayah had made her try.

"Is this one okay?" asked Tru as her finger quivered over the vein she had selected.

"Yes, perfect. Stick that sucker in." Over the comm link, Rayah could hear Tru whimper in reply.

The next urgent step was to assess Ondraus' breathing. Rayah ran her Diagnostica over his chest and confirmed he had a collapsed lung due to a broken rib. She uncapped a large 14-gauge needle and inserted it in the second intercostal space, midclavicular line. Almost instantly, she heard the woosh of air as his lung decompressed, equalizing the pressure between his lung and the rest of his chest cavity. This technique was an emergency fix because the effects only lasted for twenty to thirty minutes. She took note of the time while she affixed a non-adhesive hydrogel chest seal to the hole so it didn't suck in air.

Rayah grabbed a breathing mask and placed it on Ondraus' pale face to help push high-flow oxygen in his system. If they couldn't get to a hospital in time, she would need to insert a chest tube, but that was a doctor's job. Rayah had seen it done hundreds of times yet had never actually done one herself. She dreaded practicing such a dangerous and challenging task on her brother.

"Talk to me, Tru, how's our patient?" asked Rayah assertively.

"Um, well, she cursed me out for poking her vein too hard."

Okay, good. The needle got a reaction from Aymes. She's fine. My brother, on the other hand, is barely responsive.

As Rayah assessed Ondraus, she remembered he had complained of a headache. She didn't see any apparent contusions on his head. Rayah took out her penlight to examine his pupils and noticed one was bigger than the other. *Please no, please no,* she thought desperately as she put down the penlight and ran her Diagnostica over his head. She'd been hopeful that he only had a mild concussion, but as soon as she ran the device closer to the back of his head, she saw her screen light up with the very results she had been dreading. He had a subdural hemorrhage, a brain bleed.

This couldn't be happening. She was not equipped to handle something of this magnitude, and she didn't know if he had minutes or hours left to live. She tried her phone again. Still no answer. Rayah put down her tools and stared blankly at her brother, feeling completely hopeless and lost. What was she going to do? She tried re-reading the scan her Diagnostica had revealed. Was his brain actively bleeding? She felt alone; all the weight of this intense medical trauma was on her shoulders. If she had the time, she would have cried and had a complete meltdown, but there wasn't even time for that.

"Rayah, we're approaching a small city," announced Kaled over the intercom. "We might have better reception soon. How are they?"

She sniffed back a tear that was threatening to come out. "Aymes looks okay. Actually...hold on. Fuck."

"What?" he asked, alarmed.

"Her pulse is dropping. I gotta go. Bo! Come in here and keep an eye on my brother. You see this screen? If you see anything turn red or hear an alarm, you need to let me know."

Rayah heard him grunt in response as she ran out of the medical bay. Aymes was sitting up, her back leaning against a wall. She picked up Aymes' hand and repositioned the heart monitor ring to make sure it was working properly.

"What's wrong?" asked Tru. "Did I miss something?"

"Aymes, darling. How are you feeling?" Rayah didn't answer Tru's question. She just needed to get straight to the source.

"A bit tired, I think," responded Aymes weakly.

"Hmm." Rayah placed her finger on Aymes' wrist and counted the pulses while looking at her watch. Aymes' heart rate was low enough to make her pass out at any moment. "You need to lay down. Wilstead! Get me an oxygen mask and grab a small oxygen canister. It's green and about the size of your finger!"

"What's wrong?" asked Aymes and Tru.

"Just a little concerned with your heart rate. I'm going to take care of you."

Barely a minute passed before Aymes' eyes closed, and the small ring on her finger projected a dangerously low number. *Shit.* If Rayah didn't act quick, Aymes could lose brain function, or worse...die. *I'm sorry, Aymes, this is going to hurt.*

Somewhere in the background of her mind, she was vaguely aware that Tru was hyperventilating at the sight of her friend being unresponsive. Rayah removed the blanket covering Aymes, interlocked her fingers over her sternum, and began chest compressions. She heard a sickening crack as she began to push against Aymes' chest.

"Tru," grunted Rayah, "get out your phone and keep calling Dr. Kortez. Keep calling until he picks up his fucking phone."

Rayah kept the chest compressions going for a solid three minutes. Her arms burned with exhaustion, and she still had no idea if her brother had gotten worse or remained the same. Instead of Tru getting through to the doctor, Rayah's phone rang in her pocket. She looked at her smartwatch and noticed, with both relief and irritation, that Dr. Kortez had finally called her back.

"Tru, take my phone out of my pocket. I can't stop the chest compressions."

Dr. Kortez's voice sounded strained. "Sorry, Rayah, there was a –"

"No time!" exclaimed Tru. "Doctor, here's Rayah." She punched a button on the screen. Half a second later, a holographic image of the doctor sprang from the phone.

Dr. Kortez gasped and then immediately went into work mode. "What's the situation?"

"Both Aymes and Ondraus were shot several times. Aymes on the arm, Ondraus in the chest," said Rayah quickly while she continued with the compressions. "Both came in with severe hypothermia. I began an endothermic IV line of lactated ringers. Aymes' heart rate is really low; I'm trying to keep her perfusion going myself with CPR until she rewarms and her heart is up to the task again. Ondraus is unresponsive. He has third-degree burns all over his chest, plus a collapsed lung, which I've fixed for now with a needle decompression. He also might have a subdural hemorrhage, but I'm not sure. I need help."

A crown of sweat formed above her brow. Her arms were beginning to spasm from the continuous effort. She watched as the hologram of the doctor bent down and read the numbers on the ring's screen. "How long have you been at this?"

"Three minutes," she grunted as she continued to push onto Aymes' chest. Finally, after what felt like an eternity, Aymes' eyes flickered open, and she moaned in pain. "Welcome back, soldier," said Rayah with relief. She collapsed near her friend and hugged her.

"Keep your oxygen mask on and stay lying down," the doctor instructed Aymes. "Tru, her burns are too severe for the dermal healer. She'll need debridement at the hospital and stem cell grafts. For now, place some non-adhesive hydrogel pads onto her arm and shoulder. The pads are in the medical bay. Aymes, I'm sorry, soldier, but you'll have to wait a little longer before we can give you anything for your pain." Doctor Kortez's hologram stood up to its full height. "Rayah, let's –"

Before he was able to finish his sentence, an alarm blared from the medical bay. "Rayah!" cried Bo as he peered out the door, "you better get in here."

Both Rayah and the hologram doctor rushed to the room while Bo quickly stepped out of the way. "Stay here, Bo," ordered the doctor. "I might need you. Wash your hands and get on a fresh pair of gloves and a sterile gown. Rayah, run the Diagnostica on him again."

Rayah picked up the device and ran it on the back of Ondraus' skull. The image popped up on the large screen nearby.

"His body is warm now; that's why the bleeding has

increased," said the doctor. "How long before we get to a hospital?"

Bo relayed the question to Kaled, who stated, "Ten minutes to Tarpon Bay, thirty minutes to Oakland Regional. But I had Tye call, and he said they were both full. Each recommended we go to Lexel, and we're still fifty minutes out. I've got the throttle to the firewall already. How's my sister?"

"She's fine. Kaled, this is Dr. Kortez. Take us to Lexel. I need you to slow down and bring the aircraft down closer to tree level instead of up in the clouds. We have to operate on Ondraus, and the pressure in the cabin is not helping his intracranial situation at the moment."

Rayah felt the hum of the aircraft's engine as it slowed and could feel her ears pop as it descended. She also felt the doctor's eyes on her; Rayah knew he would ask the impossible. "He won't make it without the chest tube or without relieving the pressure in his skull. I will walk you through this." Dr. Kortez sounded so calm, so assured, but –

"I...I can't. I've never done this. This is way beyond a nurse's scope of work." Rayah had reached her limit. She wished someone would take over but knew there was literally no one on the ship who could.

"Rayah. Listen to me, soldier. He will die if we don't act now. He doesn't have thirty minutes, let alone fifty. You have to relieve the pressure in his cranial cavity."

Rayah nodded her head. Words wouldn't come out of her mouth; anxiety felt like it was giving her chest compressions of her own. She knew there was a real chance that she could accidentally kill Ondraus if she so much as did one thing slightly wrong. In her mind, even though she knew duo-com was impossible, she told him she loved him. She took out the antimicrobial scrub and prepped Ondraus for the procedure.

"Locate the fourth intercostal space," instructed the doctor. Rayah placed her finger on his side, feeling his ribs until she found what she *hoped* was the correct spot. "Now make an incision; be sure it doesn't hit his lung. That's it. Place the scalpel on the table and grab the clamps. Spread the incision and insert the tube into the pleural space." She attempted to keep her hand from trembling as she obeyed every task. Once the tube was in place, she used a suture to keep the tube secure and then connected the other end into a container that would collect both air and blood.

The doctor hovered behind her shoulder to ensure she did everything correctly and reviewed the blood's output in the clear container. "Excellent," he stated. "Prep him for the subdural procedure."

As dangerous as it had been, a chest tube was a walk in the park compared with this next surgery. Any mistake could kill or badly injure her brother. This task was dangerous enough in a hospital, let alone while flying in an aircraft. Bo handed her a vial of antibiotics, and she pushed the medication into Ondraus' IV line.

Rayah took out an electric razor and shaved off the hair from her brother's scalp in the region the doctor had indicated. Then she grabbed a marker and indicated two spots on his skull where she would have to drill. After disinfecting the area, she used a scalpel to make two incisions on his scalp to expose Ondraus' skull. The doctor continued to talk her through each step in a slow and assuring tone. Fear and nausea grabbed her by the throat as her fingers wrapped around the drill. *What if I go too far and damage his brain?*

"You'll do fine," Dr. Kortez said, as if he'd read her thoughts. "The drill has an auto-stop. It won't let you cut too deep."

That calmed Rayah enough to let her take a deep breath. She drilled two holes into her brother's skull and then irrigated them with saline, allowing the accumulated blood and fluid to pool out.

"Intracranial pressure is dropping and has stabilized. Good job, soldier," Dr. Kortez encouraged her as he read the vitals from his screen.

The entire procedure had taken only minutes, but Rayah felt as if days had passed. At last, after placing a protective dressing over the holes to keep the area sealed, she heard the doctor tell her she was finished. She nearly collapsed after the grueling emergency surgery; it was Bo who caught her. Doctor Kortez asked her to leave the medical bay and take a rest, but she refused.

"No. I can't. I need to stay with him," she objected.

"It's an order, soldier. Captain Jur, you did a fantastic job. I am supremely proud of you. You can bet I will add this to your record, and you will be rewarded for such bravery during a stressful and life-and-death situation. Honestly, you might want to look into a career in becoming a doctor. But for now, you must leave. Bo and I will stay here and watch over him. Please leave the room, get yourself a cup of water, and rest."

"I—"

"Now," he responded with finality. Bo seemed to understand the implication; he opened the door of the medical bay and escorted Rayah out.

As much as she hated the order, she knew the doctor was right. There were rules against medical personnel working on their own family because it made them think differently and not objectively. Rayah heard Bo give Kaled the directive to speed up the airship and maintain a low flying profile to prevent pressure buildup. She stopped by and saw that Aymes was still lying in the life raft; Lina, Ameena, and Tru were with her. Aymes had an oxygen mask on, and her wet hair was matted to her face, but her normal skin color had been restored and she looked fine despite all she had gone through.

"How is he?" croaked Aymes.

Rayah couldn't meet her eyes. She still had no clue herself. "Stable for now, but I'm not sure what's going to happen."

Aymes was quiet for a while. Tears welled up in her eyes as she craned her neck to try and catch a glimpse of Ondraus. "He was going to propose. Did you know that?"

Rayah nodded her head. "He was supposed to do it during the Winter Solstice holiday, but the earring wasn't ready in time. We should never have separated into non-sibling groups," she said bitterly.

"Rayah," Aymes cut in. "None of our communication systems were working. The only reason we have a fighting chance at survival is because we were able to duo-com you guys and get help. We were completely outnumbered on that airship. Trust me; no twin team would have been able to handle that. Plus, it could have been you and Ondraus out there. If both our nurses were down, no one else on board could have helped. You both would have died within minutes."

Rayah nodded silently and kissed her friend on the forehead. She wanted to go back to the medical room, but the doctor had told her to stay out, and she had to obey the order. With nowhere else to go, she staggered to the bathroom and looked at herself in the mirror. Ondraus' blood covered her hands and uniform. Her hair was a frenzy, much like her nerves. She collapsed in the corner of the bathroom and began to hyperventilate as a wave of self-doubt crashed over her. All of the decisions she'd made came back to haunt her. Her mind was going through every scenario, every step she'd taken, and making her second-guess every single action. What if her incompetence led to her brother's death? She wouldn't be able to live with herself if she lost him.

"Rayah? It's Ameena. Can I come in?"

Rayah couldn't answer. The breath kept seizing in her lungs, refusing to form itself into words. Everything around her felt like it was closing in. She was barely able to notice that Ameena had rushed in and placed her hands on Rayah's face.

"Hey, hey. Listen. You'll be okay. Just breathe, Rayah. Look at me. Slow breaths. Put your hand on my chest to feel my heartbeat. Your brother is going to be okay. You did a fantastic job. Rayah, honestly, you did so well. You kept your cool. You did what you had to do. The doctor was just praising your medical expertise." Ameena stayed with her until the crushing weight in her chest began to lift. "Here, the doctor prescribed you this. He said it would help with your nerves. I got you a cup of water as well."

Rayah recognized the pink pill as something she'd given to distraught patients in the past. It felt strange that she was the one swallowing it now, but she did as Ameena had told her, still unable to lift her head.

Another knock on the bathroom door sounded, and

Lina entered. "Hey guys, the doctor says Rayah needs to go back right now. Ondraus is losing too much blood and needs a transfusion."

That finally got Rayah to her feet. As she rushed to the small medical bay, she saw once more the red blaring alarms on Ondraus' vitals screen. Tru already had the equipment ready on a small table in the room. Rayah didn't have the mental capacity to walk her through the steps. Instead, Dr. Kortez guided her while Rayah stared at the screen. Tears streamed down Rayah's face as the red, distressing alert remained. After all they had done, she wasn't sure if it was enough to save his life.

CHAPTER 34

Aymes

The sun had spent the last five days hiding behind dreary gray clouds, which appropriately reflected how Aymes had been feeling since the terrible ill-fated trip to Clarcona. The miserable bone-chilling late midwinter weather made her want to stay inside, curled up in a warm electric blanket and drinking her sorrows away from a tall bottle of ranaq. She could almost feel the burning sensation down her throat, but Kaled had warned her off. *Trust me, alcohol is only going to dull the senses for a short while; it doesn't actually help*, he had said.

She wouldn't dare say so to her brother, but dulled senses sounded pretty good at the moment. The simplest things exhausted her strength and resolve. Her mind wasn't able to think of anything other than Ondraus, and not having him beside her made it difficult to see that even the dreary clouds above her had a silver lining.

Aymes, Rayah, and Kaled were walking hand in hand in the Heroes Vineyard. Rayah had cried herself dry but leaned into Kaled's chest as she continued slowly up the path. Aymes had her injured arm in a sling, and purple and pink bruises were still visible all over her face. Her mind was consumed with thoughts of Ondraus. She had his ring pierced in her ear though he'd never had the opportunity to properly ask her to marry him.

In Brennen, a marriage proposal was considered a binding legal arrangement. If one person proposed and another accepted in front of a witness, the marriage was official from that moment. The technicalities didn't matter to her; in her eyes, the All Creator was their witness. Wedding rings were worn on the right ear and inscribed with the couple's initials. Every five years, a small moon was etched onto the gold band to symbolize the continuation of their commitment and honor to one another. Aymes ran her fingers on the freshly engraved gold earring dangling from her lobe. She clung, like a life preserver, to the memory of the last time she'd heard him say, "I love you," and she wore the earring proudly as Mrs. Aymes Jur.

Ahead of them walked the Kortez family; Aymes could see that Evia and Ensin were having a terribly hard time coming to grips with the death of someone they had come to know and respect. Though Aymes was physically present, she was not mentally there. Instead, she stared at the wedding earring that Nerida wore so beautifully and tried to count, from a distance, how many moons adorned it.

Instead of concentrating on the impending funeral service, she tried to focus her eyes on the rows and rows of icy, emaciated grapevines. The frost covering the twisted vines up the trellises gave the place an almost magical look. Magic, of course, was not real, though she wished with all her heart that it was. She exhaled deeply, and a puff of warm breath mixed with the cold outdoor air. A small wispy trail appeared but almost instantly faded, much like the unpredictability of someone's short time on this planet.

Aymes felt numb all over, not just on her skin from the cold, but in her mind, chest, and gut. Before coming to the funeral, she'd had the difficult conversation with Niklas about why Ondraus had not come over to their apartment in the last few days. She tried to explain it as best she could, but he still couldn't understand. Such a conversation was hard to have with a two-year-old. Finally, they reached the open plot of land where the service would take place.

A podium stood a few feet from where the body lay on a bed of flowers, with a man just behind it. Aymes recognized him as Teoli Geldon, the Farmer's Apprentice, so named because one of the All Creator's titles was the Great Farmer. Teoli wore the traditional vestment for royal funerals: a long thick velvet scarf around his neck that hung over his gold-trimmed white garment. Embroidered grapevines ran up the scarf's length while the bottom had a deep purple color as if it had been dipped in the ceremonial wine.

This particular funeral site at the Heroes Vineyard sat on a hill known as Royalty Row. Toward the front, Aymes watched as King Tarrington clutched both his infants, tears silently streaming from his eyes. Captain Yosef Peterson, the king's best friend, stood beside him. Aymes imagined Yosef as a lighthouse, illuminating the dark, perilous sea the king surely was drowning in.

It was a shock, not only for the kingdom but even the entire palace staff, that the queen had been so gravely sick. Everyone knew the Utroba Virus was survivable with the correct treatment. Surely the queen would have had access to the best possible medicine, right?

Even under normal circumstances, security concerns limited the number of attendees at royal funerals, and with Rancor and Imicem still on the loose, the number had been reduced even further. Rather than the entire palace staff and a sizable group of family, only a handful of close friends were present to mourn with the king. Even The Elite were only there as guards, their weapons charged and ready to use if the need arose.

"Beloved ones," began Teoli, "we are gathered on this sad day to honor Queen Ellandra. Though her life was cut short, she was a beam of light to anyone blessed enough to have met her."

The Farmer's Apprentice continued talking. Aymes still couldn't believe her queen was gone, yet though her heart ached for her king's loss, she also grieved Ondraus' absence. Rayah stood in a daze between Aymes and Kaled, her eyes cast beyond the funeral site as she stared blankly at nothing in particular.

Nearly everyone in the palace was mourning *someone*, whether a friend or a loved one, because of all the people who had died in Rancor's attack and its aftermath. Worst of all, thought Aymes resentfully, no one knew if Ondraus would die as well or if he would survive. Though Aymes would never confess her heart's desire out loud, she would much rather have been at her husband's side in the ICU room than pulling guard duty at this funeral. When the service was over, Ensin, Evia, and their parents approached them.

"How is Ondraus?" asked Evia.

"Same, no change," responded Kaled.

Kaled knew that Aymes and Rayah were tired of talking about Ondraus' unchanging health status, and she appreciated her brother doing the talking. She felt their eyes on her, all silently wondering if Aymes would become the next widow. The fear growing in the pit of Aymes' gut somehow grew larger with every passing day. *Come back to me O,* she pleaded in her heart.

"How horrible, the poor king," said Nerida softly as she walked hand in hand with her husband Alastair. "The queen and I became close friends during the short time that we've known each other. I miss her so much." For some reason, her last statement made Rayah cry uncontrollably. Kaled wrapped his arm around his girlfriend and guided her forward.

Aymes winced in pain, her throbbing arm a constant reminder of the near-death experience she had endured a mere week ago. Since that time, the palace had enacted a curfew to go along with the buddy system and their other normal security protocols.

Can we go to the hospital now so I can see Ondraus before the curfew hits? Aymes asked Kaled through duo-com.

Her brother nodded and pulled out his keys as they neared the hovercar.

Kaled drove them back to Lexel hospital, the place where the three of them had spent almost every free moment in the past few days. They still had their military obligations to fulfill; there was, after all, a war coming. A full week had passed with no change; Aymes could feel the little hope she had left wearing thin and on the brink of dissolving completely.

Halfway down the hallway on the hospital's fifth floor, Aymes got nauseous and had to hold on to the wall for support and then ran to the closest bathroom. She threw up and then walked up to the sink to clean her face and run a disposable towel under the cold water, and put it on her forehead. The door creaked open, and Rayah walked in.

"Hey, you okay?"

Aymes shrugged. "Just threw up, but I'll be fine."

"When was the last time you slept?" asked Rayah, approaching her friend and, no doubt, scrutinizing the bags under her eyes.

She chuckled briefly; a smile on her face felt odd after the week she'd had. "When was the last time *you* slept?"

Rayah dodged the question and instead placed her hand on Aymes' forehead and then on her wrist to take her pulse.

"Are your breasts tender?"

"What?"

"Do they hurt or feel tender in some way?" asked Rayah, her fingers still on Aymes' wrist.

Aymes brought up her free hand to her chest and touched herself. They *were* tender. Her eyes widened with alarm.

"When was your last cycle?"

"Ten weeks ago, but I just figured with all the high stress we've been having, plus we use protection–"

"I think we should stop by the nurse's station," recommended Rayah.

The two ladies walked out of the bathroom and took a detour down a different corridor, much to the surprise and confusion of Kaled, who was still very much in the dark as to what had just occurred. Rayah approached the nurse and did all the talking; Aymes was far too distracted with the thought of being pregnant to think straight. The nurse cleaned Aymes' arm with an aerosol spray and then applied a small beige sticker onto the arm. In roughly a minute, the sticker would change color to reveal the results, which left Aymes only that long to get to Ondraus' bedside so they could find out together.

Ondraus lay motionless in the ICU room with a tube going down his throat and IV lines feeding into his veins. Layers of fish-scale bandages covered his entire chest to treat the severe burns he had sustained. His eyes were shut, and his rich purple hair was matted against his head. Rayah watched the unchanging monitor, the steady beep-beep-beep of his heartbeat echoing on the screen's digital display, the rhythmic whoosh in and whoosh out of the ventilator pushing air in and out of his lungs.

Aymes kissed his forehead; she wondered if he could feel her presence or if he could hear her at all when she or anyone else visited. She took out a small kit from her handbag that contained shampoo, conditioner, and shaving cream. This was her routine. She washed him; it was the very least she could do. She washed, Rayah massaged parts of his body to help prevent bedsores, and Kaled prayed.

The late afternoon sun filled the room with its warmth and made the moon bracelet on his hand dazzle with a kaleidoscope of colors. She noticed that everyone wore the moon bracelets that Evia and Ensin had gifted them during their birthday celebration. The party felt like a million years ago; that night should have been an indication of the many hardships they'd all endured since then.

The bedside table held a small basin that Kaled had filled with warm water and a washcloth. Aymes ran her fingers through Ondraus' greasy hair and added water slowly to it, and then lathered it up with his shampoo from home. She liked the idea of giving him a head massage; that was one of his favorite things, and she felt honored to be able to do it now even though there was no way of knowing if he could feel it at all.

During the hours they weren't visiting, Mr. and Mrs. Jur and Edina Behr would visit Ondraus. The Jurs stayed with Edina and Niklas at Aymes' apartment, since Aymes and the rest of The Elite still had to stay at the palace in case of an attack. Though her world was falling apart, she could not imagine how it would feel if this were happening to her own child.

"We're pregnant," she said while bent close to his ear. "You're going to be a daddy. Now you listen to me darling, you need to pull through, Niklas, this new baby and I, we need you. Your sister needs you. Come back to me. I know it must be nice and quiet where you are, probably relaxing and taking a much needed mental break, but I need you back here with us. I can't do this alone."

She wiped the tears from her face and kissed his lips. If this were a magical fairytale, he would have awakened with true love's kiss, but such things didn't happen, and they certainly weren't her story. The entire experience felt surreal, a nightmare she couldn't wake up from. She finished washing his hair but remained standing beside him, lost in thought. Never had he appeared so small and frail as he did now.

They spent an hour at the hospital before they decided it was time to return to the palace. The sky appeared to be void of happiness; it was in a perpetual state of melancholy. Aymes rested her head on the cold window. The terrible mix of sadness, exhaustion, and nausea made her grow quiet as she closed her eyes and held Rayah's hand while Kaled drove the hovercar silently.

Kaled approached the palace's landing pad, then maneuvered through a large bay door into the Fleet department. Bo and Lina, who were working on the building's fire suppression system, greeted them. Rayah and Aymes went to the medical ward while Kaled remained in Fleet to talk to Bo.

In the ward, Rayah removed Aymes' old dressings, applied the Cura Spray, and added new dressings to her injured arm. She then used her credentials to unlock a pharmaceutical cart to retrieve a narcotic drug vial and insert it into a hypo-spray. Aymes leaned her neck to one side so Rayah could inject the drug into the side of her neck in a quick and painless method. But the injection never came.

"Hold on," said Rayah abruptly, "I almost forgot. Aymes, I can't give this to you anymore since you're pregnant. It can hurt the baby." Rayah rummaged through a different drawer and pulled out a pill bottle. "Here, you can take this."

"Metozin? Really? This stuff barely takes care of low-level headaches," groaned Aymes in protest.

"I know," replied Rayah. "We have all this medicine and all these fancy gadgets and you're allowed to use almost none of them when pregnant. An early pregnancy is so fragile." Rayah suddenly grew quiet; a mixed look of shame and regret etched onto her tired face.

"What's wrong?" asked Aymes with concern.

Rayah wiped a tear from her face. "It's the reason why the queen died. Anyone who suffers from the Utroba Virus, especially to the degree Queen Ellandra did, has to be on antiviral medication for several years. This medication is non-negotiable; without it, you die. But Queen Ellandra chose to get off her medication as soon as she found out she was pregnant. It was against Dr. Kortez's medical advice. And worst of all, the king knew none of this until it was too late."

Dumbstruck, Aymes tilted her head and tried to make sense of what she had heard. All of this could have been avoided. The so-called prophesy, the queen's death, Guyad and his sickening attack on the palace...even Ondraus. If the queen had stayed on her medication, she would have miscarried, and all of this unsurvivable trauma would not have taken place to begin with.

"How long have you known?" asked Aymes after a short pause.

"I should have figured it out a lot earlier," admitted Rayah with bitterness in her voice. "When I kept seeing the queen go to Dr. Kortez late at night, I assumed something very different, and I never questioned my assumption. I should have. I couldn't really have done anything because of doctor-patient confidentiality...but maybe I would have figured *something* out." Rayah sighed. "Our queen died to give her children a chance at life; she knew the consequences. But I still wonder how things would have played out if she'd told King Tarrington sooner."

They made their way down the stairs to their sleeping quarters. They had still not moved back to their rooms in the barracks, especially after the impending invasion that Aymes had warned everyone about. She hated that gathering such vital intel had placed the man of her dreams in such a dire medical state that he was fighting for his life, but on the other hand, the information was crucial. Though it had been merely a week since their mission in Clarcona, the number of guards had tripled in the palace, and the army throughout all of Brennen was on alert. She had no way of knowing whether the battle on *Caprisor* had dissolved Rancor's plan or timetable. All they could do was prepare and wait.

"Kaled mentioned that General Peterson had sent five different spy teams, each trying to find Rancor and stop him before he attacks. Hopefully they get lucky," said Rayah. She was rummaging through her backpack when a vial of pills and a small black velvet box fell out.

"What's that?" asked Aymes.

Rayah popped a pill into her mouth and swallowed, then replied, "Dr. Kortez prescribed some anti-anxiety medication. I'm supposed to take it once daily."

"You really think you need to be on those?" asked Aymes as she removed her shoes.

"Yeah. For years I've tried to manage my anxiety attacks in silence, but it was time for me to finally get some help. It won't necessarily stop the thoughts. It just helps slow them down so I can take control. Plus, it's not just the attacks. There's plenty of times when my thoughts obsess over something, and that can be paralyzing. This is a low dose, though."

"Understandable." Aymes sat down on the bed and yawned. "But, I was actually referring to the small box."

"Oh, you saw that?" replied Rayah, her cheeks blushing.

"Mmhmm. Is it what I think it is?"

"It's going to sound silly," said Rayah.

"Say it anyway," urged Aymes with a smile.

"Well, when my brother went ring shopping, I decided to do the same," explained Rayah. "I bought my ring and Kal's. During the Winter Solstice, Kal and I had a lot of time to talk, and we decided it would be best if I were the one to propose when and if I ever find a way to trust him truly."

Rayah got into the same bed where Aymes was sitting and laid down beside her; it was a thing they did now that both of them were incapable of sleeping without the comfort of their friend.

"Do you love him?" asked Aymes as she laid her head onto the pillow and pulled the covers up to her chin.

"Of course I love Kal. But trusting him is another matter completely. I'm afraid it's going to take a long time; I just hope he doesn't get tired of waiting, because I really can't picture myself with anyone else. He's the one, and he always has been."

Aymes placed her hand on Rayah's cheek. "Just remind him of that from time to time. All he needs is to know that you love him back. He'll wait, trust me."

They embraced, and then Aymes turned over in bed so that she could try and get some sleep. The warmth of Rayah's body reminded Aymes of warm sunlit afternoons in their youth. As Rayah's arm was draped over hers, Aymes attempted to drift off to sleep. She pictured the two of them running in a field of tall green grass and yellow flowers, laughing hysterically as Ondraus and Kaled ran behind them with water balloons. The happy memory made her smile momentarily. Aymes turned over and faced Rayah and saw that her friend was still awake, her eyes red and puffy from exhaustion and fresh tears. The closeness of her beloved friend made the bed feel like a cocoon of protection was over them; without her here, this would be too heavy a burden to bear.

"Can I?" asked Rayah, pointing at Aymes' belly. Aymes smiled, taking Rayah's hand and placing it upon her abdomen. With her free hand, she gently wiped away the hot tears that streamed down Rayah's face. "It feels like the world is falling apart at the seams, and yet, a beautiful thing is happening right here within you," she sniffled.

"Who would have thought, huh? Me and Ondraus having a baby. It doesn't seem real. None of this does."

"I know," said Rayah, closing her eyes and resting her head on Aymes' good shoulder. "My parents are going to be overjoyed when they find out. They love you so much; they always have, and now with this happy news, it's almost like a part of Ondraus is here with us right now."

"I've always loved your parents too," responded Aymes sleepily.

"When are you going to call your mom?" asked Rayah.

"Oh, I guess I forgot to tell her. I'll call her tomorrow morning. I'm too tired to ring her up now."

Aymes yawned, closed her eyes, and began to drift off to sleep. Her mind still played memories of days filled with laughter and joy. Her muscles relaxed, and her breathing slowed as she recalled the first time she met Rayah, then another memory of the two of them singing at the top of their lungs while Kaled sat in the passenger seat trying to teach Ondraus how to drive his first hovercar. She thought of the way her heart soared when Ondraus first confessed he loved her.

Sleep beckoned her, and she was nearly there until

an alarm pierced through the intercom system on the far wall of the room. A jarring succession of high pitched tones resounded through the entire palace, and its sound made both women jump out of bed in a panic.

"All, this is General Peterson. Primeda Fortress has come under missile bombardment and the border radar posts have been knocked out. Everyone get into your battle stations. This is not a drill. I repeat this is not a drill."

Somehow Aymes knew, in a way she'd felt sure of anything before, that she would never have that chance to call her mother.

END OF BOOK ONE

Book 2 of the Brennen Series: Fall of the King (Summer 2022)

ACKNOWLEDGEMENTS

I've had this story in my head for several years but never felt motivated to make it happen until I saw my husband's dedication to his writing. A co-worker of mine sat me down and encouraged me to write without limiting myself or shying away from certain topics. That was enough of a push to get me to embark on this journey, and I'm glad I did!

I want to thank my beta group readers: Jennifer, Abbey, Joanna, Laura, and Stacie. These ladies truly enriched my life with their attention to detail, support, and honest criticism. Thank you, ladies, for everything. This story would be entirely different if it weren't for all of your hard work. I especially loved the midnight chats and comments in particular chapters that got quite mysterious or steamy. It was a blast!

My husband edited this entire book. I can't thank him enough. The process took forever as we scrutinized every sentence to ensure both grammatical accuracy and emotional punch.

A message from the author

I hope you've enjoyed reading *Brennen Series Book 1: The Elite*. Can I ask a personal favor of you? If you enjoyed this story, would you take two minutes of your time to leave an Amazon review so that others can experience the same thing? For independent authors like me, book reviews are our social currency, and they directly influence the way Amazon shows our books in searches. Leaving a review – for *The Elite* or any other book – is the single greatest way you can support independent authors.

If you want to connect, please follow us on Facebook, we'd love to hear from you!
https://www.facebook.com/BarringerBooks

Thank you, and be blessed!
Andrea

Andrea Barringer's Upcoming Books:
The Brennen Series
Book 2: Fall of the King (Summer 2022)
Book 3: Title TBD (Summer 2023)

Printed in Great Britain
by Amazon